CHASING SAFIYA

Ken McGoogan

Bayeux *Arts*

Chasing Safiya
Kenneth McGoogan
© 1999 by Bayeux Arts

Published by

Bayeux Arts Incorporated

119 Stratton Crescent S.W.
Calgary, Alberta, Canada T3H 1T7

Design: Brian Dyson, Syntax Media Services
Illustrations and author photo: Sheena McGoogan
Cover image: traditional Sri Lankan fire mask

Canadian Cataloguing in Publication Data

McGoogan, Kenneth
  Chasing Safiya

  ISBN 1-896209-35-1

  1. Title.
PS8575.G65C52 1999   C813'.54   C99-9107007-0
PR9199.3.M317C52 1999

The publisher gratefully acknowledges the generous
support of The Alberta Foundation for the Arts and The
Canada Council for the Arts

FOR SHEENA

without whom this novel
would not exist

Acknowledgments

Special thanks to Ashis Gupta for seizing the moment; Bob Silverstein for invoking *Om: The Secret of Ahbor Valley*; Dean Koontz for perspicacity and kind words; Vic Ramraj for counsel, sharp pencil, *Empires of the Monsoon* and the trip to India and Sri Lanka; and Sheena McGoogan for Dar es Salaam, Mombasa, the fire-mask idea, the pen-and-ink sketches — and also for instructing me in Safiya.

Contents

Prologue 7

Visions Of San Francisco 9

Casting The Runes 25

The Red Bird of Paradise 33

Viva Las Palmas 43

The Barcelona Smile 63

A Genoan Miracle 77

Satori In Rome 85

Mombasan Apocalypse 101

Lost in Al-Mayadin 115

The Magic of Meteora 125

Athenian Roulette 137

Dismay in Sri Lanka 149

Sailors of Kuwali 169

New Delhi Surprise 179

Trial by Fire 191

Trouble at the Taj Mahal 205

Do Not Come To Dar 215

Bongoya Island Bound 229

The Chinvat Bridge 245

Lighting Up Eternity 257

Magic Is Alive.

Leonard Cohen

Prologue

One thousand years after the birth of the second prophet, the fisher of men who walked on the waves, Ahura Mazda sent His faithful servant a vision. That servant summoned ashavans to a lake called Takht-i Sulaiman, or Throne of Solomon, in the hill country of northern Persia. These ashavans, followers of Zarathustra, were enduring an especially fierce religious persecution — a bloody suppression by fire and sword.

The Wise Lord wanted the ashavans to take the most sacred royal fire, the Atur Gushnasp, which had been burning continuously for two thousand years, and leave this place where they had lived since the beginning, but which had now become polluted. They were to carry the Sacred Fire — which the prophet Zathustra had built by combining the flames of sixteen holy fires — over the mountains into the ancient land of India. Ahura Mazda had appointed the mighty Verethreghna to guide and protect them in this journey, and they were to leave at once.

The ashavans listened and acted as One. The journey proved

long and arduous, but Verethreghna led them to Gujarat, a green and fertile land on the west coast of India. There, amidst peoples of many different backgrounds, the followers of Zarathustra felt they had come home.

But now Ahura Mazda sent a second vision. The Wise Lord told His servant that the journey was not done. Here in Gujarat, if they remained, the ashavans would become wealthy and content. But they would forget the revealed truths of Zarathustra, the terrible war between Ahura Mazda and Ahriman, and abandon the ancient teachings. Here in Gujarat, the ashavans could not remain without falling away. They must cross the ocean to Africa, to the Land of Zanj, where they would secretly flourish.

Again, the faithful servant addressed the people. Again, the ashavans listened. Only this time they responded not as One, but as many. In Gujarat, the people had built houses and planted crops. They had prospered. And now one amongst them rose up and challenged the faithful servant, arguing that here people were becoming strong. These ashavans would not forget the ancient ways, nor forsake the revealed truths of the prophet Zarathustra, and the unending battle between light and darkness; but here in Gujarat, where they were called Parsees, they would remain.

Ahura Mazda told His servant to make two fires of the Atur Gushnasp, and to travel south and west with as many ashavans as would follow Verethreghna. The servant listened and obeyed. He made two fires of the One and saw that both were Sacred — that both were Atur Gushnasp. Then, with three hundred ashavans — the bold, the adventurous, the creative — he travelled south by camel train to Bombay, and still further south by boat to the ancient port of Calicut. There the ashavans boarded a ship, which they called Takht-i Sulaiman, and sailed to Africa with the Sacred Fire of Zarathustra....

Visions of San Francisco

On the eve of any new millennium, a famous writer once told me, people confront elemental forces. Ancient rituals, hidden powers and forgotten prophecies erupt into our workaday lives, turning them tumultuous. Was he onto something? I don't know. I do know that until last year, unless we count a recurring nightmare, dreams and visions played no role in my life.

True, my late mother had claimed psychic abilities and dabbled in the occult. She'd devoted weekends and holidays to seances and ceremonial magic and the arcane rituals of witches' covens. But that was during my boyhood. She was a Quebecoise in exile, and my Irish-American father said that explained everything about her: her theatricality, her flamboyance, her *joie de vivre* — everything he most loved

True, too, I married a woman who, just before she died, began single-mindedly to explore her own unusual religious and cultural heritage. But how could I have anticipated that? Faithful to my father's memory and, I suppose, some image of myself, I resisted other-worldly blandishments and plunged into journalism: nothing but the facts, ma'am. I celebrated myself as a throwback to the days when "tough-minded newspapermen" paid no attention to organized religion and still less to New Age mumbo-jumbo.

Probably my skepticism was why, as a journalist, I managed to carve out a niche. A year ago, when my cosmic shock treatment began, I was writing a city column for The San Francisco Statesman. I'd been working at the paper since the mid-eighties when, fresh out of J-School, I landed a summer job and made it stick. Over the years, I'd covered education, courts, city hall, cops, even did a stint in business. Lately, under the rubric "Lanigan's Corner," I'd been churning out copy on everything from high-school reunions to a day in the life of a bus driver. Infotainment.

It was just bad luck, then, or so I believed, that the Managing Editor should assign me to chase down the "Vanishing Arsonist" who'd begun torching buildings in the Bay Area. A petite redhead with a stylish wardrobe, a big voice and a bad temper, she stormed across the newsroom late one afternoon brandishing a notebook: "Lanigan? Drop what you're doing."

Not twenty minutes before, she'd publicly dressed down three hulking police reporters for having turned up zero on the Arsonist. Now a copy runner had taken a call from a man with a thick accent who identified himself as "Chinvat or something." He said the Vanishing Arsonist was going to firebomb a bookstore in Corte Madera, just north of the city in Marin County.

While various colleagues pounded away at their keyboards, heads down, terribly busy — this didn't look promising — the M.E. handed me a scrap of paper with a name scrawled on it: Polarities. She couldn't have known it, but this was the bookstore Behroze and I had visited the night she died. And which I hadn't entered since.

"Show them how it's done, Bernie."

Apparently the M.E. remembered that, several years before, while working the police beat, I'd won a couple of awards. No sense arguing: she was famous for "drive-by assignings." I'd been polishing a column about a straight alderman wrongly "outed" by his constituents, but I stored it, grabbed my jacket and made for the cafeteria.

There, at a quiet table in the corner, reading volume two of Lord of the Rings, I found my darling daughter, Colette — the light of my life. Once a week, after school, her best friend's mother would drop her off at the newspaper and I'd take her to piano lessons. I'd wait upstairs in an anteroom, perusing dated Peoples and Newsweeks, and afterwards we'd visit a spaghetti house. I'm not much of a cook and this was one of three weekly sorties. Friday nights we'd visit a fish-and-chips place, and Sundays we'd brunch at The Cheesecake Cafe, where I'd confine myself to spicy omelettes and she'd pig out on waffles and ice cream. Sure, I indulged her: why not?

This afternoon, as we plunged into the streets of San Francisco, Colette protested: "Dad, I can't miss piano. I've got a recital next week."

"Colette, we've no choice."

"Can't you drop me off and come back?"

In fact, I could have done just that. But I'd decided that, from the bookstore in Corte Madera, I'd head straight home and then file by remote. I didn't want to drive all the way back into town. So I said, "No, we haven't time."

"And I can either like it or lump it, right?"

This had become a favorite rejoinder and I ignored it.

At the garage we hopped into my 1968 Mustang convertible, which I'd recently finished restoring to pristine condition. As we roared off I rolled down the top and, as a mutually agreeable peace offering, inserted one of her favorite tapes — Paul Simon's Graceland. The driving rhythms made us both feel better. Traffic was light and we zoomed west, nodding and tapping along to the music. I told Colette about the Vanishing Arsonist, and that he'd threatened to blow up a bookstore — though I didn't say which. She said, "Will we see it explode?"

"You won't see it at all," I said. "You'll wait in a coffee shop."

"Dad, no way. You're making me miss piano. You've got to let me share the fun."

"Colette, please." As I swung north onto the Golden Gate Bridge, the tape cut out. I glanced down to see what had happened to Paul Simon and KABOOM! drove straight into the back of a fire truck that sat stalled on the ramp to the bridge. It happened that fast. No warning, nothing. Just KABOOM!

And so the shock treatment began. I found myself floating high above the scene of the accident. Looking down, I saw my body draped over the bridge railing like a rag doll. Colette lay beside me on the sidewalk, unconscious, but even that sight didn't scare me — not yet. Detached, emotionless, I heard a muffled roar and watched my vintage Mustang explode in slow motion. Then whoosh! and away I went.

Maybe you've read about Near Death Experiences. This "NDE" of mine began conventionally. I plunged head-first, just whoosh! into a pitch-dark tunnel that ran on and on and just when I thought it would never end, the walls fell away, that sense of constriction, and I found myself tumbling, tumbling slower and slower through what had become a grey void, cavernous, empty. Drifting now, feather light, I communicated with spirit guides who resembled my parents — chatted, almost, though now I remember not a word of what we discussed. I found myself floating towards a dazzling white light . . . and that's when my NDE twisted oddly.

As I drifted towards the light, wanting only to draw nearer, the world around me shifted as if in a kaleidoscope. Suddenly, I stood on a tropical beach with the sun beating down white and nothing to see but white sand and palm trees beneath a cloudless blue sky, with turquoise ocean, yes turquoise, rolling away to the horizon. Down the beach, a slim woman emerged from a stand of palm trees. She wore white slacks and a sleeveless white sweater. As she approached I recognized Behroze, looking exactly as she did at twenty-seven, when she died. Oddly enough, I wasn't surprised to see her. Behroze took my elbow and spoke gently: "Mazda says, 'Walk with me.'"

This was a variation on my recurring nightmare. But to make that clear, I'll have to explain about my dead wife and her heritage. Born and raised in Colorado Springs, Behroze was American to her fingertips: she played baseball and loved hot-fudge sundaes and wrote her Ph.D. thesis on the novels of Willa Cather. However, she also had this unusual background: Behroze had been raised a Parsee.

The Parsees, all two hundred thousand of them, descended from the Zoroastrians who, more than one thousand years ago, fled religious persecution in Persia and settled in India. Over the centuries, they'd fanned out all over the globe, and a few had found their way to America — Behroze's parents among them.

Parsees worship a benevolent god called Ahura Mazda, who

wages a cosmic war against the evil Ahriman. So far, so dualistically typical. But Parsees reject Western notions of original sin and salvation, and likewise Eastern ideas of nirvana, karma and reincarnation. They insist that believers or "ashavans" accept personal responsibility and take an active role in shaping and justifying their own lives.

Back in the days when I was courting Behroze, a two-fisted journalist bent on becoming a soul-of-the-city columnist, I regarded all this as harmless nonsense. Besotted, I even entertained the notion of converting to Zoroastrianism — though Behroze soon discovered that for two centuries, a theological controversy had been raging over the wisdom of accepting new believers. We drove to Sante Fe and married before a justice of the peace.

It wasn't until a couple of years later, after giving birth to Colette, that Behroze expressed any serious interest in her unusual heritage, and then she described it as purely academic. I'd smile tolerantly when she waxed enthusiastic, but basically paid no attention. Behroze had been studying her roots for a year when she arrived home from grocery shopping one Saturday afternoon and suggested that we go hear some "author-prophet" speak that evening at a bookstore in Corte Madera, just a few miles from where we lived.

"He's a Parsee?" By now I'd grown wary.

"He was raised a Parsee but left that behind. They call him 'The Prophet of the Golden Flame' and say he's a John-the-Baptist for the new millennium. Apparently, he's created a new synthesis. He draws on Zoroastrianism, but also on Existentialism and Carl Jung."

"What about Colette?"

"Bernie, she's four years old. We'll get a baby sitter. It'll be fun."

I remained unconvinced. Lately I'd begun covering city hall and, during the past week, I'd endured one too many council meetings. This morning, after taking Colette swimming, I'd rented a video: Indiana Jones and the Temple of Doom. Now I proposed that we stay home and watch it, maybe order in a pepperoni pizza with mushrooms and double anchovies: "Anyway, you'll never find a babysitter, not at this hour."

"Want to bet?"

Behroze extracted a promise: if she did find a sitter, I'd go with her to hear this Prophet of the Golden Flame. Then she started working the phone. On the fourth or fifth try — my wife was nothing if not persistent — she located an ex-student who owed her a favor. This young woman turned up promptly at seven. Behroze gave instructions and, ten minutes later, we left Indiana Jones at a crossroads, piled into our battered Dodge Colt and headed for Corte Madera.

Polarities bookstore specializes in wisdom literature, as well as literary, psycholanalytical and New-Age titles, and the male owner, one half of a gay couple, greeted Behroze like a long-lost

friend. He showed us upstairs, where forty or fifty people sat in metal folding chairs. A couple of thirty-fivish men bustled around, shuffling chairs and testing the sound system. An older man, bald-headed, be-robed and beatific-looking, stood behind a podium shuffling notes — the Prophet of the Golden Flame. I disliked him on sight.

This feeling intensified when the man began speaking. He flaunted his deep, theatrical voice and mellifluous delivery, but what irritated me most was the arrant nonsense he spewed — and the way it went over with the crowd. I won't pretend to quote him verbatim. To tell the truth, I didn't listen closely. But I do remember whispering to Behroze that it sounded to me like a New-Age variation on the Parsee mumbo-jumbo I'd long since dismissed as irrelevant, anachronistic. For sure, I'd reverted to type.

The Prophet held forth for an hour while the audience listened, rapt. I couldn't understand it. Behroze had earned three university degrees to my one. How could she sit listening to bafflegab about psychic inter-connectedness and the way Taoism relates to the teachings of Zarathustra?

Finally, when I was about to explode with frustration, the Prophet announced an intermission. I asked Behroze whether she'd heard enough and she raised her eyebrows ominously. I said fine. I'd wait in the bar across the street: "When you've heard enough, come and get me."

Instead of getting angry, Behroze shook her head sadly: "Sometimes, Bernie, I feel sorry for you."

The bar was dark, dingy and dead, just a half dozen regulars. Tell the truth, in those days I drank hardly at all — but that night, nursing an inexplicable and wholly unjustifiable sense of grievance, I started knocking back beer. What did those mindless New-Agers know? I should have stayed home with Colette and Indiana Jones. Finally, as I was draining my third beer and contemplating a fourth, Behroze turned up. I suggested one for the road but she gave me such a look that I grabbed my jacket and cleared my tab.

Behroze didn't become silently furious until, approaching the car, I stumbled and almost fell. Then, tight-lipped, she said, "Give me the keys."

Behroze suffered from poor night-vision, so after dark I did the driving: "Behroze, I'm fine."

"No, Bernie, you're pathetic. And far too drunk to drive."

Probably, she was right — though often I've wondered. Shamefaced, I handed over the car keys. Behroze took the wheel. We pulled away from the curb and . . . and that's the last thing I remember.

Witnesses say Behroze ran a red light. Not two blocks from the bookstore. And wham! a fire truck slammed into our subcompact. Must have been doing sixty. Three weeks later, I woke up in hospital. Found myself alone. The car had been smashed like a tin can. Nobody could understand how I'd survived. Nor could anybody explain why Behroze hadn't.

For the longest time, I couldn't believe it: Behroze ran a red light? My Behroze? With a fire truck barrelling down on us? I couldn't believe it. No, no, a thousand times no. No, no, no, no never.

Yet half a dozen witnesses said that's what happened. And I knew Behroze didn't see well in darkness. In the end, it didn't matter whether she'd run the red light or simply hadn't seen it. Behroze had left the building. And nothing I could say or do would bring her back.

I beat up on myself endlessly, of course. If only I'd remained at the bookstore, if only I'd tolerated the Prophet of the Golden Flame, if only I'd confined myself to two beers . . . if only, if only, if only. Nobody could dispute any of this, though several people tried. And eventually, I recovered — physically. Over the years, for the sake of Colette, I willed myself back into a semblance of wholeness.

As I did so, a recurring nightmare entered my life — a nightmare comprising two vivid scenes. The first takes place in a courtroom, where I stand accused before a judge. He recapitulates the story I've just outlined, highlighting my refusal to remain at the bookstore, then peers at me over his glasses: "Anything to say for yourself?"

"I couldn't stand any more Parsee mumbo-jumbo."

"Parsee mumbo-jumbo?" The judge rises slowly to his feet. "Is that how you refer to the secret of the Golden Flame? This evolutionary advance in the spiraling spiritual realm? No. Your intellectual pride kept you from remaining, Mr. Lanigan. Your well-developed sense of superiority." He points at me and thunders: "Your hubris killed Behroze!"

"It was an accident!"

"Repent and redeem yourself, Lanigan! Repent or you'll suffer in love until the day you die."

"Her death wasn't my fault!"

"Take him away!"

Two strapping bodyguards drag me away down a corridor. They fling me through an open steel door and down some stairs into what should be a dirt-floor cell. Struggling to my feet, I rub my eyes to find myself alone on a tropical beach with a storm brewing. We've entered scene two. In the distance, a slim brown woman emerges from a stand of palm trees. I recognize my dead wife and move towards her: "Behroze!"

She hears me, I know she does, but she turns and walks the other way.

I run after her crying, "Behroze! Behroze, wait!"

No matter how fast I run, Behroze draws farther away simply by walking.

"Behroze!" Eventually, I wake up sweating and calling, "Behroze! Behroze, wait!"

That's the usual pattern. And that's what made my Near Death Experience so dramatically different. Instead of walking away, Behroze turned and approached me, looking as beautiful as she did on the night she died. Taking my elbow, she said, "Mazda says, 'Walk with me.'"

We strolled barefoot along the ocean's edge, enjoying the warm breeze and the tropical setting, neither of us feeling any need to speak. It occurred to me that Behroze had been dead for eight years, but when I turned to ask about this, she put a finger to her lips and pointed back the way we'd come. The waves had erased our footprints and I understood this to be significant: it was like we'd never passed this way. We resumed walking: "Behroze, where are we going?"

"To invoke the Sacred Fire of Mazda."

"Mazda?" The name sounded vaguely familiar. "You mean like the Japanese car?"

Behroze smile tolerantly: "No, like the Wise Lord Ahura Mazda — the benevolent god who created all good things."

"Zoroastrianism!"

"No, Bernie: Golden Flame." Behroze had stopped walking and stood staring out to sea: "It's rooted in the old Parsee faith, but has grown more complex. To access the power of the Sacred Fire, some mortal must gather fire-worthy souvenirs from sixteen scattered cities." Behroze turned again and looked me in the eye: "The millennium is upon us, Bernie. I've come to send you forth."

"You're kidding, right?"

Behroze placed one fingertip to the side of her head and looked skyward, an old familiar gesture that meant she was going to quote some literary figure from memory. Sure enough, she said: "Love is a spirit all compact of fire, / Not gross to sink, but light, and will aspire."

"Yet another obscure poet," I said. "You haven't changed a bit."

"William Shakespeare." She grinned at me, then shook her head: "You haven't either, Bernie. You've always insisted on doing things the hard way. I thought you wanted to redeem yourself."

To my surprise, she turned and walked away down the beach. "Behroze? Wait!"

I trotted after her but a mist arose, the scene faded, and I awoke in a hospital bed feeling sick, with my head bandaged and a doctor peering down at me: "You must have a guardian angel."

"Where's Colette? My daughter?"

"She's . . . alive."

"Alive? What do you mean, she's alive?" I bolted upright and passed out.

A few minutes later, the doctor said: "She's in a coma, Mr.

Lanigan. Otherwise, she's fine. No broken bones, no serious injuries."

"Colette's in a coma?"

And so began a real-life nightmare. One day bled into the next. My injuries healed but Colette did not awake. Specialists told me she might open her eyes at any moment— but she didn't. Gradually, the experts lost hope. I watched it disappear from their faces. I waited by Colette's bed, holding her hand.

In my grief, seeking answers, I played and replayed my Near Death Experience, trying to decipher it. Walking along the beach, Behroze had made a dream-like sense. Now, in the clear light of day, our exchange seemed ludicrous, more bad dream than revelation. The Sacred Fire of Mazda? Sixteen scattered cities? Where did the unconscious mind get this nonsense? I'd whacked my head and dreamed a weird dream, that was all. Best forget the whole business.

But one question I couldn't forget: why didn't Colette awake from her coma? Why had this happened to my little girl? Why, why, why, oh why? That's where I stood, at least figuratively, when Behroze turned up unannounced. She found me kneeling by our daughter's bed.

Yet another specialist had just told me, as if I couldn't see it myself, that Colette had slipped deeper into her trance. Her metabolism had slowed. They didn't know how or why or what it meant. And I don't know whether I was praying when Behroze arrived, though I was clinging to Colette's hand and calling silently, addressing somebody or something deep inside, saying, "Anything, I'll do anything, just let my little girl come back to me. Just let my darling Colette come back safe and sound."

Behroze said, "I'd hoped it wouldn't come to this."

Somehow, she'd materialized inside a hospital room whose door remained firmly closed. On the back of my neck, the hair stood up. My mouth went dry. Behroze must have registered my shock and decided to give me time because, without saying another word, she moved to the window, opened the curtain and stood looking down at the parking lot. Finally, she dropped the curtain and looked over: "You want to save our daughter? You face a ritual quest whose implications are greater than you can imagine."

I didn't trust my voice to respond.

"You remember the quest, Bernie? The gathering of fire-worthy souvenirs?"

"No need to be sarcastic." She'd brought me back to myself.

Behroze gazed at Colette, lying like death in her hospital bed: "This happened because you wouldn't listen."

"Why are you doing this?"

"I'm not doing it, Bernie: I'm fighting it. I've come to help you restore Colette. You must find the Shaman who guards the Sacred Fire."

"Behroze, this is crazy. I wouldn't know where to begin."

"He's in East Africa — the cradle of humankind."

"Tell me this is a bad dream."

She stared at me, impassive. Then she ran through it again, as if instructing a child. Zarathustra had created the Sacred Fire by bringing together sixteen holy fires. Centuries later, under persecution, certain of his "ashavans" had carried this Fire from Persia to India and then to East Africa. The Sacred Fire had been burning continuously for hundreds of years. Towards the end of each millennium, Behroze said, mortals could access the power of this Fire by gathering souvenirs from around the world — potential talismans made of metal, crystal or precious stones — and presenting them to the Shaman who guarded the now-golden flame.

"Behroze, I'm a journalist. I'm a single parent struggling to raise a twelve-year-old daughter. But you know all this! Behroze, listen, you've got to tell whoever's in charge that I'm not the kind of guy you send to find a Shaman."

"You think I didn't try, Bernie?"

"What about Colette? Don't you feel anything for your daughter? Don't you — "

"Don't YOU tell me what to feel, Bernard Lanigan. The main reason I'm here is because I love Colette." She shook her head in frustration, then resumed in a calmer manner: "Many will be called, Bernie. Some will lay down their lives." Behroze shrugged. "In this case, I agree: the choice appears to have fallen oddly — though you do possess some slight psychic ability."

"Psychic ability? Are you mad?"

"Your premonitions, Bernie. Flashes of telepathy, hints of clairvoyance. The gift you've denied for so many years?"

Oh, I knew what she meant, all right. Every once in a while,

I'd step out the front door to fetch the newspaper and I'd "see" the main headline before I unrolled it. Or else I'd glance at somebody in the street and "hear" what they were thinking. "O.K., I've had the occasional experience," I said now. "But nothing significant. Besides, these things happen randomly. I can't control it. For sure I can't undertake a job like this."

Behroze smiled grimly: "The decision is not mine."

"What do you mean, 'Some will lay down their lives?'"

"The quest is dangerous, Bernie. No mortal has yet purified a souvenir in the Sacred Fire. If it's any consolation, you'll save countless thousands of lives — maybe millions"

"The only life I want to save is Colette's. You can't expect me to leave our daughter and go charging off to Africa."

"I can keep Colette stable for three months."

"Stable for three months? I want her back now!"

"That's all I can manage, Bernie. After that . . . ."

"But how . . . what do I have to do?"

"You collect sixteen fire-worthy souvenirs, Bernie. Among them seven from sacred or magical places. Then you get the Shaman to purify one of these keepsakes in the Sacred Fire, so turning it into a millennial talisman. You bring this back and use it to cure our daughter. What could be simpler?"

"You want me to go trinket-hunting?"

"The quest functions on many levels simultaneously. Sixteen cities, sixteen souvenirs. Symbolically, you'll reintegrate the world. On another level, the process is interior — spiritual. But you'll discover the meaning of the Golden Flame as you go along."

Weak in the knees, I wobbled into the chair beside the bed. "You're serious about this, aren't you? You want to send me off on some metaphysical scavenger hunt."

"Dead serious, Bernie." Behroze began rooting through her purse. "Don't worry, I've got permission to meet you at the Taj."

"The Taj? The Taj Mahal? Why in — ?"

Behroze produced a piece of paper and glanced at it. "Check The Statesman's personal columns tomorrow. Somebody will advertise a ticket for a freighter sailing from New York to Greece. You buy that ticket and use it."

"You want me to sail to Greece? Behroze, who's behind this?"

She sighed and, ignoring my interruption, resumed matter-offactly: "You'll fly to New York. The quest could become complex, but friends and even enemies will teach you all you need to know."

"NO!" I jumped to my feet and began pacing. "I'm not going anywhere. I won't leave Colette."

"You can't not leave her, Bernie." Behroze touched my shoulder and for a moment I felt soothed. "Not if you want her to live."

Together, we stared down at our daughter. After a moment, Behroze reached out and gently removed a necklace from around Colette's neck — a gold necklace with a locket that had originally been her own. "Take this," she said, handing it to me, "from both me and Colette. Purify it in the Sacred Fire and bring it back to revive our daughter."

"What about my job?" I said, taking the necklace.

"Quit your job. Or, no: take an unpaid leave."

"Where have you been, Behroze? They don't give unpaid leaves — not at The San Francisco Statesman."

"Bernie, I'll take care of it."

She turned and made for the door.

"Behroze, wait."

She stopped and I said: "What if I fail?"

"You want to redeem yourself, Bernie? Rid yourself of that recurring nightmare? You want Colette to live? Don't even think about failing." As she stepped out the door, Behroze turned and added: "Those psychic powers I mentioned? Clairvoyance? Precognition? Develop those, will you?"

"Develop them? But how?"

"I'll be with you, Bernie. Listen for my voice."

With that, instead of passing through the door, Behroze slowly disappeared — just faded away to invisibility. I sat beside Colette for a long time, struggling to pull myself together. Was I dreaming? Hallucinating? Losing my mind? I stared at the gold chain in my hand. Had Behroze really handed me this?

For the first time I noticed a mimeographed pamphlet on a small table next to the bed: The Secret of The Golden Flame. I flipped through it: four pages, single-spaced. The pamphlet celebrated The Golden Flame as an evolutionary spiritual advance, the culmination of a process begun centuries ago.

I quickly lost patience and tossed the pamphlet aside — an action I would later regret. Obviousy, Behroze had planted the work. Or perhaps I'd read it previously and forgot — that whack on the head — and then drew from it in imagining a visitation from my dead wife. I went home and, unable to sleep, paced the living-room floor. It took most of the night, but finally I convinced myself: I'd been hallucinating because of something I'd eaten or accidentally ingested.

Next morning, just to prove it, I checked The Statesman's personals — and there discovered, to my shock and horror, an advertisement like the one Behroze had promised. I telephoned the listed number and a young man answered on first ring. He sounded desperate. A death in the family. He couldn't leave on his projected voyage. He'd failed to insure his freighter ticket to Greece. And the ship sailed next week.

"Next week?" I said. "I'll get back to you."

Again I paced the kitchen floor. No way I could leave Colette in a coma and sail away to Greece. Yet, by some bizarre coincidence, a freighter ticket had come available. Very well: I'd give it a fair test. I'd do as Behroze suggested — ask the Managing Editor for a paid leave of absence. In all my years at The San Francisco Statesman, no such leave had ever been granted. Even so, if the M.E. refused to grant me a paid leave, I'd accept that as a definitive sign: I'd remain home and watch over Colette with a clear conscience.

Visiting the newspaper office for the first time since the accident on the Golden Gate Bridge, I learned that the Vanishing Arsonist had been busy. Where originally he'd confined himself to the Bay Area — mainly San Francisco, but also Berkeley, Oakland and San Jose — now he'd begun working farther afield: Santa Cruz, Monterey, Sacramento. The police didn't have a clue. Neither did I. Difference was, I could care less.

Finally, the M.E. made time to see me. She led me into her office, closed the door and reacted precisely as I'd anticipated. She waved my request in the air: "Is this some kind of joke, Lanigan? The whole newspaper industry is moving to contract workers and you're asking for a paid leave?" She sat down at her desk, leaned back and crossed her arms: "You've been under stress, Bernie. Talk to me."

My first summer at The Statesman, when she was a city hall reporter dominating the front page, the M.E. and I had gone out a few times. I enjoyed her sense of style. I didn't share her management ambitions, though, and felt mainly relief when she dumped me to return to her now ex-husband. We got over each other quickly. Even so, when she'd visited me in hospital after this latest car accident, I knew she did so not only on behalf of The Statesman, but also as an old friend.

During her visit, I'd alluded to my Near Death Experience and she'd grown decidedly uncomfortable. Now I was supposed to tell her about Behroze's visitation? That my dead wife was sending me abroad to find a Sacred Fire belonging to some Wise Lord whose name sounded like a Japanese car? No way. Already she believed that I'd never got over the death of Behroze, that I'd never fully recovered. She'd think I'd gone nuts.

Forget the truth, then. I said that for years I'd been gathering myself to produce a book. A unique opportunity had presented itself and I needed to seize the moment. No, I couldn't reveal more about the project: "But I've got to do some research. Take a bit of a trip."

"Let me get this straight, Bernie. Your daughter is lying in a coma at the San Francisco General and you're going abroad to research a book?"

"The timing's bad. Just say no and I won't go."

"This doesn't compute, Bernie." The M.E. made a steeple with her fingers and looked at the ceiling: "Everybody knows you love your daughter more than life itself. No, Bernie. Want to know what I think?" She sprang out of her chair and leaned across her desk to yell in my face: "I think you're trying to buffalo an old buffalo shooter."

"All right! You want the truth?" I whipped out the ad in the personals, which I'd circled in red and stuffed in my pocket. "See this? If I get a paid leave, I'm travelling to Greece and India and probably East Africa. I've been ordered to find the Sacred Fire of Ahura Mazda."

"Ahura Mazda?" The M.E. looked stunned. "Did you...did you say Ahura Mazda?"

"You know the name?"

The M.E. put her hand to her eyes and settled back into her chair.

When she spoke again, she used a soft voice I hadn't heard in years: "Talk to me, Bernie."

What could I do? I told her the story. How during my Near Death Experience, Behroze had turned up. How yesterday, at the hospital, she'd visited again and this time told me to seek a paid leave. Also, to check the personals: "The ad's just a coincidence," I said. "If I don't get the paid leave, I won't go. I'll have fulfilled my obligation simply by asking."

"Remember three years ago?" the M.E. said. "When I lost my son to cancer?"

"That was terrible. Just terrible."

"Last night, Bernie, he came to me in a dream. He said, 'Mom, remember the name 'Ahura Mazda.' When you hear that name, move mountains."

"Your . . . your son said that?"

"Move mountains." The M.E. wiped away a tear, surprising me. She resumed her usual brusque manner and picked up my request for a leave. "Ahura Mazda sounds like the name of a car dealership."

"That's what I think. If you don't —"

She waved me to silence, whirled to face her computer and began punching out a letter. "I'm authorizing a three-month leave, Lanigan. Full salary and medical benefits. I'll explain that you're under stress. An irreplaceable employee. Bad car accident. Daughter's in hospital."

"But this is . . . wait! I don't know what to think."

"Get out of here before I change my mind."

As I went to the door, still in shock, the M.E. said, "Lanigan."

I turned, hoping against hope that she'd regained her senses.

She started to speak, then hesitated, smiled lopsidedly and wiggled her fingers in the air: "Bon voyage."

Casting The Runes

Next thing I knew, I was sailing out of New York on the freighter Verlandi, leaning over the railing and watching the Statue of Liberty recede into a grey and gritty, smoke-dark afternoon. A dock-area blaze had reduced several buildings to rubble, and I wondered whether the Vanishing Arsonist had followed me across the continent. I dismissed the idea as ludicrous, and stood savoring the way a solitary shaft of sunlight glanced off Liberty's torch to produce an illusion of flame. Overhead, a dozen seagulls wheeled and soared and squawked, a raucous entertainment.

As I wondered idly how long they'd accompany us, I felt a strange tingling. At the back of my neck, the hair stood up. According to Behroze, this sensation signaled a coincidence fraught with meaning — perhaps a full-blown synchronicity. My Great Awakening, she'd said, would produce curious symptoms. Down the railing, two fellow passengers had joined me on deck. Of course,

I focused first on the female — an attractive, fit-looking young woman who stood studying the cityscape through binoculars. She wore an African shirt, batiked, wildly colourful, and powder-blue jeans that fit snugly. "Nothing," she said relievedly, lowering the binoculars: "Maybe we've lost them?"

The late-summer breeze blew her words in my direction, mingling them with a spray of salt water. Her male companion looked dubious: "Don't be hasty, dear one. Those seagulls look suspicious."

I registered a British accent. The young woman threw back her head and laughed, all gleaming white teeth and black hair blowing in the wind: "We've lost them, Taggart! Good riddance to bad Chinvat."

Sounded American, but not quite. And had she really said Chinvat? Even as I wondered, I sensed her relief — and also a subterranean lack of inhibition. She glanced over and smiled absently and that's when it hit me, breaking through my depression — a psychic anomaly I now recognize as an epiphany. I experienced a dazzling flash of clarity and realized with conviction that this young woman could change my life.

Seconds later, I dismissed the perception: ridiculous. With her fine features and lovely brown skin, this woman resembled my dead wife, that was all — though I realized with surprise that she was even more hauntingly beautiful than Behroze. She looked part-Indian, part-African, and I settled on the word "stunning" as her companion pronounced her name and the wind carried it my way: Saf-EYE-ah.

I thought: must be spelled "Safiya."

But what of her companion, this unlikely Englishman who looked a dozen years older, maybe more? Would you believe a top hat, a velvet jacket and black hair falling unkempt to his shoulders? A costume, then, completed by baggy black corduroy trousers and, beneath the maroon jacket, a black T-shirt that proclaimed, in phosphorescent, lime-green lettering: "Casting The Runes."

Mentally, I ran down pigeon-holes, hesitated at "English eccentric." But no, that failed to do the man justice — because this guy fairly pulsated with intelligence. Perhaps these two counted among the significant figures Behroze had promised me? All the other passengers looked like suburbanites, long may they prosper, and I'd begun to fear for my sanity: where were my guides and mentors? So far I'd identified not a single fellow traveller, much less an expedition leader. What could these well-heeled tourists be expected to know about the Golden Flame?

Oh, I'd embarked on a singular journey.

New York City had become a smudge on the horizon. Surreptiously, I watched as Safiya made for the stairs. She moved like a panther and I thought: not an athlete but a dancer, perhaps? And was I kidding myself? Or did she not glance at me, briefly, as she disappeared into the stairwell.

Moments later, in my cabin, I checked the passenger manifest: Safiya Naidoo and Taggart Oates. They showed up as Canadians, the only two aboard — Canadians from Montreal. The manifest revealed nothing else so I closed my eyes and concentrated. This felt strange, faintly ridiculous, but lately I'd begun trying, on Behroze's advice, to develop my "latent paranormal abilities."

To my surprise, I'd glimpsed a few distant events later corroborated as having happened. Also, given a focus, I'd caught flashes of letters, articles and photographs. I remained astonished by these capacities, which would have come in especially handy, I thought, on the police beat.

But what was that? A photo of Safiya in a broadsheet newspaper? I lost the image but found it again and focused, locked onto a half-page feature and caught the gist of it. Three years before, at age twenty-eight, Safiya Naidoo had made quite a splash in the Great White North when her first novel, The Red Bird of  Paradise, won a literary prize worth twenty-five thousand dollars.

That surprised me — so young: an award-winning author. I lost focus and couldn't immediately regain it. I turned to Taggart Oates, anticipating similar revelations, and found myself stumbling around in a thick fog. This was new. These "psychic scans" usually functioned like florescent lights: hit the right switch and you could "read" anyone you wanted. Not so, apparently, with Taggart Oates. Intrigued, I continued trying to navigage the grey fog until the ship's steward, marching past along the corridor, rapped on my cabin door: "Dinner time."

Psychic exertions exacted an energy toll, I'd discovered, and to avoid dizziness I rose slowly from my bunk. As yet unaccustomed to the pitch and roll of the ship, I braced myself while washing my hands, then changed my shirt and made for the dining room. The steward, a strapping Norwegian named George, greeted passengers at the entrance. He showed me to an empty table for four and said my dinner companions would arrive shortly: an insurance broker and his wife. That's how he described them, almost gleefully: "From Omaha, Nebraska."

But now Taggart and Safiya arrived at the double swinging doors that opened into the dining room. Safiya had traded her jeans and batiked shirt for a sparkling blue sari of understated elegance. Taggart wore the same maroon smoking jacket, but he'd dispensed with his top hat and now I saw why he wore it: on top he was bald. Guiltily, I ran my fingers through my own unruly hair, which is thick and black — my sole physical blessing unattended.

George the steward led Safiya and Taggart towards a distant table occupied by two women with broad southern accents that echoed throughout the dining room. Halfway across, Taggart seized the younger man's elbow and whispered in his ear. He didn't wish to join those women. The steward shook his head, shrugged: he was helpless to change the seating arrangement.

Safiya had been gazing around the room. Now she pointed in my direction and whispered to Taggart, who nodded and led the way towards me. I rose to my feet as the three approached, the steward having given up on Taggart to plead with Safiya, who smiled brightly and shrugged: what could she do?

"Hello, I'm Taggart Oates." Quite the gentleman, no question. "I hope you don't mind if we join you?"

"Not at all. Bernard Lanigan." I shook Taggart's hand, then turned to his companion: "And you're Safiya."

"Safiya Naidoo." Her smile lit up the dining room. "You've been studying your manifest, Mr. Lanigan." She gave me her hand: so warm. And what fingers, so long and delicate. "Even so, most people mispronounce."

"Saf-EYE-ah," I said again, savoring the sound of it. "What does it mean?"

"Clear-mindedness." Again, that dazzling smile. "Purity,

wisdom — take your pick."

"Saf-EYE-ah. Clear-mindedness."

"Once they seat you at a table, that's it," Taggart said, explaining their arrival. "They don't let you shift about. And those accents would have finished me." He looked up at the steward: "Thank you, George. Just seat the doctor and his wife where you were going to put us. Problem solved, see?" He turned to me: "You're American?"

"San Francisco, born and bred. And you're — Canadian?"

"A dual citizen, actually. British, originally."

On his T-shirt, beneath the lime-green words "Casting The Runes," smaller lettering elaborated: "A novel by Taggart Oates."

At last I pegged him: celebrity author. Taggart had published half a dozen pop-culture books on mythology and religion and then began cranking out supernatural thrillers. In the eighties, People magazine had hailed him as a cross between Joseph Campbell and Stephen King, more sensational than the former, less escapist than the latter. He'd got embroiled in some scandal: "You wrote that controversial best-seller, what was it called?"

"Lord of Misrule?" Taggart beckoned the waitress. "They ran me out of England for that one."

"Taggart, they did not." Safiya laughed — yet I detected a troubled undertone. "He followed a woman to North America and got a taste of what he'd been missing."

"Winter, you mean?" To me, he added: "She's got such an imagination."

"Safiya's a writer, too, unless I'm mistaken."

The waitress arrived and Taggart ordered champagne: "No, make that two bottles."

I pointed at the Castillo di Almansa I'd already ordered: "I hope you'll share this?"

"That's a fine beginning, Bernard — but we've an occasion to celebrate. It's not every day that one sails for Greece."

"Or for Greece and India." I said, "and god knows where else."

Safiya started to speak but George the steward interrupted, began doling out food: pepper steak and pink salmon and juicy pink shrimp, a variety of vegetables. Taggart rubbed his hands together: "We'll feast this voyage."

We tucked into the meal and finished the red wine. By the time dessert arrived, we'd popped the cork on our second champagne. I chose fresh-fruit custard, Taggart chocolate mousse and Safiya lemon cheese cake. Turning to me, she said: "Are you really going to India?"

"Yes. To the Taj Mahal."

"My ancestors built the Taj. Or helped, anyway."

Safiya explained that she was born and raised in Canada, but her parents had immigrated from Trinidad and certain ancestors from India. "So says the family history, mon," she added, affecting a Trindadian accent. "I look more African than Indian, I know. But in what's left of the Commonwealth, we're all Creoles under the British Queen."

I proposed a toast: "To wayfaring Creoles."

We drained our glasses and, though Safiya protested, Taggart, red-faced and flying, called for a third champagne. Safiya told me that, from Greece, they would fly to Sri Lanka, where Taggart would spend several weeks as a writer-in-residence at the university. He'd shuttle between Colombo and Kandy, the bustling coast and the campus in tea country — one of the most beautiful, apparently, in the former British Commonwealth.

I caught myself drowning in her dark brown eyes, but managed: "Sri Lanka? Isn't civil war raging?"

Taggart said: "Civil war's over-rated."

"He set one of his novels there," Sayfia said. "The Buddha's Tooth."

"The allusion is to a Sri Lankan myth."

"To millennial nomads!" I exclaimed, raising my glass. "To citizens of the New World who go travelling on ships and planes across borders that no longer exist."

For the first time in weeks, I'd emerged from heavy darkness.

"I'll remain in Sri Lanka," Taggart said, smiling confidentially. "But Safiya will travel to East Africa, where we believe her ex-boyfriend resides. Perhaps you've heard of him: Daniel Lafontaine? He's a musician."

Safiya said, "Taggart, please don't start."

"Don't you see it in his eyes, Safiya? Lanigan, here, has a sixth sense. Sooner or later, he'll discover the truth." Taggart seized my arm and whispered theatrically: "Safiya means to find Daniel

Lafontaine."

"Taggart, you're the one who insisted we travel together."

Still affecting the conspiratorial, Taggart rolled his eyes: "Secretly, she's hoping he'll take her back."

"Even after I said I'd prefer to travel alone," Safiya said. "And you'll be just as glad to find Daniel — three must set forth?"

"Not quite as glad, my dear."

"You must excuse Taggart. He gets nasty when he drinks."

"With me, Safiya will visit Greece and Sri Lanka. With me, she'll gather fire-worthy souvenirs. But then away she'll fly to East Africa, there to cohabit with a flaxen-haired musician."

My sixth sense had gone on full alert at the mention of fire-worthy souvenirs, but I said only, "You know he's in East Africa?"

"Yes, but not precisely where. Safiya's been trying to locate him."

"So have you, Taggart." She smiled stiffly: "You'll excuse me, Mr. Lanigan."

"Bernard, please. Bernie."

In a single fluid motion, Safiya rose, pushed back her chair, spun on her heel and walked away.

"Bravo!" Taggart applauded loudly. "What a performance!"

Safiya disappeared through the swinging doors and his forced laughter turned to angry muttering. "Damn the woman, anyway." Taggart flung down his napkin. "Damn her for insolence."

Before I could respond, Taggart jumped to his feet and, while our fellow diners stared goggle-eyed, stormed across the room: "Safiya!" He barged through the doors and stomped up the stairs bellowing: "Safiya! Safiya, in the name of Mazda, I command thee: come back!"

I'd half-risen to my feet but dropped back into my chair. In the name of Mazda? How much corroboration did I require? Safiya had mentioned the Chinvat, and Taggart the gathering of fire-worthy souvenirs. Now, with this drunken imprecation, he'd removed all doubt: like me, these two were seeking the Golden Flame. Ah, but were they friends or enemies?

The Red Bird of Paradise

For watching and waiting, the Verlandi proved ideal, if only because a working freighter is not a cruise ship. Imagine trying to spy on two passengers among seven or eight hundred. On the Verlandi, a container vessel, we numbered eleven. And for the first week of the voyage, we encountered nothing but water, water everywhere. Who says we live in a global village? For days we saw no cities, visited no sights, enjoyed no diversions except those we created.

Everything Taggart and Safiya said and did confirmed my suspicion: they'd embarked on a quest that paralleled my own. But perhaps the two quests, or three, could become one? I remembered the mimeographed pamphlet, The Secret of The Golden Flame, that I'd foolishly tossed aside in Colette's hospital room. And ransacked even my unconscious mind for details.

The pamphlet spoke of the prophet Zarathustra, but also of Friedrich Nietzsche and Carl Jung and the legendary clairvoyant

Emanuel Swedenborg. It described the war between Ahura Mazda and Ahriman as "an all-pervasive duality" that would continue until the so-called Renovation. It spoke of subsuming western shamanism, and of orders of reality and sweeping time cycles and three great saviours who would arise sequentially in the Golden Flame, one at the end of each millennium. The pamphlet said nothing of shared quests, I didn't think — though it didn't rule them out, either. Almost despite myself, I began to hope. . . .

More than once Safiya and I found ourselves reading, just the two of us, in the passenger lounge, which comprised a perennially deserted bar, half a dozen wide, comfortable chairs and a small library of mass-market paperbacks discarded by previous passengers. One afternoon, as I stood studying these books, Safiya pulled out a novel called The Music of Chance and suggested I read it.

"What about The Red Bird of Paradise? I'll happily buy a copy."

"When you're ready, I'll give you one."

I didn't know quite how to take this, and Safiya just grinned, maddeningly enigmatic. She didn't produce her own novel and I plunged into The Music of Chance by Paul Auster.

Sometimes, if I didn't find Safiya in the lounge, I'd head up on deck, spread a blanket and read in the sunshine. Every couple of hours, for a change, I'd make my way to the bow of the ship and stand there, hanging onto the flag pole, as the Verlandi bobbed and plunged across the slate-blue sea. The last seagull had departed on our second day out and gazing around I'd see nothing but blue sky and Atlantic Ocean, both empty and endless.

The Verlandi did offer one organized entertainment: shuffleboard. That's how I met the other male passengers. After dinner, during the early going, we would gather on the main deck and play for an hour. I didn't enjoy this as much as I might have, but shuffleboard took my mind off Colette, about whom, though she haunted me continually, I've contrived to say almost nothing. Even now, the memory of her lying alone in that hospital bed makes me sweat and tremble. I returned to that image again and again, spent countless hours aching, hugging myself in my bunk, the pain of my absent daughter ever-present, unchanging, almost unbearable.

In retrospect, I take that pain for granted and focus instead on the passing parade. Except for Taggart and I, all the male passengers had retired, two from business, one from academia. This last, a quiet man who'd chaired the department of librarianship at Pennsylvania State, played shuffleboard only once. Safiya, I learned later, had secretly dubbed him "The Professor." Now he roamed the world with his second wife, a woman in her mid-forties, formerly a travel agent. They'd embarked on an extended honeymoon and kept to themselves.

Two ex-businessmen, Marvin and Milo, debated get-rich-quick schemes the way church scholars once argued about angels on the head of a pin. Marvin had managed an insurance agency in Omaha, Nebraska, and remained proudly a man of the suburbs — of backyard barbecues, exemplary lawn care and mini-vans that never wanted for an oil change. By comparison, Milo sparkled and shone. Swarthy and boisterous and loud about not having completed high school, he impressed me initially as more profoundly American than any of the rest of us — as the quintessential American, in fact: a self-made man, a builder.

I rather liked Milo until the third evening, when he started ranting about unionized workers: "Offer a guy a hundred bucks a day, he says his union stipulates one-forty and he won't take a penny less. These guys shouldn't get welfare. We should get rid of the whole system. Seventy per cent of their kids are illegitimate."

That's when I got it: "their" kids. Milo reminded me of a redneck trustee I'd interviewed for an article on a teachers' strike. He was bad-mouthing not just unionized workers but, incredibly, unionized black workers. The quintessential American? I didn't think so. I struck Milo from my list of sympathetic travellers, though he didn't seem to notice.

And the women? To the women I will return. Trust me: men and women together comprised a motley crew, one embarked on a physical journey, not a spiritual one. At best they sought exotica, at worst, distraction. And only Taggart and Safiya stood apart. While I'd worked away at single-parenthood in California, they'd been turning themselves into citizens of the world. To them, I would have drawn nearer even without the impetus of the quest. Nearer, especially, to Safiya, who attracted me so powerfully that, under the circumstances, I felt disturbed by my own interest: what? my twelve-year-old daughter lay comatose in a San Francisco hospital and still Safiya made me behave like a schoolboy? I'd begun a voyage of exploration, all right — and not every discovery would make me proud.

Aboard the Verlandi, nobody willingly missed a meal. George the steward would stride down the corridor ringing his xylophone and we passengers would emerge from our cabins like children flocking after the Pied Piper. As Taggart had foreseen, the captain expected us to remain at our original tables, a policy doubtless dictated by unhappy experience. That left me eating regularly with Safiya and Taggart, and for that I silently thanked Ahura Mazda.

The fare was conventional but beautifully prepared. In the morning, we'd start with cereals, fruits and juices. One day we'd choose between omelettes and soft-boiled eggs, the next between Eggs Benedict and either sunny-side-up or once-over-lightly. At lunch, we'd confront a dozen different salads and an array of coldcuts, though usually the focus was seafood: smoked salmon, herring, sardines, even caviar.

At dinner time, three servers materialized — George and the ship's two chambermaids who, for obvious reasons, pretended to speak only Norwegian. Passengers would choose between two main courses, one meat, the other fish, often including lobster. If the food lacked spice — nothing Indian or Malaysian or even Chinese — it was more than abundant. For dessert, we'd eat fruit or yogurt or perhaps watermelon, but also we'd face blueberry pie one night, chocolate cake the next, and always three kinds of ice cream.

During recent weeks, I'd eaten little. Now, aboard the Verlandi, I regained my appetite. Trying to eat healthy, however, like a good Californian, I fought a daily battle, what with Taggart showing zero restraint — hence his paunch — and Safiya behaving unpredictably. One day, she'd sample both pie and cake and the next she'd pick at a salad. When I remarked on this, Taggart shrugged: "With Safiya, you learn to expect the unexpected."

As for that first evening's blowout, Taggart alluded to it only once: "Never apologize, never explain. Don't you agree, Safiya?"

"I prefer to do nothing for which I need apologize."

These two, I realized, were fighting a psychological war.

Taggart remained opaque to me, impenetrable, but I found the silhouette of Safiya's inner life enthralling: so ambivalent. I basked in her presence — after all, I'd received no specific orders — though I swore NOT to get sucked into any emotional whirlpools. Besides, I felt perfectly safe. Experience had taught me that, though I might lapse into infatuation, I would never fall in love. The death of Behroze, or rather my guilt over it, had rendered me emotionally impotent — incapable not of performing sexually, but of humanly connecting. And now Colette lay comatose . . . .

Our third night out of New York, unable to sleep, I decided to take a starry-night stroll. As I made my way along the corridor, I heard an old familiar sound coming out of George-the-steward's cabin — not whimpering and moaning, no, but the clatter of poker chips.

Once upon a time, I'd fancied myself quite a poker player. In the days before I met Behroze, I'd gamble into the wee hours with cronies from my university days. Dealer's choice, nickel ante. Inevitably, despite the best efforts of a stalwart few, the game would degenerate into wild cards and foolishness: Baseball, Kings and Wee Ones, Fives and Sevens. Despite the levelling effect of pure, unmediated chance, usually I'd win a few bucks.

The clatter of poker chips, then. Even so, I almost walked past, immersed in thoughts of the lunatic quest on which I'd embarked. But the sound of a female voice, sudden laughter — could it be? — caused me to spin on my heel and knock on the cabin door. And then to knock a second time. Finally, George the steward opened a crack.

"You've got a game going," I said.

He looked at me blankly: "A game?"

"George, I want in."

He glanced over his shoulder, consulting his fellow players, then shrugged and motioned me into the crowded cabin. Four figures sat hunched around a green felt table. Three of them I recognized as junior officers: bosun, engineer, radio operator. And sure enough, the fourth was Safiya Naidoo, who grinned up at me as she shuffled the cards, riffling them professionally: "What took you so long, Bernie?"

Safiya had joined the game last night. As a rule, George excluded passengers, because what if one of them lost big and complained to the captain? With Safiya, who'd rambled all over the ship making friends, the other junior officers had over-ruled him. Trouble was, how now could they exclude this second voyager?

"Win or lose, George," I said as I joined the table, "we won't complain. Right, Safiya?"

George stared at me, surprised: it was like I'd read his mind.

Safiya said: "Complain? Of course not."

The game was five-card draw, Jacks or better to open. Quarter ante, two-dollar maximum. It wasn't until I picked up my first hand that I thought: wait, I can't do this — not with my growing abilities. Any time I concentrate, I can peer into an opponent's mind, and what kind of game is that?

On the other hand, night-time brought terrible doubts and agonizing visions of Colette lying alone in San Francisco. This poker game was the only distraction going. The cameraderie, the kibbitzing: damn it, I wanted to play. All I had to do was make sure I didnt't win but broke even.

Even after we began hitting ports, and spending our days ashore, we played nightly from nine until two in the morning. One night I'd win ten or fifteen bucks and the next I'd make certain to lose it. I couldn't turn myself off completely, not while concentrating hard enough to compete, but I enjoyed long stretches of normal consciousness — and plenty of time to savor card-table dynamics.

Safiya turned up every night. She loved poker and said so, adding that Taggart despised games of chance: "He's phobic about it." As for the larger question that went unasked — why these nightly absences from her travelling companion? — that Safiya never addressed. I decided the answer had to do with Daniel Lafontaine, the absent third. And focused on the game.

I found myself scanning the other players as I'd always done at poker, though I realized that I saw more deeply than I once did. I smiled grimly to think that my improved poker skills constituted a first sign of the transformation said to be part of the Golden Flame. Ha!

Three of the men played solidly, though each had weaknesses. George would draw to an inside straight; Ragnar the bosun would lose track while doggedly counting cards; and Bjorn the chief engineer bluffed too often, especially in a game where a fourth man, Sparky, the radio operator, thought he could win by remaining in every hand. He'd finish the night sixty dollars down and say: "That's it. I've lost enough."

Next night, he'd resurface and play the same game. Once, I quietly suggested: "Sparky, listen: when you've got nothing in your hand, the earlier you fold, the better."

"Cards aren't running my way," he said. "That'll change. Deal 'em up."

Safiya raised her eyebrows at me and said nothing.

Oh, she played well. But why was I surprised? She'd win forty dollars one night, fifty the next — and she never made the same mistake twice. She played more aggressively than I ever had, and ran more risks, but in her game I could find no consistent flaw. Give her a "nothing hand" and she'd fold — though every so often, when the stakes were low, she'd run a bluff expecting to lose. That way, when she held a winning hand and sweetened the pot, everybody stayed with her: after all, she might be bluffing.

More often than not, these poker games came down to a final hand. One memorable night, George and Safiya faced off. They were both ahead twenty-five or thirty dollars. Two o'clock in the morning, well into the stretch, George drew a single card and filled out a queen-high flush. Safiya drew two cards — and I deliberately tuned her out.

Towards the end of each night, by general consent, we'd raise the maximum bet from two to five dollars, and that's what Safiya tossed onto the table. Sparky and Bjorn called her and George bumped five. That meant Safiya could raise the amount of the entire pot, and she did so. Bjorn and even Sparky folded, reluctantly — but by now we're talking a pot worth forty or fifty dollars. Swallowing hard, George called: "You got a flush?"

"Yup. King high." Safiya showed the King of Hearts.

"Me, too." George turned over the King of Clubs. "And I've got a Jack to go with it."

Out that came.

Safiya leaned forward, studied the Jack: "That's too bad."

George grinned, relieved, reached for the pot — then stopped.

"Too bad for you, I mean." Safiya turned over three low hearts and then brought out the Queen. "Better luck next time, buddy."

Later, up on deck, replaying the finale in my mind, I couldn't help chuckling: "That was cruel, Safiya — the way you played that last hand."

"Yes, but did you see his face when I turned over the Queen?"

We stood leaning over the railing as the Verlandi sliced into the night. We'd taken to chatting like this after poker, both of us needing to unwind. Usually, we spoke only of the game, but tonight a full moon hung huge and off-white over the ocean. I felt Safiya's mood and said, "You're pensive."

"It's the moon, I think."

"Reminds you of meeting a certain piano-man, no?"

"Sit him down at a keyboard and he makes magic. But how did — "

"Please: tell me the story. You'd published The Red Bird of Paradise."

"Ah, Taggart must have told you."

"And you started getting invitations to book launches."

The scene came to me now, though Safiya didn't realize. "They can be pretty stiff affairs," she said. "All these people standing around talking, sipping wine, checking over your shoulder to see who else has arrived."

"You'd have been what? Twenty-eight?"

Safiya nodded, at once worldly and unselfconscious, but now her words became redundant because I joined her at the party — or rather, I felt myself both here and there. Another new sensation. Safiya and three girlfriends had driven out into the autumn evening, bound eventually for an all-night dance party. Safiya talked her friends into swinging past the book launch. Some professor's place — a redbrick mansion in Outremont, an upscale Montreal neighborhood where once my mother had worked as a babysitter.

"We weren't there ten minutes when a cry goes up and this gorgeous blond guy sits down at the piano. He warms up with some Mozart concerto and I'm thinking, oh great, the girls are going to love this — but then bam! the guy shifts gears into boogie-woogie and suddenly the whole house is jumping."

When the place can't get much higher, the piano-man cuts to a slow number, says, "Anyone see Evita?" Then, in a high, clear voice, and with just a trace of French accent, he launches into Another Suitcase In Another Hall: "I don't expect my love affairs to last for long / Never fool myself that my dreams will come true."

On the Verlandi, remembering, Safiya herself sings those lines and the next couple: "Being used to trouble I anticipate it / But all the same I hate it, wouldn't you?" She pauses, shakes her head. "By the time he finishes, I've fallen in love — along with every other woman in the place. I'm applauding, but also I'm yelling, 'Yes! Yes!'"

The piano-man spots Safiya and blows her a kiss but well-wishers surround him, most of them women, and she beats a strategic retreat. She picks up the young man's name: Daniel Lafontaine. She's trying for more but her friends get restless: "They have a real-time party to attend," she explains. "A big blowout downtown and never mind this literary stuff, they want to meet some guys."

Her friends threaten to leave without her and finally Safiya says, "Okay, okay, enough already," and follows them into the night. That's when it happens, the magic moment. Safiya's making for the car when, directly above Mount Royal, the so-called "mountain in the middle of town" that my Quebecoise mother used to talk about, she sees the full moon hanging so white and huge and glorious that she can't understand why she didn't notice it earlier.

"That's when the ringing starts," she says. "This insistent, oddly silent ringing coming from somewhere deep inside me. I stop and stare up at the moon and then Time stands still, or that's how it feels, and I realize the full moon's an omen. It's telling me I've arrived at a fork in the road, one of those rare moments, maybe two or three in a lifetime, when you make a crucial choice: this way or that? Daniel Lafontaine, yes or no? I realize that he can be important to me, play a role in my life. But if I leave now, if I disappear into the night? I'll never see him again."

"You didn't need a full moon to tell you that."

Safiya shrugged. "I told my friends I'd changed my mind and plunged back into that launch-party. As I strode across the room, I spotted this vase full of red roses and plucked one and kept walking, and there stood Daniel chatting with this well-known woman poet, but I stepped into the circle and handed him the rose: 'Daniel Lafontaine, will you marry me?'"

"He thought you were nuts."

Safiya chuckled: "Maybe you'll get to meet him."

"He's in East Africa?"

"Yes, teaching music."

We fell silent and stared out over the railing. After a moment, laughing ruefully, Safiya said: "He waited until after we'd made love to tell me that soon he'd be leaving for Africa." She chuckled. "He knew I'd think that he was the crazy one."

"To that, I can relate," I said.

"It was okay for me to be nuts, but not him."

"Ahura Mazda does funny things to people."

Safiya had been staring out over the water. Now, slowly, she turned to face me: "What did you say?"

"Ah! That got your attention."

"Did you just say what I think you said?"

"Ahura Mazda? Yes, I do believe we share a common quest."

"I don't believe it! Why didn't I realize?" Safiya slapped her forehead. "Wait until Taggart hears this."

"You think it's wise to tell him?"

"Of course, you goof! Only two will approach the Shaman, yet three must set forth together. This changes everything." Seeing my confusion, she continued: "Your presence renders Daniel expendable, don't you see? Or that's how Taggart will see it. You're less of a threat."

"Are you trying to flatter me?"

"Taggart will absolutely rejoice at this revelation."

I wanted to say: "And you, Safiya? What about you?"

But in a way, she'd already answered: I presented less of a threat.

Viva Las Palmas

Safiya proved wrong in suggesting that Taggart would be pleased about my questing, though she proved right, and even prophetic, about everything else we discussed that night on the deck of the Verlandi. I'd registered Safiya from the moment I saw her, as faithfully reported, but for her I became real only now. Given her serious attention for the first time, did I talk? No, I babbled. With the full moon above, and the Verlandi bashing into the night towards Spain, Italy and Greece, I connected the dots between moments I'd already revealed. I told Safiya how I'd been called to the quest: that I'd survived a freak car accident but denied a calling forth and now my darling Colette lay comatose in a San Francisco hospital. Safiya shook her head in dismay — but showed no surprise. I told her about Behroze — not how guilty I felt about having caused her death, but how she'd fixed it with the Managing Editor so I could seek The Shaman.

An auspicious departure, Safiya called this — adding ruefully

(I couldn't help noticing) that Daniel Lafontaine had departed under less happy stars. Instead of going with him, she said, or at least bidding him farewell, "I tried to shake him out of his trance." When he persisted in his obsession, insisted on pursuing this quest, she told him goodbye. "That was my version of the second refusal," she said. "Not long afterwards, my sister got cancer." She turned away: "It's in remission — at least for now."

Thrilling to her honesty, which implied such trust, I responded with my own baffled observation: "What kind of 'benevolent god' summons people using car accidents, comas and cancer?"

"My sister's cancer is the work of Ahriman, the father of envy, hatred and destruction. The remission is Ahura Mazda's. Don't you see? Scratch a religion or a metaphysical philosophy and you'll find a dynamic polarity. Yahweh and Satan, Vishnu and Shiva."

"Yin and Yang. One reality, countless polarities."

Safiya nodded: "The calling to the quest shines a spotlight on you. Attracts the wrong kind of attention. Light brings forth dark."

"And refusing the call?"

"Renders you still more visible — and vulnerable. So says Taggart, anyway. All I know is that my mother died after I rejected the first calling, which came to me in a dream." She shook her head sadly: "I dismissed the timing of my mother's death as a coincidence. I was immersed in my second novel and didn't want to hear about Golden Flames and Sacred Fires. Then came the freak disasters. The Fleuve St-Laurent overflowed into Montreal. A lightning storm started a fire in the east end that killed hundreds."

"What's that got to do with anything?"

"Ahriman is awakening after a millennial sleep. The world-wide explosion in natural calamities? Earthquakes and hurricanes, wildfires, volcanoes? Taggart says Ahriman's behind all of it."

"The Vanishing Arsonist?"

Safiya nodded: "To put the Evil One back to sleep, some mortal must purify a talisman in The Shaman's Fire."

"Wait a minute. Nobody said anything about an Evil One to me. The only reason I'm here is Colette."

"Are you sure, Bernie? Don't you ever get the feeling that somebody else is pulling the strings? That we're marionettes?"

"Absolutely not! Free will is ours — that much I know." I thought then of my recurring nightmare, and how my guilt over the death of Behroze regularly reduced me to pleading for a chance to redeem myself: "I do recognize secondary motives."

"Bernie, we've all got personal considerations. But tens of thousands have already been sacrificed. Volcanoes in the Phillippines and Japan, earthquakes in Mexico and Central America, bombings and ethnic cleansings in the Balkans."

"That's not fire."

Safiya shook her head impatiently: "Death and destruction, Bernie — the Evil One wears a thousand different masks. Until somebody accomplishes the quest, innocent people will continue to die — and they'll die in the tens, the hundreds of thousands. Maybe even the millions."

"Is that what convinced you? Natural calamities?"

"Not alone, no. But Daniel predicted omens and signs, and then I met Taggart at a literary conference on the millennium. When he casually mentioned the Golden Flame, I told him my story and he clarified my situation: I'd ignored a dream and rejected a personal invitation. My meeting with Taggart was a last-chance synchronicity. Either I got with the program or my sister would die."

I was tempted to joke: "That's quite a line." But I heard the sadness in her voice, the seriousness, and I said, "The long arm of the awakening Ahriman." Then, as another thought came to me: "I hope this doesn't make us . . . competitors?"

"Friends and uneasy allies. That's the demented beauty of it, according to Taggart. Only one of us can succeed. But two ashavans must approach The Shaman together, and before that, three must set forth — three seekers of deeper meaning."

"Taggart knows all this?"

"Bernie, superior knowledge is his gift."

"Like creativity is yours?"

"And extrasensory perception your own." Safiya laughed at my discomfort. "Everything is finally fitting into place. Did you think me completely unaware?"

I shrugged: "And Taggart? What does he know?"

"He'll rejoice to learn you're one of us, Bernie."

I smiled ruefully: "The lesser threat."

Safiya laughed, impulsively kissed my cheek, then turned and walked away, leaving me suddenly alone under the stars, and far,

far away from home. I'm not proud of what I did next, but don't feel I can honestly withhold it. After standing a few more moments on deck, I returned to my cabin, stretched out on my bunk and, well, deliberately turned my attention to Safiya. In my mind's eye, I went down the corridor, entered the double cabin she shared with Taggart and found her hunched over a table, writing in her notebook by flashlight.

Taggart lay snoring in his single bunk. Clearly, she didn't want to disturb him. I waited until she finished writing and closed her notebook. She clicked off the flashlight and then brushed her teeth in the small washroom before undressing. In the darkness I couldn't see clearly, but as she pulled a light shift over her head, I registered her heart-stopping beauty.

Back in my own cabin, as I returned to consciousness, Behroze danced a few words through my mind: "Return to the depth of your soul," she said. "That is where you will always rediscover the source of the sacred fire . . . ."

The source of the fire, indeed. It wasn't quite a rebuke, yet a tidal wave of shame swept over me — not just for having invaded Safiya's privacy, but because somehow Behroze knew what I'd done. I vowed never to repeat this terrible invasion, no matter how desperately I yearned. And realized only then how exhausted I felt, how psychologically drained. But of course: psychically, I'd just run a marathon.

Next morning, Taggart greeted me ambiguously: "Welcome aboard, Mr. Lanigan." But he didn't acknowledge that we shared a life-and-death quest until we reached Las Palmas, and then his recognition came only after we'd shared a bizarre misadventure and several beers, and I'd raised the subject myself because I felt haunted by yet another bit of paranormality.

The trouble with clairvoyance is you can't always control it. One of my main motivations in developing my incipient powers was to keep tabs on Colette back in San Francisco. With the help of Behroze, whose rivetting presence had enabled me to locate that distant hospital room, I'd locked onto my comatose daughter. Now, the instant Colette registered any change in consciousness, no matter how miniscule, I would know about it.

Meanwhile, however, since our second day at sea I'd been receiving telepathic flashes from East Africa: Swahili proverbs mostly, but also nursery rhymes, newspaper articles and, occasionally, full-blown rushes from a beach or a hotel bar. These came, I'd deduced, courtesy of Safiya Naidoo. Her pining for Daniel Lafontaine had created a channel of sorts, or perhaps the two of them had established a psychic rapport outside of Time. Either way, I recognized these flashes as arising from a deeper, spiritual reality that's embedded in the profane reality of our mundane lives.

Don't ask me to explain when all I can do is describe. Even now, as I write these lines, I don't pretend to understand. Then, all I knew was that I'd be sitting alone on deck, relaxing with a book, when suddenly, whap! I'd register a snatch of Swahili complete with English translation: *Mafahali wawili hawakai zizi moja.* Two bulls do not live in the same cowshed. And again: *Kamba hukatikia pembamba.* A rope parts where it is thinnest. And yet again: *Avuaye nguo huchutama.* He who is naked squats low.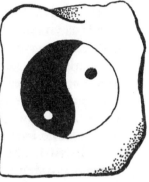

We're talking quick hits every time. So that's how it began.

The first indelible dream didn't arrive until the Verlandi neared its first stop: the Canary Islands. I'd eaten a hefty breakfast and lay on my bunk, enjoying the gentle rocking of the ship, when look out! suddenly I'm in Tanzania with Daniel Lafontaine, who's stuffing clothes into a canvas bag while babbling excitedly to a friend: "You've got that map? And your fire-worthy souvenirs?"

Daniel looks nothing like your stereotypical Quebecois. He's blond, six feet tall, beautifully put together. He speaks Canadian English with just a hint of French accent, and so reminds me of my mother. His friend, Victor, is a striking man of mixed heritage. I register African-American, Cherokee Indian, Caucasian-Greek and don't know what else. Victor's older than Daniel, more mid-thirties, like me. At the International School, where Daniel teaches music, he teaches English and Art.

It's school break, a week-long holiday for teachers, and these two buddies are packing to visit the coastal town of Mombasa in Kenya. Daniel, who has waited weeks for "the right moment," is bent on invoking The Shaman. He's absolutely focused. Victor is going along for the ride, though he's keen to get out of Dar es Salaam: his wife has flown home to Chicago because her mother is dying and he doesn't want to be alone.

Amazing the information that comes to me. Both men would rather fly but can't afford it. Daniel would borrow the money but Victor intends to return to America at the end of the school year, when his contract expires, and needs every cent he has saved to re-establish himself: "I've got to get some traction under me."

"Forget the plane, then." Daniel has told him. "A bus leaves Dar every afternoon around four o'clock. Arrives in Mombasa next morning at eight. It'll give us a taste of the real Tanzania."

"Tell you one thing, bro. If we want to get a seat on any such bus, we'd best arrive early."

Early it is, just quarter past two, when Daniel and Victor arrive at the bus depot, pile out of a cab and find a dozen women standing in line. They wear colourful patterned dresses — lime green and flame red, patchwork elephants and zebra stripes — and talk and laugh excitedly: this trip is an event.

The two men join the line-up. The sun beats down, the afternoon shimmers. Victor settles into himself but Daniel remains strangely on edge, tense and looking around

"Daniel? Why so uptight?"

"The Chinvat."

"Ain't no Chinvat skulking around Dar." Victor swaggers out of the line-up, thumps his chest and shouts at the sky: "Yo! Hey! Any Chinvat in the vicinity? Any Chinvat looking to tussle with this upstanding American boy?"

Daniel says: "Spare me the jive talk, Victor. The Chinvat killed my father."

"Sorry, I forgot."

"I wish you'd take this quest more seriously."

"And I wish you'd relax."

Finally, an ancient bus rumbles into the depot. Daniel sounds out the words written on its side: "*Ukitaka uzuri sharti udhurike.*" He raises his eyebrows: "If you want beauty . . . ."

Victor finishes the translation: "If you want beauty, you must first be injured."

"Not exactly propitious."

"Just remember," Victor says. "This is no place for Quebecois manners and Canadian *politesse*. You want a seat? You stick with me."

"*D'accord*, Vic." Daniel figures they're near the front of the line, how can they miss? But when the driver opens the door, the crowd surges forward. It's like a rugby scrimmage. Daniel finds himself in a mad crush of large women. Victor cries, "Grab my shirt!"

He charges grunting into the melee, elbows high, legs churning, driving like a fullback for short yardage. The crush squeezes the breath out of Daniel, but he hangs onto Victor's shirt and pop! the two men explode into the quickly filling bus. Near the middle, they find an empty seat and fall into it laughing. Looking up, they find themselves identifying with the other clamorous passengers, a couple of whom glance over with grudging respect: yes, that's how we do it in Dar.

The bus fills up in seconds. Sari-clad women remain in the aisle, talking and laughing like friends meeting after a long absence — which is precisely what they are. Daniel feels a part of this, yet also apart. He can't help noticing that he's the only white person on the bus and reflects that, back home in Canada, this is what Safiya must feel all too often: highly visible and therefore vulnerable, exposed.

Up front, the ancient engine coughs to life and settles into a rough, roaring rhythm. The safari-suited driver wheels out of the station into the chaos of downtown Dar es Salaam. He leans on his horn and pedestrians scatter. Soon the bus is rattling through the outskirts of town. From the walls of twelve-story apartment blocks, large chunks of cement have fallen. Tenants have covered the gaping holes with hanging blankets.

Gradually, these battered highrises fall away. The bus rumbles through a shantytown of dirt floors and tin roofs. Gradually, even these dwellings yield to empty fields. The driver swerves back and forth to avoid crater-like potholes in the two-lane highway and doesn't always succeed. At some point the pavement gives way to dirt and stone and the highway becomes a two-lane track. Sisal plants dot the green fields that roll away into the distance, where tiny, bent figures work late into the day. The setting sun streaks the sky with vivid colours.

The bus swings through a village of sod hots and Daniel realizes that night has fallen. He still hasn't got used to the sun setting so suddenly: now you see it, now you don't. He spots half a dozen flickering fires and dark shadows moving among them. Somewhere in the darkness, a lone villager relentlessly pounds a drum. A woman carries a basket on her head. A young girl follows behind her, skipping along in time to the distant rhythm of the drum, and suddenly I get an image of Colette skipping off to school, my darling daughter at age seven.

It's like interference on a television channel, but then I'm back in Africa, tuned in again, with half a dozen new passengers crowding onto the bus. Back on the road, the activity settles to a hum. A large woman suckles her baby. At her feet sits a basket with a checkered cloth sewn on top. A few passengers have brought suitcases, but most use these baskets. The bus smells of sweat and milk and cigarette smoke. Near the back, another baby begins to cry.

The bus jerks and bumps along at thirty miles an hour, stopping at villages to collect and disgorge passengers. At every stop, vendors gather at the open windows to offer hard-boiled eggs, cashew nuts, various fruits. New passengers greet old ones: "*Jambo! Habari?* Hello, how are you? *Mzuri*, I'm fine. *Habari wa mama*? How is your mother? *Mzuri. Habari wa toto?* How are your children? *Mzuri.*"

Daniel dozes off. He's dreaming of Safiya Naidoo when the engine dies. One minute, the bus is roaring through darkness. The next, it coasts silently to a halt. The driver rises and makes an announcement in Swahili, speaking too quickly for Daniel. Laughing, everybody gets off the bus. It's pitch dark but for a great canopy of stars, and dead quiet except for cicadas and the drums of a distant village. So this is the African night. People slip away into the bushes, then reappear.

The bus driver opens the hood of the bus and flames light up the night. Has the engine caught fire? The driver smothers the flames with a canvas bag that clearly he has used before. Male passengers crowd around the open hood, gesticulating, speculating, advising. The driver ignores them, fiddles with the engine. Finally, satisfied, he shuts the hood, climbs back into his seat and yells a few words out the open door. The male passengers move to the rear of the bus and begin pushing it along the empty road. Daniel and Victor join the others. The men push the bus faster and faster until the driver pops the clutch and the engine catches with a mad sputtering and resumes the old-familiar roaring. The passengers clamber back inside, Daniel and Victor among them, laughing and knocking and . . . knocking? what's that knocking?

"The Canary Islands." George the steward? "You've got twelve hours."

The transition back to ordinary reality took a moment. Slowly, I awoke and reoriented myself: the freighter Verlandi. George the steward had rapped on my cabin door as he strode down the hall proclaiming our first stop. I thrust Africa from my mind, shook off my sudden tiredness and turned to *Las Islas Canarias*.

I'd read the guidebook. Though closer to Morocco than Spain, the Canary Islands, so celebrated for their balmy climate, remain proudly Spanish. Of the thirteen islands, only seven are of any consequence and the Verlandi put in at the largest of these: Grand Canary Island, properly known as *Gran Canaria*. Shortly before noon, the freighter docked at Las Palmas, the provincial capital.

I felt odd, sick at heart, about heading off on a touristic ramble while Colette lay comatose in San Francisco. Despite myself, I kept returning to that hospital room where she lay motionless in an adjustable bed. My darling daughter. About beginning my quest in earnest, however, I felt good: here I would purchase a fire-worthy souvenir. Taggart had long since gathered a sufficient number, but Safiya, like me, would be seeking crytals, metals and precious stones. I made a decision I'd repeat several times before this adventure was done: I decided to "go with the flow."

We'd read enough about Las Palmas to make directly for the *Playa de las Canteras*, where a promenade of shops and restaurants fronted a spectacular two-mile beach. Trouble was, the Verlandi had put in at *Puerto de la Luz*, some distance away, in an area devoted to merchant vessels and the loading and unloading of cargo. We found the dock deserted: no stevedores, no scampering children, no teenage hooligans — not even a taxi stand. We'd arrived on a Sunday.

We stood on the dock, eleven voyagers contemplating their situation, when here comes a taxi after all. Turns out the Professor and his wife, the ex-travel agent, have made arrangements. They hop into the car and the rest of us gather round. The driver's English is shaky but no matter: Taggart speaks fluent Spanish. He tells the driver to send three more cars. The man says "si, si," and spins away.

After a few minutes, sure enough, here comes a second cab.

By now we're strung out along the dock. Some of us have despaired of waiting and decided to hike to the *Playa de las Canteras*. The two businessmen, Milo and Marvin, and their wives are twenty or thirty yards ahead of everyone else. Milo has been loudly complaining that the Verlandi should have arranged to have cars here, waiting for us, and what kind of service is this?

I yearn to remind him that the Verlandi is a working vessel, that passengers are secondary, and in signing on for the voyage he explicitly accepted this. But then: what's the use? Wait for Safiya. She's hanging back, fretting over Josephine and Rosella, the two white-haired women from the Deep South whose accents I thoroughly enjoy, though they annoy Taggart no end.

Rosella looks the quintessential spinster, and in fact she taught high-school English for years. Along the way, she divorced one alcoholic husband and outlived another. She'd told Safiya all about it. Tall and slim, neatly dressed, Rosella wears her white hair in a bun and revels in the role of an aging Scarlett O'Hara.

Josephine has proven more elusive: a heavy-set woman with sloppy eating habits and weak hearing: "Huh? Huh? What'd you say?"

Finally, I'd sorted it out. To go on this voyage, Rosella needed a travelling companion. She'd brought along her cook and housekeeper — and why not? Trouble is, Josephine has bad feet. She can shuffle around, but not easily. On the Verlandi, we'd know when Josephine was arriving for a meal because we'd hear her scuffing down the hall.

With this in mind, on the dock at Las Palmas, Safiya says: "Wait a minute, now. Maybe we shouldn't stray too far." Because she can see that Josephine will never make it to the *Playa de las Canteras*.

Up ahead, Milo flags the second taxi and berates the driver for arriving late. The young cabbie doesn't fully comprehend Milo's American slang, which is probably for the best because any fool can see he doesn't appreciate being wrongly chastised. Milo tugs at the rear door, which is locked, and begins yelling again: What the hell is this? We paid good money for this voyage and blah, blah, blah. The taxi is a small white Renault, room for the driver and four passengers, max. Having taken my cue from Safiya, I'm thinking: what about Josephine? when Taggart steps past me: "Excuse me, Milo. Aren't you forgetting something?"

He apologizes to the cabbie for Milo's behaviour and I can't help admiring the fluency of his Spanish. Taggart waves Rosella and Josephine forward, and soon all nine remaining passengers have gathered around the little car. Taggart opens the back door and Milo says, "What the hell do you think you're doing?"

"Rosella and Josephine need this car," Taggart says. "You can wait for the next or walk, like everybody else."

"This is our taxi," Milo says. "We saw it first and we're not going to let some stupid limey cheat us out of it."

To my amazement — it's like witnessing road rage — Milo shoves Taggart hard and seizes the door handle: "Come on, Marvin. Let's get out of here."

Taggart, who's physically awkward, stumbles backwards and sprawls across the trunk of the car. But here comes Safiya, swinging her shoulder bag. Instinctively, I reach for her arm — but I miss. She whacks Milo on the arm, but her bag glances upwards and smacks the side of his head. Strangely, I watch this part happen in slow motion and think of Behroze — same spirit, same sense of injustice.

Milo leans back to avoid the blow and falls onto the dock.

"Take the bloody car!" his wife shouts — mainly at me, oddly enough: "Go ahead! Take it!"

Rosella stands wringing her hands: "Oh deah, oh deah."

Taggart recovers and, while the cabbie shakes his head in disgust and disbelief, helps Josephine into the back seat. Rosella gets in on the other side and Safiya waves the driver away.

Two staring white faces disappear into the afternoon.

That leaves seven of us on the dock. Milo sits on a pile of wooden scaffolding to catch his breath while his wife and friends cluck over him, more embarrassed than angry. Fully recovered, Milo curses and swears. We're far enough away that Safiya and Taggart can't hear, but all my senses are fired up: "That black bitch," he says. "Did you see that? Hit me when I wasn't looking! I'll sue the bitch!"

Hearing none of this, Safiya says, "I didn't mean to knock him down. Maybe we should check to see if he's okay?"

"No, no, he's fine." I hustle my fellow questers along the dock, and soon we've opened up enough distance that I, too, lose Milo's vile mutterings in the wind. By the time we reach the promenade that runs along the beach, the so-called *Paseo de las Canteras*, Taggart and I are chuckling while Safiya entertains: "Did you see his face when I whacked him?" She opens her eyes in shock: "How would you describe that in Spanish, Taggart? That eye-popping astonishment?"

We haven't planned to spend the afternoon and evening together, but somehow we've entered into a post-adrenalin-rush solidarity. Cafes, bars and restaurants line the promenade: Indian, African, Chinese, you name it, offering everything from pakoras to baboti and won-ton soup. Most of them are low-end eateries but we happily grab a table with a view at an Ethiopian place and order a coffee.

The late-afternoon sun blazes down. People throng the white-sand beach, mostly families. They kick beachballs, snap towels, bury each other to the neck. Taggart is strangely watchful and I don't understand it — and then suddenly I do: he's looking out for Chinvat. Safiya spots a change room and draws our attention to the signs over the entrances. "*Senoras* and *Caballeros*," she reads aloud. "Don't you just love the Spanish language? *Caballeros*! It's so much more expressive than Men or even *Hommes*."

Safiya wants to go swimming. I've brought my bathing suit in the small green knapsack I carry, but she's left hers on the Verlandi. "Look at the fun they're having!" She points at a group of twenty-somethings swimming and splashing in the white-breaking waves. "Taggart, let's rent suits."

"Water must be freezing," he says. "Look at the ratio."

I like the idea of seeing Safiya in a skimpy bathing suit. But I'm more concerned with the quest and second Taggart's implied motion: "Many sun-worshippers, few swimmers."

"What's the name of that place?" Safiya says. "Where we can get souvenirs?"

"The *Pueblo Canario*," Taggart says. He stands to gain by our preparedness, if only because three ashavans must set forth together. Three ashavans armed with fire-worthy souvenirs.

— 54 —

At a kiosk we buy a map and away we go on foot.

Safiya wants to mail a letter to Africa. She's got a lead on Daniel Lafontaine, so despite the afternoon heat we hunt a post office, venturing up and down winding back streets. I can't decide whether to tell Safiya about my dream of Daniel in Africa — so dark, so ominous. Taggart says the post office will be closed today, Sunday, and I figure he's right. But Safiya takes to stopping people, her phrase book open: "*Buenas dias, senor. Donde esta el oficina de correo?*"

Nobody knows. Even the Spanish here are visitors. Finally, an old man pushing a bicycle with a flat tire points along a street. Surprise! the main post office hums with activity. We've forgotten, Taggart and I, that in Las Palmas, tourism is the number-one industry.

Safiya joins a line-up that extends into the street. I step into the shade of a giant palm tree. Taggart paces the sidewalk, irritated. When Safiya emerges from inside, mission accomplished, we visit a nearby kiosk and gulp down soft drinks. We resume walking and finally locate the *Pueblo Canaria*, a replica of an early Canary-Island village. We've just missed the Sunday afternoon folk dancing, but visit the craft shops and the *Museo Nestor*, where we examine paintings and memorabilia. Some of the shops are closing down, their owners heading home for the day. Safiya says: "This doesn't look good."

"Not to worry," I answer, because I feel a tingling, and I chase it around a corner and down a back alley and sure enough, a tiny old woman sits waiting behind a table of curiosities, many of them made of metal and clearly fire-worthy. Safiya selects a silver ankh, a cross with a loop for its upper arm, while I choose a miniature lantern that shines like gold. For these items, as Taggart has suggested, we don't haggle but pay the asking price. As we walk away, Safiya chirps: "Trinkets from Las Palmas — nothing to it."

Looking this way and that, Taggart says, "If you think they'll all come this easily, you'd better think again."

Our main objective accomplished, we make for the *Vegueta*, the historic centre of Las Palmas, hiking along a broad, bustling street thronged with shoppers. Taggart's still pensive, hyper-alert, and suddenly I don't feel like playing tourist: visions of Colette haunt the outskirts of my conciousness and colour my mood and

I seriously consider heading back to the Verlandi. On the other hand, if I stick around, maybe I can squeeze a few clarifications out of Taggart.

The *Vegueta* is all peaceful cobbled streets, balconied-buildings and quiet, tree-lined squares. We swing past a fifteenth-century cathedral renowned for its magnificent Flemish and Castilian paintings, but of course it's closed. Safiya doesn't care. She strides along, leading us up one winding side street and down another, Spanish phrase book in hand, exchanging greetings with kiosk owners and newspaper vendors.

Taggart and I have visited Europe before, but Safiya can't get over the numbers of people in the streets — old men sitting on doorsteps and mothers doing laundry, and here's a group of giggling teenage girls parading around in their Sunday finery, bursting with pride at their new platform shoes: "Everybody lives outside!"

And the Spanish language: Safiya revels in its familial resemblance to French. She has taken to reading signs aloud, several times each, striving to perfect her accent: *Calle Mayor de Triana, Calle Galicia, Calle Nestor de la Torre, Plaza de Santa Ana, Museo Diocesano de Arte Sacro.*

We reach the *Museo Canario,* which houses mummies of the Guanche, the original inhabitants of the Canaries, one hour after closing. Already it's seven, so no wonder we're hungry. Where to eat? Safiya wants to return to the *Paseo de las Canteras,* which offers that lovely view of the beach: maybe we'll see a sunset?

But those restaurants cater to low-end package tours, Taggart says, and what we want now is a quaint bistro with checkered table-cloths and handsome waiters who drape white linen napkins over their arms. We ramble a while, searching, and we're about to head beachward when we stumble upon the perfect plaza. Safiya searches vainly for a sign to read aloud, but the square is alive with people and seven or eight outdoor cafes.

We find a vacant table in the thick of the action and congratulate ourselves on having got off the beaten track because look: locals throng the square. Not ten feet away, a short, muscular man with thin grey hair has set up a portable shoeshine stand. Safiya can't believe how many men want their shoes shined and regrets that she's wearing sneakers. The grey-haired man makes everybody laugh while he polishes, his sense of fun the secret of his success, and all kinds of workers, from waiters to busboys, stop to kibbitz, to poke him and punch him and trade insults, and he slaps them back, his portable stand a non-stop action centre, and Safiya says: "So this is Spain."

Our waiter arrives without napkin but he's black-haired, mid-twenties and decked out in white shirt and red vest. Taggart pronounces him the perfect matador. Safiya flirts shamelessly in broken Spanish and, with images of Colette washing over me for no apparent reason, I marvel at how she can drive her worries beneath the surface. Occasionally, I catch her staring pensively into space, but never for long before, like a cat, she shakes herself into the present.

Suddenly impatient with her flirting, Taggart uses his impeccable Spanish to take charge and order for all of us. An avocado salad and endless bowls of rice provide a base, and then there's *chicharros*, which Taggart says is mackeral, and *cazuela canaria*, a casserole of salted fish, and *cancocho canario*, a fresh fish cooked with both sweet and regular potatoes and served with broth-like gofio. The meal crackles with *mojo picon*, a hot seasoning that mixes paprika, coriander and peppers — a welcome change from the hearty but bland freighter fare.

For dessert Taggart and I order flan, a custard topped with caramel, while Safiya goes for the *helado*, the ice cream. By now, at Taggart's urging, we've switched from the passable house white to sangria, which mixes red wine with lemonade and sugar, and I can't help remembering that I've tasted sangria before, when I visited Madrid with Behroze. While we eat, Safiya makes small talk with the nearest families and we're all surprised at how late they stay out with their children, the five and six-year-olds playing energetic tag around the table.

A tall black man in African dress wanders over and, speaking broken English, asks Safiya for a light. She catches some inflection and responds in French: sorry, she doesn't smoke. The young man asks: is French her first language? No? Then where did she learn to speak so fluently? Despite my mother's drills, I can't understand a word he says. Even the fluently bilingual Safiya struggles with his accent. But gradually, she determines that the man comes from Senegal and works on a cargo vessel. He wants to talk about Quebec. People speak French there? How does one immigrate?

Safiya talks happily, blithely unconcerned, yet I register discomfort in Taggart, who fears that the young man might be Chinvat. I scan the Senegalese, detect no supernatural darkness and whisper to Taggart, "He's clean — a civilian."

Taggart regards me strangely — how do I know? — but nods acceptance.

Meanwhile, we're knocking back sangria — though not in any great quantities. Eventually, the young Senegalese returns to his friends, strongly encouraged by Taggart. The night air grows cool and we move to an inside table. Somehow, we get talking about mythology. Taggart says the Verlandi takes its name from one of three Scandinavian sisters who spin the web of destiny, and I say, "That's just what we need — a Ship of Fate."

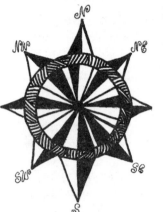

"That's why Safiya's so at home on the freighter," Taggart says. "She's a child of destiny."

"I noticed that, now you mention it."

"Would you two stop discussing me as if I weren't here?" Safiya stands up. "On second thought, talk away: I'm going to the washroom."

Since morning I've been troubled by Africa. That haunting dream of Daniel and Victor making for Mombasa raised difficult questions. I've said nothing for fear of upsetting Safiya, but now, alone with Taggart, I say: "What can you tell me about the Chinvat?"

"The Chinvat?" Taggart glances around the bar, then lowers his voice and says: "What do you know?"

"Only that they're to be feared. Who are they?"

"They're a splinter group, a cult. They're fundamentalist Zoroastrians with a fanatical sense of mission. They're shock troops who'll lay down their lives to prevent people from invoking the Sacred Fire. They take their name from the Bridge of Judgment, the Chinvat Bridge. And they've sworn to destroy not only The Shaman but all those who enter the Golden Flame."

"How do we recognize them?"

"They're young men, mostly: clean-cut, short-haired, muscular. Not unlike that young Senegalese, though most are of European heritage. They look like martial arts experts. They ARE martial arts experts. They contend that The Shaman should never have removed the Sacred Fire to Africa. That by doing so, he committed a sacrilege, disrupted the natural unfolding." Taggart eyes me keenly. "You don't know the background?"

"I know that three ashavans must set forth together." On the other side of the bar, Safiya stands chatting with two African women. "Tell me, Taggart: does everybody know that?"

He sips his drink, shakes his head no: "It's common knowledge that two ashavans must approach The Shaman. Also, that they must present sixteen fire-worthy souvenirs, including seven from sacred places, and answer three questions or riddles. But that three must set forth? No. I discovered that myself only recently." He eyes me shrewdly: "Why do you ask?"

I shrug, tell him: "If I hadn't turned up a freighter ticket and received an unprecedented leave of absence, I'd consider this whole quest, the gathering of talismans, the three setting forth — well, don't you find it a bit crazy?"

I half-expect him to laugh, but instead he turns intellectual: "We're battling elemental forces, Bernie. At any new millennium, they manifest in archetypal patterns. Ancient rituals, hidden powers and forgotten prophecies emerge into our workaday lives and turn them tumultuous." He shrugged. " Ah, but too many odysseys lack flamboyance, don't you think? You find yourself wondering where, oh where are the narrative fireworks? the cosmic pyrotechnics?"

"Now you sound like my Quebecoise mother."

Taggart chuckled: "Consider the fire-worthy souvenirs, Bernie. Any Vahran or Sacred Fire comprises sixteen holy fires, all of which derive from guilds connected with metal work."

"So the sixteen are symbolic."

"Both symbolic and real, but that's not the point. They're outrageous. The quest demands ritualistic recognition of a reality that's so over the top, it's outrageous. We're talking demented beauty. On a deeper level, ceremonial recognition translates into healing — into healing and transformation."

"Okay, you've lost me."

"Golden Flame is a process, remember? A quest that implies increasing understanding and gradual integration. We place sixteen mementoes in the Sacred Fire and trust that seven will survive the flames — one each for Ahura Mazda and the other six Amesha Spentas or Bountiful Immortals." To my surprise, Taggart begins unbuttoning his shirt: "Answer three questions and The Shaman will turn one of those keepsakes into a magic talisman. But look here." Opening his shirt, Taggart reveals a sheath strapped around his chest. From this, he takes a small dagger that gleams despite the gloomy darkness of the bar.

"Is that real silver?"

He winces that I'd even ask and hands me the dagger: "Comes from Persia. Signifies the penetrating power of the intellect."

I admire the dagger, its razor-sharp blade and intricate handle: "Some say the intellect is an enemy of creativity, that it impedes the natural flow of the unconscious."

"And I say, don't leave home without it." He nods at the dagger: "A gift from Esmeralda Esteban."

"The folksinger?"

"Folk, blues, jazz," Taggart says. "The singer-songwriter, yes."

"Truly, it's amazing. I've never seen a more beautiful knife."

Satisfied, Taggart restores the dagger to its sheath and rebuttons his shirt. "But you must have a primary keepsake?"

The question makes me uncomfortable. But what can I do? I open the small green knapsack in which I carry my valuables and show Taggart the gold necklace and locket that Behroze retrieved from Colette's neck.

"This, too, is beautiful. Look at the craft!" As Taggart admires the locket, I return to my original question: "You said not everybody knows that three ashavans must set forth." I hesitate. "What about Daniel Lafontaine? Does he know?"

Taggart looks up from the necklace: "I've been wondering about that. I discovered the admonition in a fragment from the lost Avesta. I don't know whether Daniel's father managed to translate that particular passage. I suspect not. Maybe that's why he died."

"He died while engaged in the quest?"

"Didn't Safiya tell you? They found his body on a beach in Kenya, burned to a crisp. That's how Daniel got involved."

Safiya arrives: "What's this about Daniel?"

"We're talking about his father," Taggart says, returning my talisman. "Just speculating, really."

Safiya has already admired my gold necklace and shown me her own favorite souvenir — a silver bracelet she acquired in Colorado while visiting the cliff dwellings of Mesa Verde. Now, as she resumes her seat, the voice of Behroze comes to me, quoting William Butler Yeats: "The darkness drops again but now I know / That twenty centuries of stony sleep / were vexed to nightmare by a rocking cradle, / And what rough beast, its hour come round at last, / Slouches towards Bethlehem to be born?"

I'm still recovering from that bit of incongruity when, instead of asking to take another look at my necklace, Safiya regards me strangely: "Bernard, have you learned something about Daniel? Something you haven't shared?"

What now? Should I tell Safiya that, bent on invoking The Shaman, Daniel Lafontaine has set forth with a single fellow ashavan? What purpose would that serve? Besides, I don't know if it's true. Maybe my African dream was merely a fantasy. "Don't be silly. I've never even met Daniel."

"Don't lie to me, Bernie. Lying and 'bad speaking' weigh heavily at the Bridge of Judgment."

She's only half kidding, but I have nowhere to go: "Safiya, I know nothing about Daniel — nothing at all."

The Barcelona Smile

Taggart Oates liked nothing better than an audience, and in Las Palmas he'd discovered an avid professional listener. Ah, but Taggart needed me as much as I needed him. And he needed me to be relatively well-informed, so that I could play the disposable third. The morning after Las Palmas, as we sailed up the Mediterranean coast of Spain, he showed me more of his fire-worthy souvenirs. I remember a five-pointed star, an iron watchtower, a curiously doubled Cross of Lorraine and a hanged man he identified as a zodiac element. He also produced a tiny crystal ball, which he called a shewstone: "Certain people use this for 'skrying,'" he said, studying me intently. "They gaze into it to obtain visions?"

I kept my face bland: "Safiya says you gathered most of these mementoes and keepsakes during a speaking tour."

"I travelled with the so-called Prophet of the Golden Flame while researching a novel."

"Did you visit California?" I fought to keep intensity out of my voice. "Eight or nine years ago? The Bay area around San Francisco?"

He studied me intently: "Just before we went our separate ways."

The night Behroze died, Taggart had been present. A terrible wave of remorse swamped me with regret, sorrow and guilt. Why couldn't I have remained for the lecture? Behroze wouldn't have died.

"Bernard, you look pale. Are you okay?"

"I'm fine." I knew better than to reveal more. "Where's The Prophet now?"

"I don't know and I don't care." His vehemence surprised me. "I don't mind discussing metaphysics, Bernie. But my personal history is nobody's business."

"Hey, understood."

"Besides, it would just distract you. And you were sufficiently distracted, I thought, as we explored Las Palmas."

"You're right. I've been worried sick about Colette."

"When you're ashore, you've got to pay closer attention — remain in The Now." Taggart finished stuffing his souvenirs into a small leather sachet. "Three journey-related questions lie ahead."

"That I understand. The Golden Flame as millennial revelation I find elusive."

"Zarathustra himself, whom the Greeks called Zoraster, laid the first of three cornerstones." Leaning over the railing, Taggart elaborated: hundreds of years before Jesus, and maybe even a thousand, Zarathustra had kicked off a final "trillennium" in the struggle between Ahura Mazda and Ahriman. We ourselves live within that period, he said, but when exactly? Did a millennium mean precisely one thousand years? Or could the concept be applied figuratively?"

"Yeats believed in two-thousand-year Platonic cycles," I said, remembering a gleaning from Behroze. "The first began with Helen and the burning of Troy, and the second with Jesus. The third will begin with the birth of that great beast slouching towards Bethlehem."

"Yeats intuited the cyclical nature of history," Taggart said. "But he was born too early and remained within the narrowness of the West. I would guess that he never even heard the names Hashedar, Aushedar-Mah and Sashoshyant."

"Sorry, who?"

"The three Zorastrian saviours. They're scheduled to arrive amidst omens and portents, one at the end of each millennium. All three are descended directly from Zarathustra, though I don't expect we must take that too literally. If one broadens the concept of the 'good religion,' one could argue that Jesus was Hashedar, the first of the three great saviours. But then one has to explain his acceptance of the Judeo-Christian Fallacy."

He glanced over and saw my confusion: "The notion that Evil entered the world through human agency at the Fall of Adam — an apocryphal event that gives rise to a ludicrous historicity and an endless debate about free will. The Avesta teaches rather that Evil is an original principle, the dark side of an all-prevasive polarity. Ahriman existed before we did. We can choose to follow him or not."

"We choose our destinies — but so what?"

"So after Jesus came the prophet Muhammed, in whose name certain zealots drove the ashavans from Persia."

"Thus ruling out Muhammed as the second saviour?"

"Looks that way. As an alternative second, are you ready for this? Some Golden Flame radicals propose Friedrich Nietzsche."

"The German philosopher? Thus Spake Zarathustra?"

Taggart nodded: "That revolutionary work repudiated Christianity, especially the way it devalues this world while proclaiming the kingdom of heaven. Nietzsche argued that Christianity teaches men how to die, not how to live. And called for a revaluation of all values."

"Didn't he also declare that God is Dead?"

"That he did." Taggart smiled happily: "And so became the father of existentialism, the second great cornerstone of Golden Flame."

"Now you've lost me."

"Existentialism introduced the dialectic: thesis, antithesis, synthesis." Taggart checked my face and continued: "It's an advance on the dynamic interplay of opposites. Nietzsche's Zarathustra battles Jesus Christ and out of that confrontation comes the Overman — a Jungian symbol of the Self."

"Golden Flame as dialectical transcendence. But didn't the Overman give rise to Nazism?"

"The deliberate misuse of the idea played a part. Nietzsche didn't mean to establish the Overman as an evolutionary objective, but rather as an internal image against which to measure ourselves."

"Man is something to be overcome. Or make that humanhood. Still, I see gaps."

"Nietzsche's Zarathustra gave rise to the 'godless existentialism' of Jean-Paul Sartre, who insisted that all people choose, and cannot avoid choosing, their characters, goals and perspectives. Existentialism argues that we ourselves determine who we become: that we freely make choices and so must take responsibility for ourselves. As against Christianity, with its problematic determinism, existentialism reiterates the original Zoroastrianism."

"But what of Mazda? Golden Flame is anything but godless."

"You're forgetting the third great cornerstone — the paranormal. The fundamental recognition and acceptance, if you will, of such contemporary concepts as synchronicity and clairvoyance and the multi-dimensional nature of reality. The notion that, in different dimensions, the same event manifests in different ways." He took a beat. "In my view, that's why Nietzsche eventually went mad. He recognized the eternal truths of Zarathustra, and sought to penetrate the symbolism to the irrational human heart, but then couldn't face what he discovered. He couldn't accommodate magic."

Taggart searched my face as he spoke, but I saw no reason to express anything but innocence: "So the Golden Flame combines Zoroastrianism, existentialism and the paranormal."

"Along with the Tao and Carl Jung and western shamanism and a cyclical vision of Time, yes." Taggart grinned, having returned to his own current obsession: "Speaking of which, some scholars say Zarathustra lived around 600 B.C., while others say 1200. Given the latter time frame, Jesus fits well enough as Hashedar, the first saviour. And as for the second, well, Nietzsche doesn't accord with what's happening around us, so maybe we missed someone? Who says the saviour had to become famous? Or maybe the concept of 'millennium' is more elastic than we realize. Maybe —"

"Maybe it's time to go ashore." Safiya spoke as she arrived looking radiant, her black hair blowing wild in the wind. "Come on, Taggart. Give it a rest. We're arriving in Barcelona."

While we'd been discussing the mysteries of the Golden Flame, she'd been reading guidebooks. Already she regretted that we'd have only five hours to expend. "But that's perfect." Taggart said. "Just enough time to buy a fire-worthy souvenir. Maybe a zodiac element? Say, a high priestess?"

Safiya rolled her eyes skyward. "Taggart visited back in '92," she said. "Just before the Summer Olympics. He'll be able to show us around: *La Sagrada Famila, Barri Gotic, Las Ramblas.*"

Safiya assumed I would tour Barcelona with them. But as she spoke, I realized Taggart hoped I wouldn't. Nothing personal. With regard to our mutual quest, he'd settled on a purely professional approach. Three ashavans would set forth together, and at some point, I might become useful, even necessary. To leave me in ignorance might prove dangerous. Yet Taggart saw this voyage as his last chance to wean Safiya from Daniel Lafontaine. And so wanted to be alone with her.

Safiya desired my presence at least partly because I served as a buffer. In the presence of any third party, Taggart granted less scope to what she called his "windigo-side." This she derived from a dream in which Taggart had appeared as an ice skeleton, a cannibalistic windigo she later identified as coming from Inuit mythology. She'd shuddered: "I don't want to talk about it."

Now she said: "So what do you think? Shall we rent a car in Barcelona?"

She smiled eagerly and I yearned to reach out and gently touch her face. Instead, I turned and stared out at the coast of Spain: "Sure, why not?"

Taggart glowered: "Why not, indeed?"

To hell with you, I thought. Why don't you bow out gracefully?

I didn't need psychic powers to understant that Taggart suspected my feelings for Safiya. Clearly, we were heading for the sort of trouble that might get in the way of invoking The Shaman. Sure, I could back off — but I had no such intention. And that left only the white-lie option. "Something you should know, Taggart," I said casually, as Safiya hurried ahead and we followed more slowly towards the stairs. "That car accident I mentioned?"

"What about it?"

"It left me, well . . . unable to function." Too late, I saw a plausibility gap yawning before me: who would honestly volunteer such a confession? Surely Taggart would see through my lie?

"Unable to function?"

"With women, I mean." I plunged ahead, already committed, as an image of Safiya donning her shift invaded my mind — an image I'd stolen by shamefully invading her privacy.

"Good god!" Taggart said. "Are you serious?"

"Just thought I'd mention it." People believe what they want to believe. "So you don't get the wrong idea."

"No, no, I never . . . but I am sorry to hear that, old boy. Can nothing be done?"

"Apparently not, no." Secretly, I renewed my vow never again to use my burgeoning paranormal powers for personal gain. And prayed that Mazda or Whoever would forgive my single transgression.

We reached Barcelona at two-thirty in the afternoon — the continent at last. From this port city, five centuries before, Columbus had sailed for the New World. Now came this reverse exploration, far more modest in scope, though with a large secret purpose: New Worlders exploring the Old and the Ancient with a view to saving The Whole Shebang.

The first time I'd visited Europe, as a back-packer, I'd travelled to experience difference — to immerse myself in "the foreign." This time, I proposed to concentrate on the transaction of travel, on the spiritual impact of a "foreign place," mainly because I secretly believed The Shaman would focus on this area. For example: "How did the experience of Las Palmas change Taggart's feelings about you?" On the other hand, I didn't dare ignore the mundane.

A city of three million, Barcelona remains the second largest port in the Mediterranean. I'd visited Madrid in the eighties and thought I knew what to expect, but Taggart said no: "Barcelona is far more an art city — and also the capital of Catalan nationalism." Seeing my blank look, he added: "If Canada were Spain, Quebec would be Catalonia. Toronto would be Madrid, and Montreal, Barcelona."

— 68 —

"My mother always identified Quebec City as the heart of Quebec nationalism."

"The analogy is not exact."

Having docked, we quickly found a taxi stand, unlike in Las Palmas. Taggart haggled separately with three drivers before choosing one. As we drove into town, Safiya noticed that the street signs were bilingual, Spanish and Catalan, and Taggart said the latter language had started turning up in the late seventies, after the death of Franco.

Before he could launch into a full-blown lecture, we arrived at the original walled city, a medieval town dating back to the fourteenth century and known as the Gothic Quarter — or, as Safiya preferred, the *Barri Gotic*. We piled out and traipsed winding streets, past cathedrals and palaces and government buildings, some of which are still in use: the *Catedral de Barcelona*, the *Palau de la Musica Catalana*, the *Museu d'Historia de la Ciutat*.

Again Safiya revelled in pronouncing names aloud. She counted twenty-seven churches and claimed she'd missed entire streets. Taggart pointed out the *Museu Picasso*, but said: "His great work is elsewhere. Here in Barcelona, the artist to experience is Antoni Gaudi, creator of *La Sagrada Familia*."

He'd led us in a circle, a notable feat, and surprise! here was our taxi-driver, patiently waiting. This time, as we drove, Taggart held forth on Gaudi and his *Sagrada Familia*, which he called "Barcelona's answer to the Eiffel Tower."

Safiya said: "*La Sagrada Familia*, The Sacred Family. You've got to love the way language works."

Taggart resumed talking about Gaudi, the Catalan architect whose buildings grace Barcelona. I paid attention, knowing that he was trying to prepare us all for any questions The Shaman might ask. Gaudi began working on *La Sagrada Familia* in the 1880s and kept at it for decades: "This was his masterpiece, his obsession. During the last eight months of his life, he lived in a builder's hut on the church grounds, where he could oversee work on his creation."

Taggart made the cabbie drop us off two blocks away, insisting that the only way to approach *La Sagrada Familia* is to march up the broad *Avinguda de Gaudi*. As we did just that, I found myself marvelling at the imaginative genius that had conceived this cathedral more than a century before, and at the force of will which had driven that conception this far into the future. The stained glass windows, the sculpted religious statues, the gargoyles — these you'd expect from the Gothic tradition. But a handful of finger-like spires reaching skyward? Never had I seen such audacity, such futuristic flamboyance. Yet Gaudi's contemporaries had not thought him mad.

Scaffolding extended around both sides of the cathedral, and Taggart explained that workers had completed only one of four facades. During the Spanish Civil War, anarchists had burned the original plans. Nothing but rough sketches remained. The question arose: to complete or not to complete? In 1979, the Catalans voted and decided that, if it took forever, they would finish *La Sagrada Familia*. They'd been at it ever since.

At the cathedral entrance — for once we weren't too late — we paid four hundred *pesatas* each and joined a short line-up. As we made our way forward, a tiny old woman suddenly flung herself at Safiya and me, knocking us both off our feet. As we landed on our backs, a huge piece of metal scaffolding crashed to the ground precisely where we'd been standing, narrowly missing Taggart. We looked up in time to see three young men duck into a window about halfway up the nearest spire.

Safiya and I dusted ourselves off. Taggart said: "They've found us."

The tiny woman who'd saved our lives had disappeared into the crowd. Safiya said, "Why am I not surprised?"

Two worried officials, overweight men, arrived exclaiming that nothing like this had ever happened before. Somehow, the three lunatics who'd done this had got away. But they intended to conduct a full investigation. They had witnesses. Safiya exchanged glances. We assured the officials that we weren't hurt, and finally they let the three of us enter the cathedral — though all joy had fled the experience.

We rode an elevator into the dizzy reaches of the main spires. Barcelona sprawled before us in every direction. I looked out through some bars in a window and, despite my best efforts to remain in The Now, saw my daughter lying still as death in San Francisco: Colette, oh Colette: what am I doing here?

Safiya sensed my mood because she touched my arm and said: "Don 't worry, Bernie. We'll do what has to be done."

Back at ground level, Taggart led the way out the door.

"*Hasta luego*, Gaudi!" Safiya cried. "*Hola, Las Ramblas!*"

Forget the Chinvat, she meant. Let's get our fire-worthy souvenirs.

Las Ramblas is a glorious, tree-lined pedestrian mall with a single lane of traffic running along either side. Chock-a-block with flower stalls and newspaper kiosks, cafes and clubs, cinemas and taverns and tapas bars, it's one of the world's most colourful promenades. *Las Ramblas* runs for almost a mile along what was once a river bed — a drainage canal, really — from a bustling square, the *Plaza de Catalunya*, all the way to the harbour.

The cabbie dropped us near the square at the covered entrance to *La Boqueria*, Barcelona's main market. On the sidewalk, and despite the warmth of the afternoon, an old man in rags squatted, feeding twigs into a small fire that burned in a rusted water pail. He glanced up at me, his sharp eyes belying his unkempt appearance, and smiled conspiratorially, as if in recognition. A shiver ran through me as he nodded once, abruptly, then picked up his portable fire and disappeared into the throng.

To Safiya, I said: "Did you see that man?"

"What man?" She'd been investigating a magazine kiosk.

Taggart finished paying the cabbie and declared that from here we'd walk. An ironwork structure encircles *La Boqueria*, which overflows with fresh produce — forests of hanging sausages and hams, piles of wild mushrooms as big as your fist. We passed heaps of candied fruits and nuts, and coffee stands where sailors jostled and joked with tiny ladies dressed in black, who would sell you a single apple or a tiny bag of olives.

Safiya insisted on buying three coffees. Then, while we stood drinking them, she said, "Enough with the long faces, gentlemen! The Chinvat aren't going to make a second move in one day. We're safer than we've been all trip. Let's forget the scaffolding and get on with it."

We drank to that and strolled onto the mall, where buskers

and birdsellers mingled with sailors and hustlers. Tourists sifted through everything from lottery tickets and Arabic newspapers to German bridal magazines and pornographic comic books. Safiya admired the sidewalks: "We're walking on wrought-iron tiles!"

I'd begun to worry about not finding souvenirs — we had only a couple more hours — but we came upon a kiosk devoted to metal jewelry and trinkets. I purchased a finger-length sceptre that Taggart identified as a miniature "athame" or ceremonial sword. Safiya considered a copper sphinx, but opted for a tiny *Sagrada Familia*, which we had to admit perfectly signalled "this place."

I said: "This is almost too easy."

"The real challenge," Safiya said, "will be emotional."

"That scaffolding wasn't emotional."

We walked down *Las Ramblas* to the bottom, where a monument to Christopher Columbus, a two-hundred-foot column and statue, commemorated a 1493 visit. Taggart said, "The statue faces the wrong way."

"Ah, but only if you're a literalist," Safiya said.

Taggart said: "You'll pay for that."

Safiya and I rode an elevator to the top of the monument. We looked out at the harbour through decorative ironwork and counted forty-six ships. Was that the island of Majorca in the distance? As we stood speculating, a bearded man in costume, looked like Christopher Columbus, stepped onto the deck where we stood. He approached us purposefully, glanced over his shoulder, then whipped a sword out of its sheath and, brandishing it over our heads, said something fierce and threatening. Safiya and I looked at each other: was this a joke? Columbus grabbed Safiya's bag, in which she'd stored our souvenirs, but she knocked away his hand.

Chinvat! I swung at the man, missed and then narrowly evaded a sword thrust. Columbus whirled to attack again, but out of nowhere came the ragged old man I'd seen at the entrance to *La Boqueria*. Now he showed incredible agility, leaping onto Columbus's back and driving him to his knees. Columbus fought furiously but the old man locked him into a choke hold, obviously painful, and gestured with his head: get out of here now! We did as he indicated, charging both into and out of the elevator, and surprising Taggart with our urgency: "Let's go!"

As we headed up *Las Ramblas* describing this second attack, Taggart nodded unhappily: "The Chinvat have found us."

Safiya said: "What makes you so sure?"

"The Columbus costume. That's their idea of a joke."

I said, "And the old man?"

"Who knows?"

Obviously, we had to get out of Barcelona. But the Chinvat had just taken not one but two shots, and surely we could relax for an hour or so. At a bar with white chairs and tables, we ate seafood tapas and washed them down with ice-cold beer. "Forget the scaffolding," Safiya said. "Forget Christopher Columbus. Look at those facades! And the human scale of this place! What a city! I kept expecting to round a bend and stumble into 'the real Barcelona,' an area like Bay Street in Toronto, where grey men in suits stride along muttering that time is money. That never happened."

"What about those sailors?" I said. "Down that side street, dickering with hookers?"

"Every world city has its seamy side," Safiya answered. "Barcelona celebrates the human being over the automobile. Instead of the *autopista* you get the *bocacalle* and the *bulevar*."

Back to language, then. Safiya said, "Catalan sounds more like French than Castilian Spanish. I can almost understand it."

"France is just across the Pyrenees," Taggart said. "The links are historical, cultural, linguistic."

Seeing a full-blown lecture coming, and frankly disbelieving that The Shaman would care a whit about any such links, I excused myself to visit an underground washroom. By the time I returned, Safiya and Taggart had embarked on a different discussion. They weren't fighting, exactly — more like playing psychological poker.

On arriving in Barcelona, and just before we debarked, George the steward had distributed letters to various passengers. Safiya had received one from a woman friend in Montreal, and now it lay open on the table. Safiya wore a tight smile: "You lied to me, Taggart. You slept with Esmeralda when I visited Quebec City."

"Maybe I did," Taggart replied coolly. "But you lied to me, too."

"I did not."

"You spent that weekend with Daniel Lafontaine." Taggart

sipped his beer. "My friend Joseph saw you walking in Old Town."

"I've never even met Joseph!"

"I'd sent him a photograph. You're quite exotic-looking, you know. Joseph recognized you in the street, billing and cooing with a gorgeous blond man, and called to ask me if it was over between us."

This story rang false — clanged like a tugboat bell — and I decided to try an extrasensory scan. I'd been experimenting with a new method of probing embedded realities. Taggart's thick psychic fog had impressed me enough that I'd created a fog of my own, then developed a means of exploring within it. It was like donning night-vision goggles. Trying this now, I found I could indeed penetrate Taggart's fog — though with difficulty. Even so, I turned up three surprises.

In her letter, Safiya's friend mentioned seeing Taggart at a Montreal jazz club with Esmeralda Esteban. In fact, he'd spent the night with Esmeralda — a remarkably talented woman with whom, before meeting Safiya, he'd intended to approach The Shaman. That was the first surprise: Esmeralda Esteban had sought the Sacred Fire.

Second revelation: when Safiya, suspecting the truth, had accused Taggart of sleeping with Esmeralda, he'd denied it barefaced. He'd known she would use his infidelity as an excuse to renew her affair with Daniel Lafontaine. The eyeopener? Safiya had not lost touch with Daniel before Taggart turned up, as she'd claimed. She'd left Daniel in the dark about her new sense of mission out of a bizarre sense of loyalty to Taggart, knowing at this point only that two must approach The Shaman, but not yet that three must together set forth. Call it a period of emotional confusion.

And the third surprise? Taggart was bluffing. True, a friend named Joseph lived in Quebec City, but they hadn't spoken in months. Taggart had received no phone call wondering about Safiya. And if she hadn't felt so guilty about saying a final goodbye to Daniel, and letting him go off unassisted to seek The Shaman, she would have realized this.

Perhaps all of us had sins to expiate? Guilt to burn off in the Golden Flame? Ah, but Taggart had read Safiya correctly. She'd travelled to Quebec City ostensibly to visit a friend who published a literary magazine, but really to bid Daniel adieu before he flew to East Africa, not knowing where, precisely, he'd alight. Now, at a tapas bar in Barcelona, Taggart was running a bluff on an expert poker player and — call this a fourth surprise — making it work.

"We didn't bill and coo in the street," Safiya said, flushing. "Anyway, why shouldn't I have said goodbye to Daniel? I didn't betray our quest. Though I know now it wouldn't have mattered."

"One day, Safiya, you'll realize how badly you've treated me."

"Maybe so." Safiya stood up. "Right now, we'd better head back to the Verlandi. Coming, Bernie?"

Taggart had bluffed her out! Safiya had held a Royal Flush and he'd blown her away with a pair of deuces. As we headed for the Verlandi in a taxi, my head began to ache. For the first time, I understood that Safiya had reason to fear Taggart — and I did, too. As he blathered up front with the cabbie, I said quietly: "I've seen photos of Esmeralda Esteban. To you, Safiya, she can't hold a candle."

Safiya smiled and I flushed like a teenager.

A Genoan Miracle

"People create their own luck." So Safiya declared on the deck of the Verlandi. We were enjoying our habitual post-poker-game chat, a late-night ritual I'd come to anticipate almost more than the game itself. The sky sparkled with stars and we stood at the railing as the ship travelled north along the Mediterranean coast of Spain.

"Surely we've just seen Destiny playing favorites?" I answered. "Who would have believed that third Jack?"

Safiya chuckled: "That was lucky, I admit."

Less than two hours before, she'd been down seventy dollars on the evening. Thanks to the Jack of Hearts, she'd ended up thirty ahead. "But if Destiny plays favorites and I'm one of them, what happened to Florence?"

The captain had changed the itinerary. Instead of staying three days in Genoa, we would remain only twenty-four hours. Originally, Safiya and Taggart had planned to zip back and forth to Florence: "A magical place — one of the requisite seven."

"A bitter loss," I agreed. "But how do you feel about Rome?"

"Rome's farther south even than Florence."

"Ah, but it's more than halfway to Naples — the Verlandi's next stop. Where they've pencilled in a three-day stay."

"I see where you're taking this. What if they change plans again?"

"We telephone. From Rome, unlike Florence, we remain within striking distance: three hours away, not nine or ten."

Safiya insisted on checking my maps and guidebooks.

Three o'clock in the morning, hunched over a paper-strewn table in the library, suddenly she looked up: "You're right. Rome's an option."

Next day, at lunch, Taggart made it unanimous: "I've always wanted to see the catacombs." He paused reflectively, then added: "Maybe we're meant to visit Pompeii, as well."

I couldn't help myself: "You're not going fatalistic on us."

"Not at all." He smiled his wintry smile. "But I'm not blind to synchronicity, either. Mount Vesuvius covered Pompeii with ashes and pumice stone in A.D. 79. It erupted last in 1944 — just over fifty years ago. Perhaps it's due to blow again?"

Incredulous, I said: "And you want to be there?"

Safiya, who had remained hunched over the map, said: "Pompeii isn't far south of Naples."

"It's beyond Naples," I stressed. "Out of our way."

Taggart said: "Just a thought."

If necessary, I knew, I could probably "scope out" Pompeii without leaving the Verlandi. But I remained uncertain of my ability to conduct a long-distance astral expedition, and hoped to avoid it. The thought of the energy drain, and how tired I'd feel after such an undertaking, didn't attract me.

Late that afternoon, when we docked in Genoa, we expected to meet an immigration officer. He'd stamp our passports and away we'd go. We waited thirty minutes, forty minutes, seventy-five. We waited ninety minutes and then Safiya said, "Forget this. Visa or no visa, I'm out of here."

She climbed under a braided maroon rope and marched down the gangway. I shucked on my miniature green knapsack and called: "Taggart, let's go."

Shaking his head and clucking like a flustered hen, he grabbed his bag and followed.

Genoa does not rate as one of Italy's attractions. It's dreary and dismal, a tangle of narrow, cobblestone streets that twist away down hills into shadows and darkness. "Cold War Russia," Taggart offered. And Safiya: "Edgar Allan Poe country."

We flagged a taxi and rode to the train station, the *Genova Principe*, where Taggart's Spanish proved useless. Nor did the ticket clerk speak French or English, so Safiya whipped out her Italian phrase book: "*A che ora c'e il primo treno per Roma? De quale marciapiedi?*" To us: "Don't you just love the way it sounds? You can winkle out the meaning from the sound alone. '*Aspetti, cerco la frase nel libro.*' Wait, I'll circle the phrase in the book. You've got to love it."

Safiya determined that the Rome train left at midnight and bought three second-class tickets. By the time Taggart found out — "you bought first-class tickets, right?" — we'd hailed a second cab and were making for the house of Christopher Columbus, tempting fate. We arrived as the place closed, though the cabbie, a fatherly man who spoke some English, had assured us it would be open: "*Aperto! Si*, is open."

This fatherly cabbie argued with the gatekeeper. He pointed at his watch and flailed his arms to no effect. We suspected a ruse but the driver refused to accept payment, even when Safiya insisted: "No, no, it would not be right."

This was an Italian cabbie? Surely one of a kind.

Pedestrians again, and ignoring countless stray cats, we rambled narrow streets and walkways that wound beneath tall, dark houses with overhanging gardens. Small statues of the Madonna graced the corner of every second alleyway. Sailors put them there, Taggart said, as they left Genoa to explore the world. On impulse, I photographed Safiya with one of the more attractive Madonnas.

Eventually, we found the city's commercial centre — an assortment of dreary shops rebuilt after the Second World War. As we explored it, streetcorner lotharios hissed invitations at Safiya, who ignored them. Taggart grumbled about the second-class tickets: "Have you ever seen an Italian train?"

By unspoken consent, none of us said a word about the Chinvat. If they'd found us in Barcelona, they could find us here and we all three kept an eye out. We stumbled into a lively area of antique stores and palm readers and bakeries selling bread and pastry slices hot out of the oven. We found a jewelry store, bought a ring and a bracelet — no magic in Genoa — and figuratively breathed a sigh of relief. Mission accomplished. And no sign of Columbus, though this was his birth place.

Safiya said, "He already took his best shot."

Taggart grunted non-committally and kept gazing around.

The idea of facing The Shaman's questions would drive us to explore every city we visited. Here in Genoa, on a sidestreet, we chanced upon a cosy family restaurant and realized we'd been seeking precisely that. We lingered eating *spaghetti alle vongole*, which involved prying open clamshells with a special knife while drinking more than one carafe of dry red wine. Again Taggart mentioned the train tickets. He wanted to travel first-class.

Back at the train station, phrase book in hand, Safiya exchanged the tickets: "*Per piacere, ha tre posti di seconda prenotati. Vorrei tre posti per la prima serie. Ci sono dei posti in prima?*"

We paid almost double the original fare, but Taggart insisted that later we'd thank him. In this, he was right — though not as intended. Watch what happens. See a busy redcap give us impatient directions. We end up standing on a platform beside sunken train tracks. It's too cold to remain outside so we crowd into a shelter with two dozen working men, all laughing and joking in Italian. They don't stop staring at Safiya until one of them shouts: "*Eccola*!"

Safiya translates: "It's here."

Out we go with the workmen. Glancing down the track, I spot an old man sitting cross-legged on the platform, warming his hands over a bucket of smouldering embers. No, it can't be — not the same man I saw in Barcelona? He wears a similar cloth cap, but when he raises his eyes and smiles directly at me, I see this guy has a gold tooth.

Holding my gaze, and without chuckling or gesturing, he communicates anticipation and . . . amusement? I step towards him but a dozen Japanese tourists come between us. I lose eye contact, and when the tourists have passed, the old man is gone. To Safiya, as the passenger train shunts and hisses to a halt, I say:

"Did you see that man?"

"What man?"

With everybody else, we clamber aboard the train. Safiya leads the way to a first-class compartment occupied by a single sleeping man. We settle ourselves, well-satisfied. After a couple of moments, the train starts to move, heading back the way it just came. Surprised, I glance at my watch: we're leaving ten minutes early — on an Italian train? That strikes us all as unlikely. Safiya flips through her phrase book: "O.K., I've got it."

The train slows and clanks to a halt. Then it starts moving again, heading back into the station. I wake our fellow traveller and Safiya says: *"Scusi, e questo il treno per Roma?"*

"Il treno per Roma? No, no: il treno per Milano."

Safiya says, *"Milano??"*

Taggart cries: "Wrong train!"

Wide awake now, the Italian tries to tell us something, but nobody can figure out what. *Binari? I binari?* The train is picking up speed. Safiya grabs her bag and charges out the compartment door. Taggart follows. I concentrate on our fellow passenger and try telepathy, but he's thinking in words and I hit a language barrier.

I scramble out into the corridor.

Between cars, Safiya has pried open a door. She moves onto the lowest step and leans out but now we're travelling around a wrong-way curve and can't see where we're going. The train begins to slow but it's still travelling ten or fifteen miles an hour. Here's the end of the platform, so we're almost back in the station. This track runs right on through and out the other side, and what if the train keeps going? Safiya swings off onto the platform, makes it look easy, then trots along beside us, bag in hand.

The train is still travelling too fast for my liking, but none of us is thinking straight. *Milano?* No thanks! Behind me, Taggart says: "What if the train shoots through without stopping?"

"Precisely." I jump and hit the ground running. I've got both hands free because I'm wearing my miniature green knapsack. I touch down with one hand but stay on my feet and regain my balance. Taggart's alone and afraid to jump — and not without reason. I trot alongside, encouraging him. Incredibly, the train picks up speed. Two cars ahead, a conductor leans out a door and starts yelling angrily, waving his arms. He wants Taggart to get back inside, that's clear, but now Safiya has caught up and Taggart wails: "Safiya, help!"

She flips me her bag, runs along beside the open door and extends one hand to Taggart. Two cars ahead, beside himself with fury, the red-capped conductor begins a cursing frenzy.

Taggart jumps as the train lurches. He hangs onto the metal handhold too long and comes off at a funny angle. He gets one foot on the platform and Safiya grabs his jacket but she can't hang on and down he goes. It's ugly — an awkward twist and roll, an explosion of dust and stones.

By the time I get there, Safiya is cradling Taggart while he howls and moans, clutching his ankle: "It's broken! Broken, I tell you."

Together, Safiya and I help Taggart to the nearest bench.

The conductor arrives, red-faced and furious, but too worried to resume cursing and yelling: "Change tracks. *El treno* change tracks."

So that's what our fellow passenger had been trying to communicate.

Sure enough, the train has ground to a halt two tracks over from where it began.

"*Roma?*" I ask the conductor.

He points to the train we've just left: "*Milano.*" Then, not without contempt, he indicates another train three tracks over: "*Il treno per Roma.*"

Safiya hovers over Taggart looking worried.

Wincing, clearly in pain, he clutches his ankle: "It's broken, I tell you."

I hand Safiya her bag and address Taggart: "Let me see that."

Kneeling, I grasp Taggart's ankle and immediately realize he's right: it's broken.

At the back of my neck, I feel the hair tingle, and I hear myself say: "Taggart, relax."

Something in my tone makes him obey.

Feeling strangely detached, I clasp his ankle with both hands, close my eyes and feel the world recede into nothingness. I get an image of that old man warming his hands beside the train tracks, fairly glowing with suppressed amusement. But that, too, disappears. Gone the noise of the trains and the loudspeaker announcements. Gone the people jostling to get a better look. I'm alone with a broken ankle. I feel heat, a steady surge of heat, course down my arms to emerge through my hands and my fingers. I don't know how long I remain rivetted, one minute, two at most, but again, in my mind's eye, I glimpse the cloth-capped man and sense his amusement — only this time I understand that Taggart is about to become the butt of a cosmic joke. The energy stops flowing and I release the ankle.

"The pain!" Taggart says. "It's . . . gone."

He stands and gingerly tests his foot.

"You can't walk on it," I say. "Not for a while. But it's just a bad sprain."

"I'd have sworn it was broken." Taggart walks back and forth, limping slightly: "I felt heat." He stares at me hard. "How'd you do that?"

I shrug and look away: "I didn't do anything. It's just a bad sprain."

This is no simple accident, I realize, but a synchronicity. Where is it taking us? I notice the fatherly cabbie in the crowd, the one who refused to accept payment, and glimpse a possibility. To Taggart, I say: "You'll have to stay off that for the next couple of days."

"I can't travel, that's for sure." He pulls himself together: "I'll go back to the ship. You two go ahead."

Safiya digs deep: "I'll go back with you."

"Don't be silly," Taggart says. "You and Bernie should go to Rome."

"What about you?"

"Remember that cabbie, Safiya?" I gesture at the man in the crowd, wave him closer: "He'll see that Taggart gets back to the ship."

"Back to ship? Bring back to ship? No problem."

I almost add: "That's why he's here."

But Taggart is scrutinizing me, so instead I say: "We'll rejoin the Verlandi in Naples, as planned."

"He's right, Safiya. The cities we've visited — Las Palmas, Barcelona, Genoa — they'll count among the scattered sixteen. But Rome is a magical place, and could be one of the requisite seven. No sense you missing out because I've hurt my ankle."

A few minutes after midnight, when the Rome train pulls out, Safiya and I sit staring out the window of a first-class compartment. Taggart limps along the platform, waving bravely, following the cabbie, and soon disappears from view.

We're both reeling, but Safiya more than me.

Taggart's absence, I can handle: out of sight, out of mind. I don't know why Destiny has spun events this way, but I'm keen to go with the flow. That second cloth-capped man has suggested a hypothesis: if all things remain dynamically in balance, Yin versus Yang, then surely, opposite the Chinvat, there would stand a team of . . . Watchers?

How else to account for numinous old men who huddle over fires?

Have these Watchers contrived to get me alone with Safiya? There lies the deeper question. As I settle down to sleep, I warn myself: don't jump to conclusions. But I can't help relishing my situation: I'm alone with Safiya Naidoo, the most desirable woman in the universe — and not without Destiny's blessing. Surely that bodes well?

Satori in Rome

Both Safiya and I sleep soundly as the train rumbles through the Italian night, but I go especially deep, probably in reaction to the energy drain of working that minor miracle. Yet even as we rumble south, again I find myself travelling north with Daniel Lafontaine, swaying through Tanzania on that all-night bus rocking with noise, and trying to sleep while women near the front shout to those near the back and men joke and argue and slap hands.

At the rear of the bus, three young men begin chanting. No way Daniel can hear rhythm without joining in, so he abandons sleep, digs out his flute and starts playing along. At first, nobody knows what to make of this odd addition. But then crying babies fall silent and adults begin grin at each other, and when, after half an hour, Daniel pauses for breath, two dozen people loudly insist that he resume playing.

Daniel plays for another half hour while passengers chant and clap along, but finally even he grows tired. Laughingly, honestly flattered, he resists appeals to continue, gesturing that he needs sleep. A calm descends on the bus and Daniel dozes off, scrunched up in his seat.

He awakes to find his head on Victor's shoulder and sits up straight:"When's the next Howard Johnson's?"

Victor smiles: "Pit stop's just ahead."

Grimly, Daniel responds: "It better be."

Shortly after one in the morning, the bus arrives in Tanga, their half-hour stop. Daniel stumbles out of the bus and finds two dozen Masai warriors standing out front of a shelter on one leg, leaning on spears and dozing — flamingoes at rest. One young man opens his eyes and stares at him — not with hostility, he realizes, but wonder: wonder and curiosity, almost a yearning.

Daniel spots a sign saying "*Kuvalia*," meaning washroom, and points: "Let's go."

Victor shakes his head: "I don't think so."

"I thought you had to go?"

"Everybody else's using the bushes."

"Why use the bushes? The facility's right there."

He strides to the building, opens the door and steps inside. The stench almost knocks him down. Nor does he like what he sees. He wheels and explodes out of the building. Victor starts laughing and can't stop: "The look . . . on your face."

"Enough, already." Daniel makes for the bushes.

Every few minutes during the next hour, Victor bursts out laughing. Daniel ends up laughing along with him.

More passengers have crowded aboard, among them several large women who arrived with baskets on their heads and babies on their hips, and three smallish men in American clothing, holes at their elbows and knees. One of these entertains his friends by smoking a cigarette wrong-way round and drawing the burning ember into his mouth.

The windows remain open but provide no relief because the bus stirs up a silken, choking dust. Fitfully, Daniel sleeps. In the middle of the night, from the luggage rack above, an empty suitcase falls onto his head and jolts him awake.

The nearest passengers click their tongues in sympathy and say, "*pole, pole*," meaning "sorry, sorry," all seriously concerned, and one woman produces a wet cloth and holds it against a goose egg emerging on his forehead.

Victor checks that Daniel's okay, then says he's lucky the suitcase was empty: "The owner means to carry illicit goods back from Kenya."

When next he awakes, Daniel sees a sky of many colours, thinks: this day dawns like a rainbow. The bus approaches the border crossing at Lunga Lunga. Daniel has nothing to declare but relations between Tanzania and Kenya do not always run smoothly. He feels a knot in the pit of his stomach. An omen? Victor tells him not to worry — yet he, too, looks nervous.

At the border, passengers pile off the bus. Guards direct them into a line-up that winds into a building. Daniel has never felt so freakishly out of place. Up ahead, beautifully black, Victor jokes with the armed guards and sails through. A young guard, eighteen or twenty, points a long finger at Daniel: "*Twende*. Come with me."

Feeling suddenly sick, Daniel follows. As directed, he sits down in a hard-backed chair. Three men question him intensely. How much money does he have? Is he bringing anything illegal across the border? Four different men search his travelling bag, one after the other. Three of them leaf page by page through his journal. Another examines his flute. The youngest guard flips through the paperback he's carrying, entitled Satori: Insight Into The Unconscious.

One of the guards cries, "Aha!" Out of a hidden pocket, he produces the small bag full of fire-worthy souvenirs that Daniel has gathered during the past several months, among them coins and earrings and a shining Piscean scale. These attract far more interest than anything yet, and also some heated but incomprehensible discussion. Daniel is wearing two of his most valuable souvenirs — a cross from Ethiopia, a silver ring from Iran — yet the remainder look  sufficiently valuable that the senior officer lays them out on the table in front and asks: "How much money do you have with you?"

Another guard rubs his fingers together, says: "*Kitu kidigo*," which Daniel recognizes as Swahili for "something small." He understands that these men want a bribe. In the heel of his shoe, he has stashed some emergency money. But he's just received a letter from Safiya, hopes to see her again soon and can't afford to spend that money, not now. He indicates his wallet: "That's all I have."

The guard looks grim. Daniel is wavering when Victor pokes his head through the door: "Everything all right?" He points to Daniel: "He's my friend — *rafiki*."

Behind Victor stands a large woman with a baby. She says something in Swahili, then makes like she's playing a flute. The guards change their manner. One of them hands Daniel his flute, tells him to play, and so he does.

When he stops, the guards are all smiles: "Ah, *karibu*."

They hand Daniel his duffle bag.

With Victor and the large woman, he returns to the bus.

As he arrives, a second bus pulls up at the border, heading the opposite way. A young man sticks his head out a window and shouts: "White capitalist! Fascist pig!"

Victor says, "Just ignore it."

Daniel climbs into the bus and, as he makes for his seat, his fellow passengers erupt into spontaneous applause. "What's this?"

"You may be a white man," Victor says, "but you're their white man."

At that I snapped awake in Italy, found myself rattling south with African applause ringing in my ears — and oh, what a terrible sense of foreboding. I waited until the train approached Rome before saying to Safiya, as casually as possible, "What happens, do you think, if only two set forth?"

"To invoke The Shaman's Fire? Nothing I'd want to imagine. Why do you ask?"

"Just wondering. Hey, look! We're here!"

The *Stazione Termini*, cavernous transportation hub of the Eternal City, throbbed with noise and activity. People stood in line for information, currency, baggage, food, drink, even shoeshines and haircuts. Safiya plunged into this tumult, considered the line-up at the nearest information booth and said: "Forget that." She whipped out her phrase book and strode through the main doors, where instantly a dozen men surrounded us crying: "*Pensione!*"

Safiya revelled in these situations. Laughing, she kept repeating two sentences: "*Desidero una camera con due letti.*" She wanted a room with two double beds. And: "*Quanto costa al giorno una camera?*" What is the daily cost?

"*Pensione! Pensione!*" Neither of us could make sense of the situation, but then through the crowd came a burly guy in his early fifties who wore a hat saying "Official Tourist Guide." He said: "You want a room with two beds, yes? My name is Angelo. Come, please, to the Hephaistos."

To me, Safiya said: "The Greek god of fire and metal workers."

"A Greek god in Rome? Fire and metal workers? Sounds right to me."

At Safiya's insistence, and while shooing away competitors like pigeons, Angelo reduced his original asking price. He led us to a taxi stand, put two fingers into his mouth and whistled. A stoop-shouldered man limped out from beneath some trees. Angelo told us to follow this man, Stephano, to the Hephaistos.

As we followed him through the streets, we saw signs in the windows: *pensiones* everywhere. Next time we visited Rome, we agreed, we would stride past the *Stazione* throng and go door-knocking. These places would have to be cheaper if only because they didn't pay an "Official Tourist Guide" to buttonhole tourists.

Stephano responded to Safiya's phrase-book Italian by nodding, smiling and saying, "*Si, si.*" Eventually, we arrived at a five-storey apartment block. We rode a creaking elevator to the top floor and stepped out into a lobby that doubled as a dining area. To a matronly, no-nonsense woman named Clara — Angelo's wife, we later determined — Safiya said: "*Desidero una camera con due letti.*" Clara led us down a hall to a small, neat room with two single beds and a tiny balcony overlooking the street. Safiya pressed for a private bathoom: "*Ha una camera col bagno?*"

Clara shook her head no and showed us the communal facility down the hall. Finally, Safiya said, "*Va bene, prendero questa camera.*" To me, she added, "You've got to love the family resemblance!" And offered a French translation: "*Tres bien, je prendrai cette chambre.*"

While Safiya finalized arrangements in the lobby, I put my bag on one of the beds and stepped onto the balcony. Half a dozen pedestrians, a small bicycle shop, a busy grocery store — I was still enjoying the view when Safiya returned and announced that we were set for three nights: "Bernie? We're in Rome!"

"Alone at last," I said, trying for a jocular tone.

Safiya emerged onto the balcony and I tried awkwardly to put my arm around her shoulder. She moved away: "Bernie? Don't get any ideas, eh? Because we're sharing a room?"

"Safiya, I wouldn't — "

"I'm not going to sleep with you"

She hesitated but I found myself speechless.

"There's chemistry between us, Bernie. And we share certain objectives. But I'm committed to rejoining Daniel, okay?"

"Safiya, no problem. We're here to gather fire-worthy souvenirs. All I want to do is restore Colette."

She patted my shoulder: "And maybe redeem us all into the bargain?"

"Hey, why not?"

During the next couple of days, we learned that Angelo's "official tourist guiding" consisted of leading new arrivals from the *Stazione Termini* to the taxi stand. Clara ran the Hephaistos with their two sons: the older one, twenty-three, strove to perfect his English while the other, a sulky, good-looking teenager, clearly had better things to do than hang around making nice with tourists.

Clara served a superior contintental breakfast — cereal, croissants and coffee — and our biggest problem was that she kept the shower taps at the front desk, and made them available only in the morning and evening, between five and seven. Late the second day, having sorted out this schedule, I returned from the shower to find Safiya sitting cross-legged on her bed, studying photographs: "What have you got there?"

"Haven't I shown you?" Here, against the skyline of Montreal, Daniel Lafontaine stood drinking from a canteen. There, on the Plains of Abraham, he made like a lookout. Again, surrounded by admiring women, he pounded away at a piano. Daniel playing with a puppy, blowing a penny whistle, emerging from a blue tent. "Algonquin Park," Safiya said wistfully. "We went camping."

"I still don't get it, Safiya. You miss Daniel so much, how come you're travelling with Taggart?"

"Because I said I would — before I realized. We'd bought the tickets, made arrangements."

"Before you realized what?"

"That I would have preferred to pursue the quest with Daniel."

"Did you tell Taggart?"

"Of course! He said I couldn't back out now. That he'd booked hotels, paid the freighter deposit. Finally I said, okay: I'd travel with him to Sri Lanka — but then I'd go find Daniel." She took a beat, remembering. "Taggart knew that three must set forth. But now I suspect he was thinking of a different third party."

A commotion directly outside our door interrupted this discussion — some new arrival complaining that the shower didn't work. Safiya went to translate.

During the next couple of days, as we rambled around Rome, we returned more than once to her love life. Needing to talk, she cast me as confessor — not the role I wanted, though for now it would serve. After all, she'd admitted to "chemistry" between us, and surely that gave me reason to hope?

For beauty, Rome can't compare with Paris or Barcelona, but from the tree-lined Juniculum that runs along a ridge, you can look out and see how the modern city grew out of the ancient one. Strolling along, I recalled a golden afternoon with Colette and felt weak in the knees. We'd stood on a hill near Golden Gate Bridge and looked back at downtown San Francisco. Remembering made me want to weep, but I'd vowed to keep my pain private and blurted, "The absence of skyscrapers! That's the wonderful thing about these European cities."

Safiya glanced over: "Bernie? You look pale."

"No, no, I'm fine. You were saying?"

"Joseph Campell? The Hero With A Thousand Faces? He works with mythology, draws on Carl Jung?"

"Yes, yes, Behroze introduced me."

"Campbell talks about changes in consciousness, and how refusing the call for change leads to stagnation and spiritual death. You cling to the old forms instead of accepting life as a series of deaths and rebirths."

"A series that could end with The Shaman's Fire."

"We broke out of the patterns, the old forms, Daniel and I, because we were driven to do so. Initially, I hoped we could reconstruct those old patterns. But Campbell got me thinking that a three-way marriage might work better."

"A three-way marriage? Wait, let me guess: you, Daniel and Taggart."

"I'm giving you background, Bernie. The only way to approach The Shaman is synchronistically: right place, right time. Three ashavans must set forth together, but from where? That's the question. And the sacred texts are silent. Taggart thinks the three must set forth from some shared emotional base."

"And Campbell?"

"He affirms the need for new arrangements, don't you see?"

In fact, I didn't see. All I saw was Taggart hanging onto Safiya and using this protracted quest to keep her involved with him. That was the real meaning of this three-way marriage scheme, though I didn't dare say so — not yet. Instead, I tried a gentler approach: "How'd you get into Campbell?"

"Taggart lent me the book."

In response, I said nothing.

Back in New York City, before boarding the Verlandi, Safiya had seen clearly that she'd have to choose between men. Indeed, before leaving Montreal, she'd chosen Daniel over Taggart. But now, travelling with Taggart, she'd slipped back into confusion.

Not two hours later, apropos of nothing, Safiya said: "Carl Jung made it work."

"Made what work?"

We'd just explored the Roman Forum, which Safiya insisted on calling the *Foro Romano*, and discovered that the birthplace of western civilization had devolved into a wasteland of crumbling temples, broken statues and two-thousand-year-old arches leading nowhere. We'd entered the Colosseum and caught the tail end of a tour, heard about the retractable awnings, the eighty entrances, the fifty thousand roaring spectactors and how gladiators fought to the death.

Where now, this mighty Empire? That's what I was wondering when Safiya mentioned Jung. The imperial power that had once ruled the Mediterranean with an iron fist had eventually self-destructed. Later another empire, one vaster than any Roman could have imagined, extended around the globe, linking far-flung corners of the earth through a common language, English — a *lingua franca* that might one day constitute the foundation for an empire of transnational consciousness.

Emerging into contemporary Rome, a city of honking horns and jostling crows, I remained lost in these reflections. Hence: "Made what work?"

"A three-way marriage, Bernie. The emotional base from which three ashavans can set forth."

"Can we take this from the top?"

"The traditional marriage is dead. Look at the divorce statistics. It's time to abandon the old forms and develop new ways of living together, men and women."

"Enter Carl Jung?"

"Jung and his wife, Emma, and a woman named Toni Wolff."

"All this you learned . . . wait, let me guess — from a biography of Jung that Taggart lent you?"

"I don't know why I confide in you."

That's when it happened. Did I mention the scooters? In Rome, they buzz around like mosquitoes in a swamp. As we strode along the edge of a sidewalk, a motorbike drew alongside. The passenger, a big guy with short black hair, grabbed my miniature knapsack and hung on as his buddy gunned the machine. The straps held but he jerked me off my feet. I sprawled into the street and lay spread-eagled on my back, helpless as a truck barrelled down on me. Only the quick reflexes of the driver saved me. He spun the wheel hard and, amidst a squealing of breaks, rammed a small car while narrowly avoiding my head.

Having seen that I'd survived, Safiya turned and dashed after the scooter, disappearing into the crowd. Didn't stop to think. Several people helped me to my feet, exclaiming angrily. After a couple of moments, to my relief, Safiya reappeared, breathing hard. The truck driver and a well-dressed woman were exchanging heated words. I thanked the young man for saving my life, though he didn't speak English. The woman translated and, as I slipped away, having handed the man an American twenty, the two of them resumed arguing.

To Safiya, as finally we made our escape from among concerned by-standers, I said: "What were you thinking of? Chasing after two muscular men."

"I wanted to get a closer look. See if they were Chinvat."

"And did you?"

"They were Chinvat, all right."

"That's impossible. We came here by chance. Bought souvenirs without incident." At the Victor Emmanuel monument, a young woman had sold us a gorgeous pair of silver earrings. We'd split the cost and taken one each.

"Without immediate incident, you mean." Safiya shrugged: "Taggart and I thought we'd lost them in New York."

"What would they want with my bag?"

"Maybe your souvenirs. Maybe a copy of the Avesta fragment. Maybe they wanted to kill you."

"What Avesta fragment?"

"Taggart found it years ago in Iran. He memorized it and locked it away in a vault — though probably the Chinvat don't know that."

"Anyway, you've witnessed my vindication."

"Vindication?"

"This green knapsack of mine? It's fabulous."

We resumed walking, but talking less and watching more.

The Chinvat had found us in Rome.

Safiya insisted that we carry on regardless, and the following morning, at the *Stazione Termini*, we boarded the number 64 bus, the so-called "Wallet Eater," and made for the Vatican. "It's a tiny separate state, right?" Safiya said as we rode. "Governed by the Pope? And featuring Saint Peter's Cathedral and that balcony where the Pope stands when he wants to tell the world how to think and behave?"

"That's one way of describing it."

Physically, the Vatican knocked us out. As you arrive, a series of spectacular linked columns guide your attention towards the architectural glory of Saint Peter's Cathedral. Here a dome by Michaelangelo, there a chapel by Raphael. Everywhere else, breathtaking paintings and sculptures — the opulence overwhelms.

"Oooeee!" Safiya said. "All this in the name of Jesus." We'd gone inside and stood gazing up at paintings of popes. "Look at the royal robes, those sleek, well-fed faces."

"Safiya, not so loud."

"Not a bad little game they've got going here. Surrounded by splendor, they run a kingdom: fly their own flag, make their own coins, sell their own postage stamps."

Faithful pilgrims glared at us stone-faced, rightly furious. How could they know that, if we rejected their faith as moribund, yet we shared an identical yearning. Safiya wasn't helping. In desperation, as I hustled her back outside, I tried to distract her: "What will Daniel think of this new arrangement?"

She looked at me blankly, so I continued: "This three-way marriage business. Setting up house, the three of you."

"I haven't had a chance to discuss it with him."

"And Taggart?"

"I'll go to East Africa and spend time with Daniel. Taggart will arrive later."

"One woman, two men."

"When the time is right, we'll set forth to invoke The Shaman. Meanwhile, we'll share."

"Taggart agreed to that? Funny: he strikes me as insanely possessive."

"I thought so, too. But look around, Bernie" We'd emerged into the square. "We're in Rome, just the two of us. Taggart didn't object."

Obviously, he hadn't told her about my alleged incapacity, either. Instead, he'd racked up points for broad-mindedness. Never mind. The question that plagued me was: how could a woman like Safiya, so bright and sensitive, have got so lost in matters of the heart? Oh, I underestimated Taggart and his predatory voraciousness. And only later, when I felt its effects, would I appreciate his dark gift for sowing confusion. Now, I tried another tack: "So what's in this for Daniel?"

"Daniel's into the East, didn't I tell you? Hinduism, Taoism, Zen Buddhism. He believes in karma and reincarnation, that we all live countless lives, and so regards possessiveness and jealousy as self-indulgent."

"Karma? Reincarnation? Those aren't Golden Flame."

"My, but we've become doctrinaire."

"But karma's so self-righteousness, don't you think? It says, 'Hey, I'm spiritually advanced enough to seek enlightenment because I've lived wisely and generously during countless past lives. You're a thief and a beggar because you've sinned horribly and deserve no better.' Pretty convenient, if you ask me."

"My point, Bernard, and I repeat, is that Daniel sees jealousy as self-indulgent."

"And in that, you find hope."

"But of course. African wives have no trouble sharing a husband."

"You think not?"

"And in some corners of the world, several men share one woman. It's we in the West who've got it wrong. Monogamous marriages don't work, but we've yet to create alternatives."

"Like three-way marriages? Give me a break."

"Hey, you brought it up."

I thought I'd made zero headway. But that afternoon, I discovered that on some level, at least, Safiya had listened. We'd rode a bus to the catacombs, and I felt sad to discover that the celebrated Appian Way of ancient Rome had become a blaring, traffic-congested highway. Where now the imperial legions returning from distant conquest? Having glanced at a guidebook the previous night, Safiya told me Rome boasted fifty-one catacombs, five of them open to the public. At the largest, *San Callisto*, you could explore fifteen miles of tunnels on five different levels. Santa Domitilla claimed the most beautiful paintings, among them the first known painting of Christ as a good shepherd.

But the *Catacombe de San Sabastiani*, our chosen destination, had once housed the bodies of Saint Peter and Saint Paul. It took its name from a Roman soldier who tried to help a couple of Christian prisoners, Safiya said: "His fellow soldiers tied him to a tree and used him for target practice. Now, he's the patron saint of archers. You've got to love it."

At the catacombs, which were tailor-made for a Chinvat ambush, guides conducted tours in half a dozen languages. Safiya proposed joining the Italian one, now leaving: "*Demain, domani, manana* — how tough can it be?"

Thanks, but no thanks. We waited twenty minutes for an English tour. Our guide spoke the language with a British accent. He said people believe the early Christians held secret meetings in the catacombs, but the tunnels were too extensive ever to have remained secret. Fact is, burials were expensive and most Christians were poor. The catacombs provided a cheap way of burying people: "You went along a corridor, found an empty spot and dug out a hole. Then you wrapped the body in a sheet, stuffed it into the hole and walled it up."

All this in a bustling square where anybody could listen.

As we followed the guide towards the tunnels, a white-haired woman caught my eye. She stood a dozen yards to the left of the entrance, poking at a smoking bowl of incense that hung suspended from a metal stand. She looked up and we locked eyes: white-haired, worn, the woman looked eighty, yet radiated both wisdom and beauty. I found her incredibly attractive.

As the tourist group carried me forward, I heard myself think: "Are you a Watcher?" The woman nodded, faintly smiling, and beyond language communicated: "Golden Flame." Taggart had spoken of a transformative process. Now I realized that my indelible African dreams and the collusion of these fire-bearing well-wishers proved beyond a doubt that the Golden Flame had become part of my life.

To Safiya, as we followed the guide towards the tunnel entrance, I said: "Did you see that beautiful woman?"

She joked: "I beg your pardon?"

"No, no. That old woman. She absolutely radiated."

Safiya smiled up at me: "You're the clairvoyant, Bernie. Not me."

Yin versus Yang, Light versus Dark, Chinvat versus Golden Flame. It made sense, but where was it leading me? Was I getting any nearer to restoring Colette? To absolving myself of the death of Behroze? At that thought, my dead wife whirled T.S. Eliot through my mind: "And what the dead had no speech for, when living, / They can tell you, being dead: the communication / Of the dead is tongued with fire beyond the language of the living."

Baffled, I followed Safiya into the catacombs.

Initially, the tunnel ceilings stood high enough that we could walk upright. But soon we found ourselves stooping — first me, then Safiya and the others. Down we went, down, down, down, pausing every twenty or thirty yards while the air grew thicker, and trying to ignore the increasingly unpleasant odor while our guide made observations about this animal mosaic or that bit of graffiti, or else speculated on the meaning of a wall painting.

Dim lights lined the tunnel walls, adding to the eeriness. The deeper we went, the thicker the air: the bad smell became a stench. The guide offered no explanation and nobody sought one. Most of us just wanted out.

We were climbing slowly towards the surface when Safiya shielded her eyes with one arm and fell sideways against the wall.

"Safiya? You okay?" I touched her hand and plunged into yet another impossibly vivid dream. Safiya bustled along a marble hallway with fifteen or twenty others and I strode along with her, identifying completely, experiencing the scene through her senses.
. . .

The dream-state lasted only a few seconds, and then we returned to the mundane reality of the *Catacombe de San Sabastiani*, where our guide remonstrated, calling: "Please, everybody, stick together."

We caught up with the others and, within a few moments, emerged into startling daylight. Badly shaken, Safiya said: "I just had a strange experience, down there in the catacombs."

"Come, sit down." I led her to a vacant bench. "You had an unusually vivid dream, right?" I decided against adding that I'd experienced it right along with her, and that it reminded me of my own recurring nightmare — a nightmare I hadn't experienced since boarding the Verlandi. Did questing after The Shaman's Fire somehow keep it at bay? Was this change a result of the transformative process? Further evidence that the Golden Flame had begun to burn in my life?

"I'm bustling along this corridor with a crowd of people," Safiya said. "Together, we enter a glorious court room, a magnificent hall with balconies, almost an ampitheatre. Spectators pour into the place, chattering excitedly, vying for seats. I spot The Accused sitting at a table in front of the judge."

"A young woman," I said. "Tired-looking, shabbily dressed."

"How did you know?"

I shrugged and resolved to keep my mouth shut. "Go on."

"Her crime is minor, I happen to know. So the intensity of the ensuing debate surprises me. One expert follows another to the witness stand but I find their double-talk boring and pretentious, their testimony a waste of time. The Accused, too, sits indifferent, unconcerned. All around her: increasing turmoil, excited speeches. I begin to focus. Suddenly, I find myself in the thick of the action. I sit at a table in the centre of the courtroom, right down in front of the judge. Turns out I'm a lawyer. A witness finishes testifying and, one table over, a man rises to his feet — the prosecutor."

"Very eloquent, very theatrical."

Safiya eyed me strangely but kept talking: "I find myself admiring his performance, enjoying his fluency, but then he points at The Accused and cries: 'Death by hanging!' What? I can't believe it. We're talking about a minor offence, something on the order of a traffic ticket. I make my way over to the defence lawyer, who slouches in his chair, decidedly bored."

"Looks like a recalcitrant high-school student."

"I ask him how much power this court has but he doesn't know. Is an appeal possible? He doesn't know."

"He's not just indifferent but truculent, accusatory."

"He doesn't give a damn — suggests, oddly, that I myself should be acting for The Accused. That I've shirked my responsibilities."

"You do feel you could have done a better job."

"I haven't wanted to get involved. But I've forgotten why. And that's when I spot you, Bernie, sitting three rows up."

"Larger than life and twice as worried."

"I climb up and ask you whether an appeal's possible, but when I try to speak, I can't. Somehow, my tongue has come unstuck. That's how it feels, though when I reach up and check, I discover a second tongue in my mouth. Very embarrassing. I turn my back and remove this extra tongue. Now I can talk. I whisper: Is an appeal possible? This time, you understand what I'm saying."

"But instead of answering, I suggest you do something about that second tongue."

"Yes, but what? Hiding behind my raised elbow, I try to stuff it back into my mouth. Those nearby find this disconcerting. I realize that I've been trying to insert it backwards. I turn it around and try again. You grow embarrassed for me."

"I suggest you visit a mouth specialist. Somebody should be able to do something."

"Suddenly I remember. This problem with my tongue is why I'm not defending The Accused. I can't speak properly. To make myself understood, I have to keep removing this extra tongue. To you, I start explaining but the judge pounds his gavel, demands silence. Then, speaking clearly, his voice ringing in the courtroom, he declares: 'Only the two who approach The Shaman need be lovers.'"

"From the balcony, someone cries: 'Three ashavans must set

forth!'"

"The judge offers a clarification: "Three must set forth — but only two need be lovers.' The judge rises deliberately and points at The Accused: "Only two need be lovers. You're guilty as charged."

"The ampitheatre erupts."

"The judge roars like a maniac: 'Death by hanging! Take her away!'"

"Death by hanging? What? No! This can't be final."

"I've got to find somebody who knows how to appeal, because suddenly I'm no longer a bystander, or even a hapless lawyer. I've become the shabby young woman — The Accused! And two burly police officers start dragging me away."

"Then whoosh! You awake."

"You shared the whole dream, Bernie." She fixed me with her brown eyes. "What do you think it means?"

Mombasan Apocalypse

My darling Colette went deeper.

I felt the drop as it happened. She'd been floating just beneath the surface of consciousness. Then, suddenly, down she went. Behroze halted her plunge almost immediately and stabilized her at a deeper level. Yet even Behroze didn't have the strength to raise our daughter back up to where she'd been.

On the Verlandi, as all this registered, I plunged into an agony of frustration. I pounded my pillow and cursed myself for ever having left Colette alone. If I'd remained in San Francisco, I might have been able to help. I might have been able to — to what? That's what Behroze wanted to know. What could I have done? Nothing. Colette had slipped deeper, yet remained perfectly safe. And Behroze knew where to find help if she needed it.

As for me, if I wished to restore our daughter, then I'd best focus on doing what needed to be done: I'd best gather the requisite souvenirs, get The Shaman to purify one of them and bring the resultant talisman back to San Francisco. Oh, and by the way: if achieving this meant lingering in a howling inferno of unrequited love, so be it. I had a job to do. Over and out.

Behroze never failed to make me think.

But I didn't return to myself until next morning, when I stood on deck with Safiya and realized she'd been battling her own demons. I said: "You want to talk about it?"

She raised one eyebrow: "About what?"

"Our visit to that privileged space. That embedded reality, that dimension hidden somewhere within ordinary Time and Space." I took a beat, then added: "The tongue dream."

"Damn it, Bernie. You've been snooping again."

I shrugged: why try to deny? She knew I was developing telepathy. We stood gazing out at the Syrian port of Al-Mayadin. I waited, expecting her to comment on the dream's key revelation: that the two ashavans who approach The Shaman must be lovers. A communication tongued with fire. Yet again she surprised me, and demonstrated our different priorities, because she said: "Taggart's got me mouthing his ideas."

She found this hard to admit, I could tell, because she stared straight ahead. On entering into her relationship with Taggart, she'd acted on the conviction that she was younger but equally talented — and also, like Daniel Lafontaine, far more intuitive: Safiya Naidoo could certainly hold her own against Mr. Taggart Oates. Now, her unconscious mind had suggested otherwise.

I said: "Sounds about right."

"He threatened suicide, you know. In Montreal. I told him I wanted to seek The Shaman with Daniel. He said if I left, he'd kill himself."

"That's how he got you to come on this voyage."

"He also said he'd discovered the secret of how to succeed in this quest. I suspected a ploy, but he produced a fragment of scripture, said it came from the lost Avesta. I went to McGill University and had his translation verified. Eventually, he showed me the complete message. Three ashavans must set forth."

It was my turn to stare out at the minuets of Al-Mayadin. "If three must set forth, why didn't you both leave with Daniel."

"Taggart said the time wasn't right. He prevaricated until Daniel left. Now he says you've vindicated his strategy, and we should invite you to Africa — given that we need a third."

"Instead of going the three-way marriage route?"

She nodded: "Not necessarily. But Taggart prefers you to Daniel."

"Ah, yes, I remember — less of a threat."

Safiya said nothing. By now, we knew each other well enough that we felt comfortable staring out at the city in silence. If Taggart was willing to forget Daniel Lafontaine, why couldn't we do that? Clearly, Safiya didn't wish it. But where did that leave me? My growing feelings for Safiya had begun to distract me. My darling daughter lay comatose in San Francisco and I'd fallen slave to this subsidiary obsession — an enchantment not unrelated, because Safiya listened gravely and had begun to feel for Colette. But distracting all the same.

That thought sparked another: maybe this growing passion was further evidence of the Golden Flame at work in my life? And surviving it constituted the essence of my quest? By beating my way through this emotional fire, maybe I'd redeem myself? Become worthy of approaching The Shaman? This I knew: my yearning for Safiya had become part of who I was.

But The Now. I needed to focus on The Now.

A hundred ships lay scattered around the harbour, maybe more. Most flew Chinese flags, but also I spotted a Liberian, a Dutch, even a British — though no American. We weren't especially welcome here. Beyond Al-Mayadin, near a blue range of mountains, black smoke billowed skyward. This land, Syria, had once formed part of Ancient Persia, Zarathustra country, and I found myself thinking that we would never come closer than this city to the original home of the Sacred Fire.

The dock at Al-Mayadin can accommodate only fifteen or twenty vessels, which explained our wait. George the steward said that last time the Verlandi put in here, it remained only five hours and nobody left the vessel. Time before that, the ship sat waiting for a week. He'd met a Sudanese sailor who claimed that here he'd waited three months.

All of which had galvanized Safiya and I to wait on deck for Boutros the shipping agent. An hour ago he'd arrived by motor launch and closeted himself with the captain. We'd positioned ourselves near the bottom of the stairs. At dinner last night, the captain had made a brief speech. Mr. Boutros didn't want any passengers going ashore that evening. Tomorrow morning, he would send a tourist guide to bring us to Ugarit, the birth-place of writing.

Nobody liked the "tomorrow" part of this message, but Safiya and I liked it least. We needed to buy fire-worthy souvenirs in Al-Mayadin, which certainly qualified as a magical place. Safiya thought we should send an emissary to the captain but couldn't drum up enough support. We'd resumed speaking with all our fellow passengers except Milo and his wife — but barely, and most didn't share our sense of urgency: If Mr. Boutros didn't want us rambling around Al-Mayadin, no doubt he had a good reason.

This morning, after breakfast, Boutros had arrived alone in the boat launch except for the driver. No sign of the promised tourist guide. Now Safiya paced the deck, panther-like, while I leaned against the railing. On the deck above us, a door opened. The shipping agent descended the steps and Safiya, smiling broadly, flagged him down: "Mr. Boutros, when can we expect this tourist guide?"

"Tomorrow," Boutros said. "Tomorrow, a guide will come."

"Today," Safiya said. "I want to go ashore today."

"Tomorrow, he will come."

"No, today. I want to go today."

"Okay, today," Boutros said, smiling thinly. "I'll send another launch."

"Why can't we come now, with you?"

"I'm going now to other ships. Excuse, please."

Boutros had zero intention of sending another launch today. Safiya knew that, yet insisted that we prepare to leave. She returned to her cabin, packed a small bag and organized Taggart. Into my miniature green knapsack, I threw a toothbrush and a change of underwear. Then we waited. At noon, we ate lunch. At one o'clock, Safiya said, "O.K., we've given Boutros long enough. We'll get our own launch."

Taggart said: "I'm going back to the cabin." And disappeared down the corridor.

He'd visited Tehran a couple of years back, and had already procured a Persian souvenir — a metal chess piece, an armed knight he'd described as symbolizing fire.

To Safiya, I said: "We need visas to go ashore."

She looked at me, then started up the stairs. I followed.

The ships waiting in Al-Mayadin harbour formed a loose semi-circle around the dock. The Verlandi lay two-thirds of the way out, roughly three miles. Every few minutes, we'd see a launch or a motorboat whiz past. Most were over-crowded — but not all.

From the top deck, Safiya began shouting and waving, trying to flag down one of these passing boats: "Hey! Over here!"

Milo's wife, Shirley, poked her head through their porthole and cried: "Do you mind, up there? We're trying to nap!"

"Sorry about your nap," Safiya said, "but I'm flagging a boat."

She resumed shouting and waving.

After half an hour, I began to lose hope. Then Safiya caught the eye of a motorboat man wearing a monster straw hat. He turned his boat around and headed our way. As Safiya raced down the steps to negotiate a price, she cried: "Get Taggart! We're out of here."

During our windblown trip across the harbour, the moustachioed mortorboat driver developed a passion for my modest blue sailor's cap, necessary protection against the blazing sun. He began gesturing, pointing first at his monster straw hat and then at my more modest headgear. When I understood that he wanted to trade, I shook my head emphatically no. But as we pulled up to the pier, he snatched the cap from my head.

Immediately, he replaced it with his monster straw hat, broad-brimmed and spectacular — but three sizes too small. He refused to trade back and, short of using force, I could only accept defeat. He waved us off and we walked up a dirt road under construction, Safiya laughing merrily as I struggled to keep this grotesque hat on my head.

T-shirted men stopped working to gape as we passed, and I realized that, yes, we constituted a spectacle. Despite the blistering heat, Safiya wore a long-sleeved blouse and an ankle-length caftan. She also sported a floppy hat, but her long neck was bare and alluring enough that Taggart muttered, "We've got to get you a headscarf." He'd warned her against exposing anything but feet, face and hands. Earlier, in response to our pleading, he'd agreed to leave his top hat on the Verlandi. But with his batiked shirt, shoulder-length hair and silver-mirror sunglasses, he remained hard to miss.

At the top of the hill, where the dirt road met a highway, we arrived at a check point. Armed soldiers demanded to see our passports. They also sought visas but we feigned mystification. To my surprise, Safiya whipped out a paperback called Learn Arabic in a Month and began sounding out words and phrases: "*Ismi Safiya. Ana kanadiyaa. Hal tatakalam Inglezzi?*"

A young officer emerged from a shelter: "Can I help you?"

Safiya explained that we'd debarked from a freighter. We wanted to stay overnight in Al-Mayadin and needed a hotel, not too expensive. Obviously smitten, the man said: "No problem." He snapped his fingers and the original soldier handed back our passports. The officer began shouting, waving his arms. Several middle-aged men in white shirts, sleeves rolled up, stood leaning against the wall of a nearby barracks. Now one of them stepped forward. The officer spoke a few words to him, then turned to Safiya and said, "This man will take you to a hotel."

Safiya said, "*Ma'a salaama*," and we followed the man to an eighties vintage white sedan. Taggart said: "Where'd you get that phrase book?"

"The Verlandi's library. Didn't you see it?"

The driver wanted Safiya to sit up front next to him, but I hopped in and refused to budge. Finally, away we drove along a two-lane highway thick with scooters, cyclists and pedestrians. The dusty streets grew congested and we slowed to a crawl. We saw no highrises here, just ground-floor shops in two-storey buildings and, everywhere we turned, throngs of people, almost all of them men.

Safiya drew attention to the signs — the Arabic script. Street signs, shop signs, nothing but Arabic script. Giant billboards advertised American movies, you could tell from the colourful posters. But the lettering, the words beneath the garish illustration? Incomprehensible. Safiya pointed at huge billboard: "Legends of the Fall. And look! there's Shakespeare in Love!"

The driver pulled over and indicated that we'd arrived. But

the surrounding hurly-burly looked more like a flea market than a tourist area. Lots of signs to be seen, but all of them incomprehensible. Safiya sought clarification using the phrase book and sign language, but the driver insisted only that, yes, we'd arrived. He hadn't forgiven me for sitting up front, and out we tumbled. Taggart gave the driver five American dollars and away the man drove. Safiya said: "Welcome to Al-Mayadin."

As we stood on the side of the street gazing round, I realized that we'd left the West behind. Italy and Spain? From where we now stood, they looked a lot like America. We'd become aliens who'd beamed down into the wrong world. Yet, as we stood wondering which sign said "hotel," I spotted passers-by wearing western clothes and realized that Al-Mayadin lay at just one remove — that it wasn't completely Other. Rather, East meets West. To Safiya, I said: "Welcome to No-Man's Land."

"No-Person's Land?" She cocked an eyebrow to show she was teasing.

A tall, thin man wearing a bright pink shirt and matching slacks crossed the street and addressed us in German.

Taggart said: "This is surreal."

I said, "No, no — it's a borderland."

The thin man tried French and I cried: "See what I mean?"

Turned out he knew more English than French. He nodded understanding at the word "hotel" and said, "Follow, please."

The pink-shirted thin man led us around the corner, up some broad stairs, through swinging doors and into an ornate, second-floor room where another man sat behind a desk. Safiya whipped out her phrase book and got as far as saying, *Ana kanadiyaa.* The man jumped to his feet: "Canadians?"

Taggart and I looked at each other, shrugged. Turned out our host had once spent two months in Peterborough, Ontario, visiting a cousin: "Great country, Canada."

Hakim, his name was. Thirty years old, clean-shaven, neatly dressed. Quite well-muscled. Could this guy be Chinvat? I scanned, found no sign and relaxed.

Hakim owned this establishment, the Hotel Rahmsis. He'd inherited it from his father, who'd died in a great fire that had wiped out much of Aleppo. He pointed to a massive portrait on the wall behind his desk: a bearded man wearing white. Our arrival constituted an event. Yes, yes, he had rooms. Very nice rooms, very nice. But first we had to register. Hakim produced a thick ledger and flipped it open: Father's name, mother's name, citizenship, place of residence, passport number, date of entry.

The column ran down the right hand side of the page, not the left, but why not? this was Arabia. Hakim spent extra time examining my passport. "American," he said. Coolly, he handed it back.

While we filled in blanks, Hakim talked heatedly with the pink man, doubtless discussing a finder's fee. We rented two rooms without seeing them because, after all, where else could we go? When we'd finished writing, Hakim insisted on breaking out cold orange drinks to celebrate our arrival.

He changed money for us: "Very good rate." And he produced a tourist map of Al-Mayadin, said it included all the sights. "The museum? You want to see the museum?"

Safiya took the map and opened it.

To Taggart, I said: "Maybe the museum will have something on the Sacred Fire?"

Before he could respond, Hakim slapped his own forehead: "Today the museum is closed. What about beach? You want to see beach?"

Safiya said: "Hakim, this map is in German. Have you nothing in English?"

Hakim dug furiously through his desk and turned up an Italian brochure. Nothing in English, nothing in French. But look! Triumphantly, he produced an English map of Aleppo. Unfortunately, we weren't going to that city. Never mind. "See beach? I will take you to beach."

We looked at each other: why not? First, though, we wanted to see our rooms — one single, one double. Each had a balcony and a small bathroom with toilet and sink, and the one in the double featured a shower. By North American standards, none of this sparkled. But before any of us said a word, Hakim cried: "We clean. I take you to beach, we clean bathrooms."

Taggart and Safiya left a few small items of clothing in their room. I trusted to my fabulous green bag and left nothing but my new straw hat, which wouldn't stay on my head. Soon, ensconced in Hakim's van, we found ourselves careering through crowded streets. Hakim leaned on his horn every time he approached a bicycle, a scooter or another car. He passed everything on the road and scared us all white — especially Taggart, who'd insisted on sitting up front.

By the time we reached the beach, Taggart looked ashen, but Hakim noticed nothing. He had delivered us to the beach, lickety-split. And isn't that the way Westerners do things? Now he wanted to know when he could pick us up. Half an hour? One hour?

We felt crowded by this Middle-Eastern hospitality, overwhelmed. Safiya said we'd make our own way back to the hotel, but Hakim pretended not to hear. She was a woman. Taggart wiped his brow, still pulling himself together, so I stepped forward: "Hakim, we don't know how long we'll stay at the beach. We've got to do some shopping. We'll find our own way back."

Hakim didn't like this. He enjoyed showing us off — but also, I realized, felt concerned for our safety. Reluctantly, he agreed to leave us. Safiya had already waved and strode off down the beach. With Taggart in tow, she headed for an outdoor cafe about one hundred yards distant.

As I trotted along the beach to catch up, suddenly I felt dizzy, light-headed. Too much heat? Weak in the knees, I slowed to a walk, then stopped and braced myself against a palm tree. A white light throbbed and I closed my eyes and shielded them with my arm. After a moment, the dizziness passed — but now I felt unbearably hot. And what humidity!

When I opened my eyes, day had become night. I blinked repeatedly before understanding that I'd entered a privileged space, an embedded reality. I'd plunged more deeply than ever, and so found myself experiencing more vividly. A full moon hung low in the sky. I stood on a beach that proclaimed tropicality: palm trees soared from a lush jungle and swayed in the breeze high above. Ocean waves rolled steadily shoreward, cresting white-capped in the moonlight, muting an orchestra of night sounds. The insistent calling of a redbird made me realize: Africa!

Details came in a rush. I stood on a beach on the Kenyan coast, just north of Mombasa. Daniel and Victor sat cross-legged before a campfire. Early today, they'd stumbled out of that overnight bus from Dar and found a hotel in Mombasa. They'd napped for three hours and then gone souvenir-hunting in the Old

Town, a hilly warren of streets and alleys and tall houses with intricate metal balconies.

In the busiest streets, together with silk dealers, perfume makers and spice merchants, goldsmiths and coppersmiths displayed their wares. Daniel bought a copper bracelet studded with semi-precious stones and Victor a tiny shield bearing the Mombasa coat of arms. Their business concluded, the two men made short work of Biashara Street, where women in head-to-foot Bui Buis or brilliant Kanga outfits sorted through textiles, musical instruments, palm bags and assorted mats, spoons and winnowing trays.

They climbed the hill to Fort Jesus, a pink-walled stone structure which the Portuguese built in the sixteenth century to serve as the heart of the African slave trade. They ventured onto the flat roof of Omani House and stared out at Mombasa Harbour and the sprinkling of dhows and sailboats at anchor, and marvelled at the tranquility of the scene. Five hundred years before, the Portuguese Vasco de Gama had sailed into this harbour and proceeded to change Africa forever.

Here in Mombasa, the Portuguese had tortured recalcitrant Arabs, massacred thousands of Turks and abandoned others to die at the hands of the Zimba, a man-eating tribe from the interior. Here, at the end of the seventeenth century, they'd endured a final seige by Omani Arabs, who eventually wiped them out. Mombasa had borne witness to both the beginning and the end of the Estado da India, the Portuguese empire, in East Africa, and also to many of its worst excesses.

Daniel and Victor explored the Hall of the Mazuri, where centuries before Portuguese sentries had scratched graffiti into the walls, and also examined an exhibit celebrating the Mombasa excavation, a lengthy recovery project devoted to retrieving the seventeenth-century wreck of the Santa Antonia de Tanna, which remained in the harbour eighteen metres down.

Finally, sobered, they put history behind them. They hired a car and left Mombasa, heading north across the Nyali bridge. Daniel felt ambivalent about leaving the island city because at least one legend alluded to invoking the Sacred Fire from an island. Yet he'd done his homework and knew the city itself boasted no acceptable beach. He'd decided on the north coast as more private than the south and awaited synchronistic guidance. They'd driven past the Nyali Golf Club and Mamba Village, declining a suggestion by their driver, a cheerful university type, to visit a crocodile farm set amidst streams and waterfalls.

They'd looked in briefly at Bombolulu, where a handicrafts centre offered hundreds of original designs in metals and local woods, but bought only sandals: they'd already acquired their Mombasan souvenirs. They whipped past a series of beach hotels with names like Neptune Beach, Ocean View and Whitesands, and stopped again at Jumba La Mtwana, the fifteenth-century site of a legendary Swahili community.

Their young driver showed them a jumble of tombs. At Daniel's urging, he translated a number of inscriptions, and both visitors were taken with one of them: "Every soul shall taste death. You will simply be paid your wages in full on the Day of Resurrection. He who is removed from the fire and made to enter heaven, it is he who has won the victory. The earthly life is a delusion."

Daniel took this as propitious. He strolled down the hill onto Jumba Beach and stood looking out at the ocean: in the distance, a white yacht sat etched against the blue sky. To Victor, he said: "This is the place."

The driver left them nearby at a newly opened beach hotel called the Whispering Palms. After checking in, Daniel and Victor went to the dining room and ate seafood. Victor flirted shamelessly with three attractive Dutch women seated nearby. Daniel fretted that his friend wasn't taking the quest seriously. But later, when darkness fell, Victor turned grim and resolute. The two men took their sachets of fire-worthy souvenirs and walked along the beach to a deserted spot overhung by palm trees. Here they gathered driftwood and started a bonfire, feeding it steadily until the blaze reached shoulder-height.

Now, as I watched, Daniel spread souvenirs and mementoes, most of them European, on a small tray he'd brought for this purpose. On the far side of the bonfire, Victor did the same, laying out a variety of mainly Caribbean keepsakes, among them stone dwarfs, a sheet-metal warrior and a three-horned Bosu figure.

Daniel began chanting, repeating the same words over and over, and Victor joined him. After a while, I realized that the rhythmic chant comprised the names of the "Amesha Spentas" of whom Taggart had spoken, the seven Bountiful Immortals: "Ahura

Mazda, Vohu Manah, Asha Vahishta, Khshathra Vairya, Spenta Armaiti, Haurvatat, Ameretat." Round and round they went for a good fifteen minutes. Then, simultaneously, they fell silent.

Flinging his keepsakes into the blaze, and indicating that Victor should do the same, Daniel cried: "I announce and complete my worship to thee, the fire, oh Ahura Mazda's son! Together with all the fires, and to the good waters, even to all the waters made by Mazda, and to all the plants which Mazda made." He paused, then shouted: "Verethreghna! Keeper of the sacred flame! Come forth."

In response, the bonfire blazed brighter — or was that a trick of my imagination?

Daniel tried again: "Mighty Shaman! Two ashavans approach! Come forth."

Still nothing. After a moment, Victor said, "Now what?"

"We're missing something."

From outside Time and Space, I wanted to shout: "You set forth without a third! And you're not lovers!"

"We're not on an island," Daniel said. "Maybe that's the problem."

"Verethreghna!" Victor cried. "Get your butt out here."

"Victor, don't fool around."

"Come on out, you old witch doctor. Come out and fight like a man."

"Victor, knock it off." Daniel moved around the bonfire towards his friend. "We'll let the fire cool and reclaim our souvenirs."

Victor danced out of reach, jigging first on one leg, then the other: "Verethreghna! Mighty Shaman! Let's see some lightning."

"For god's sake, Victor!" Daniel darted around the fire to tackle his friend, but the ex-tailback eluded him easily, shouting skyward: "Come on, Verethreghna! Strike me dead if you dare."

"Stop acting crazy, Victor. You're fooling with elemental forces."

Victor howled at the moon, then turned and raced for the

water: "Yo! Mighty Shaman! Where's your lightning?"

Daniel trotted after his friend but Victor charged into the whitecaps shouting: "You out there, Verethreghna? Strike me dead if you dare!"

At waist level, Victor plunged into the waves and started swimming straight out..

Knee-deep in ocean swells, Daniel stopped and called: "Victor! Come back!"

His friend disappeared into the darkness beyond the moonglow.

From behind him, a deep voice said: "Daniel, your friend is lost."

Daniel whirled. A wizened old man in a white robe stood ankle-deep in ocean.

"What do you mean, lost? He'll come back in a minute."

The tiny man pointed out to sea: "Chinvat."

Daniel looked where the old man indicated: beyond the moonglow, for the first time, he discerned a white yacht — the same ship he'd seen that afternoon. Panicking, Daniel cried: "Victor! Come back!"

A few seconds later, as if in response, a shot rang out. Then came a howl and, in quick succession, two more shots. Then, nothing. Nothing but the sound of the ocean. Daniel plunged into the whitecaps and began swimming, making for the yacht, raising his head and treading water occasionally to look around wildly and shout: "Victor! Where are you?"

The yacht had disappeared. Treading water, breathing hard, Daniel thought he heard the sound of an engine receding into the night. "Help! Somebody, help!"

But he'd chosen this spot for its isolation.

For twenty minutes, shouting and crying, Daniel swam in great circles. Finally, nearing exhaustion, he located and made for the beach. There he stumbled ashore and fell onto the sand weeping, knowing he'd never see Victor again. After a while, he felt a touch — a hand touching his shoulder. He looked up, saw the wizened old man etched against the night sky and for a moment forgot his sorrow: "You're not . . . Verethreghna?"

Smiling grimly, the tiny man helped Daniel to his feet: "I'm not, no."

"Then who are you?"

"You need know only that I can make your music happen, Daniel. I can make you world famous."

"How'd you know my name?"

The old man shrugged and exposed his palms: "Once, people called me a prophet." He paused, then added: "You seek recognition, do you not? Fame and glory as a musician?"

Daniel stood clenching and unclenching his fists: "You'd want something in return."

The tiny man took his arm: "Come walk along the beach."

Lost in Al-Mayadin

The emotional math of love triangles challenges even Einsteins of feeling. But love quadrilaterals? One woman, three men? They're more difficult still — especially when three of the four must work together or die trying. I'd fallen in love with Safiya Naidoo. I knew it, she knew it and Taggart Oates suspected. Safiya loved Daniel Lafontaine, the absent fourth — and hence that shocking psychic missive from north of Mombasa.

Safiya's love for Daniel made me wild, but right now I faced Taggart. And that meant keeping my objective in focus, though our quadrilateral equations grew increasingly complex. I'd embarked on this quest for the sake of Colette, whose life remained ominously in danger. By answering the call, I'd launched a transformative process which had brought into play my guilt over the death of Behroze. Now my own psychic survival hung in the balance. How much of this was conscious? On some levels, most. On others, none. But all of me knew that I had to succeed or die trying.

If success involved collaborating with Taggart Oates, my enemy in love, then collaborate I would. Obviously, Taggart had come to a similar conclusion. He'd realized I might be useful, even necessary, to his own success. At one point, half joking, he'd even suggested that he and I might be the two ashavans who would eventually approach The Shaman. He hadn't yet learned that the two must be lovers. I'd urged Safiya to keep secret the tongue dream we'd shared in Rome, and after thinking about it, she'd agreed. After all, she and Taggart qualified to approach. Likewise, she and Daniel Lafontaine. Full disclosure would only give Taggart extra leverage and make him watchful. She preferred to encourage our unspoken pact of mutual toleration.

Meanwhile, I'd begun to hope that Safiya's relationship with Taggart would self-destruct, and resolved to do whatever I could to aid that process. The tongue dream had complicated our friendship. In Rome, even while sharing a room wth Safiya, I'd respected her wishes and controlled my yearnings. Now, I worried that if I declared myself more fully, she'd think I was doing it merely to qualify — that I was seeking to use her. No, surely not. She knew how I felt. And surely her relationship with Taggart was dying?

As the three of us quit the beach at Al-Mayadin, I shared nothing of that African night — nothing of Daniel's failed invocation and its terrible aftermath. Instead, I insisted that the heat had induced a momentary dizziness. Safiya suspected a waking vision but couldn't be sure. She tried teasing the truth out of me but I didn't respond. Again I'd been reminded that this was no game: Victor wasn't the first to die, and he wouldn't be the last.

As we hiked from the beach into the heart of downtown, I willed myself into the present, The Now, and realized that Al-Mayadin was a city of men: men sitting on doorsteps in hardbacked chairs, men leaning against walls and smoking cigars, men sucking contentedly on mouthpieces attached to gigantic brass water pipes that sat respelendent beside them. We saw men arguing in groups, and men spilling out of cavernous rooms whose open doors offered glimpses of still more men sitting in circles on the floor, shouting and laughing while playing cards and backgammon. I saw no sign of Chinvat, felt no psychic traces.

Here on the sidewalk sat another group of men, all of them

staring up at a small colour TV mounted on a wall, watching . . . an American beauty pageant? Young women in bathing suits paraded around on stage wearing sashes across their fronts: Miss Alabama, Miss Oklahoma, Miss Kentucky. Safiya made a face but said nothing. We all three kept walking.

We stumbled into a covered bazaar and spent half an hour wandering among carpets and woven bags and caftans, not to mention pungent barrels of basil and clovers, brassware and decorative daggers and swords and water pipes, and also tacky souvenirs, hieroglyphic drawings and Ayatollah-Khomeini wrist watches. I considered buying one as a novelty but Safiya gave me such a look when I whispered this that I didn't even pick it up.

In the bazaar, at last, we encountered women. A couple of the younger ones wore modest European clothing, skirts that reached below the knee, but most wore ankle-length caftans like Safiya's. A few wore widow's weeds, nothing but black, and hid their faces behind veils even while furiously negotiating. Safiya purchased a golden scarab that glowed in the sunlight, and I bought a silver "caduceus," two snakes entwined on a vertical staff. Taggart said this item symbolized the alchemical energies of Yin and Yang: "Also, it's an emblem of the medical profession."

Before leaving the bazaar, urged on by Taggart, Safiya bought a colourful headscarf — "*marhaba, ureed kaffiyeh*" — and donned it then and there, covering her neck. I spotted a green sailor's cap that looked vaguely like the one I'd "traded." It was too small, but not dramatically so. I paid the asking price and Taggart snorted with contempt: "They expect you to haggle."

Without exchanging a word on the subject, we all three became more vigilant. Buying fire-worthy souvenirs, we'd begun to believe, had a way of galvanizing unwanted attention. On some level, it transmitted a signal — or perhaps made waves. Outside the market, Safiya studied our German street map before striking out for the restaurant Hakim had declared the best in Al-Mayadin. This would be our splurge. The streets grew increasingly congested and Safiya observed that, even if we had an English map, we'd still be forced to count streets and alleys because we couldn't decipher signs.

In Italy or Spain, even when we didn't understand, we could sound out words and often they'd hint at meaning. Here in Al-Mayadin, every sign proclaimed the place foreign: nothing but

Arabic script. Incomprehensible. For Westerners like ourselves, oriented to the printed word, the experience proved unsettling. We couldn't get our bearings. Safiya said: "This is what it's like to be illiterate."

Reflectively, having stopped at a street corner, she added: "It's the perfect symbol for our condition. Do we go this way? That? We're the foreigners here, lost and relying on instinct." She whipped out her notebook and began scribbling. "Lost in Al-Mayadin. Not a bad title, eh? For my next novel?"

"Which novel is that?" Taggart said. "The one about you, me and Lanigan, here? Or the other one, about you, me and the absent fourth"

"The one about the woman fighting to survive in a world full of arrogant men."

She kept writing, then read aloud: "Lost in Al-Mayadin, by Safiya Naidoo.'"

"Lost in Al-Mayadin," Taggart repeated. "That's got a ring to it. But maybe make it Lost in Al-Mayadin . . . by Taggart Oates."

He chuckled but Safiya didn't laugh with him.

And in that I glimpsed not a crack but a fault-line: these two competed professionally. Give their relationship time and it would self-destruct. So I told myself, anyway.

Eventually, by counting streets, Safiya found the restaurant. We devoured a superb meal, vaguely North African, and couldn't help noticing as we finished that diners at a nearby table had commandeered a magnificent, silver-plated water pipe that stood maybe three feet tall. The waiter, in response to our questions, said they were smoking "special tobacco."

We requested the same and shared an after-dinner smoke out of yet another elaborate hookha. Taggart inhaled but just ended up coughing. Safiya observed that we had no way of knowing whether every pipe got the same "special tobacco."

She led us back to the Hotel Rahmsis, where we found the lobby deserted. No sign of Hakim. In the two rooms we'd rented, chambermaids had cleaned the toilets and changed the linen. They'd left our worldly goods, including my new straw hat, untouched. In my room the window stood open and, because of the lingering heat, I left it that way.

Three stories down, the city began coming to life: men yelling, their words untelligible; men blowing car horns and gunning motorcycles. Around two o'clock in the morning, as Al-Mayadin settled into almost quiet, a sudden hammering woke me. From down the hall came the sound of male voices talking loudly — somebody giving orders?

A man yelled, "Chinvat!" Taggart? A woman cried out: Safiya?

In a single motion, I sprang from my bed, crossed the room and jerked open the door. Down the hall, people were scuffling — among them, Safiya. A burly man in a white T-shirt was dragging her by the wrist to the stairwell. She kicked and punched and jabbed with precision, fought like a trained kickboxer, but he absorbed this punishment without losing his grip.

This guy never saw me coming. I tackled him viciously, drove my head into the small of his back. He smacked the cement wall with his face and slumped to the floor, bleeding from the mouth and nose. I kicked him twice in the stomach, and then once more, and whirled and ducked and felt a second man go flying over my head to sprawl on his back. He sprang to his feet like a cat.

There were three of them, then — and fighting on our side, an older man, grey-haired and determined, a martial artist past his prime. Taggart, winded and wheezing, had regained his feet. Safiya and the older man were together battling the biggest and toughest of the Chinvat. Amazingly, the big man I'd tackled and kicked had struggled to his feet. Footsteps and shouts heralded the arrival of newcomers. The Chinvat leader cried out and instantly the three intruders retreated down the stairs.

Hakim arrived from the other end of the hall: "What is happening, mister? What is happening?"

Hakim took us downstairs for coffee. Nothing like this had ever happened here before. Nothing like this in the history of the Hotel Rahmsis. Nothing like this. He felt so badly that he tried to refund our money. Saifya refused, telling him: "Hakim, this has nothing to do with you. It's not your fault."

Who was the older man who'd melted away as Hakim arrived? Nobody knew. Hakim hadn't seen him. All these intruders. He wanted to call the police, but Safiya talked him out of it. What good would that do? They'd keep us up all night, answering questions. And think of the reputation of the Hotel Rahmsis: better to post a watchman and keep the incident quiet, no?

Later, as the three of us said another goodnight, Taggart said: "Good thing they didn't have weapons."

"They were trying to kidnap us," Safiya said, "not hurt us. They think we know something they don't."

"Do we?" I said.

Taggart shrugged: "The hurting would have come later."

To Safiya, as I went to the door, I said, "By the way, where'd you learn to kickbox?"

Exhausted, she managed a grin: "That's a little something I picked up in your mother's home town."

Next morning, I woke to the sounds of a muezzin calling the faithful to prayer. I washed and dressed, checked the mirror and decided that I looked not much worse. Down the hall, I found Taggart favoring his left shoulder, nothing serious. Safiya had been up for an hour, scribbling impressions of the late-night battle in her notebook. She'd considered going for a walk — "I wanted to ramble the streets alone, just for a while" — but decided that, in view of last night, it would be unwise.

We all agreed that we'd best make for the ship right away. In the second-floor lobby, where last night we'd drank coffee, we saw no sign of Hakim. Probably still sleeping. I left my monster straw hat on a chair and followed my fellow travellers into the quiet morning streets.

Map in hand, Safiya led us to a tourist bureau. Out front stood a wooden sign declaring its identity in a dozen languages, among them German, Spanish, Italian, French and English. A metal pull-down door remained closed and padlocked. No telling when or even if the place might open.

Safiya had brought the phone number of Boutros the agent, just in case, but if he learned we were rambling around Al-Mayadin, he would no doubt be furious. As for battling Chinvat at the Hotel Rahmsis, the less said, the better. Our best bet would be to find someone who spoke English, someone who could guide us back to the docks.

We moved to a busy streetcorner. Safiya studied our German map. We were conspicuous, no question. People gawked and went wide, making room, and I began casting about psychically. Catching a snippet of an old Beatles tune, I picked out a middle-aged man — potentially, our good Samaritan. He strode toward us amongst half a dozen other men dressed similarly: neatly pressed slacks, a short-sleeved white shirt. I said: "Excuse me, sir. Do you speak English?"

He looked surprised: "Why, yes. What can I do for you?"

I explained that we needed to get back to our ship and the man said he'd be happy to help. He extended his hand: "Jahed Khouday." Would we join him for coffee? By now I'd become so suspicious of strangers, even those I approached, that I thought: Chinvat? A quick scan told me no. Even so, I protested a shortage of time. But Jahed Khouday wouldn't accept a refusal. He led the way to his shop on a busy side-street while explaining his fluent English: as a youth, he'd spent three years in New York and briefly attended Columbia University. Then his father had died and he'd come home to run the family business, a Singer Sewing Machine agency.

As he led us into his shop, Jahed barked orders in Arabic. Two young men scurried to produce chairs. We visitors sat down in mid-shop, as directed, and spent the next half hour sipping Turkish coffee out of tiny cups while customers came and went, buying mostly needles and wool, and curiously inspected these three outlandish Westerners.

We saw widows in black, young girls in army uniform and men wearing *argales*, those white head-dresses, circled on top by colourful kerchiefs or bands, that hang down the back of the neck. In a quiet corner, an old man clacked worry beads. Safiya observed that empty sewing-machine cases lined the top shelves of every wall: "Does that mean business is good?"

Jahed sat with us in the heart of the shop, but kept jumping up to chat with customers and suppliers. With us, he conferred in the most urbane and civilized tones. With his minions, he shouted imperiously. They scurried in and out of a back room. Customers stepped behind the counter to use the telephone. They carried on angry discussions. We sat sipping coffee, waiting for Jahed to show mercy, but clearly he wanted us to see and be seen.

Finally Safiya, out of patience, leaned over and whispered in

Jahed's ear. The man looked horrified. He leapt to his feet, clapped his hands and barked an order. One of his young men raced out the door. Jahed whipped a business card out of a drawer and, on its back, scribbled a note in Arabic.

Ignoring Safiya, speaking mainly to me, he said that if we encountered difficulty, we should show this note to anybody who could read. With that, he led us outside to where a young man waited in a car. Jahed gave him orders, then bundled us into the back seat and waved goodbye. Away we went, back to the docks.

The driver spoke broken French with Safiya and drove directly to the military checkpoint above the dock. He conferred with the soldiers, then said the Verlandi had docked not far away. We could hardly believe it. With so many ships in the harbour, we'd anticipated a terrible time finding our own. The young man backed up, turned around and swung down a rutted track that emerged onto the dock. He drove slowly along the busy pier through workmen and cyclists, insistently blowing his horn. Suddenly, Safiya exclaimed and pointed. Incredibly, there sat the Verlandi.

Safiya insisted on paying the driver out of her poker winnings. As we stood waiting, Taggart said to me: "What did she say to get us out of that shop?"

Joining us, Safiya heard the question and grinned: "I told him I needed to return to the ship immediately — that I was having female problems."

Taggart said, "Safiya, you're ruthless."

She threw back her head and laughed in that way she had, and I felt such a pang of yearning that I feared I would declare myself right then and there, despite my best interests, and so wheeled and fled to my cabin.

At lunch we learned that the Verlandi would sail tonight, as soon as it finished unloading. Not only that, but agent Boutros had come through. We'd arrived in time to catch an organized tour to Ugarit, a dozen miles away. Once the most important city on the Mediterranean coast, now it lay in ruins. Still, as Taggart said, writing itself was born in Ugarit, home of the earliest alphabet known to man. I made a mental note: possible Shaman's question.

And of course we took the official tour — what could be safer? The three of us squeezed into a car with Rosella and Josephine, the southern ladies, for the hot, bumpy drive. Rosella wore long white gloves and, despite the heat, refused to remove them. They protected her from infection. Back home, somebody had warned her against contracting a disease in the Middle East: "All you have to do is touch your eye."

Josephine spotted a bunch of men loitering outside a building: "That must be the unemployment office, huh?"

By the time we reached Ugarit, even Safiya needed a break. She marched on ahead while Taggart chatted with the tour guide. I matched her pace: "Our fellow passengers getting to you?"

"Look at them, Bernie," she said, indicating not just our party, but the dozen or so other European visitors. "They've come not to grapple with a living place, but to see ruins. Museums, statues, monuments, castles — ruins, ruins, ruins and more ruins."

"Where's your sense of history?"

"I love history. But also I love the pulse and throb of today. These people want nothing to do with that. What did they want to know about the hotel where we stayed last night? Were the bathrooms clean?"

Twenty minutes later, as the tour guide showed us around the ruins of Ugarit, I caught Safiya paying close attention and she smiled ruefully. A proud university graduate in his early thirties, the guide proved efficient, well-informed and eager to share the history of this place.

Seven hundred years ago, Canaanites lived here, followers of Baal. They made Ugarit a thriving city. But writing had arisen here hundreds of years before that, when Ugarit was just a town. The elders would meet and make decisions. Using the earliest alphabet known to man, they inscribed these decisions on wet clay tablets. People would bake these tablets in ovens and carry them home.

The guide expounded proudly on the birth of writing, which he rightly described as a seminal event in the history of humankind. What would we know about the past if the alphabet and writing did not exist? Safiya smiled as she scribbled in her notebook. A few moments later, when the tour guide suggested a break, I asked her what she'd found so funny. She said the guide had given her an idea for a cartoon.

Taggart rolled his eyes but I wanted to hear more.

"In the background," Safiya said, "you've got palm trees, a

couple of camels, maybe a sand dune — enough props to hint at ancient Arabia. In the foreground, two figures: a turbaned Sultan and a young woman with a clay tablet draped over one arm. She looks abashed. The tablet has gone soft — like the watches and clocks you get in Salvador Dali? The Sultan thunders: "Have you gone mad, Fadilah? Equality for women? Get out of here with your half-baked ideas."

I laughed: "You should send it to the New Yorker."

Taggart made a face and said: "Readers' Digest, maybe."

He strode off towards the washroom. I said: "What's eating him?"

"No sense of humour." Safiya took a beat, then added. "Maybe it's because I mentioned Daniel."

"The distant lover grows daily nearer."

"You'll like Daniel, I think. I meant it, you know, when I said come to Africa." She reached out and touched my arm. "This trip, Bernie, I don't know what I would have done without you."

"You need another man like a wet clay tablet."

Safiya grinned brightly, all gleaming white teeth, but I heard sadness in what she said next: "When it comes to men, Bernie, I'm lost in Al-Mayadin with an arm-full of half-baked ideas."

The Magic of Meteora

Safiya traced her heritage to both Africa and India, yet regarded the Indian subcontinent as "the land of my forebears." On the Verlandi, she perused my maps and guidebooks of India, focusing mainly on the area near Agra that had produced her ancestors. Yet she refrained from speaking her desire to visit because here we were sailing to Greece, and from Greece she would travel to Sri Lanka and East Africa. She felt that only a spoiled brat would pine for India, and didn't realize I could read her yearning like a flashing neon sign.

Taggart Oates knew what she felt, yet remained intransigent. This he regarded as HIS time with Safiya, dammit, and he had no intention of letting her wander off to India with anybody else, not even briefly. That much he shared, though again he'd become impervious to scanning, which I found both intriguing and ominous.

For a while, I'd made progress and ascribed it to living in the

Golden Flame. But now, again, whenever I'd try to visit, I'd find myself stumbling around in a pitch-dark room, bumping into furniture while hunting a light switch. Never mind. I'd discerned, as anybody would have, that for Taggart, Safiya meant far more than just a second ashavan with whom to approach The Shaman. He'd stood an equally good chance, or so he once said during a heated exchange, of confounding The Shaman with Esmeralda Esteban.

Safiya, however, had become his "kwarenah" — his final cause, his destiny, his heart's desire. I think he meant to use the power of the Sacred Fire to bind her to him forever.

Did I oppose this? Only with every fibre of my being — though I could understand his passion and, on some level, even empathize. Physically, Taggart had never been beautiful, not like Daniel Lafontaine, and he'd long since lost even a mitigating youthfulness. He'd turned forty-six and looked older. True, as a famous novelist, Taggart attracted literary groupies, but most of them bored him. Where would he find another Safiya? So insightful, so articulate, so emotionally reckless? So completely his equal in intelligence, and quite possibly his superior in talent, although that he would never admit. Creatively, she fed him. And beautiful? Exotically so. Quite ravishing, really.

To this litany, I could add only: yes! And tremble, alone in my cabin aboard the Verlandi, as Behroze brought me the love poetry of Sappho: "For when I see you even for a moment, then power to speak another word fails me, and at once a gentle fire has caught throughout my flesh, and I see nothing with my eyes, and there's a drumming in my ears, and sweat pours down me, and trembling seizes all of me. . . ."

Behroze had caught my drift. I'd fallen foolishly, irrevocably in love.

Yet even so, Taggart went beyond. Take a yearning not unlike my own, add a selfish, exploitive disposition and what do you get? A monstrous possessiveness. Whenever Safiya chatted with another man, Taggart secretly longed to lash out and destroy. The intensity of this impulse, which I discovered during the brief period when I'd mastered his fog, had shocked me into responding with my white lie. I'd acted to diffuse it. Now I'd become the exception who confused the rule, the professedly impotent male who posed no sexual threat and so gave Taggart an opportunity to display his apparent broad-mindedness.

Taggart believed he loved Safiya. Yet she'd dreamed of him as an ice-skeleton, an insatiable Windigo. Certainly, he did appear to feed off her in some curious way, almost to devour her psychologically. I tried to look at this objectively: maybe Safiya needed the catharsis of death and rebirth? Maybe she needed to be psychically devoured? Maybe she did — but I didn't think so. And even if she did, I needed her more than she needed destruction — or even Daniel Lafontaine, for that matter. I loved Safiya, dammit! Apart from that, and my own psychic survival, only Colette mattered.

That's why I agreed, on the night before we arrived in Athens, to travel north to Meteora, the strangest agglomeration of monasteries in Greece, and probably the western world. I could blame this decision on drinking too much red wine, or explain that I didn't want to gather fire-worthy souvenirs alone, not even for a while, before following Safiya to East Africa.

But instead I'll acknowledge the truth: I'd fallen unrequitedly in love. And when, with Greece looming on the horizon, Safiya extended the invitation, I did not think, "Oh, oh, look out, this decision might precipitate a crisis that will jeopardize your entire quest." No, I thought: "I can bask in her presence for a while longer."

I'd told Safiya that in Greece I would hunt fire-worthy mementoes in Delphi and Crete, the first a recognized sacred site or "magic place," the second an island on which, after Behroze died, I'd lived with Colette for three months, drinking too much ouzo and trying to forget. Safiya said: "Don't do that to yourself, Bernie. Come to Meteora!"

Because of the Sri Lanka commitment, she and Taggart could spend only five days in Greece. They'd agonized and chosen the monasteries: "You can see ancient ruins anywhere in the country," Safiya said, "starting with Athens and the Parthenon. But these monasteries perch atop giant hoodoo-fingers of black rock. They're unique in the world. You want magic, Bernie? Meteora!"

The quintessential Safiya, then: intense, enthusiastic. Irrepressible, really. So exuberant, so alive, so . . . oh, give it up. I loved, I ached, I accepted her invitation.

We three were the only passengers debarking anywhere. All the others had signed on for a round-trip. As we made our way down the fly-away stairs to the boat launch that would take us to the dock, Safiya blew a kiss to George the steward, who stood leaning over the railing. She cried: "Any time you want a poker game!"

George had the grace to chuckle, but then he wasn't the big loser. In the end, Safiya had taken nine hundred dollars out of the game. To Taggart, as we descended, I said: "I'm amazed they let her walk."

"Ha! You know what she left George as a tip?"

"Let me guess: an American fifty?"

"Took it out of our JOINT winnings."

Taggart had fronted Safiya fifty dollars at the outset on the understanding that he'd share in any winnings. He'd taken half, though he didn't need it, and I didn't feel he should be complaining about the size of George's tip. Never mind. In Piraeus, we debarked at the international dock, as distinct from the domestic one, which accommodated mainly island ferries, and hired a taxi to drive into Athens.

The cabbie grumbled about the amount of baggage: besides the usual suitcases, Taggart — ever the eccentric Englishman — had brought a small trunk and two wicker hampers. But Safiya gave the man a carton of cigarettes and so moved him onside: he tied the luggage on top, whisk, whisk, no problem. And away we went.

Athens worked no magic on any of us. Dusty and crowded and loud with honking horns, the city suffers the worst smog in Europe, the Nefos. Late afternoon, we drove straight into it. The cabbie, now friendly and garrulous, told us we'd just missed the worst heat wave of the century. It had killed several hundred Athenians. We traded glances all round and Taggart muttered: "Ahriman."

We checked into the Hotel Helios on Patrou Street, a three-star establishment, minutes from Syntagma Square. The place not only took its name from a sun-god, but a fiery-sun logo hung over the front door and adorned everything inside from towels and stationery to tiny shampoo bottles. Safiya and Taggart had booked in advance and the desk clerk — a middle-aged man, white shirt and tie, who spoke beautiful English — welcomed them enthusiastically. As for me, he regretted that he had no single-room vacancies. Perhaps tonight I would take a more expensive double and tomorrow he'd move me?

Great, we'd arrived. Twenty minutes later, the three of us set out for the American Express office. Safiya wanted to arrive before six in case the place closed. And we made it. Having left no forwarding address, I expected no mail and received none. But both Safiya and Taggart collected a bundle. Taggart received the larger haul, most of it professional, but in her smaller pile, Safiya found the treasure she sought: an airmail letter resplendent with colourful animal stamps: "Bernie, look! Tanzania!"

Taggart said nothing. The set of his jaw spoke volumes.

Safiya refrained from tearing open Daniel's letter on the spot. But as we made our way through the rush-hour streets, I could feel her anticipation: she yearned to read the newly arrived missive but didn't wish to offend Taggart. At Syntagma Square, an outdoor cafe, we ordered retsina all around, and why not? We watched tourists dash in and out of the airlines offices that encircle the square — PanAm, TWA, Olympic Airways. And Greek lotharios, "kamakia" as they're called, working the tables, trying to pick up North American girls. Some of these men, Taggart said, carried cards attesting them free of AIDS.

Safiya disappeared to the washroom and I tackled Taggart with small talk — with how strange it felt, for example, suddenly to have no floating hotel in our future. He grunted in response and finally I let him suffer in silence. When Safiya reappeared, beaming, Taggart said: "You've read Daniel's letter."

"What if I have?"

I said: "From Dar es Salaam? Planning a trip north?"

Safiya nodded, but before she could speak, Taggart said: "You couldn't wait, could you? Couldn't enjoy our arrival in Greece. Couldn't imagine that — "

"O.K., folks, I've seen this movie." I knocked back the last of my retsina and shucked on my green knapsack. "I'm going to check out old haunts."

"What about Meteora?" Safiya said. "We haven't finished planning."

"How about lunch tomorrow? I'll swing past at noon."

She nodded, I spun on my heel and made for Plaka. It's a hodgepodge of nineteenth-century houses and classical ruins, a warren of narrow, winding streets lined with tiny shops selling plaster figurines and lambswool sweaters and hand-made leather belts. At a kiosk that offered a glimpse of the Parthenon, I bought a beautiful Coptic cross made of brass.

As I paid the delighted merchant, full asking price, three young girls swept past on the sidewalk behind me, laughing and giggling. One of them, all big brown eyes and dark lashes, reminded me so forcefully of Colette that I went weak in the knees and steadied myself against the wall. Half a dozen times a day, I'd been checking that distant hospital room, and now again, as I stood trembling in Plaka, I registered the reality that kept me going: Colette lived! But, oh, god, how I missed her.

Colette filled my mind as she did every night, only now, as I resumed exploring, I tried to heed Safiya's advice: "Just stop, Bernie. Stop wallowing in self-pity and give thanks that you've been summoned to this quest. That you've been given a chance to restore her."

Forget self-pity, then. Focus on the present, on The Now, because who could guess what questions The Shaman might ask? Plaka boasts dozens of kafenions and tiny shops, and as I wandered among them, recovering my equilibrium, I realized that the blaring rock music I remembered from the eighties had disappeared, replaced by a hubbub typical of any crowded, downtown neighborhood and the occasional sounds of traditional bouzouki — a major improvement.

At the Areides Taverna, I sat out front and admired the centuries-old Tower of the Winds while sipping ouzo, savoring the pungent licorice taste. Last time in Greece, I'd learned to drink it straight, the way Greeks do, and I enjoyed feeling superior to a table of German tourists sipping ouzo gone cloudy because they'd weakened it with water.

Greeks eat dinner late — half past nine at the earliest. From a street vendor, to tide me over, I bought a donair and a brown bag of roasted peanuts, which kept me rambling happily until well past ten. The most popular tavernas had yet to open their doors, but I discovered an obscure, nameless place that looked inviting, its walls adorned with happy cartoon figures romping amidst ruins. Once inside, I noticed blue-checkered table cloths and remembered the old question: When does a taverna become a restaurant? Answer: When the owners replace paper with cloth and double their prices. Even so, I decided I'd made the right choice when, on the price list, I discovered a classic disclaimer: "All on the menu under the police control to the prices overcharged."

I wolfed down a Greek salad, easy on the olive oil, and then some *moussaska* and *arni youvetsi*, otherwise known as lamb and macaroni. A muscular young man stepped into the restaurant: not Chinvat? Thankfully, no: he collected his girlfriend, the pretty cashier, and together they quickly departed. Out came a guitar player, a grey-haired man in a brown pin-striped suit, white shirt and tie. He moved from table to table serenading the diners, many of them couples, with sorrowful Greek ballads. I found myself missing Safiya, remembering Rome and thinking how much she would enjoy this taverna. I heard her laugh and spun around — but no, it was somebody else.

Next morning, early, I hiked across town to Mount Lycabettus, which at nine hundred feet is the highest hill in Athens. I rode the funicular to the top and drank too much coffee at the outdoor restaurant. From Lycabettus you can see all of Athens: the best-known symbols of ancient Greece, the Parthenon and other temples on the Acropolis, overlook even the contemporary metropolis. Beyond them, in the distance, lay the Mediterranean Sea, and I wondered: where now the Verlandi?

I returned to the Hotel Helios and found my fellow travellers packing bags. A quick read on Safiya told me that, yes, last night she'd argued with Taggart. They'd called each other vile names and almost come to blows. But that was last night. This morning, she'd bounced out of bed and gone to inquire about travelling to Meteora. Turned out you had a choice: either rent a car at an extortionate rate or take both a train and a bus. This last sounded fun. Trouble was, unless we left immediately, we'd have to wait a day and a half.

Safiya had four days left for Greece and no intention of wasting any of them in a city she hated. She'd opted for the scramble.

Bought three tickets, dashed back here to the Helios and talked to the desk clerk, who worshipped her. What else was new? Now she cried: "Pack your worldly possessions, Bernie! They'll lock them into the safe. Our train leaves in an hour."

Back into the shared frenzy, then.

We made the train with thirty seconds to spare.

Rattling north in a first-class compartment, we sat looking out the window and marvelling at this latest synchronicity: a family of three had cancelled their tickets as Safiya arrived at the wicket. In this I recognized the Golden Flame, but said nothing. The train took almost an hour to get outside the city, but then we started seeing donkeys tethered to olive trees and sheep-dotted hills rolling away into the distance.

We clattered through towns where grizzled men sat on wooden benches in the shade or else strolled proudly with home-made walking sticks, and Safiya waved to a shop-keeper who stood in his front door chatting with two white-bearded priests wearing black hats and caftans. We saw white-shirted men pedalling one-speed bicycles through groups of skipping children and fruit markets spilling over with produce and hagglers, and an old woman in widow's weeds riding side-saddle on a donkey, bringing home three baskets of kindling.

The real Greece? It doesn't exist. But if it did, we all three agreed, we would get no closer than this, not during this frenzied quest. We would get no closer than to see Greeks working and playing, living their lives while we looked out at them from a speeding train.

Safiya said, "Doesn't that make us voyeurs?"

"Tourists might be voyeurs," Taggart said. "But we're questers. I refuse to feel guilty."

Safiya said: "This guilt I can live with."

"Playing tourist," Taggart said, "is the least of your sins."

"If that's not the real Greece," I said, pointing at a young man herding goats up a winding dirt road, "it's near as makes no difference."

Late in the afternoon, we transferred onto a crowded bus. With bouzouki music blaring and the driver honking his horn at children, chickens and braying donkeys, we careered along a two-lane highway at twice the speed any sane person would consider safe. At Kalambaka, our dusty destination, we emerged relieved, happy to find ourselves whole, and stood awestruck, looking up: behold the monasteries of the air!

Safiya recovered first: "They look dangerously phallic."

I said: "You've got a dirty mind. Think giant stalagmites."

"I'll try but it won't be easy."

Twenty fingers of rock soared hundreds of feet into the air. If these natural phenomena weren't sufficiently amazing, many of them bloomed at the top into monasteries built during the first centuries of the millennium. Clearly, the fanatical monks who created these stone fortresses did not relish contact with the world.

We'd arrived too late to hunt souvenirs. But as a swarthy young guide led us up empty back streets towards the only open hotel — tourist season had ended weeks ago — I thought to ask Taggart what The Shaman might make of the Coptic cross I'd bought in Athens: "It's such a Christian symbol, after all."

"As long as the souvenir can be burnished by fire," he said, happy to pontificate, "the most significant variable is Place: where you obtained the memento, not how it sparkles. Then comes emotional resonance. And obviously your primary talisman, the one you hope to purify, carries special weight. Likewise, to some extent, the seven from magic places. But the symbolism itself, whether Christian, Hindu, Buddhist or Islamic? Think allegorically, Bernie. At the Purification, which immediately precedes the Renovation, all teachings and dogmas will be melted down into a complex, all-encompassing truth — a single molten metal. How could the specifics matter?"

"I take your point." But secretly I wondered: Had we all three gone mad? True, a certain strangeness had emerged into our lives. But I remembered Taggart suggesting that the wilder the metaphysics, the better. Just how seriously did I have to take his preposterous extrapolations?

That night, at the Hotel Divina, we ate dinner and retired early. After checking on Colette, I fell into a fitful sleep and, for the first time since entering the Golden Flame, experienced my hateful recurring nightmare. Again I stood before a roaring judge who declared that my intellectual arrogance had killed Behroze: "Take him away!" Again I ended up running along a tropical beach, chasing after Behroze to beg another chance. Again I woke up crying, "Behroze! Behroze, wait!"

Afterwards, as I stood at the bathroom sink splashing water into my face, I realized that this was my answer: I was expected to take Taggart's extrapolations very seriously indeed. For me, that was the challenge, and also part of the cure, I began to understand, for the hubris that ailed me — my narrow intellectualism.

Of the original two dozen monasteries, six remain open to the public. We spent the next day and a half exploring them — climbing stairs, navigating swinging bridges, examining religious icons. The first surprise is how easily one can reach these retreats via twisting roads and rickety bridges. Tourists can hike even to the Monastery of the Metamorphosis, the so-called Great Meteora. Bearded monks welcome you into a museum area, though visitors must dress modestly: no sleeveless dresses, no immodest shorts. If you arrive unprepared, you can rent cover-all slickers — but neither Taggart nor I fancied shorts and Safiya, having done her homework, wore jeans.

Rambling around the courtyard, studying the fortifications, we found ourselves shaking our heads at the fanaticism that created these places. In the early days, around 950 B.C., none but expert rock climbers could have reached these sites. Later, monks rigged up pulleys and attached giant baskets so they could winch each other up and down, sending delegates into the world for food, drink and firewood — the necessities.

"Well may you marvel, gentlemen." Safiya, hanging onto her hat in the wind, stood gazing out over the red-tile roofs of Kalambaka and Kastraki: "This is what happens to men without women."

I said: "They accomplish great deeds?"

"They erect monuments to madness."

Moments later, Taggart refused to traverse a rickety suspension bridge. Neither Safiya nor I would back down so we made our way, whistling, across a rocky gorge, the bridge swinging madly beneath us. The monastery on the far side was the smallest, the most rustic. The bearded monk who kept the place insisted on posing for photos. At his chest he made a steeple with his fingers, then tilted his head and rolled his eyes skyward. This pose, we understood, signified holiness. The monk produced a box for our donation, thanked us profusely — then asked if we'd brought cigarettes. At first, Safiya didn't understand his request because of his accent. When the monk asked a second time, Safiya threw back her head and laughed.

Using mostly sign language, Safiya inquired whether the monk had any religious icons for sale. He led us into a back room and showed us small statues. Finally, at Safiya's urging, he produced a cardboard box of jewels and metal objects and let us poke around in it. Safiya purchased a Madonna with child, and I chose a silver representation of the Biblical burning bush. The monk quoted a terrible price, expecting us to haggle, but again, we swallowed hard and paid up.

We stuffed our purchases into my green knapsack and headed back across the rickety swinging bridge, holding onto the railing and taking our time. Halfway across, Safiya cried, "Look out!"

A solitary raven swooped and dove straight at us. We ducked to avoid the bird and shook the bridge — not much, but enough to tear it loose at the monastery end. Next thing we knew, we were clinging to the rope railing while dangling in the air hundreds of feet above ground.

Safiya managed to get her feet onto the criss-crossed rope railing and I followed her example: "You okay, Bernie?"

From farther up, Taggart cried, "Hang on!"

"We've got to climb up," Safiya said. "Think you can make it?"

Swinging in the wind, I cried: "Lead on!"

We managed to climb the rope railing to where Taggart and a half a dozen horrified monks could help us onto solid ground. The monks insisted that we sit and drink a whole bottle of eucharistic wine before we returned to town. Safiya assured them that the accident wasn't their fault, that dark forces were at work, but gave up when she realized they wanted to absorb the Golden Flame into Christianity, and not the other way arounnd.

Safiya and Taggart didn't argue once in Meteora. We all three remained under the spell of the monasteries during the return trip to Athens. We didn't articulate it, but we became aware — especially Safiya and I — that in two days we would go our separate ways: me to India and the Taj Mahal, Safiya and Taggart to Sri Lanka.

That night, for dinner, I insisted on treating. I led my fellow ashavans to the nameless taverna with the jolly cartoon figures, the blue-checkered table cloths and the grey-haired guitarist. They loved the place. We ate too much and drank too much and I remember Taggart arguing that even ancient Zoroastrianism is superior to Christianity because it insists that individuals take responsibility for themselves instead of relying on somebody else for salvation. Safiya added that she preferred the idea of The Renovation to the Christian expectation of the End of the World, but described both religions as authoritarian, paternalistic and, in their teachings on women, antiquated and shamefully male chauvinist.

I said: "Yet you've sallied forth in the name of Mazda?"

"The Golden Flame's gone beyond the old teachings. On some levels, Ahura Mazda's just another name for Over-woman. Besides, like you, I had no choice, remember?" Candle-light danced in her dark eyes. "Now that I'm into it, I mean to succeed, though — not just for myself, but for women in general. That's part of my kwarenah."

I hadn't got disgracefully drunk in years, but Taggart kept ordering and the guitar-man kept playing, and somehow I got onto the subject of Colette, lying in a coma in San Francisco, and how much I missed her, and how afraid I felt. And then came Behroze, and how I blamed myself for her death, and if only I hadn't been so prideful, such an intellectual snob, she'd be alive even now. In short, I got stupid. I got maudlin and blubbering and feeling sorry for myself. Safiya, who'd long since stopped drinking, ran out of patience. Sympathetic to a fault, yet she couldn't bear this self-indulgent whining and insisted that we call it a night.

She led the way back to the Hotel Helios — Taggart had matched me drink for drink — and steered me into my room. I tumbled into bed with the room spinning and didn't wake up until noon next day, when the maid arrived to clean the room. I didn't feel too bad, considering — not until after I'd shaved and dressed and plucked my room key from the top of the dresser. That's when I noticed, while gathering myself to apologize to Safiya for my behaviour: where was my fabulous green bag? The miniature knapsack in which I kept fire-worthy souvenirs?

Athenian Roulette

You wouldn't know it to look at me, given my unruly black hair and rumpled sports shirts, but I take an ex-boy-scout's pride in being prepared. I might appear an unimpressive non-entity, but deep down inside, having submitted to the Golden Flame and put my skepticism on hold, I saw myself as a clairvoyant action hero ready to rumble — an Indiana Jones blessed with sensitivity and second sight. Okay, the fantasy wouldn't stand much scrutiny.

Yet back home in San Francisco, when I'd undertaken this around-the-world scavenger hunt, I'd remembered my fabulous green bag. I'd bought it a dozen years before, during the magic days with Behroze, and packed it away soon after she died. When she resurfaced with her terrible ultimatum, I thought: sentimental value and talismanic significance. Whatever magic the green bag possessed, I wanted with me. I dug it out of a trunk and paid a shoe-maker to add leather strap, metal gromets, a water-proof lining: make it state-of-the-art and hang the expense.

So far, this miniature knapsack had performed flawlessly. I'd strapped it on in Las Palmas, Barcelona, Genoa, Rome, Al-Mayadin, Meteora — just strapped it on and forgot about it. Sure, I had to remove the bag to sit down on anything but a bar-stool. Yet no way anybody could wrest it out of my possession. Remember Rome? My fabulous green bag had withstood a Chinvat assault.

That miniature knapsack was more secure, I believed, even than the safe at the Hotel Helios. Think about it: if a committed thief turned up at the Helios, where's the first place he'd look for valuables? The safe.

Now, having discovered my loss, I panicked. I flipped open cupboards, tore blankets off the bed, jerked open drawers and slammed them shut. The green bag had disappeared. Panting, I stood in the middle of the shambles I'd made of my room, clenching and unclenching my fists. I closed my eyes, reached out psychically and couldn't concentrate. Couldn't focus my energies. What? Had the Golden Flame deserted me?

The nameless taverna! Down the hall I raced and forget the elevator, too slow. Four flights of stairs I took, two steps at a time. I dashed through the lobby and out the front door, sprinted along the sidewalk, spun around half a dozen pedestrians, almost knocked over a fruit stand and found the nameless taverna closed. I peered through the window, spotted a man cleaning up last night's mess and began pounding: bam! bam! bam! The man hurried over. He pointed at the sign, but I shook my head and pounded away until the cleaner ran to get the manager — who turned out to be the guitarist. He recognized me and opened the door.

I rushed to the table we'd occupied last night: no fabulous green bag. I got down on my hands and knees and whirled like a break-dancer. Nothing. The manager helped me up. What was I looking for? A green bag? No, he'd found nothing. He spoke Greek with the cleaner, who'd seen no green bag. My green bag was gone. I felt dizzy and collapsed into the nearest chair as the manager called for water.

My green bag had contained all the usual valuables except my passport, which I'd stuffed into my jacket pocket the last time I'd changed money. More specifically, it contained travellers cheques, credit cards, airplane tickets, a paperback Music of Chance, two hundred dollars American and one hundred more in drachmas.

Worse, the green bag contained three scribblers in which I'd been writing since San Francisco. These rough journals included a seven-page description of my Near Death Experience, which I'd written immediately afterwards; I'd described Behroze's visitations and traced the subsequent development of psychic abilities: mind-reading, clairvoyant flashes, Taggart's ankle, the whole testimonial.

At the back of my mind, I'd thought: one of these days, who knows? maybe I'll write about what's happened. I told myself I could recreate my experience from memory. But I'd counted on having my scribblers handy. Without my notes, I might complete the project, but it wouldn't be the work I'd conceived. I'd give birth, all right. But mine would be a baby born with tiny hands where arms were meant to be.

All this washed over me as I sat in the nameless taverna keeping my head between my knees. And that wasn't the worst of it. In retrospect, it seems unbelievable, but the fire-worthy souvenirs I'd gathered? The rings and bracelets, the Coptic cross, the athame, the caduceus? The mementoes I needed to invoke The Shaman and restore Colette to health? I'd kept them in a leather pouch at the bottom of my fabulous green bag. I held off facing that as long as I could. When the reality hit me, I stumbled into the washroom and vomitted until my head hurt. And then did it again.

Still in shock, I returned to the Helios. Safiya met me in the lobby. The desk clerk had told her he'd seen me race past. She took one look and said: "Bernie, what's wrong?"

Reeling, distraught, I could do nothing but shake my head. Safiya led me back to my room, where the maid toiled over the the chaos I'd wrought. She glanced at me reproachfully, then grew concerned. I stretched out on the bed. The maid fetched a cold wash cloth. At Safiya's request, she left us alone.

Recovering language, I said I'd lost my green bag. At first, because she didn't know what it contained, Safiya didn't grasp what this meant. She figured airplane tickets, credit cards — and these I could readily replace. She began pacing, planning, preparing to do what had to be done. "Safiya, it's not just cards and tickets. That bag contained notes. It contained my . . . my souvenirs."

"Your souvenirs?" Safiya went wide-eyed. Speechless, she slumped into the arm chair and stared into space. After a minute, she jumped up: "We've got to get them back." Again she resumed pacing. "You'll offer a reward."

Pacing the room, Safiya sketched out a plan. She divided responsibilities, then disappeared into the afternoon. I washed my face, changed my shirt and visited American Express. I reported my travellers cheques stolen and received replacements. I located the relevant police station and reported the theft. Or rather, the loss. Finally, I returned to my hotel room, stretched out on my bed and waited. Inevitably, my thoughts turned to Colette. I located her psychically, detected no change. Withdrew in shame and horror and cursed myself ferociously one more time: how could I have been so careless?

Safiya arrived and resumed prowling. From a distance, I noticed that she radiated energy and purpose. So focused, so fierce, so fine. Safiya gave me hope. While I'd visited American Express, she'd worked with the front-desk clerk. They'd drafted a sign in both English and Greek: "REWARD — $500 American." She showed me a photostat copy. I was offering five hundred dollars for the return of a small green knapsack, no questions asked. I wanted the notebooks and souvenirs, which had sentimental value. In other words: keep the money you've stolen and I'll reward you as well, just give back my baubles, please, please, please. The sign included my phone number at the Helios.

While I'd chatted with the police, Safiya had papered the neighborhood with notices. Everywhere she spotted a "Rent Rooms" sign — Jimmy's Place, John's Place, The Metropole — she'd stapled a copy. Now she said: "Bernie, I've been thinking. Maybe I should stay a while in Athens to help you retrieve those mementoes."

"Safiya, that would be great."

"Make you a deal, Bernie. I help you retrieve your souvenirs here…and you take me to India. Just as friends, mind. My poker winnings are burning a hole."

"You've got plane tickets to Sri Lanka."

"I want to see the land of my forebears." She took a beat. "Besides, I'm not happy with my collection. I've got keepsakes from North America, Europe and the Middle East, but none from Asia. One or two from Sri Lanka just don't seem enough."

"But you and Taggart leave tomorrow."

"I intend to change that." She extended her hand and insisted we shake: "To retrieving your souvenirs."

"And visiting the Taj Mahal."

Into the late afternoon we plunged. I followed Safiya in a daze of self-censure. At the Air India office, I stood outside while Safiya talked with front-deskers. A man in a blue cap pushed a cart along the sidewalk towards me — a cart in which he roasted chestnuts over a smoking hibachi. He offered me hot chestnuts in a brown paper bag. I mumbled, "No, no thanks."

He pressed them on me: "Free for you."

Then he turned and wheeled away into the crowd. Maybe the Golden Flame remained with me? Maybe this dark cloud bore a synchronistic silver lining? I entered the airlines office and found Safiya sitting with the manager. She waved me into the open office, impulsively plucked the chestnuts from my hand and said: "A small token of our sincerity."

The manager, a cherubic, curly haired man who'd decorated his office with photos of his family, reached into the bag. We all ate a few chestnuts. Safiya resumed pleading her case. Laughing, the manager threw his hands in the air and produced the requisite forms. I excused myself and went back outside. Fifteen minutes later, when Safiya emerged, she'd arranged for both of us to travel to India. She'd used her credit card, and I owed her. Oh, and one more thing: we'd travel via Colombo, Sri Lanka, with a ten-day lay-over.

"Colombo, Sri Lanka? What?"

"Have you counted your souvenirs, Bernie? Even if we get them all back, you've got what? seven or eight? And you need sixteen. Anyway, this was the only deal I could swing. If you don't like it . . . ."

Wait a minute. Why was I arguing? Ten days sounded long for Sri Lanka . . . but then Safiya and I would travel to India. We'd visit the Taj, just we two. "No, no, please: sounds great to me. And thanks! But what about Taggart? He won't like this a bit."

"Leave Taggart to me," Safiya said — though for the first time today she sounded worried.

Back at the Helios, Safiya went to find Taggart. I returned to my room to lie on my bed and worry: what had I done to my last chance for redemption? Worse: what had I done to my hopes for

Colette? If I didn't retrieve those souvenirs, I'd have to start over. To visit city after city, buy a whole new set — and how long would that take? What if I ran out of time? What if Taggart —

The phone rang, interrupting: Safiya calling from the dining room downstairs. Taggart had accepted the change of plans, albeit reluctantly. Why didn't I join them for a bite? Downstairs, Taggart made all the right noises: told me how sorry he was, said he would stay and help out himself if he didn't have a professional commitment in Colombo. I said: "The Chinvat did this."

"Stole your green bag? Quite possible."

Safiya said: "Yes, but why?"

"Because they're ignorant," Taggart said. "They've been tracking me for years, trying to find out what I know. They hope I'll lead them to The Shaman so they can destroy him." He smiled at me: "Maybe they think you're the weak link."

"They think they can destroy The Shaman?"

"Certainly they can't invoke him." Taggart sipped his beer: "They're misguided, know-nothing fundamentalists, Bernie. They've got it into their heads that The Shaman shouldn't have taken the Sacred Fire to East Africa. Out of Persia, yes. Into India, yes. Across the water, no. They cite Avestan scripture."

"And they're murderous."

"Not as long as they think you might be ueful. Believe me, Bernie, we face far worse perils than the Chinvat."

Taggart declined to elaborate. And next morning, he left for Sri Lanka.

We shook hands in the hotel lobby and he wished me luck: "Stiff upper lip, old boy."

His departure went almost too smoothly. I made a mental note to ask Safiya about it, then forgot. She accompanied Taggart to the airport. I stayed in my room, waiting for a call that didn't come.

That afternoon, Safiya phoned the Athens Daily News and inquired about advertising rates. We didn't buy because they were exorbitant, but also because Safiya and I agreed that the thief, Chinvat or otherwise, had stolen the green bag at the nameless taverna. That's where he'd see the REWARD sign — or else in one of the nearby rooming houses. Not in the Daily News.

Unable to remain forever indoors waiting for a phone call,

Safiya and I rambled the streets and alleys of Plaka. We drank ouzo at outdoor kafenions and watched a sunset bathe the Parthenon in apricot and violet. Next afternoon, we climbed the Acropolis to take a closer look and bought a photo of ourselves sitting cross-legged on a broken column. Afterwards, Safiya wanted to visit the Temple of Hephaestus, supposedly the best-preserved classical structure in Greece. But I couldn't work up the enthusiasm. I returned to the hotel and let her wander alone.

More than once, I reached out psychically to locate and retrieve my green bag. Always I ended up stumbling around in a fog. Where was Behroze when I needed her? The Golden Flame continued to burn: I'd seen it produce chestnuts for a cherubic airline manager. But this devastating inability, after so much growth and development, to reach out and locate my own most valuable possessions . . . incomprehensible.

I toyed with the notion that my usual abilities derived from the gold necklace Behroze had given me in San Francisco, but that didn't make sense. My clairvoyance had come first. Was it the stress of the loss? What about Taggart? Could my prolonged exposure to his interior darkness have undermined me? Surely, this wasn't the beginning of some terrible forgetting? Maybe the Golden Flame was testing me?

Psychically, and not for the first time, I called out to Behroze — and heard a knock at the door. Could it be? No, but Safiya had come to commiserate. In this darkest hour, and with only two nights remaining in Athens, certainly I felt the need to confide. We ordered room service meals and sat drinking coffee. As I gathered myself to broach the failure of my Golden Flame gift, the telephone rang.

I answered and a deep male voice, heavily accented, said: "You have reward money?"

The man told me to go to John's Place, a run-down rooming house located halfway between the Helios and the nameless taverna. At the top of the stairs, the man said, in a corner behind an open door, I would find what I wanted. "You go alone. You leave money."

The phone went dead. I yanked on my desert boots and grabbed the reward money.

Safiya said, "Where we going?"

"I'm going to John's Place."

"Not without me, you're not."

"He said I should go alone."

"I don't care what he said."

Safiya beat me out the door. To tell the truth, I preferred having her with me. We trotted down the stairs and through the lobby. The desk clerk realized in mid-greeting, too late, that we'd received a phone call: "Wait!"

Out the door we ran, down the street and around the corner. Safiya raced along so focused and grimly determined that if I'd seen her coming my way down a street, I'd have crossed to the other side. At John's Place, she hesitated, looked this way and that: half a dozen pedestrians, nobody suspicious. We entered the lobby, climbed the stairs two at a time. Behind a closet door, as promised, we discovered my fabulous green bag. Inside, I found my three notebooks and yes! my small leather bag of fire-worthy souvenirs.

Trembling, I laid them out on the floor. They were all there but one — the gold necklace Behroze had taken from our daughter's neck. My primary talisman. Desperately, I searched the green bag. No sign of the missing necklace. I turned the bag upside down and shook it. Finding nothing more, I hurled it into the corner. My primary talisman had disappeared.

Safiya said, "We'd better get out of here."

I pulled the envelope out of my back pocket and tossed it onto the floor.

"Not so fast." Safiya picked up the envelope. "They've already stolen a couple of hundred dollars — not to mention the necklace."

She opened the envelope and counted the reward money. Half of it she removed and stuffed into my shirt pocket. Then she tossed the envelope into the closet and grabbed the green bag.

"Safiya, they'll come after us."

"If they'd left the necklace, we'd have left the five hundred." She led the way down the stairs. "Under the circumstances, if they want more, let them find us in India."

I chased her down the stairs into the street.

Back in my hotel room, we examined the souvenirs: New York, Las Palmas, Barcelona, Genoa, Rome, Al-Mayadin, Athens, Meteora — all here but San Francisco. "Why did they take that one?" I picked up the bracelet I'd bought in Rome. "This one's worth more. It's almost like they knew."

"Have you nothing else from San Francisco?"

"No, nothing." I must have sounded despondent. For sure, I felt torn and confused. I'd regained most of my souvenirs, but the gold necklace I'd lost had been the talisman I proposed to purify. None of my remaining keepsakes packed anything like the same emotional punch.

"You'll have to choose another." Safiya had been sitting in the arm chair while I sprawled on the bed, but now she rose and crossed the room. "Look here, Bernie." She sat down beside me and fingered the bracelet she wore — a silver bracelet with a turquoise stone. "This comes from Mesa Verde in the American southwest. I visited as a girl."

As she leaned forward her shirt fell open at the neck, and I noticed that the top button had come undone. Safiya had left girlhood behind. I stuttered: "It's lovely. But I couldn't — "

"Close your eyes, Bernie."

I did as she directed, afraid to think, afraid almost to breathe. I heard rustling. Surely Safiya couldn't be . . . removing her clothes?

"You may open now."

Safiya stood at the foot of the bed wearing nothing but a white shirt that reached to mid-thigh. "The two who approach the Shaman . . . must be lovers, remember?"

"Yes," I said, my voice thick.

"I'm doing this for me, too, Bernie."

Slowly, deliberately, Safiya undid the buttons on her shirt. "To improve my odds, understand?"

I nodded, not trusting myself to speak, not wanting to break the spell.

Safiya let the shirt fall open. Beneath it, she wore nothing. No brassiere. No underpants. Nothing. She reached up behind her neck and removed a clasp from her hair. Her breasts were high and firm and tightly nippled — but they weren't symmetrical, I discovered now. I thought: an imperfection! And felt flooded with tenderness and yearning and loved her all the more. My breathing grew ragged.

Safiya smiled brazenly and rested one hand on her hip. In response, I let my eyes slide down her naked body: her black bush, defiantly untrimmed, took my breath away — the hair so thick, so luxuriant, reaching upwards almost to her navel. "What are you waiting for, sailor? An inscribed invitation?"

I'd like to report that I exploded off the bed in a single motion. That I tore off Safiya's shirt as she tugged at my jeans and together we fell into bed ripping and tearing at my clothes. And that then I took her as she'd never been taken before.

The truth is more humbling. The truth is: I froze.

Safiya slowly removed her shirt and let it fall to the floor. She stood naked and lovely at the foot of the bed. I felt overwhelmed — overwhelmed not just by her beauty, but by her womanhood. Neither of us said a word. The room echoed with the raggedness of my breathing.

Safiya joined me on the bed and helped me out of my clothes.

I said: "Do we need a condom?"

Safiya shook her head: "No, I can't have kids."

Silently, we both dismissed any darker concerns.

With both of us naked, Safiya stretched out beside me.

I groaned to feel the warmth of her, to feel her softness. We kissed and I ran a hand lightly over her body. How long had I waited for this? How many times had I imagined it? Yet, now that it had arrived so unexpectedly, and though Safiya ran her hands gently over my chest — nothing. The strength of my desire had rendered me helpless.

"This has never happened to me before."

She put a finger to my lips: "I'll take care of this."

Safiya gently kissed my forehead, my cheeks, the hollow at the base of my neck. Slowly, while I lay frozen, she worked her way down my body, kissing my chest, my belly. Finally, lovingly, she took my limp penis in her mouth. Inside me, some trigger snapped at this gesture, at the intimacy of it, at the way she took charge — or maybe what she did just felt so good. In seconds, I stood erect and ready for action.

Yet now Safiya wouldn't stop and her enthusiasm threatened to carry me away. I tried to think of something else, anything else. I settled on fire omens and began counting, remembered the flame I'd seen in Liberty's torch, the fire that burned in Barcelona in the old man's bowl, the fire in the distance off Al-Mayadin, until finally Safiya took mercy and slid back up along my body and kissed my mouth whispering, "Take me, Bernie."

As I entered her warmth I almost lost control, so I stopped and held still and told myself to count fires, count flames, because this was Safiya, so wet, warm and welcoming, Safiya saying, "yes, Bernie, yes." This was Safiya so wide open and encouraging, so rocking gently back and forth, Safiya who'd stood laughing at the rail of the Verlandi, Safiya hugging me tight and whispering, "take me, Bernie, take me," Safiya so brilliant and funny, so self-possessed, this was Safiya who'd smiled at me in the ship's library, Safiya so cat-like, so lovely, Safiya who'd taken my arm as we traipsed around Rome and kick-boxed her way out of Al-Mayadin, this was Safiya crossing her ankles behind my back, Safiya saying "take me, Bernie, take me," Safiya suddenly so active, so wild and thrusting and crying my name and take me, Safiya, take me, oh take me, and oh I was loving Safiya I was loving Safiya I was loving Safiya, Safiya, Safiya, SAFIYA!

I must have passed out. I don't know how long I remained unconscious. When I awoke, I found myself staring into Safiya's lovely dark eyes and felt suddenly afraid. What if she'd spoken the truth at the outset? What if she'd done this only to increase her chances of invoking The Shaman? She might roll out of bed, stand up and depart. Technically, we'd become lovers. Now, Safiya could approach The Shaman with any one of us: Taggart, Daniel or me.

Instead of rolling out of bed, however, Safiya snuggled closer.

I gazed into her eyes. I smelled her hair. I kissed her tender lips.

"Bernie?" she said. "Where are we?"

"What do you mean?" Even as I spoke, I understood. I sat up. Our surroundings remained unchanged, physically, and yet everything looked . . . different: "We've shifted into another dimension."

"We've entered a garden, Bernie . . . a magic garden."

Safiya didn't glow, exactly, and yet she'd gone numinous. She stood out sharply against the rest of the room, yet no longer felt separate from me. It was as if, in the whole wide world, only we two existed. For a long time we sat grinning foolishly, staring into each other's eyes.

I said: "Can we stay here forever?"

Safiya laughed, wrinkled her nose and drew close: "We can try."

I went to the washroom, and then Safiya did, too. When she returned, she kissed me gently on the lips — and instantly I was aroused. Safiya slid her hand back and forth across my chest, played with my chest hair and reached farther down. "Such a naughty sailor boy," she said. "Look what you're doing."

"Oh, no, you don't," I said. "It's my turn."

I buried my face in her breasts, and fondled and kissed them, and after a while I slid down her warm brown belly, using my mouth and my tongue, and kissing and licking and taking my time, and Safiya said, "yes, Bernie, yes," and I rubbed my face back and forth in her bush, enjoying her glorious bush, and loving the smell of her, and the taste, oh the taste, and she said, "yes, Bernie, yes," and I plunged into her bush with my mouth and my tongue, and yes, Bernie, yes, she said, deeper and deeper, and yes, Bernie, yes, and then my Safiya went wild, and I went chasing after her, Safiya, Safiya, Safiya.

All night long, we made love. I'd never experienced anything approaching it. Where did we find the energy? the appetite? Somehow, we fed off each other. Certainly, Safiya's physical beauty, so long merely imagined, could drive any man to frenzy. But the way she responded to my passion — with so much passion of her own. Oh, god, but I loved her enthusiasm, her shameless responsiveness, her willingness to show pleasure and her wanton self-abandon. Oh, god, but I loved making love with Safiya.

As morning approached, we fell asleep in each other's arms. When I woke, fully aroused yet again, Safiya was gone. On my night table, together with her Mesa Verde bracelet, I found a note: "Oh, Bernie, what a night! But that's not why I'm writing. No talisman could replace the one you've lost. But take this silver bracelet, please, and keep it in memory of what we've now shared. In return, Bernie, I want you to behave as if last night never happened. Yes. To pretend, certainly with Taggart and Daniel, but even when we two are alone, that we've never been more than friends. If last night was special to you, Bernie, as it was to me, and if you value our friendship, you will do this for me, no questions asked. Forgive me, Bernie, but I must insist. Safiya."

Dismay in Sri Lanka

For six years, following the death of Behroze, I remained celibate. When I did venture beyond flirtation, I discovered that making love can be dangerous. You're playing with fire. You unleash forces you can't control. And a night like the one I'd shared with Safiya? That couldn't happen without some special conjunction. If it did, it would fan the embers of even a lukewarm romance into an inferno of passion.

And what of the magic garden we'd found? Together, we'd entered a sacred space, a dimension in which the act of love symbolizes the union of the polar opposites that suffuse existence — Yin-Yang, Male-Female, Ahura Mazda-Ahriman, call them what you will. We'd sought and briefly achieved transcendence. Yet Safiya wished to pretend that nothing had happened? I could hardly believe it.

Secretly, I'd begun to fear that, because of my feelings for Behroze, my guilt over the way she died, I would never be able to love again. That I deserved to endure that recurring nightmare. On the Verlandi, with Safiya, I'd caught a first glimmer of hope. If I ould succeed in this quest, if I could restore Colette, I would exonerate myself, and then maybe, just maybe. . . .

Surely, Safiya was kidding herself. Sooner or later, she'd wake up and realize what we'd discovered. Until then, what could I do? Ignore her wishes? No, I'd play it her way. And keep gathering souvenirs.

Safiya's obsession with the quest — that's what I overlooked.

Forget normal relations. We'd left those behind. In the context of the Golden Flame, I'd needed a lover with whom to approach The Shaman. Now, thanks to Safiya, I had one. Even so, we both needed a third ashavan with whom to set forth. Until now, worried sick about my daughter, concerned with meeting the challenge of the quest, and increasingly obsessed with Safiya in her own right, I'd assumed that this third would be Taggart. I hadn't focused. Now, Daniel Lafontaine exploded into possibility.

Trying to spare my feelings, Safiya waited too long to tell me.

Having arrived in Sri Lanka, we'd spent three days, both with and without Taggart Oates, zooming around Colombo in "tuktuks" or motorized rickshaws. Three curious days during which we pretended we hadn't made love. Safiya was so good at this that finally I began to wonder: had I dreamed the experience?

I'd read her note the morning after and could quote it from memory. Yet that note had gone missing. It no longer existed. True, I now possessed the Mesa Verde bracelet. But what did that prove? Maybe Safiya had given herself to me only in some other dimension? Maybe she hadn't given herself at all? Yes, I'd begn to question my own sanity.

I kept waiting for Safiya to make some gesture. Instead, she insisted on racing around Colombo. For me, tourism had begun to pall — how much information did we need to ingest? — but of course I accompanied her. We were exploring the Buddhist temple at Kelaniya on the outskirts of the city, just the two of us, and with me still watching anxiously for some signal, some validation, when she said, "Daniel's arriving tonight, did I tell you?"

"Daniel Lafontaine?" The shock made me stupid. "He's coming to Colombo?"

"He recently lost his best friend and needs a holiday."

"But you and I are going — "

"We'll all three go together."

"To India. You, me and Daniel? What about Taggart?"

"He can't get away. But he thoroughly approves."

"Maybe you should take this from the top."

"It goes back to Greece," she said, leading me to a stone bench.

In Athens, while I'd been agonizing over my lost souvenirs, Taggart had negotiated coolly. In exchange for allowing Safiya to stay and help me during "his" scheduled time, he'd made her promise that she'd test his three-way-marriage fantasy in Sri Lanka: Daniel, Taggart and Safiya.

"So that explains —" I held my head with my hands. "The penny drops."

If it worked, this trial would provide a template for Dar es Salaam. While waiting for the right moment to set forth, they could all three share a house, why not? "Three-way love, trust and co-operation," Safiya said brightly. "Sometimes I'm with Taggart, other times with Daniel. Sometimes we're all three together."

The lunacy of this proposal took my breath away. Talk about madness! Worse, far worse, where I figure in this menage? As far as I could tell, nowhere. Yet I remained cool: "What does Daniel say?"

"This is not the kind of thing you discuss on the phone." Safiya looked at her hands. "I'll wait until he arrives. Or maybe until we're down the coast, you, me and Daniel."

"Count me out, Safiya. Looks like you already have."

"Don't be ridiculous, Bernie. It's all part of the deal."

"The deal according to Taggart Oates?"

"You've travelled with me and Taggart. Why not me and Daniel?"

"So that's all I am to you? A glorified chaperone?"

Safiya looked at her hands: "You're not taking this well."

"Let me get this straight." I jumped to my feet to pace up and down in front of a small stone Buddha. "While Taggart holds forth at the university, you, me and Daniel —"

"We gather souvenirs around Sri Lanka, visit Kandy and Galle and —"

"Wait a minute! What about India? We leave next week, you

and me."

"Daniel will come too. He's taken sick leave. Hopes India will heal him spiritually."

"This is Taggart's doing." I smacked my fist into my hand. "He doesn't want us to be alone. Safiya, what about you and me?"

"We're expendable, Bernie. Only the quest matters. If we get a couple more souvenirs here in Sri Lanka, India will put us over the top. We'll be ready to approach The Shaman."

"The prophecies say nothing about three-way marriages that exclude me."

Safiya had tears in her eyes. "Bernie, I bought into this for your sake, remember? So I could remain in Athens and help you retrieve your souvenirs."

I turned my back in frustration and found myself staring up at a full-lotus Buddha. What could I do? Try to approach The Shaman alone? Forget that. Yet Taggart had extracted this ludicrous promise, and how could I ask Safiya to go back on her word? We both knew The Shaman dealt harshly with promise-breakers.

In the end, what choice did I have? With little grace, I acquiesced. At the Taj Mahal, I would talk with Behroze and ask her advice. Meanwhile, I would suffer — and simmer — in silence. Daniel Lafontaine arrived that evening, but I didn't meet him until the next, when he and Safiya joined me for dinner at the Hotel Renuka. They'd taken a double room in this modest establishment, where I'd been staying in a single since arriving in Colombo. Until now, Safiya had been living with Taggart, who as a visiting panjandrum commanded an air-conditioned apartment.

Daniel's physical beauty hit me like a blow. My strange dreams had merely suggested it: techicolour movies. In the flesh, Daniel proved three-dimensionally gorgeous. Late twenties, blond hair to his shoulders, he looked every inch a musician. Without thinking, I greeted him: "You play a mean flute."

He glanced at Safiya: "Did I tell you I've taken up flute?"

Safiya shook her head no: "Bernie's like that. You get used to it."

Over dinner, as we developed our souvenir-hunting plans and I struggled to avoid images of these two in bed, Daniel suggested we visit the east coast of the island: "Especially if we're going to

Kandy. That's halfway to Trincomalee, where I hear the beaches are spectacular."

"Daniel, the civil war, remember?" Tamil insurgents controlled the north and east of Sri Lanka. No tourists allowed. This morning, Safiya had taken Daniel tuk-tukking around Columbo. She'd shown him bombed-out government buildings and a neighborhood reduced to rubble. Daniel had registered the city as the battleground without realzing that the war raged everywhere. Now he laughed, embarrassed: "In Dar, we don't get much news of the world."

Fair enough. Yet that's what I seized on to dull my pain and block a torrent of excruciating images of the two of them making love: Daniel's lack of political savvy. This beautiful man threatened my relationship with Safiya. Unable to face that, I asked myself: which of my two rivals would serve better as the third ashavan? Wouldn't we have three questions to answer? What Taggart Oates didn't know about people, places and politics didn't matter, as he frequently suggested. And the other-worldly Daniel? I registered his spirituality and his intuition, but this last fell short of clairvoyance and surely I had that covered?

No, I didn't want to like Daniel. He was too alive, too animated, too drop-dead gorgeous. I did a superficial sounding and found an Achilles heel: Daniel had been deeply wounded by the death of Victor. That experience had shaken his resolve. In time, he'd probably regain it, given his spiritual constitution. But time was something none of us had.

Deeper than that, fearing sexual images, I chose not to go.

When Daniel excused himself to visit the washroom, I said: "Has he talked about Victor?"

"Not much."

"I wonder what that loss has done to his resolve?'

Safiya smiled grimly: "You're getting more like Taggart every day."

Late next morning, I went to see the man himself.

We met on the terrace at the Galle Face Hotel, which looked out over the Indian Ocean. Taggart said every visitor to Colombo should breakfast there once. For the occasion, he'd worn his top hat and red running shoes and I arrived to find him gazing out to sea, his feet crossed at the ankles on a chair.

"You want Otherness, Bernard?" He gestured expansively.

"I give you Sri Lanka."

"Safiya wants Otherness." I pulled up a chair. "I want to restore Colette — and perhaps heal myself."

"*Touché*!" Taggart chuckled. Why not? For him, the universe was unfolding as it should.

"I see Otherness here," I said, because with Taggart, you could never just cut to the chase. "But that Otherness is superficial. The heat, the indecipherable street signs, the mostly brown faces. Yet beneath these surface differences, I see not just universalities, like a common sense of humor, but parallels."

Taggart raised his eyebrows.

"Rambling around Colombo with Safiya has been like gazing into a fun-house mirror. We recognize ourselves, and even see ourselves clearest, in distortion or reversal."

"Which is, you so quaintly believe, the kind of spiritual transaction that might interest The Shaman."

I nodded vigorously: "Take the ubiquitous Buddhism. Sri Lankan Buddhists feel they've been chosen to create a unique Buddhist nation here at the bottom of the Indian sub-continent."

"Their vaunted sense of mission."

Nobody would ever accuse Taggart of being slow.

"Right! But Safiya points out the parallel with Quebec. Not so long ago, and even into my mother's time, many French Canadians believed they'd been chosen to create a Roman Catholic nation in North America."

"Lately, that's evolved into ethnic nationalism — but I take your point."

"Or look here." I snatched an English-language newspaper from a nearby chair and flipped through it: "Fighting in the north of the country. Bombs exploding all over Columbo."

"A civil war rages. You're not suggesting —"

"No, no, I don't expect that in Canada. But Sri Lanka's civil war began as ethnic trouble, right? Between the majority Sinhalese and the minority Tamils?"

"It was partly religious: Buddhism versus Islam. But the fighting began over language issues. In the mid-fifties, when Sri Lanka's newly independent government changed the country's official language from English to Sinhala, the well-educated, English-speaking Tamils began lobbying for a separate state."

"My point, exactly. Language tensions, minority rights issues — sounds like our neighbor to the north, no?"

"Your neighbor to the north, perhaps." Taggart smiled a Buddha smile: "You asked me here to talk about . . ."

"Our shared quest, of course. This business of three ashavans setting forth from some emotional base. Why three, do you think?"

"Right thinking, right speaking, right action."

"And the two who approach?"

"They symbolize the escalating struggle that marks the final millennium, the beginning of the end: Light versus Dark, Good versus Evil, Ahura Mazda versus Ahriman."

"And the success of The One?"

"That signifies the victory of Mazda and the emergence of the Overman, living symbol of the Self. It announces The Renovation, the rebirth that follows hard on a difficult purification." Taggart sipped his coffee and stared out at the ocean. He'd spent hours pondering what the quest might mean in psychological terms. Now he put down his coffee and looked over at me: "But you didn't come to talk about symbolism."

"Safiya wants me to explore Sri Lanka with her and Daniel."

Again Taggart gazed at the ocean: "I'd rather you travel with them than see them go alone."

"So I gather. But I'm feeling abused. This three-way marriage business. I don't under—"

Abruptly, Taggart rose to his feet and began pulling bills out of his pocket. "I don't care what you talk about with Safiya," he said, tossing a bill onto the table. "But I don't feel inclined to discuss my domestic arrangements with you or anyone else."

"I'm not trying to offend, Taggart. I just can't see it."

"Three ashavans must set forth, Bernard."

"Safiya will be torn apart."

"Surely you don't expect me to derail a train that left the station even before we met?" He noticed his reflection in the window and adjusted his top hat: "You might think twice, Bernie, before letting your personal feelings reduce your chances of invoking the Shaman."

"I thought we were having breakfast."

"Sorry, old chap, but I've got a lecture to give." Walking away, Taggart called over his shoulder: "Otherness, indeed."

Alone on the terrace, watching the tide roll in, I cursed my stupidity. All I'd accomplished was to put Taggart on guard. Had I really imagined that because I asked, he'd immediately stop exploiting Safiya's sense of responsibility? Talk about hubris. But maybe Taggart was right about one thing: maybe my feelings were clouding my thinking. This much remained clear: Taggart's three-way marriage threatened to make me the odd man out — the fourth ashavan, unnecessary, extraneous. Was this, too, the work of the Golden Flame?

During the next few days, while souvenir-gathering, I grew accustomed to seeing Safiya with Daniel Lafontaine. There was more to the man than I might have wished. Having grudgingly admitted this, I soon found myself enjoying him: his enthusiasm, his resourcefulness, his spiritual disposition. The death of Victor had profoundly changed him. Even so, you couldn't get the guy down.

The day after I accomplished nothing with Taggart, Safiya, Daniel and I missed the express train to Kandy. We'd crossed the city by tuk-tuk through a light rain, arrived forty minutes early and joined the line-up for tickets. A young couple directly in front of us snapped up two of the last three seats, leaving only a single. I wanted to sit on a bench in dejection, but Daniel whipped out a map: "Bus depot's just down the street."

"I make it a mile through mud puddles," I said.

Safiya said, "Maybe we should try again tomorrow?"

Daniel made for the stairs. "Tomorrow? Where's your sense of adventure?"

Safiya followed: "Time's a wasting, Bernie!"

We muddied our shoes, but Daniel got us to the bus depot, which was really a noisy parking lot crowded with colourfully painted buses, half of them revving their engines. Safiya located the right bus and we found three empty seats separated, two and one, by an aisle. We shoved our bags into the luggage rack and sat down to wait.

Daniel predicted the bus wouldn't leave until all seats were occupied, including those that flipped down into the aisle. Safiya drew my attention to a series of framed pictures of the Buddha that ran across the top of the windshield, then opened her notebook and wrote madly. After ten minutes, she snapped shut her notebook and, pleased with herself, grinned over at me. I felt an all-too-familiar flush of love: god, I adored her! To hide my confusion, I resorted to The Now.

A scratchy sound system brought us soft rock music with Sinhalese lyrics. The airplane-style air-conditioning, which ran along above our heads in lieu of a second luggage-rack, blew just enough cool air to keep the bus bearable. I decided against moving into an aisle seat and a young man sat down between Daniel and me. I felt vindicated in my decision once we got outside Colombo. I'd wondered about the two handles welded into the seat-back in front of me, and now I understood: you hung onto these handles as the bus careered around corners. Aisle-seat passengers had to rely on the sardine effect.

The bus slowed to merely dangerous speeds at villages and towns and Safiya observed that, on most storefront signs, English complemented the cursive but unreadable Sinhalese: Jayantha Texties, St. Anthony's Shoe Mart, Buhair Stores, People's Bank. We saw water pumps where people took turns pumping and drinking, and roadside stands spilling over with oranges and mangoes and bananas and fruits we didn't recognize. Here a flatbed truck loaded with soft drinks had pulled over onto the side of the highway; the enterprising driver sold soft drinks to thirsty workers. Farther back in the fields, their counterparts dowsed each other with pails of water.

Around eleven we arrived in Kandy, a picture-postcard town that circles a lake. We hired a car and driver, ate lunch at the Hotel Suisse in an elegant bar, then visited a batik factory where Safiya dickered over a shirt and eventually walked away: "It's cheaper in Colombo." We visited the botanical gardens and the university campus and took close-up shots of a massive white-painted Buddha, once covered in real gold, that sat overlooking the town.

Safiya had brushed up on Sri Lankan history and drew our attention to the forests surrounding the town. British troops had marched through these woods in 1815. That's when the English, Colombo-based governor attacked Kandy and looted it, she said, and so took control of all Ceylon — a milestone in the creation of the Empire. The governor justified this aggression by falsely portraying the king of Kandy, a pleasure-loving pacifist, as a "remorseless tyrant."

We visited the gold-coloured Temple of the Tooth, and admired what purported to be the sacred tooth of the Buddha. A thief had snatched it, or so the story goes, from the funeral pyre in 543 B.C. Later it was smuggled into the country in the hair of a princess. Where Taggart would have analyzed this myth, and apparently did in one of his novels, Daniel simply savored it. Travelling with him was far easier than with Taggart, who fretted and worried and refused to relax. When I mentioned this, Daniel grinned and responded with a Swahili proverb: "*Mpiga ngumi ukautani huumiza mkonowe.* He who beats a wall with his fist hurts only his own hand."

At the main market, we found no fire-worthy souvenirs. We'd grown concerned by the time Safiya spotted a nondescript stall down a sidestreet. There, thinking it appropriate, I bought a miniature Buddha. Safiya found a silver bridge and Daniel, who had already gathered more than enough keepsakes, purchased a tiny elephant: "Force of habit."

We caught the express train back to Colombo. As we thundered through the tree-clad hills and valleys of tea country, Safiya made me admit that we'd seen more of Sri Lanka, more of the people, towns and villages that morning, during the swaying, two-and-a-half-hour bus ride we almost hadn't taken. Though she wouldn't have missed this train ride for the world: look! weren't those pine trees? Sri Lankan tea country looked a lot like the high plains of midwestern America.

The train rattled and clacked along at crazy speeds — sixty, seventy miles an hour — and the cars lurched so violently that Safiya had trouble scribbling in her notebook. I went to stand in the open area between the cars, the better to savor the glorious rattling ride. The door was open from about waist level and I leaned out to feel the wind blow. I couldn't hear a thing but the clacking of the wheels and the roar of the wind, but a sudden dark premonition made me duck back inside just as two men joined me between the cars — two furious, filthy sailor-types, one of whom said, in an English accent, "It's 'im all right,"

before grabbing me by the throat.

The other one started ripping at my fabulous green bag, in which I'd stuffed our latest fire-worthy baubles, but I swung around and gave him such an elbow in the face that he let go and stumbled backwards, cursing. He rejoined the fray and managed to get the door open while his partner and I exchanged blows. The two of them together were trying to shove me out the open door, and probably would have succeeded if Safiya hadn't arrived just then. She thrust her foot into the lower back of one of the desperadoes and sent him spinning out the door, howling. The other fought on, and almost swung me out the door, but at the last moment I grabbed an iron handle and out he went after his friend, rolling and tumbling into the brush.

Now Daniel arrived: "What's going on?"

"You picked a bad moment to go to the washroom," Safiya said, breathing hard.

"Maybe the Chinvat waited for that moment," I said.

None of the other passengers had seen a thing, apparently. Back in our seats, after I'd filled in a few blanks, I wondered aloud: "Why were they disguised as nineteenth-century British sailors? They looked like they stepped off the movie set for Mutiny on the Bounty."

"I've been wondering about that," Safiya said. "Obviously, they've got to assume some appearance. And I've told you about the perfidy of the British here in Sri Lanka, which they called Ceylon. Maybe it has something to do with the ghosts of colonialism? Ghosts that have to be exorcised along the way? Columbus the conquerer in Barcelona? British sailors here?"

Daniel and I remained dubious, but as neither of us could propose any better explanation, we let that one ride. Back in Colombo, early evening now, we stuffed ourselves at a Chinese restaurant before returning by tuk-tuk to the Hotel Renuka. We deked into the downstairs bar for a nightcap and quickly knocked back three beers. I was waving at the waitress for another round when Daniel put his hand on my shoulder and got to his feet: "No thanks, Bernie. We're going to turn in."

He waggled his eyebrows at Safiya and I remembered that he didn't know she and I had shared a magic night. And realized he didn't begin to suspect how I felt about her. Safiya had the grace to look away: "Night, Bernie."

I heard mixed emotions in her voice, or so I told myself as I sat alone in that dark bar, nursing my Heineken. This was The New Reality, then — the latest bed of hot coals I was obliged to traverse: watching Daniel and Safiya head off arm in arm, whispering sweet nothings in French. I didn't think I could survive it.

Half an hour later, when I arrived at my room, I found it ransacked. Bureau drawers pulled open and emptied onto the floor. Two chairs turned upside down. The bed tipped over and the mattress ripped open from top to bottom. The perpetrators had taken nothing — that's what the staff found strange. I'd stored my valuables in the hotel safe. But I'd left some American dollars on the bureau and there they remained. The hotel manager couldn't understand it. He gave me another room and had a porter carry my effects from this one to that. He insisted on summoning the police, and I told them nothing had been stolen. The police, too, found the case baffling: was I a spy or something?

I said not a word about the Chinvat or the "British sailors" we'd thrown off the train. I couldn't imagine trying to explain.

Next morning, over breakfast, Daniel and Safiya shook their heads in dismay. Safiya cried, "Bernie, you should have woken us!" They agreed with my analysis: the Chinvat didn't want my money. They wanted to send a message, to let us know they'd found us in Colombo. We'd escaped a couple of hitmen on the train. But any time they wanted, they could strike again.

If I'd had my doubts about travelling down the coast with Safiya and Daniel, the ransacking had dissolved them. We had to get out of Colombo. Safiya had studied her Lonely Planet guide and proposed as a main base the resort town of Hikkaduwa, about one hundred kilometres south of the city. We left a message for Taggart, telling him that my room had been trashed: he'd know what that meant. Then away we went in a rented car — which, in Sri Lanka, meant a rented car with driver.

The two-lane highway out of Colombo flirts with the coast: here a crowded shantytown, there a sandy beach awash in drift wood, and everywhere the smell of fish and salt sea air. We drove slowly and gradually our collective mood lifted. Daniel and Safiya took turns reading the signs aloud, revelling in the sounds of the names: Wellawatta, Angulana, Kalutara, Bentota, Balapitiya, Ambalanangoda. We stopped to watch the stilt fishermen mending their nets and, and the driver explained that the sea was too rough for the men to go out.

A short while later, we stopped again, this time to view the "toddy tappers," high-wire artists who climb towering palm trees barefoot and walk tight ropes from one to another. Daniel offered another Swahili proverb: "*Usigombe na mkwezi, nazi imeliwa na mwezi.*" Seeing our faces, he grinned and translated: "Don't argue with the coconut-palm climber. The coconut has been eaten by the moon."

Safiya said: "You live in a world of your own."

The climbers were tapping the palm trees for a liquid "toddy" which, fermented, becomes the knock-em-dead alcoholic drink arrack. Safiya insisted on sipping toddy from the roadside stand, though both Daniel and I fretted — unnecessarily, as it turned out — and warned her against it. This only encouraged her and she took a second great swig and then wiped her mouth with her forearm: "Just consider me a coconut-palm climber and quit arguing."

"*Kupanda mchongoma, kushuka ndio ngoma,*" Daniel responded. "You may climb a thorn tree, but coming down again is a dance."

I laughed along with them, but their banter made me sad. It revealed a reality, a shared intimacy, that I didn't wish to face. If I hadn't needed fire-worthy souvenirs from down the coast, I would have made an excuse and returned to Colombo. But Colette, Colette...for Colette, I carried on. We'd booked nothing in advance, not wanting to tip our hand to Chinvat, and when we reached Hikkaduwa, Safiya suggested we try the five-star Coral Sands Beach Hotel: "They'll never find us there. We'll splurge."

The driver parked out front and she went inside to talk price. The desk clerk quoted her a reasonable rate. But when Daniel and I hopped out of the taxi, the clerk realized he'd made mistake: he'd taken Safiya for a resident, but clearly Daniel and I were "Europeans" — tourists! He revised his quote upwards by fifty per cent. Daniel shrugged — "we're only here once" — but Safiya, outraged, insisted that we climb back into the car and find another hotel.

We ended up staying down the highway at the Hotel Serendib. It rated four stars, not five, but Safiya said: "Here, at least, one price fits all."

Daniel overtipped the driver. We deposited our gear in our respective rooms (they were sharing a double) and met in the lobby. A sign informed us, in both English and German, that entertainment happened nightly: calypso music, magic night, acrobatic act, fire limbo. Hey, why not?

Daniel got chatting with a Dutch tourist and mentioned the double-pricing at the Coral Sands. The man laughed and said we'd lucked out: the Coral Sands catered to package-tour groups, mostly German. But the Serendib aimed at independent travellers. The grounds didn't photograph as well, and we wouldn't encounter any old men offering elephant rides, but wait until we sampled the buffet breakfast — incredible Sri Lankan specialties, all you could eat.

Daniel waved his hands in the air: "We've arrived in paradise."

Safiya looked around, wide-eyed, agog: "And we're paying half price."

Together, they dissolved in laughter. I retreated to my room as Behroze brought me Shakespeare: "Thou art a soul in bliss; but I am bound / Upon a wheel of fire, that mine own tears/Do scald like molten lead." With that, my own tears came: Colette! Oh, Colette! I endure this for you.

That afternoon, we lounged around the palm-studded grounds. Thatch umbrellas, chaise lounges you could wheel like carts, chasing shade, and a dog-leg pool big enough for swimming lengths — Daniel pronounced the whole *"absolument merveilleux"* and got no argument. We strolled off the grounds onto the beach, all three of us, grinning at a smiling guard as we passed through a double gate in a rough stick fence.

The white-sand beach stretched for miles in both directions, nothing but palm trees and a few dozen families playing in the warm water. We stood ankle deep in the Indian Ocean, savoring the sunshine and magic of this fabled island, whose gifts to the world, I suddenly realized, included the word serendipity. Would this place work magic for me?

Safiya said: "We're on the far side of the world."

Daniel pointed at the empty horizon: "Tanzania."

"What strikes me about here," I said, "is the absence of so much we in America take for granted. No motor boats. No water skiers."

"No hang gliders," Safiya said. "No roller bladers, no fitness fanatics, no cute little pastel outfits."

"No concession stands," Daniel said. "No hollering ice-cream vendors, no crowds of people baking themselves brown." He looked down the deserted beach: "The civil war's wreaking havoc on the tourist trade."

Safiya punched his shoulder: "You're not completely out of it, after all."

A young man trotted onto the beach dangling half a dozen marionettes, their huge heads consisting of colourful masks: "Best quality! Cheap!"

Safiya fell in love with a dancing puppet but declined to buy it. Daniel understood her refusal — purely financial — before I did and insisted on getting it for her. As Safiya protested, he wheeled and trotted back to the hotel to fetch his wallet. The young salesman squatted in the sand to wait.

I pointed to a flapping red flag down the beach and he confirmed, in broken English, what we'd surmised. The flag indicated that the sea was too rough for swimming. To Safiya, I said, "Ah, but what about wading?"

Together we waded into the Indian Ocean. Unlike the Pacific off northern California, it felt warm. Thigh-deep in the undulating ocean, the rolling waves, we stood splashing ourselves and rejoicing in the bright sun, the cloudless blue sky, the great slow curve of the palm-fringed beach sweeping away forever.

Safiya walked out farther and I followed. Waves crested at my hips, then my waist, but Safiya plowed forward and a giant wave loomed and she glanced over at me, grinning in anticipation, and whoosh! The huge wave dragged me shoreward, tumbling, but I got my feet under me and staggered upright, coughing and rubbing my eyes and tasting salt water. When I looked around, I saw Safiya flashing her "good-times grin" and we both felt such a rush of exhilaration that we burst out laughing: here we stood on the far side of the world, playing in the Indian Ocean.

We'd put the Chinvat behind us to savor a tropical moment. But even as I stood in the sun-dappled waves, laughing with Safiya,

I felt a now-familiar tingling and registered dark foreboding. Epiphany eluded me, however, as suddenly I lost the moment in Safiya's laughter as Daniel Lafontaine came thundering towards us, high-kicking through the water. He charged past and didn't stop galloping until he tumbled face first into the waves, then came up crying: "Touchdown! Lafontaine!"

To me, Safiya said: "That's what I missed about Daniel."

"His ability as a fantasy halfback?"

"His *joie de vivre*, you jealous man."

Safiya patted my face, then turned and raced into the water after him, left me to emerge alone. I could see what she meant about Daniel's enthusiasm, especially compared with Taggart's pompous rationality. That didn't mean I had to like it. Or that I didn't find it strange, given the recent death of his best friend. While Safiya and Daniel romped and splashed like children, I sat pondering.

When she came ashore, Safiya made her marionette dance. Then she snapped a towel and provoked Daniel into chasing her down the beach. Again I was struck by his beauty. I'd known he was roughly my height, six-foot-one, but I hadn't registered his athlete's physique. In a bathing suit, with his long blond hair and his muscular physique, Daniel looked like he'd stepped out of Baywatch — the quintessential California surfer. As he chased Safiya, lithe and panther-like, down the beach, I felt my heart sink: together, they looked perfect.

That night, we watched a fire-eater perform — a slim, wild-eyed man I scanned carefully: Chinvat? Golden Flame? He proved devoid of quest-related significance, though I assured Safiya that he served as a synchronistic marker evidencing that we remained on the right, true path. To avoid a repeat of the Colombo experience, when Safiya and Daniel had left me alone with my Heineken, I fled before the show ended, retreated to my room and lay awake a long time.

Whenever I wondered how much I could bear, how much more of this emotional trial by fire, loving Safiya and watching her love someone else, I'd touch base with Colette and draw the same conclusion: I would endure however much I had to endure. Safiya knew this, I felt certain, and though we'd never discussed it, I believed not only that she approved, but that she identified and suffered with me.

Next morning, after a superb breakfast highlighted by succulent fruit and tiny pancakes called hoppers, we hired a car and driver. We drove south to Galle, an ancient port believed to have been the Biblical city of Tarshis, where King Solomon bought gems, spices, muslins, silks and peacocks. The port had remained under Arab control for hundreds of years, part of a peaceable Indian Ocean trading empire. The Chinese seized it early in the fifteenth century. Then, in short order,  came the Portuguese and the Dutch. By the middle of the seventeenth century, Dutch East Indiamen were using Galle as the final gathering-point for their home-going fleets, traditionally beginning voyages on Christmas Day after praying in the Calvinist church.

If now Galle seemed a sleepy Dutch town, judging from the streets, the architecture and several old churches, we agreed that its ancient history took priority and found a shop in which we bought evocative souvenirs: a tiny incense bowl, a crystal pendulum that glowed red in the morning light and a silver engraving of a lovely Indian maid. As Safiya finished paying the merchant, a smiling old Dutchman, I felt a tingling at the back of my neck and knew something bad was coming. Safiya and Daniel stood between me and the door, and I spun on my heel and leapt at them, carrying them both out the door into the street as an explosion erupted from the rear of the shop.

Even before we got to our feet, the place was engulfed by flames and thick black smoke. Within minutes, the shop had burned to the ground. Fortunately, it stood alone, unconnected, at the end of a small street. Safiya, Daniel and I felt badly shaken, and couldn't get over the fate of the shopkeeper, but then police arrived and searched the rubble and found no trace of a body. An old Dutchman had closed the shop a decade ago, they said, and died a couple of years after that. None of us saw any reason to argue.

We told police we'd been walking along the street when the explosion happened. We checked our newly purchased souvenirs, which remained entirely tangible, then returned to our rented car. As we drove back up the winding, two-lane highway, we congratulated ourselves on our success in Galle — and warned each other not to get too complacent. We drove past Hikkaduwa to Ambalangoda, home of Sri Lanka's most famous mask carvers, and there visited three different shops, exclaiming as we went. Safiya and I confined ourselves to looking but Daniel spent fifty dollars American on a garish "devil-dancing" mask celebrating fire, complete with protruding eyeballs, lolling tongue and flaming, red-and-yellow hair. "It drives away evil spirits," he said. "Think of it not as decoration but technology."

I said, "We'll unleash it on the Chinvat."

"You're a bit of a devil yourself," Safiya said. "When do we get to see you dance?"

"This is it! I'm dancing as fast as I can."

They both laughed and I reflected that we'd reduced our recovery time: already, we'd returned to the kind of silly exchanges that made me weep inside. I stepped outside to wait alone.

Back at the hotel, we changed into our bathing suits and went to the beach. The sun blazed down but the red flag continued to flap in the breeze: swimming was prohibited. On the other hand, how many chances would we ever get to swim off the coast of Sri Lanka? Daniel and I left Safiya standing waist-deep and beat our way out beyond the breaking waves to where the ocean rolled and swelled. While Safiya kept an uneasy watch, we swam together in giant circles, pausing occasionally to loll on our backs.

"This quest has its moments," I shouted, expecting an equally light-hearted rejoinder. But Daniel responded with Swahili: "*Usimwamshe aliyelala; utalala wewe.*" Then, treading water, he translated: "Do not wake one who is sleeping; you will fall asleep yourself."

He turned and swam for shore and I got a flash of darkness. Yet again epiphany eluded me and I surmised that he was thinking of Victor. No, wait: maybe it was that wizened old man. The one who'd turned up afterwards on the beach. A strange old bird I'd almost forgotten, but who'd clearly arrived with some purpose in mind. He'd offered Daniel fame and recognition, but what had he wanted in return? I tried a paranormal scan and hit a fog-wall. This only I knew: Daniel remained sombre for the rest of the afternoon.

By evening, he'd returned to himself. This was our last night down the coast — the Chinvat knew we were in the vicinity — and Safiya suggested we eat dinner in an open-air restaurant belonging to the hotel next door. We strolled down a winding, flagstone path and there it sat: thatched roof, rolled-up bamboo curtains, table-top candles providing the only light. What else? Nothing but palm trees and the roar of the ocean. This had to be the most romantic spot in the world.

We shared spicy curry dishes and chased them down with beer.

As we finished, we heard music wafting from the hotel lounge. Safiya and I would have been content to linger a while longer, but Daniel needed to see the music. A jazz ensemble had taken the stage. They played big-band standards, mostly Duke Ellington, with the leader switching from saxophone to piano and back again. We took a table, ordered more beer and sat grooving on the entertainment. When the musicians took a break, Daniel went to chat.

Twenty minutes later, when they came back on stage, Daniel commandeered the piano. Two minutes into the first number, the boys in the band knew someone special had arrived. A few minutes later, when Daniel took a solo, the audience got the message: this guy wasn't just good, he was just smoking great. And that's when, with a cold shiver of fear, I understood what, beyond the physical, Saifya found attractive: Daniel wasn't verbal but musical. I'd been comparing him with Taggart and mistaking his relative lack of political sophistication for stupidity. In fact, the man was an intuitive genius — though you didn't see that until he went musical.

Now I remembered his Mombasa trip and how, with a cheap flute, he'd charmed a busload of restless passengers. I'd glimpsed his talent then, but now I watched a full-scale demonstration. As Daniel sat hunched over the piano, driving those Sri Lankan jazzmen places they'd never been, I found myself wondering how, after loving such a one, Safiya could have got involved with Taggart Oates. And smiled grimly to think that I'd reversed myself.

An even darker moment ensued: how had Safiya got involved with me? Maybe she'd spoken the truth? Maybe to her, that night we'd shared — if in mundane reality we'd shared it at all — maybe to her it meant nothing? She'd just been increasing her chances of approaching The Shaman. I hadn't admitted this possibility, not viscerally. In my besotted innocence, I'd secretly believed that Safiya, so fiercely capable and intelligent, would grow bored with her California surfer and turn at last to me.

Now I glimpsed a much bleaker prospect. The dark moment lingered, became two moments, twenty. And then this dark hour grew darker still. The jazz band, exhausted, took another break. The crowd applauded while Daniel, sweating profusely, rejoined our table. Safiya suggested that we go outside, get some air. We gravitated to the ocean, drawn by the roar, and found ourselves strolling along the deserted beach. Looking up at the star-studded sky, we recognized not a single constellation and I marvelled once again that, as people from the western hemisphere, we stood on the far side of the world. So far away from my darling Colette.

I turned to share this thought with Safiya and found her staring into Daniel's eyes. Together, without me, they made "perfect": a beautiful young couple enjoying a star-lit tropical beach. Disheartened, dismayed, I slipped away in silence, started back towards the hotel. Safiya neglected to call my name. And the voice of Behroze offered nothing but Byron: "I am ashes where once I was fire."

Sailors of Kuwali

That night, as I prepared for bed, I felt movement in San Francisco. Alarmed, I focused and found Behroze enlisting reinforcements — four white-bearded men. She stationed them at the corners of Colette's hospital bed and my fear and concern gave way to relief: Behroze needed to gather her energy for the Taj, that was all; but with the help of these four, she could sustain Colette forever.

Reassured, I drifted into my nightly ritual of reviewing images from Colette's childhood, as if flipping through an old-fashioned book of photos: Colette as a baby, dancing gleefully in her Jolly Jumper; Colette saying her first words, taking her first steps, racing around with her favorite Teddy. And later: Colette at Disneyland, wide-eyed and wondering, bent on trying the scariest adult rides; Colette at the beach down the coast in Carmel, determined to win a castle-making contest; Colette hunched over her piano in the living room, preparing for yet another recital.

I could have wallowed longer, but experience had taught me that I'd reached the point of no return: from here, either I could cry myself to sleep, missing Colette, or apply myself elsewhere, to some task that might help bring her back. With an effort of will, I turned to Daniel Lafontaine and focused. Lately, he'd become more opaque and less readable, this Quebecois musician with a penchant for Swahili proverbs. Had Mombasa changed him?

Daniel had always felt doubly marginalized. His mother traced her ancestry to Ireland so he'd never been *un de nous autres*, a Quebecois *pur laine*. He'd grown up "half-and-half," speaking French at home and English at school. That's not as dramatic as arriving into a "visible minority" in white-bread Ontario, like Safiya, but it did mean feeling always on the outside looking in. And that experience, Daniel believed, created a unique sense of self, making him more like Safiya, say, than like Taggart, who'd grown up feeling part of a dominant culture.

With all this, I empathized. Born and raised in San Francisco, and profoundly American, yet I grew up feeling part and not part — a complexity I'd only now begun to appreciate. I had my mother to thank. Her Quebecoise influence pervaded my youth, and even today remains constantly at odds with the practical, no-nonsense American my father wished me to be.

Yet the way Daniel approached this, imbuing it with so much significance, struck me as oddly Canadian. In Colombo, I'd raised the subject with Safiya, obliquely challenging Daniel's contention that they'd bonded as outsiders, and she'd responded with exasperation: "What could you know about being an outsider, Bernie? About feeling alien in your own country?"

"Hey, I'm half-Quebecois, remember? I've always been a counter-culture guy."

"But you don't even speak French."

"You're coming at this too narrowly. Selfhood is larger even than language."

Now, in Hikkaduwa, a particular tingling interrupted this contemplation — a tingling I'd learned to recognize as presaging a dimensional shift. Dar es Salaam: late afternoon — I recognized it immediately: Daniel's apartment. Yet this time the place feels subtly different, provisional somehow. . . .

Daniel Lafontaine finishes playing Lady, Be Good, a favorite warm-up tune, before turning to his latest composition. For two days, he's been fretting over an intractable problem but now he hears a possible solution: maybe, at the transition, he should move to the minor key? He's working away, sounding out this solution, when he hears someone knocking.

Daniel crosses the living room and opens the door to Nathan and Rachel Finklestein, recent additions to the school staff. Rachel hands him a blender: "Safiya did say seven?"

He looks at his watch, which says five-twenty: "Damn thing's died."

Nathan says: "Humidity will do that."

Ushering his friends into the living room, Daniel says, "She and Bernard must have stopped at the Yacht Club. They went sailing, did she tell you? Let me fix you a drink."

What's happening here? Looks like I've entered the future.

Daniel carries the blender into his sparkling kitchen.

Four months ago, flying into Dar es Salaam — a city first Arabic, then German, then British, now Tanzanian — he didn't know what to expect. But certainly he didn't envisage this air-conditioned, two-bedroom apartment three minutes from the International School.

He opens the fridge and takes out a tray of ice cubes.

The apartment comes with the job: teaching music to the sons and daughters of expatriate diplomats and engineers and of local businessmen, mostly "Asians" of Indian heritage. No, correction: he qualified for the extra bedroom, and moved into these upgraded quarters, only after Safiya arrived and began teaching French. And here I think: Safiya teaching French in Dar? Surely this future isn't fixed?

But what a difference Safiya makes. Today, after teaching music from seven until noon, Daniel came home and ate lunch with her — fresh fruit piled high in a split papaya and doused in lemon juice. Then they'd changed into their swimsuits. Ignoring the mid-day heat, which I felt even in my visionary state, they crossed the green expanse of school yard and entered the pool through a gate, nodding hello to the seated attendant, an old man in a blue uniform.

They'd timed their arrival to catch the single hour reserved for adults. A dozen teachers and a few parents lolled and splashed in the lukewarm water. Daniel swam sixty lengths, roughly one mile, and Safiya eighteen — the most she'd done yet.

After the swim: siesta. Coming from a northern country, Daniel had never appreciated the wisdom, almost the necessity, of napping through the worst of the heat and humidity. Now, with Dar on the ocean and so near the equator, he not only understood, but revelled. Safiya hadn't joined him today. Instead, she'd sat at the dining-room table marking French papers, rushing to finish and go sailing. He'd tried to dissuade her: "I've got a bad feeling about it."

"This isn't like you."

"Safiya, please don't go."

"Come with us then."

"Can't, remember? I've got that curriculum meeting."

Twice before, Safiya had sailed in The Askari. Today, for the first time, she would take the helm as captain. As she called goodbye from the door, Daniel heard the excitement in her voice and beat back a senseless wave of panic. Bernard would be with her. If trouble arose — but why should it? The day was bright and clear and he'd seen no sign of Chinvat.

Daniel napped for an hour and awoke refreshed. Again he crossed the school yard, this time to attend the meeting. Ninety minutes, deadly dull, nothing accomplished — a complete waste of time. He went to the music room to correct papers.

The school formed a rectangle around an open court. While he worked, Daniel glanced occasionally at the gardeners as they swept and raked the courtyard and tended the blazing bougainvilleas. He enjoyed listening to them speak Swahili. The explorer Richard Burton had encountered the language first in India, among slaves nobody could understand. Later, Burton recognized it here in East Africa, and realized that Swahili had once been the *lingua franca* of a trading empire encircling the Indian Ocean — an empire predicated on the predictability of the monsoon winds, which carried trading vessels now one way, now the other. Spoken quickly, Daniel reflected, Swahili sounded almost like singing.

Before leaving the school, Daniel stopped by the pool, now

silent and deserted. The water shone in the sun like a mirror. He used his "borrowed" key to unlock the gate. He removed his T-shirt and sandals, plunged into the water and swam a dozen lengths, before turning over to float on his back. Again he fought off a foreboding, told himself to stop worrying. Safiya would be fine.

He gazed up at the blue sky, dotted now with fluffy clouds, and spotted a yellow kiskadee wheeling and soaring on the wind. Still higher up: a passenger plane flew north towards Mombasa. Why not? A Swahili proverb presented itself: "*Heri nusu ya shari kuliko shari kamili. Better half a disaster than a whole one.*"

But now it's seven-thirty and Daniel's smashing icecubes in his kitchen, thinking: Safiya, where are you? He tells himself: don't panic, don't worry, entertain your guests. He pauses in his work and, from the living room, hears Nathan and Rachel whispering.

Nathan has become his best friend in Dar, though nothing like Victor. Daniel has told him not a word, for example, about seeking The Shaman's Fire. Nathan's wife, Rachel, is a willowy blonde who has worked in Guatemala and Saudi Arabia but hails from a small town near Chicago. From back home in America, she'd recently brought half a dozen "new-fangled toys," among them this four-speed blender. Later this evening, perhaps, Daniel would whip up a mango dessert.

Now he carries drinks into the living room: "*Alors, vous imprudents.* Cinzano on ice."

Rachel says, "The real thing? Here in Dar?"

"Bernard found it. I can't believe that guy."

"Nathan says he's . . . different."

Nathan sips his drink. "I told her about the wayward tarantula."

"Which reminds me." From the hall cupboard, Daniel retrieves a towel, something he forgot to do on the night of the tarantula. The memory triggers a flashback. Again Daniel sees the giant spider scuttle in under the front door, its hairy, grey-brown body as big around as his fist: eight sturdy legs, antennae waving, their ugliest visitor yet. The tarantula pauses mid-living-room, pulsating, startled by the dramatic change of environment: the tile floor, the quiet music.

Instinctively, all four humans — my god! I'm one of them — lift their feet from the floor. The tarantula skitters off, fiendishly mobile, less like a spider than some awful lost hand. It takes refuge beneath the sofa. Daniel has long since realized that light draws these giant insects and silently curses himself for having forgotten to stuff the towel into the gap at the foot of the door. Now what choice do they have? No way they can leave the flat without dispatching the tarantula. Return home not knowing where it lurks? Forget that.

While Nathan and I watch, Safiya retrieves the heavy-duty insect spray from her study and moves to one end of the sofa. Daniel fetches the broom from the kitchen and stations himself at the other. He indicates readiness and Safiya begins blazing away.

Twice already they've been driven to this extremity, and both times they've marvelled at how much spraying a tarantula will endure before it breaks for freedom, so giving the broom-holder a clean shot: whack! But even wonky and disoriented from spraying, a tarantula remains fiendishly mobile, difficult to hit. Now, hating even the thought of killing it, Safiya starts spraying, but I say: "Wait a minute."

All this is filtered through Daniel. The doubled point of view reminds me of Rome and the catacombs, but the provisional feeling, the lack of fixity — these are new. I'm watching, participating and analyzing all at once. Nathan says: "That thing could inflict serious pain. They can't just leave it."

"Let's try something." I cross the room and open the front door, then kneel in the centre of the room and hold out my hands, palms up: "Close your eyes. You can feel it."

Daniel wonders: Is this guy for real? Yet he closes his eyes and surprise: he can "feel" the intelligence of the trapped tarantula, and also the great, billowing waves of hatred it emanates.

I tell him: "It knows we're trying to destroy it."

Now Daniel feels a different emanation: a wave of kindness? Of fellow-feeling? The tarantula feels it too, the warmth passing through my hands. Daniel opens his eyes, watches the spider emerge from beneath the sofa and make a bee-line for the open door. Zip! It disappears into the night.

Nathan says: "How'd you do that?"

I laugh uneasily: "Just a trick my dead wife taught me."

Now, to Rachel, while stuffing the towel beneath the door, Daniel says: "You'll meet Bernard tonight. I'll be interested in your reaction."

Having wandered to the window, Rachel stands looking out at a back garden Daniel has come to love: three palm trees, a couple of baobabs, one lemon tree, one papaya, six sisal plants and two trees whose names he doesn't know, but whose pods can be turned into maraccas; not to mention a colourful riot of shrubs, lush and flowering, about which he knows nothing. For a Montreal boy, living in Dar is like living in a greenhouse.

Yet again that sense of foreboding: Safiya, where are you?

Turning back into the room, Rachel plucks The Daily News from a magazine rack and says, "Did you see today's front-page editorial?"

"About witchcraft?" Daniel refills Nathan's glass. "It's classic."

Nathan says, "Here, let me see."

Instead of handing him the newspaper, Rachel reads aloud: "Police in Dar es Salaam have been compelled to issue a statement refuting the prevailing notion that evil spirits are roaming the city and threatening the lives of residents. We would have ignored the statement were it not for the fact that some people need to be disabused of false fears and unscientific beliefs."

"That's got a ring," Nathan says.

Rachel reads on: "The world is made up of matter in different forms of material existence. There are no spirits of any kind, either living on their own or hidden in the material things we see, hear or feel around us."

Nathan says, "I like it."

"There are no spirits, good or bad," Rachel continues, "which can bring about a good harvest, heal the sick or fly aeroplanes. That is the objective reality."

Daniel can't help himself: "Nothing there about communing with tarantulas? Nothing about Chinvat or wizened old prophets?"

"Sorry, what?"

Rachel resumes: "We would like to join the police in assuring people that there are no evil spirits, otherwise called *mumianis*, in Dar es Salaam or anywhere else. All talk of spirits is stupid and nonsensical. *Mumianis* exist only in the imaginations of ignorant and superstitious folk."

Nathan applauds loudly: "No *mumianis* in Dar."

Daniel says: "What time is it?"

"Seven-forty," Rachel says. "Give them a few more minutes."

Daniel steps to the front window and looks out.

Rachel digs into her purse, produces three American quarters and picks up a paperback which, before sitting down to play piano, Daniel had placed carefully on the coffee table: a well-thumbed copy of the I Ching, the Chinese Book of Changes: "Come on, Daniel. You go first."

Nathan looks at the ceiling: "I can't believe you two."

"You never leave, I notice," Rachel says.

Daniel says: "Maybe we should wait until Safiya and Bernard arrive?"

And Nathan: "You're not going to inflict this on Bernard?"

Daniel picks up the quarters. During the past few weeks, they've made a parlour game of it: Daniel and Rachel consult the ancient oracle while Nathan plays skeptic. The readings they find in this "new interpretation for modern times" resonate for all of them — though Nathan admits nothing.

Daniel shakes the coins in his cupped hands and tosses them onto the table. Rachel counts the heads and tails and records the results. Daniel focuses on Safiya. He can think of nothing else. It's not like her to be late.

When he's finished rolling, Rachel reports that he has thrown hexagram number fifty-one: "The Thunderclap — and with two moving lines." She flips to the appropriate page and begins reading: "This is a time of sudden…"

She stops and looks up at Daniel.

"Of sudden what? Go on."

Rachel begins again: "This is a time of sudden catastrophic events. Remain cool. Expect a general reaction of shock and fear and then hysteria. Do not get caught up in it. If you retain a deep acceptance of the inevitability of the present moment, then you will ride out the widespread catastrophe wiser and stronger than you were before."

Nathan says: "The syntax needs work."

Alarmed, Daniel reminds himself that he likes this version of the I Ching because, in offering interpretations, it draws on the Hindu concepts of artha, kama and moksha, which pertain to the outer world, sexuality and spirituality. "The moksha," he says. "Read the moksha."

Rachel reads: "A time of catastrophic 'acts of God' is a good time to examine the depth of your spiritual commitment." She hesitates, then continues: "In the face of the present disasters you are rediscovering fears and anxieties in yourself. Thus you do not completely, deeply, effortlessly accept the will of God."

Nathan says: "Talk about bunk."

Rachel ignores him: "You have not thrown off your ego so thoroughly that you can face these times with a Buddha-like calm. It is good that you have discovered this."

"Ahura Mazda works in wondrous ways," Daniel says.

Rachel glances up, puzzled, and quickly he adds: "You mentioned moving lines."

"The Thunderclap transforms into hexagram forty, Release," Rachel says, flipping pages. Again she reads: "'This is the hexagram of climax, of the dramatic finale, of the miraculous release.' Listen to the moksha: 'Enlightenment comes to some after a close brush with death. Enlightenment is death of a sort. The Zen Buddhist experiencing satori "dies" as he loses his identity. The yogi abolishes his ego and —'"

"Dan? You all right?" Nathan helps Daniel into a chair, makes him put his head between his knees. After a moment, Daniel, looking pale, raises his head: "I want to phone the Yacht Club."

"I'll do it," Rachel says, placing the I Ching on the table. "You two wait here in case Safiya gets back."

The three step outside and Rachel strides off across the school yard to use the only nearby telephone. Daniel notices the growing wind, sees that night is falling. Here in the tropics, it happens so suddenly. He's still not used to it.

Rachel is gone a long time. Daniel and Nathan are discussing going after her when she emerges out of the darkness, looking grim: "They did a boat count and came up one short." She lets that register. "Maybe we should go to the Yacht Club."

Daniel feels his mind flare: oh, god, what has he done? Safiya's not part of the deal. Surely the very name of the sailboat makes disaster impossible: "Askari" means "guard" or "night watchman." Unbidden, a Swahili proverb dances through his mind: "*Mwanamaji wa Kuwali, kufa maji mazoea.* To a sailor of Kuwali, death by water is a common experience."

Reality slugs him in the stomach: "They did a boat count?"

New Delhi Surprise

In New York, during a final North American visitation, Behroze had mentioned that even vivid premonitions represented nothing fixed and unalterable, but only one possible future among many. Now her admonition brought hope. Somehow, I had to ensure that the permutation I'd witnessed never became the fixed reality, because obviously something terrible had happened to Safiya.

The day after this precognitive experience, I casually asked Daniel whether he'd ever encountered a white-robed old man on a beach. He looked at me oddly: "Not that I recall. What a strange question. Why do you ask?"

"The archetypal-journey idea. Taggart's influence."

Was Daniel hiding something? Had he really forgotten? Maybe that dream, too, had been provisional — though in memory it felt irrevocable. This much I knew: Daniel had changed since the death of Victor. As we flew together towards New Delhi, I tried to scan him and encountered a fog thicker even than Taggart's.

"History boasts countless empires of the sword," Daniel was saying, "but only India has created an Empire of the Spirit." He was describing a documentary film, rambling really. "Where we Westerners celebrate materialism, rationality and masculinity, India looks to non-violence, the inner life and the female. Westerners abhor the material poverty of India, but Mark Twain rightly observed that, 'In matters of the spirit, it's we who are the poor ones.'"

I thought of Colette, lying comatose in her hospital bed. How much longer would I have to remain away? I reviewed my souvenir count: New York, Las Palmas, Barcelona, Genoa, Rome, Al-Mayadin, Athens, Meteora, Colombo, Galle and Kandy. Eleven plus Mesa Verde, the bracelet Safiya had given me. Twelve of sixteen. And of the seven I needed from magical places, I counted four: Mesa Verde, home of the lost Anasazi; Rome, the catacombs; Meteora, the monasteries; and Kandy, the Temple of the Tooth.

I glanced across Daniel at Safiya, snoozing in the window seat, and felt a now-familiar yearning. I'd developed an elaborate rationale proving not only that Safiya's relationship with Daniel was doomed, but that ultimately she would turn to me. Its premise was that she had her own emotional centre: her writing. Given that, why had she allowed herself to get involved with Taggart Oates even before Daniel went off to Africa? Answer: because she needed to be the centre of somebody else's universe.

Taggart had long since established himself as a novelist. He'd stopped climbing short of the highest peaks but happily explored a lofty plateau. By comparison, Daniel Lafontaine, in his music, still scrambled obsessively upwards. Question: which man could better afford to make Safiya the centre of his emotional universe? Answer: the eccentric Englishman. And Safiya preferred me to him. See how it worked?

We're talking desperation. In truth, Safiya proclaimed her independence and self-sufficiency with every word and gesture. She felt no need whatever to inhabit the centre of anybody else's emotional universe. Yet I'd convinced myself that all I had to do was wait. As a mental contortionist, I'd achieved a personal best. Pathetic, really.

In the airplane to Delhi, noticing that he'd lost my attention, Daniel switched to Swahili: "*Asiyesikia la mkuu huvunjika guu.*"

He took a beat, then translated: "He who does not listen to an elder's advice gets his leg broken."

"So now you're my elder?" Still, I couldn't help smiling. I'd listened with only one ear, yet Daniel's enthusiasm stayed with me. And India itself taught me that, contrary to popular opinion, beggars CAN be choosers.

I think of a young man I encountered in New Delhi. Late afternoon, a major downpour had just ended. I'd emerged from our downtown hotel, the Bombay Jack, wearing sneakers and realized they'd never do: the streets and sidewalks were awash inches deep. In places, the water reached my calves. I returned to my room, removed my sneakers and donned plastic thongs I'd bought in Sri Lanka. Back outside, I rolled up my pantlegs and, head held high, strode lordly through puddles and temporary lakes eliciting smiles of recognition. I'd been walking for an hour when a light rain began falling, threatening worse, and I decided to return to the Bombay Jack.

At a pedestrian underpass, I trotted down stairs and at the bottom, just out of the rain, I discovered a thin young man wearing nothing but shorts, kneeling on the pavement with his hands clasped in supplication. Beside him, a small fire burned and I thought: Golden Flame. I checked, discerned nothing significant, gave him my coins and walked on.

Later, as I towelled my hair dry in my room, I realized that, in scanning the youth, I'd detected no hidden malice. Perhaps that's what I'd been meant to discover? Despite desperate circumstances, that young man had become not a mugger but a beggar. In America, and even in Europe, big-city beggars don't importune — they subtly threaten. India's not free of muggers. But the general tendency, the national disposition, I realized, is profoundly pacifist. This temperament could prevail only in an empire of the spirit. Daniel Lafontaine had been onto something.

India made me ruminate — and wasn't that what The Shaman intended? What, indeed, the Golden Flame demanded? Not tourism but transformation — a transactional grappling with Otherness. It had been easy enough, rambling around the Mediterranean, to forget this and bog down in superficial experience. But in India? Somebody should hang a sign at every airport and border crossing: "Indifference not an option, all ye who enter here."

Those visitors who dislike India, I decided then, and still believe, are those who can't get beyond the material poverty — and poverty there is, poverty enough to break your heart. Travellers who love the subcontinent are those who look through that to the people — not just their warmth and hospitality, but the courage they display, so many of them, in fighting on though they stand with their backs to the abyss.

At that I stopped and wondered: where now the hard-nosed journalist who'd left San Francisco? The Golden Flame was changing me — though I didn't know yet precisely where this fiery quest was taking me. I thought of our favorite auto-rickshaw driver and how we would emerge from the Bombay Jack and find him waiting with six or eight other "rickshawmen," standing amongst their motorized three-wheelers beyond a makeshift fence that separated them from the princely cabbies who charged three or four times their rates.

This rickshawman, a turban-wearing Sikh, had taken a Bachelor of Arts degree from a university here in New Delhi: "Even so, I could not get a job. So, I have started driving rickshaw."

He'd cocked an ear one afternoon when Safiya got talking about the caste system. We'd just emerged from the Bank of Baroda where, to change American dollars into rupees, we'd stood sweltering in a small room for forty minutes. As we careered through the streets in the back seat of the rickshaw, Safiya reminded me of how, in downtown Colombo, she'd gone to the Hong Kong bank, inserted her Canadian client card and presto! out popped Sri Lankan rupees: "Welcome to the global village."

Here in New Delhi, the automatic teller machines had rejected her card and so ordained our visit to the Bank of Baroda, where three different men got involved in the money-changing. One fellow took Safiya's visa and stamped it. He carried it to a man at a second counter, who made Safiya sign a form. This second man brought both visa and form to a man in a glass cage, who sent out the money with yet another clerk.

"The system's a product of over-population," Safiya said. "Each worker does a very specific job. That's the genius of the caste system."

"The what did you say?"

"Okay, it has drawbacks. But so many people need employment

that the system has to subdivide the work. Have you looked around the lobby at the Bombay Jack? Not one desk clerk, but five. Not one bellman, but seven. Same at any restaurant. Never one or two waiters but half a dozen."

"Somewhat lacking in efficiency, no?"

"The needs of the people take priority. Here in India, except in upper-class enclaves, this Western notion of slashing jobs for the sake of efficiency would inspire incredulity and charges of madness. Why destroy your own economy?"

"Very good question, madam," the rickshawman pronounced over his shoulder.

I said: "You come into your own when Taggart's not around." Then, realizing I'd crossed an invisible line, I offered: "India makes us all ruminate."

Originally, in visiting the subcontinent, I'd planned to fly into New Delhi, take a train to Agra and go straight to the Taj Mahal. There I'd meet Behroze and demand answers: what purpose did this mandated rambling serve, besides exposing me to constant danger? Why didn't she do something about the Chinvat hooligans hounding us?

Somehow, with Daniel's enthusiastic support, Safiya had turned this bee-line approach into a circle-tour of Rajasthan, land of the maharajahs. We'd spend a couple of days in New Delhi, then fly to Udaipur and stay at the Lake Palace Hotel, a palatial edifice that had served as the setting for an early James Bond movie. Then we'd travel by car to Jaipur and Agra, where we'd visit the Taj (and I'd see Behroze).

In this amendment, on reflection, I discovered wisdom. It gave me four cities in which to gather mementoes, two of which would qualify as magical: Udaipur, with the legendary Lake Palace Hotel, and Agra with the Taj Mahal. Even so, when Safiya and Daniel started investigating low-end accommodation, I began to worry. In Rajasthan, a visitor can sleep dorm-style for pennies a night. It's also possible to stay at nothing but five-star hotels, or to hook up with a tour group of twenty people and cruise around in an air-conditioned bus. To me, neither extreme appealed.

My travelling companions, having decided to splurge on the Lake Palace, had wanted to go down-market in New Delhi, maybe stay at Nirula's Hotel, which caters to twenty-something Westerners. I'd travelled "rough" in my own twenties and didn't feel like doing it again, not here and now, when I needed all my physical and mental resources, so I swallowed hard: "Listen, I'll pay the difference."

That's how we ended up at the Bombay Jack, a four-star high-rise frequented by commercial salesmen, cut-rate tour goups and serious travellers in their thirties and forties. The Bombay Jack boasts a modest outdoor pool and a decent restaurant. We'd scarcely arrived and scoped out the bustling lobby, the five desk clerks and seven bellhops, when India delivered its first jolt.

During check-in, one of the desk clerks asked to see our documents. Safiya and I complied but Daniel couldn't find his passport. No immediate problem. The senior desk clerk told him to produce it later. Upstairs, in the double room he shared with Safiya, Daniel searched his luggage. No passport. Safiya glanced at me and smiled grimly: "Shades of your fabulous green bag."

None of us could think straight. Flying is never easy, and we'd endured an especially gruelling and roundabout trip from Sri Lanka. Seventy-two hours before departure, we'd confirmed our seats by telephone, as directed. Yes, yes, everything was fine: three seats confirmed to New Delhi.

Four hours before our late-night flight, we checked out of the Hotel Renuka and took a cab to the airport. We arrived three hours before take-off and stood in line for twenty minutes, nothing too onerous. We got our passports stamped, cleared emigration and made for the Air Lanka counter. There, to our dismay, we found a crowd of disgruntled ticket-wavers.

We'd all heard horror stories about how airlines overbook flights in this part of the world. Apparently, it makes economic sense to ensure that paying passengers occupy every seat, even if the airline ends up booking disgruntled left-behinds into first-class hotels. Trouble was, we all three shared an unshakable North American optimism: What could go wrong? We'd paid several hundred dollars for plane tickets to New Delhi and simply didn't believe that The Worst could happen, not to us.

Daniel chatted with a distracted Dutchman. He'd bought a

special-fare ticket and already Air Lanka had bumped him: "Can you believe this? I'm a tour guide. We're travelling to Nepal. Half my group has already boarded the plane. The rest of us are still here. I'm the leader."

Even so, we waited. The senior ticket agent talked to someone on the telephone. Then he waved a group of seven through the gate. He picked up a loudspeaker and urged all remaining passengers to chat with an Air Lanka representative. Half a dozen people trundled dutifully to the counter. We waited with half a dozen more. The agent kept returning to the telephone. We kept hoping he'd find three seats.

In fact, he did. He gave them to a couple with a baby, the husband waving an official-looking piece of paper, and to a young man heading off to New Delhi to attend university. As this youth walked away down the corridor towards the plane, he glanced over his shoulder. We locked eyes and whap! I realized that, on some level, he served the Golden Flame.

The plane left without us. Daniel and Safiya couldn't believe it.

"The Shaman had a hand in this," I said.

"It's just a snafu," Safiya said. "Why would The Shaman get active?"

"To teach us a lesson? To make the quest tougher? I don't know why."

Safiya grinned at me: "Where now the skeptical journalist?"

Doggedly, I said: "I don't know why, I just know that."

At the counter, Air Lanka representatives laid out our new itnerary. For tonight, what remained of it, the airline would put us up at the five-star Oberoi back in Colombo, twenty miles distant. Tomorrow morning, early, they'd send a car to return us to the airport. Then they'd put us on a flight to Madras.

Safiya said: "But that's on the wrong side of India."

In Madras, Air Lanka officials would whisk us to another fine hotel, as yet unspecified. Late that afternoon, we'd fly Indian Airlines from Madras to New Delhi. Any questions?

As Safiya and I climbed, sullen and silent, into a taxi for the drive back into Colombo, Daniel said: "So we spend another night in Sri Lanka. It adds texture to the adventure. Besides: *Amnyimae punda adesi, kampunguzia mashuzi.*"

Safiya said, "Okay, we give up."

"He who withholds lentils from a donkey reduces his passing of wind."

Neither of us could find a suitable response.

Now, having finally arrived at the Bombay Jack Hotel in New Delhi, we decided to worry later about Daniel's missing passport. I went to my room and fell into bed.

Next morning, Daniel phoned the Canadian High Commission and they confirmed his worst fears: To leave the country, he needed that document. If he didn't recover the original, he'd have to get a new one — and that meant red tape and hassle. He could start by getting someone to fax his birth certificate from Canada, and he'd finish by laying out hundreds of dollars he didn't have.

He told me all this at breakfast. He'd ransacked his luggage. He'd telephoned Indian Airlines and lost-luggage at both airports: nothing. He'd called the Trident Hotel in Madras, where we'd stayed for three hours: also nothing. If he'd dropped the passport somewhere, then for sure it was gone.

Safiya said: "Chinvat?"

"I don't think so." Daniel shook his head sadly. "What would they gain?"

I said, "Maybe you left it at that money-changer's office?"

I meant in Madras: a hole-in-the-wall outfit. We hadn't taken the name, and Daniel had tossed away his receipt. He would have to remain in Delhi and get a new passport. Safiya and I could go on ahead to Udaipur.

I said: "That money-changer's had a name."

"What difference does it make?" Daniel said, more frustrated than I'd seen him. "If I left the passport there, do you think they'd admit it? Probably I lost it at the airport."

Safiya said, "Bernie?"

"Give me a minute." I rested my elbows on the table, buried my face in my hands and — how best to describe this? — ventured deeper into reality. Starting in Colombo, I replayed our journey. Air Lanka bumped us and we spent the tag end of the night at the Hotel Oberoi. We rose at four in the morning, made our way downstairs and piled into a waiting taxi for the return trip to the airport. Departed on schedule.

In Madras, we spent more than an hour hunting the Air Lanka

manager. Eventually, he provided us with a voucher for the Trident Hotel. Our connecting flight didn't leave until late in the day. We ate lunch and, knowing the city would shut down during the hottest part of the day, splashed around in the pool. Safiya suggested we venture out into Madras to purchase fire-worthy souvenirs. As well, Daniel's travelling bag had lost its handle en route from Colombo, and here he could buy a new one.

Safiya checked with the Bell Captain, an Anglo-Indian who sounded like he'd grown up in London, though he claimed he'd never left India. If we departed right away, he said, we would have just enough time to visit the Tip Top Shopping Mall, where we'd find both jewelry and luggage.

The Bell Captain summoned a rickshawman and, in what looked like hard bargaining, negotiated a round-trip fare of one hundred and fifty rupees, roughly five dollars American. Climbing into the rickshaw, I caught the driver's eye and felt such a wave of hostility that I almost didn't board. A quick scan turned up not Chinvat, exactly — but something affiliated. Safiya said, "Times a wastin'" and hauled me aboard.

Ten minutes down the road, the driver pulled into a gas station. He spoke no English but communicated that he needed fifty rupees for gas. None of us had any small bills and Daniel handed him a one-hundred rupee note — two-thirds of the round-trip fare. The driver filled the tank and pocketed the change. He then proceeded to the Tip Top Mall, took twenty minutes, where three or four auto-rickshaws sat out front. Yes, yes, the driver would wait, no problem.

I continued to feel uneasy. The Bell Captain had negotiated hard on our behalf, maybe too hard — though I felt that wasn't the problem. I kept "feeling" almost-Chinvat but couldn't pin it down. In any case, we had no time to waste. The mall proved circular, a bustling, two-storey affair. Daniel spotted a money-changer's office and deked into it to trade American dollars for rupees. Safiya went hunting for jewelry and spotted luggage.

Daniel emerged with rupees and bought a suitable bag while Safiya and I failed to locate a souvenir shop. Pressed for time, we abandoned the search, rushed back outside — and found that our rickshawman had disappeared. Few of the other drivers spoke English, and disaster threatened: if we didn't get to the airport on time, what then? We'd miss our flight and our plans would be thrown into disarray. Fortunately, Safiya managed to find a driver who recognized the name "Trident Hotel." She convinced him to take us by meter. When we arrived, it read thirty rupees and I slipped him one hundred.

This sortie had taken longer than expected and immediately we left for the airport. We arrived to hear Indian Airlines loading our flight. We'd received tickets and boarding passes in Colombo and nobody asked to see our passports. After all, we weren't leaving the country, but merely flying from one side to the other.

Now, in the restaurant at the Bombay Jack, I said: "In Madras, nobody asked to see our passports."

"*Mfa maji hukamata maji*," Daniel said. "A drowning man catches at the water."

Still with my face in my hands, I revisited the Tip Top Shopping Mall and replayed our arrival: "That money-changer's office? It's called LKP Merchant Financing."

I opened my eyes.

Daniel stared at me strangely and Safiya patted his arm: "Let's make a phone call."

With the help of the hotel operator, Daniel phoned LKP Merchant Financing in Madras. He got the manager on the line and said: "This will sound crazy, but I've lost my passport and I'm wondering if I left it there?"

He paused, then said. "No, I'm Canadian." Again a pause: "Daniel Lafontaine."

The manager had the passport on his desk. In his rush to change money and buy a bag before the rickshaw disappeared, Daniel had left it on the counter. Now, he offered to pay to have it shipped — but the manager insisted on shipping it for free. LKP Merchant Financing had an office in New Delhi, just off Connaught Place, and Daniel would be able to pick up his passport there. Not tomorrow, because today's mail had already left. Not tomorrow, but the next day.

Almost immediately, I had second thoughts. If I'd minded my own business and just forgot the missing passport, Daniel would have ended up battling red tape in Delhi — but Safiya might have come alone with me to Rajasthan.

I was still mentally kicking myself that evening when events revealed this self-deception for what it was. We'd decided to celebrate the imminent return of the missing passport by dining at the Gaylord Restaurant, where you find waiters in maroon jackets, sixteen-foot ceilings and mirrors built into walls. Through a pane of yellowed glass we watched a white-hatted chef make kebabs. We'd had to extend our stay in New Delhi by a day and a half, but Safiya had changed our tickets and reservations and we dug into our spicy meals with gusto.

Later, Safiya likened the surprise to a twist in a Paul Auster novel, while Daniel shook his head over "the Yin-Yang contingency of events." If he hadn't misplaced his passport in Madras, we would at that moment have been winging our way towards Udaipur and the Lake Palace Hotel. Nobody could have caught us until Jaipur, and who knows how events might have unfolded?

As it happened, I'd proposed a toast in the Gaylord and we were drinking to the character of the Indian people when I looked up and saw a top-hatted man walk past the window. No! It couldn't be. But yes, of course, it was: Taggart Oates in full regalia — top hat, black T-shirt, red sneakers. He spotted us immediately, waved off the maitre d' and crossed the restaurant grinning: "Hey, everybody! Surprise!"

Trial By Fire

The quest had become a trial by fire, as I've noted. Yet now the fire intensified, certainly for we three males. Bound by mutual need, tormented by jealousies, we agonized each in his own way. One night Daniel recounted the death of Victor, not knowing I'd witnessed the entire tragedy. He described his friend's insistence on taunting The Shaman, how he'd plunged into the ocean and never come back. But he said nothing about the Chinvat yacht. Nothing about three shots ringing out. Nothing about a wizened old prophet accosting him. Had that part really happened? I let it go. Daniel had learned, because Safiya had told him, that three ashavans must set forth together. As for Victor's death, he said: "I can't stop blaming myself."

I thought of Behroze: "I know how you feel."

Next night, I listened while Taggart fretted over what would happen when he approached the Chinvat Bridge. The Avestan scriptures said nothing about an overture by the living. They described how, three days after you die, you meet an embodiment of your conscience at the Bridge of Judgment, which spans the abyss of hell. The worthy soul, in whom right actions outweigh wrong ones, encounters a beautiful maiden who leads him across the bridge to paradise. The unworthy soul confronts the evil Vizaresha in the shape of a foul-smelling hag.

"A crew of devils tries to drag you to the Seat of Judgment," Taggart said, sipping dry red wine. "But let's say you elude them. You race onto the Bridge. Know what happens then? The bridge narrows to a razor-sharp edge. Or else flips onto its side. Either way, you plunge into the abyss — the abyss of hell."

"You speak metaphorically."

"What's metaphorical here, in mundane reality, happens all too literally in some other dimension. And hell's hell either way."

"You're scared to death, aren't you?"

Taggart sipped his wine. "At the Chinvat Bridge, any approach by a living person might be considered premature, disrepectful. Events could turn nasty. Does that scare me? Bloody right!"

As for me, in addition to my usual anxieties and torments, I felt haunted by two sets of images. First, Safiya had told me more about Vasco de Gama, the celebrated Portuguese explorer. Five hundred years before — halfway through the millennium — he became the first European to reach India by ship. De Gama put an end to an Arabian trading empire, and indeed to a way of life, that had lasted more than eight hundred years. And fair enough, I thought. Yet the way he did it sickened me — as it would any civilized being.

Not content with demonstrating his vastly superior fire-power, the product of European technology, De Gama had sailed around the Indian Ocean committing one atrocity after another. In the coastal city of Calicut, a flourishing port not far to the southwest of Udaipur, the European flag-bearer had decided to teach the ruling Zamorin a lesson. He began by seizing eight hundred prisoners and cutting off their hands, ears and noses. From there he descended into depravity. De Gama's nightmare-inducing barbarism represented Ahriman at his most hellish, his most hateful — Ahriman beyond words.

Second, more personally, more selfishly, more trivially, I couldn't stop chastising myself for what might have been. I kept returning to the moment when I learned that Daniel had lost his passport. Instead of keeping my mouth shut, I'd grandstanded as Mister Nice Guy and helped him retrieve it. What if I'd done nothing? Taggart would have missed us in Delhi. I might have ended up rambling around Rajasthan with Safiya, just the two of us, gathering fire-worthy souvenirs. Instead, I found myself bearing witness to a far less pleasant scenario — one featuring images of the woman I adored making passionate love with two other men. This was another kind of horror, another kind of hell — negligible, perhaps, when set against the onslaught of European colonialism in the lands encircling the Indian Ocean, yet terrible enough on a personal level.

But who knows? Maybe I needed that deep-rooted awareness of the relative insignificance of my suffering? Maybe I needed that particular juxtaposition? Consciously, I kept going for the sake of Colette. And because I could do nothing else and survive. The Golden Flame burned within me. Eventually, Safiya and I would approach The Shaman. How, I didn't know. We'd cross the Chinvat Bridge when we came to it. But to get that far, we'd need at least one of our two fellow ashavans. "It's a torture test, Bernie," Safiya said in the wilds of northern India. "An emotional torture test that reflects the metaphysical quest."

A trial by fire, then. But let's take it from the Gaylord Restaurant and the surprise arrival of Taggart Oates. He'd expected to catch us at the Taj Mahal and overtook us in New Delhi only because we'd been delayed by Daniel's missing passport. Taggart had checked into the Bombay Jack and inquired, just in case. A helpful bellhop had sent him to the Gaylord. He couldn't believe his luck, and later wondered whether the Golden Flame hadn't worked some magic on his behalf.

Judging from their faces, neither Daniel nor Safiya shared his enthusiasm. Originally, Taggart had taken a miss on this expedition because of his writer-in-residency. But three hours after we departed Sri Lanka, insurgents had fire-bombed the building in which Taggart had been scheduled to lead workshops. His commitments postponed, he contrived to fly north on short notice: "Mazda works in wondrous ways."

Daniel muttered: "Sounds more like Ahriman to me."

Taggart rubbed his hands gleefully: "I hope this means we can start immediately."

"Start what?" I said.

"Not you, old boy." He pointed around the table. "We three."

We'd returned to the three-way marriage scenario. As we travelled around India, Safiya would sleep one night with Daniel, the next with Taggart. Back and forth she'd shuttle. As I pieced this together from the ensuing conversation, I wondered: has Taggart gone crazy? And answered: Yes, crazy like a fox. Oh, but he understood hubris and how to exploit it.

Creative artists are pioneers, don't you know? Writers, musicians: the normal rules don't apply. What the non-artist wouldn't even attempt, these three avant-gardists would go out and achieve. These trailblazers, these Golden Flame Overpeople could make of themselves whatever they wished. They would rise above mundane jealousies to create "a relationship template for the new millennium." Nothing could stop them. Taggart gestured magnanimously: "Lanigan, here, will be our witness."

Easy enough to see what drove Taggart: He couldn't bear the thought of losing Safiya. She played along because in Greece, for my sake, she'd promised. She couldn't back out now without breaking her word, a "wrong action" that might jeopardize her survival at the Chinvat Bridge. More mundanely, she feared Taggart's instability. If she insisted on sleeping only with Daniel, the Englishman might do something drastic. Secretly, she feared he might kill himself.

As for Daniel, Victor's death — or perhaps something darker? — had plunged him into Eastern fatalism. He subscribed to the Golden Flame, yet clung to the notions of karma and reincarnation, and vowed to resolve in this life all the contradictions remaining from his last. Probably jealousy was one of them. Certainly, now that he'd arrived in the Empire of the Spirit, he'd be watching for signs and synchronicities.

At the Gaylord, when I asked him point blank what he thought of Taggart's scenario, he shrugged. "*Mbio za sakafuni huishia ukingoni*," he said. "Running on a roof finishes at the edge."

Away we went to Rajasthan, land of the Maharajahs.

I've mentioned the Lake Palace Hotel, a sparkling white, two-storey edifice that emerges out of the middle of a huge man-made lake. Its effusion of arches and cupolas, turrets and crenellations, suggest nothing so much as Tales of the Arabian Nights. Once the summer home of the Maharana of Udaipur, the well-foundationed Lake Palace looks like it floats on water.

A motor launch delivers visitors to a hotel dock, where uniformed doormen take your bags. You follow them inside and try not to gape at the splendour: marble floors, crenelated columns, courtyards and gardens open to the sky, lavishly decorated rooms and a sizeable swimming pool surrounded by ornate arches that frame charming views of the encompassing lake. From the front of the hotel, looking out through still more arches, you can marvel at the massive City Palace complex that looms over the lake like the impregnable fort it once was. Today it contains a museum, a five-star hotel, several fine restaurants and the permanent residence of the Maharana and his family. . . .

Back in New Delhi, Taggart had phoned book-industry acquaintances, made promises and threats and turned up a plane ticket to Udaipur on the very flight we'd already booked. As we drove into Udaipur from the airport, rattling and banging along the national highway, we saw hundreds of workers — both sexes, all ages — swarming over great piles of stone. The cabbie said they were sorting: hand-sized rocks, middle-sized stones, semi-boulders. Other workers carried tools along the road — shovels and hoes and sledge hammers.

Welcome to Rajasthan. Cows sprawled in the middle of the highway chewing cud while traffic streamed past on both sides. Two yoked oxen hauled a load of rocks. A camel pulled a flat-top cart piled high with slabs of marble. Scooters and bicycles veered around gaudily painted trucks, many of which sported colourful signs with strange lettering. This wasn't Arabic but Hindi, though it was equally indecipherable. "The advantage here," Safiya noted, "is that English is present, too. And not just in the signs."

Like me, even before me, Safiya drew comparisons with Al-Mayadin. In some ways, that Middle Eastern city was less a hybrid than any Indian one: here, as a legacy of British colonialism, so many people spoke English. Why was Al-Mayadin a no-man's-land, Udaipur not? Safiya pin-pointed religion: in the Middle East, the hard edges of Islam clashed with those of other faiths, notably Christianity: "But the Empire of the Spirit accommodates all gods and prophets."

For Daniel, who looked out at India through the lens of East Africa, the heat and material poverty proved familiar. Likewise, the hard-working people and the shops that lined the roads. "Difference is, you can see the history," he said later, as a guide showed us around the City Palace. "People live amidst the ruins of another age, and not in the shadow of an encroaching jungle."

This was no time to elaborate, however, because we found ourselves surrounded by ancient splendour. Built in the sixteenth century, and occupied successively by twenty-four generations of the same family, the City Palace is a labyrinth of galleries decorated with inlaid mirrors and sculptures, frescoes and wall-paintings. We spent an hour wandering, and then a guide led us through the nearby Garden of the Maids of Honour, built early in the eighteenth century. Safiya sniffed: "Maids of Honour, indeed." We explored five different gardens, each with a distinctive vegetation and atmosphere, a unique fountain, and Safiya fell in love with Slow Rain in the Forest.

Emerging from the gardens, and acting on impulse, we hired two auto-rickshaws to drive the four of us around the hilly streets of Udaipur. We discovered those streets, too narrow for cars, to be lined with one-room hovels housing families of six and seven. We couldn't help contrasting this with the magnificence we'd just explored, and also with the Lake Palace, where we ourselves were staying. Even Taggart, who rode with me, fell silent.

On our way back to the boat launch, Safiya spotted a puppet show under a canvas awning. She insisted on stopping, but the performance ended as we arrived, and Daniel wondered if we'd missed more than we realized — some cosmic communication, perhaps. Behind the stage, Safiya discovered women making tie-die shirts and men decorating copper pots and plates — a whole world of stalls. She found puppet-makers dressing their creations in colourful clothes. Finally, she located an old woman selling handmade jewelry. Both Taggart and Daniel had long since exceeded their souvenir quotas, but like me, they bought stone-laden bracelets. Safiya turned up an Egyptian ankh and exclaimed: "Symbol of eternal life!"

As she spoke, the setting sun turned the sky a thousand different hues, and for an instant, from where I stood, Safiya wore a golden halo. For the first time I perceived her not just as the embodiment of the gifted, intelligent and sensual female, but as primarily a spiritual being. And I surmised that, like me, Safiya was changing in the Golden Flame — becoming not less earthy but more ethereal.

With that thought, I felt a tingling at the back of my neck. I whirled just in time to avoid having my head split open, as a costumed man delivered a savage blow with a two-foot length of pipe. The pipe glanced off my shoulder, numbing my left arm. The man aimed another blow at my head and in avoiding it I stumbled and fell to the ground. This was no costumed man, I realized, and no ordinary Chinvat. This was Vasco De Gama, a warrior prince — and he was bent on killing me. I lunged to one side as De Gama narrowly missed me with a third smashing blow, and with that Daniel and Safiya tackled him simultaneously, knocking him to the ground.

Daniel landed two vicious punches to the face and Safiya a kick to the groin that would have incapacitated any normal man. De Gama cursed and rolled to his feet, looking around for his length of pipe. Now Taggart joined the fray, swinging the pipe at the intruder like a baseball bat. De Gama caught the pipe with both hands and ripped it out of Taggart's grip. By now I'd regained my feet and, even though my left arm was useless, for De Gama I made a raging fourth opponent. Against three, he would have fought on. But against four such as these? No. He wheeled and disappeared into the bazaar, leaving the four of us to treat our wounds and make of his attack what sense we could — which wasn't much.

As we made our way by launch back to the Lake Palace Hotel, I slowly regained feeling in my left arm. Safiya attributed my healing to the Golden Flame, and Taggart said the whole experience reminded him of Antaeus, the Greek figure who, thrown to the ground by a stronger foe, would draw strength from the earth and rise up stronger and fiercer than before: "As a group, we've gained strength from that confrontation," he said — and none of us felt inclined to contradict him. Not openly.

Still, Udaipur no longer felt like a haven. The Chinvat had found us. The unpredictability of their assaults and methods —

that's what I found demoralizing, debilitating. Their attacks showed no pattern. Either none existed, or randomness itself formed part of the plan. Bottom line? We'd booked two nights and did not intend to be driven out early. We'd carry on regardless — but watchfully.

That evening, after freshening up in our rooms, we recrossed the lake to the City Palace. Three of us enjoyed a spicy dinner while Taggart, suffering a mild case of Delhi-Belly, stuck mainly to rice. Afterwards, we sat sipping wine in a bar with a view. As we looked out at the Lake Palace and the almost-full moon shining soft in the night sky and revealing dark hills in the distance, I realized that we'd arrived at another of the most romantic spots in the world. Oh, what wouldn't I have given to be sitting here alone with Safiya?

Originally, she'd reserved two double rooms — one for me, another for her and Daniel. Taggart's arrival had complicated matters, but not impossibly because both double rooms boasted two single beds. Taggart changed the number of guests from three to four and claimed the reservations clerk had made a mistake. That night, he bunked in with me and Daniel stayed with Safiya. The next, Taggart joined Safiya and Daniel stayed with me.

If the staff noticed anything odd about these musical beds, they pretended they didn't. And I'd resolved to let nothing faze me. The quest demanded no less. When I felt my self-control weaken, I'd swim in the pool or read and drink tea in the courtyard. With Vasco De Gama loose in Udaipur, we all stayed close to home. Each morning, I awoke expecting one of the others to snap. It didn't happen. The Lake Palace worked magic enough, I decided, to postpone the crisis I felt had to come.

The pink city of Jaipur lay far enough away that we flew. Taggart insisted that we stay at the Rambagh Palace, sister hotel to the Lake Palace. We'd originally booked far humbler accommodations, but he juggled reservations and picked up the tab. Called it his atonement for upsetting our plans. Even so, the gesture surprised me. I'd pegged Taggart for a tightwad. Was he trying to demonstrate that questing with him brought benefits?

In Jaipur, we saw no sign of Chinvat. We visited the Palace of the Winds, that famous five-storey pink facade with honey-combed windows that long ago enabled women of the maharaja's harem to look out over the city while remaining modestly hidden. And we visited Amber Fort, where Safiya insisted we celebrate the purchase of three metal keepsakes — the sun-god Surya, the fire-god Agni and Nataraja, lord of the dance — by taking an elephant ride.

As we wobbled slowly uphill, a tout trotted alongside and badgered me to buy an eighteen-inch puppet. I spent most of the ride haggling as we tossed the doll back and forth. Safiya found this puppet-tossing hilarious. She threw back her head and laughed, all tumbling black hair and sparking white teeth, and what could I do? I bought the puppet and made her accept it as a gift.

The Rambagh Palace proved to be a walled-estate in the heart of Jaipur, its grounds dotted with well-kept trees and shrubs. Women swept pools of water from courtyards and three men worked with two bullocks and a plow-like mower to cut grass. We'd arrived during monsoon season and, in the sunken outdoor pool, the water spilled over onto the ground.

The setting was magical — but brought more musical beds. I tried not to think about Safiya with Taggart, Safiya with Daniel, but felt so jealous, wounded and sick at heart that I wondered whether I could keep going. Swimming in the pool late one afternoon, a strategic withdrawal, and with a light rain falling, I listened to the sounds of the city, of traffic and voices beyond the walls, and found myself contemplating perspective.

Early that day, before the heat built up, Daniel and I had gone walking. We'd brought plenty of coins and believed ourselves ready to face the worst India could offer — yet now, in the pool, two encounters came back. I remembered a ragged youth on crutches, one of his legs amputated above the knee, who pounded along beside us for half a block, demanding more coins; and then a legless women on a cart, who paddled directly at us, shrieking, enraged, who knows why, and who suddenly flung back the cloth covering her lap to expose hideously amputated limbs.

Floating now on my back, I heard the laughter of children and imagined a boy peering through a chink in the wall. What would he see? A fabulously wealthy white man enjoying an existence so privileged as to be almost beyond imagining. He would never guess that I might be struggling for psychic survival, that I might, for example, have a daughter his age lying back home in a coma. Or that here I might be bearing tormented witness to a horrible three-ring circus as the woman I loved shuffled between two other men and — no, don't think about it.

Next stop, Agra and the Taj Mahal. Behroze would bring not just advice but eye-witness news of Colette. Given that, and the material desperation of the legions beyond these walls, what did it matter, who slept with Safiya tonight? So I consoled myself, and turned to my preparedness. Sixteen fire-worthy souvenirs we required, among them seven from magic places. Counting Mesa Verde, my totals stood at fourteen and five. But Agra, home of the Taj, would certainly qualify as magical, and so would Dar es Salaam, celebrated "Haven of Peace."

Now enter contingency — or did the Shaman himself, acting in the Golden Flame, decree that the physical quest should become more difficult, less predictable, as we neared our objective, and so mirror the emotional situation? Before I'd left San Francisco, well-meaning "India hands" had advised me to avoid the subcontinent during monsoon season. I couldn't choose my schedule and so ignored their advice.

In retrospect, I wonder: were they right? Safiya suggested, as we thumped and banged along a dirt road in the pouring rain, that monsoon is to India as winter is to Canada. In its presence, daily life becomes difficult, surface travel impossible: goodbye roads, hello floating cowsheds. On the other hand, does a traveller experience Canada if she doesn't confront winter?

The night before we left Jaipur, heavy monsoon rains flooded the city. When our driver, a handsome man named Govinder Singh, collected us at the Rambaugh Palace, he said water had reached the top step at Nero's restaurant, where he'd dropped us just yesterday for lunch. And the bookstore next door? Where Safiya had bought a guide to Hindi? "That is flooded completely."

On the outskirts of Jaipur, at a traffic circle, a police officer stood directing vehicles off the main highway. Govinder rolled down his window and exchanged words with the man. Heavy rains had washed out the road ahead. We'd have to take this secondary artery, then double back. Amidst angrily honking horns, we followed cars and buses and trucks along a potholed two-lane highway. Shops and houses lined the road. Mothers and children sat out front, watching the honking parade. We'd crawl forward one hundred yards, then stop. Govinder would jump out and stand on the running board to see what he could see: never anything of significance.

Taggart dubbed the traffic jam "Kafkaesque." We'd travelled for an hour and covered maybe two miles when three tourist cars, white Ambassadors like our own, came rumbling towards us on the quiet side of the road. Govinder flagged the third and, through open windows, exchanged words with the driver. "Can't get through up ahead," he said, pulling a U-turn. "The driver in front knows a shortcut."

We caught the other Ambassadors and whipped along at thirty miles an hour. I sat in front, stoically enduring the rough ride, while my three companions, wedged into the back, muttered darkly among themselves that we should rotate positions. I ignored them. A fifth vehicle, a tourist van, had joined the chase by the time we swung left onto a red-dirt road. This one-laner ran along beside railroad tracks. Rain had begun lightly falling, which reduced visibility, but Govinder used the wipers sparingly. He didn't want to run down the battery. Daniel wondered where we were, and Govinder cheerfully admitted he had no idea.

"We're lost in the wilds of northern India," Taggart said. "It's monsoon season. Rain's pounding down. What more do you need to know?"

Safiya said: "Did you drink your coffee this morning?"

The three cars ahead slowed to a stop. We pulled up behind them. Govinder jumped out and talked with the other drivers. When he returned, he said water had washed out the road ahead: "We're going to try it anyway."

Behind us, surprisingly late, the white van arrived. Safiya said: "Look! No windshield."

Sure enough, the front of the van lay open to the elements. The turbaned driver and three Europeans stood outside, conferring in what had become a steady drizzle. Daniel hopped out and walked back to visit. When he returned, he said that just before the vehicle had turned off onto the dirt road, a truck had knocked a stone up onto the windscreen and shattered it: "A freak accident."

"They can't drive in this weather," Safiya said. "Not without a windshield."

Govinder said: "Probably they'll return to Jaipur."

We watched the Ambassador immediately in front of us navigate a small lake. It regained the muddy road thirty yards ahead. Govinder revved our engine and popped the clutch. Away we went. The water rose to the bottom of the car but we churned steadily forward. Halfway across, suddenly, the engine coughed and died.

There we sat, islanded. Govinder rolled his eyes skyward.

"Water, water everywhere," Safiya said. "And not a fire at which to warm our hands."

Govinder removed his shoes and socks, puzzling and transfixing all of us. He rolled up his pantlegs and whipped a rag from under his seat. Then he stepped out into the rain, opened the hood and disappeared beneath it. After a moment, he jumped back into the car. Still in his bare feet, he turned the key and yes! the engine caught and chugged to life. We completed the crossing.

The other three drivers, who'd stood waiting, waved and drove off. Behind us, on the other side of the road-swallowing lake, the van's passengers stood in the rain, obviously still debating what to do. Govinder pulled on his shoes and socks, got back behind the wheel and resumed bouncing the Ambassador along the red-dirt road. We hadn't travelled another half-mile when a cow sauntered into the track. Govinder swerved to avoid it and thunk! the car pitched sideways and slammed to a halt.

Govinder jumped out and the rest of us followed. In turning to avoid the cow, he'd steered into a cement culvert that lay hidden at road's edge. For the first time today, he looked seriously concerned. The car's right front wheel dangled uselessly in the open part of the culvert. The other three Amabassadors had long since disappeared. Behind us, no sign of the van. We were alone and badly stuck.

Taggart began swearing.

Daniel said: "At least the rain's letting up."

Safiya pointed: "Look!"

A dozen people approached along the raised train tracks.

Govinder said: "Must be a village on the other side of the ridge."

I counted fifteen people, then twenty: old men, middle-aged women, children and even a few thin teenagers. The villagers surrounded the car. Govinder tried three different languages, elicited nothing but baffled grins.

Daniel stepped forward: "This is like getting stuck in a blizzard."

Using gestures and sign language, he positioned eight or nine males around the car, including Govinder and me. Taggart watched intently — not unwilling to help but awkward and uncertain. Daniel cried, "Now!" Everybody understood. Together, and without difficulty, we hoisted the Ambassador out of the culvert and back onto the muddy road.

Govinder jumped into the vehicle and gunned it. He skidded forward through a rough stream. Taggart, Daniel and I followed along a spit of land, but now Safiya stood stranded on the wrong side of an ankle-deep stream. Sharp pebbles made bare feet impossible and she'd worn her best travelling shoes.

As she stood weighing options, Daniel waded over in his soaking-wet sneakers. He presented his back and told Safiya to climb aboard. Laughing, she complied. Daniel picked his way gingerly across the stream. Halfway, knowing he had an audience, he pretended to lose his balance. The villagers roared with laughter. When Daniel finished, they broke into applause. To Taggart I said: "This is it — the real India."

"You think so?" As he moved towards the car, he spoke with unusual feeling: "This backroads misadventure is no more real than haggling over carpet prices or whirling around Delhi in a rickshaw."

"Surely it exemplifies India's unpredictability?" I responded. "Anyway, I hope you've been paying attention. Never know what The Shaman will ask at the Chinvat Bridge."

Taggart scowled and climbed into the car.

Daniel, overhearing this exchange as he approached, offered a proverb: "*Usicheze na simba, ukamtia mkono kinywani.*" Then he translated: "When you play with a lion, Bernard, do not put your hand in its mouth."

Before we left India, I would fervently wish I'd listened.

Trouble at the Taj Mahal

Photos don't do justice to the Taj Mahal. In reality, the monument overwhelms: so beautiful, so huge, so incongruous. In a land of macho, fiery-red forts, suddenly, on the banks of a winding river, you confront this delicate, white-marble ode to ever-lasting love. Up close, you discover the attention to detail, the superhuman intricacy. If you've visited the Taj, you've experienced the magic. If you haven't, think unforgettable.

In responding to the stories that the Taj has inspired, people reveal who they are. Going in, Safiya and I knew that the monument celebrates the perfect love of Emperor Shah Jahan for his wife, Mumtaz Mahal. On details, we were vague. Oh, but we were eager to learn — to learn and to empathize and, above all, for the sake of our meeting with The Shaman, above all to remember.

On arriving at the Taj, we gleaned that early in the seventeenth century, Mumtaz bore thirteen children and died giving birth to a fourteenth. She'd foreseen her own death and made Shah Jahan promise to build over her dead body "such a beautiful tomb as the world has never seen."

Now comes the twist. Having created this fabulous mausoleum — eighteen years, he devoted — Shah Jahan lost his kingdom to one of his sons, who imprisoned him in the so-called Red Fort. From there, he could see the monument he'd built only by reflection. More specifically, by peering into a tiny mirror. "Don't you just love it?" Safiya said. "You get this image of the once-mighty emperor confined to a fetid cell, holding up a mirror so he can see his masterpiece through a barred window high overhead."

This she said later, while rambling around the Red Fort itself, where Shah Jahan's "tiny cell" had proven to be a suite of palatial rooms. Glance through any large window, step out onto any one of several balconies, and you can enjoy a magnificent, naked-eye view of the Taj. True, in one room, a marble column boasts a small, embedded mirror. But instead of trying to find the Taj in it, why not turn your head: *voila*!

The journalist in me bridled. Turned out I hadn't capitulated after all. Tiny cell, indeed. View the Taj by mirror? Oh, please. The myth-makers had sacrificed truth to story: "I think it's deceitful."

Safiya laughed uproariously. In the extravagant fabrication we'd discovered, she delighted: "That's one of India's charms, Bernie. That fantastical embroidery."

"What about truth?"

Taggart said: "Ah, truth."

That was Day One in Agra, with a light rain falling and all of us carrying big black umbrellas. At the Taj, I saw no sign of Behroze, but then I'd expected none. I knew she was present, more present than usual, and that she wanted to watch, perhaps take a few readings.

Day Two, our second visit, we enjoyed sunshine. As we stood near the front gate, admiring the Taj across a series of pools and flower gardens, Behroze brought me Shakespeare: "The flowery way that leads to the broad gate and the sacred fire." As if on cue, the fountains sprang to life and the Taj appeared to float magically above the spray.

Today, I realized, she would meet me.

As we approached up the walkway, a guide materialized and, despite our protests, began running through meaningless statistics: the top of the parapet over the entrance reached a height of one hundred and eight feet, and the tip of the dome, two hundred and thirty-seven. We ignored him and eventually he went away.

In the glass palace, the Aina Mahal, a Muslim steward chanted verses from the Quran, his voice echoing back to us from the dome high above. In the subdued, shadowy light, we stood marvelling at the artistry of an octagonal marble screen that surrounded the cenotaphs and symbolized the mortal remains of Shah Jahan and his wife — remains entombed directly below us.

On Day One, I'd suggested descending into that burial chamber, but Safiya, remembering the catacombs, shivered and declined. Both Taggart and Daniel expressed indifference, and so we left without descending. Now, again, I felt the call of the mortuary chamber — and with it, this time, a sense of urgency that proclaimed the presence of Behroze: "I'm going down. Meet you back at the hotel."

Taggart had begun to tire and even Daniel, enthralled by the chanting and the echoes, by what he called "the music of the Taj," looked like he'd heard enough.

Safiya said: "We don't mind waiting."

"Never mind, really." I joined a short lineup at the top of the stairs. "Meet you in the lounge before dinner?"

Slowly, following others, I descended the stairs into the chamber, which housed two dim-lit tombs. Pilgrims shuffled painstakingly around them — shuffled and stood, shuffled and stood. The oppressive heat made me feel faint. As my eyes adjusted to the gloom, suddenly I saw her: my dead wife stood alone in a corner. I'd travelled halfway around the world to meet her here, and had fully expected to do so — yet now I went weak in the knees. I steadied myself against a pillar. Behroze wore a vivid African dress, a riot of colour and pattern, and an old familiar lopsided grin that brought tears to my eyes.

A great wave of remorse washed over me, at once familiar and devastating, and almost swept me to the floor: If only I hadn't been so proud, so narrow, if only I'd remained and listened to the Prophet of the Golden Flame, if only, if only, if only....As I hurried towards her, I felt the world shift and — how can I describe this? The mortuary chamber faded to background and the shuffling pilgrims became living scenery. I'd stepped through a veil into another order of reality. Behroze and I embraced, then held each other at arm's length: "Darling, we've got to stop meeting like this."

"Congratulations, Bernie: you're halfway home." Seeing my confusion, she clarified: "You've fallen in love with Safiya Naidoo."

I shrugged: no sense trying to conceal it. "How's Colette?"

"No change." Her face clouded with sadness and worry and I got a flash of our daughter lying comatose in that San Francisco hospital. Four figures stood around her, one at each corner of the bed: "Who are your pals?"

"They're keeping Colette from slipping away."

"Damn it, Behroze! I should be there to —"

"To do what, Bernie? To sit by the bed? You leave Colette to me and . . . what did you call them? my pals." She smiled thinly. "We can maintain Colette for a few more weeks. But I won't kid you, Bernie. We can't bring her back."

I realized that Behroze had secretly hoped, with the help of her four friends, to retrieve Colette from the shadows, and blurted: "To you, my quest represented nothing but an insurance policy."

"Not true. Certainly, I hoped to restore Colette without your help. But can you stand here in the Taj and tell me that she's the only reason you've persevered?"

I started to answer affirmatively, then thought of my recurring nightmare, of my guilt and yearning for redemption, and looked down at the floor and said nothing.

"You've grown wiser, Bernie. And you're right: I underestimated Ahriman. To restore Colette, we need the power of Mazda. You've got to invoke that Shaman, Bernie — not just for your sake, but Colette's."

This intensity, this near-panic — it frightened me more than I can say.

"That gold necklace you gave me?"

"You lost it in Greece, I know."

"I tried to locate it, psychically. Turned up not a trace. Do you think we could . . . get it back?"

"I can't find it either, Bernie. I've tried."

"But it's not just symbolic. I felt its power."

"The silver bracelet Safiya gave you should do the job."

"What about this millennium business? Taggart's speculations: where are we in Time?"

"Bernie, nobody knows."

"Taggart says we're near the end: earthquakes, heatwaves, fire-bombings. He thinks Jesus was Hashedar, the first of three saviours. That we missed the second and now —"

"Maybe Jesus was Hashedar, maybe he wasn't. Maybe Christians are incipient ashavans, maybe they're not. The Wise Lord and the Demon of the Lie have been contending since the dawn of Time, Bernie. Good and Evil, Light and Dark, Chinvat and Golden Flame — they'll battle until The Renovation, whatever names we use. Don't worry about 'when,' Bernie. Focus on here, now and what's next."

"Should I go to Tanzania?"

"What did I just finish saying? You must go. You've got to invoke The Shaman's Fire."

"But that dream of the future? Safiya and I go sailing and —"

"That was provisional, Bernie. A particular ordering, a permutation. If you don't like what you saw, change it. Safiya can help."

"Safiya's shuffling between Taggart and Daniel. It's all so . . . so sordid."

"Safiya's not just any young novelist, Bernie. She has the potential to make a difference. Think Nadine Gordimer, Toni Morrison. We're talking Nobel-Prize material." Behroze hesitated. "There's something else about her, too, I believe. Something transcendent and more important still . . . ."

"More important than her literary career?"

"Possibly, yes."

"Does it have to do with the way she's changing? She seems to be growing more . . . I don't know, more spiritual. At the same time as —"

"To succeed in the quest, Safiya will stop at nothing. She'll make any sacrifice, endure any passage, suffer any rite of purification. You couldn't find a more worthy partner."

As she spoke, I saw sadness in her eyes: "You were worthy, Behroze!" My voice cracked. "You, too, were worthy."

Behroze smiled, touched my face and brushed away my unbidden tears. "You must think of me now, Bernie, as a John the Baptist figure."

"Not another one." We both laughed, and then I added: "I'm not sure what you mean."

"You'll see, I hope. Though nothing is fixed."

"What about Daniel and Taggart? What can you tell me?"

"Daniel's gone utterly opaque since the death of Victor. He won't be setting forth again any time soon. And Taggart I wouldn't trust."

"That enshrouding fog!" My exclamation resonated in the chamber and the chanting steward, vaguely irritated, shook his head as if to ward off a buzzing insect. I lowered my voice: "I think Taggart's unbalanced. Either that, or someone's . . . with him."

Behroze raised her eyebrows and I plunged on: "The same way you're with me only . . . I don't know, obscenely closer. Maybe Taggart's a pawn? Maybe he's being used."

"We're all pawns, Bernie."

"But with Taggart, it's different, somehow. Daniel thinks it has to do with past lives and karma, but I sense —."

"Karma, Bernie? We'd better get you out of India." She turned serious again. "Taggart's devious, but he knows what he's doing. Three must set forth and Daniel's not ready. You've got a tight deadline and can't afford to be odd man out."

"At least we've eluded the Chinvat."

"You've eluded nothing. They're biding their time."

Behroze hesitated. She wanted to reveal more but decided: too dangerous. Instead, she hugged me for a long time, then let me go and stepped back: "Bernie, we both hate extended goodbyes. Already I've lingered too long."

"Surely this isn't goodbye."

"I had to get special dispensation even to come here once."

"What are you talking about? You can't abandon me now."

"Not to worry, Bernie. You're approaching redemption. For the first time since I crossed over, you've fallen in love. And love is an Ariadne's thread: it can lead you out of a labyrinth or through a Shaman's Fire."

"Behroze, wait." She was fading. "Talk to me about Colette."

"I love her as you do, Bernie. But three months is all they've granted me. After that, it's up to you."

As Behroze withdrew into the shadows, she cried: "Don't get lost in the music."

"What music? Behroze?"

The Muslim steward stopped chanting and glared at me: "Please."

I'd snapped back into ordinary reality, the mortuary chamber at the Taj Mahal, and hurried up the stairs into the sunshine. What did Behroze mean, don't get lost in the music? The music of chance? The music of the Taj?

Our discussion had raised so many questions and evoked so many memories, however, that I forgot her admonition, simply failed to make the connection, when that evening we chose a restaurant.

Our hotel, the Mughal Sheraton, offered a choice of four. We settled on the best, despite white-linen table cloths and a too-formal atmosphere; first because we wanted Indian cuisine, not Italian in India, and second because, when we peaked in, we discovered two musicians performing on a small stage. One played percussion and slapped out complex rhythms on a drum, while the other, clearly the leader, sang and played a stringed instrument.

Classical Indian music can be entrancing, and these two proved expert enough to impress even Daniel. Yet that's no excuse. I should have noticed when Taggart began taking an aggressive tone with Safiya. He'd started drinking upstairs, in the lounge, and I should have known from the Verlandi where that led. But instead of paying attention, I relaxed. I got lost in the music. When the performers finished their set, Daniel and I applauded with enthusiasm. We sat near enough the stage that the singer smiled and asked if we came from America.

"Canada," Daniel said. "I'm a musician, too."

The singer said one of his sisters lived in Calgary, near the Rockies, and Daniel insisted that he join us. This new arrival, Sudhir Narain, had recently released a cassette of original compositions. It had sold well enough in America that next month, he'd return to the studio and put together a second. Maybe he'd include some Urdu "ghazals" he'd translated into English: what did we think?

Daniel asked if he could buy a copy of the first cassette and Sudhir said no, impossible — but he'd give him one. The two went backstage through a curtain — and that's when Taggart snapped. This is a five-star restaurant, right? White linen table cloths, a maitre d' in a tux, waiters hovering in white shirts and vests. Put down an empty glass and whisk! it's gone. The place is full: twenty-five or thirty diners, half of them wealthy Indians, the other half tourists from all over the world.

"You slept with Lanigan, didn't you?"

"You don't own me, Taggart. Who do you think you are?"

Taggart pushed away from the table, leapt to his feet and banged his glass with a spoon: "Ladies and gentlemen, your attention please." He climbed onto his chair, although not without difficulty. Red-faced, slurring his words, he said: "You're all familiar with the *menage a trois*? Two women, one man? Or else one woman, two men? Now try to imagine a *menage a quatre*. One woman, three men. I'd like propose a —"

Inside me, something snapped. Three waiters had stepped forward, but I arrived first. I reached up, grabbed Taggart by the jacket and hauled him off the chair.

Taggart cried, "Get your hands off me!"

"Shut your face!"

"You fucked her, didn't you, Lanigan? You fucked her and think it matters."

"That's none of your business."

"Last night it was my turn. And you — "

Okay, I lost it — I who'd been evolving, or so I'd convinced myself, into an increasingly spiritual individual. I've never been a fighter, yet somehow I flung Taggart Oates across a table of Belgians who'd been discussing the Euro. I was moving around the table, going after him, when a young man stepped out of the shadows and slammed his fist into my stomach. I doubled over, fell to my knees. The young man whipped out a knife. Chinvat!

I rolled under a table as he slashed at me, missed. He raised his arm to try again but somebody kicked the knife out of his hand — Safiya! He wheeled, astonished, and then, realizing he was badly outnumbered, leapt to his feet and sprinted up the stairs and out the door into the night.

Two waiters helped me to my feet. In the confusion, nobody knew what had happened. In a corner of the room, Daniel administered to Taggart who was bleeding from the nose. "He fucked her, Daniel," Taggart was saying loud enough that the whole restaurant could hear. "Two of us weren't enough."

Daniel wiped at his face: "What difference does it make?"

If it weren't so mortifying, the scene would have been ridiculous.

Sudhir Narain stood alone on the stage. The look on his face said it all: Barbarians. Uncouth barbarians from the West. He wheeled and disappeared behind the curtain and I found myself wondering if he wasn't right.

Safiya had returned to the table and sat knocking back wine, looking flushed and magnificent. I said: "Safiya, thanks: you saved my life."

"You're welcome, Bernie. But right now I need to be alone."

From over in the corner, Daniel glared at me — then deliberately looked away. I needed fresh air and made for the door. I'd got lost in the music. Obviously, to the Chinvat, I'd become expendable. But that wasn't the worst of it. Safiya preferred solitude to being with me. God, but that hurt!

Do Not Come To Dar

"You talk as if Africa were uniform," I said. "As if Ghana, Malawi and Tanzania were interchangeable. And that's just not so." It was late afternoon in Dar es Salaam, sweltering hot. Daniel, Safiya and I sat under a colourful umbrella on the patio at the New Africa Hotel.

"I take your point." Safiya sipped orange squash, which tasted to me like soda gone flat. "Yet even so, most African countries share attributes or characteristics that distinguish them from a country like Canada. Characteristics which, to a Canadian at least, render them alien, exotic — primordially Other."

"Africa hot, Canada cold," Daniel said. "Africa black, Canada white. Africa outdoors, Canada indoors."

"Africa poor, Canada rich." I said. "Who cares?"

But this was their favorite game and they wouldn't quit.

"Africa is congregating at night to dance and beat drums," Daniel said. "Canada is screaming yourself hoarse at a hockey game."

"We know they're stereotypes, Bernie," Safiya said. "Yet Tanzania reminds me that I come from a cold country full of rich white people. Wouldn't Nigeria do the same? Or Ghana?"

"But why focus on differences?" I said. "What about universalities? Those things that as humans we share?"

"Not nearly as much fun," she said. "Though I can see where a visitor accustomed even to the semi-tropics — an American from Florida, say, or Louisiana — would probably find Africa's palm trees and giant snails less exotic than we do."

"And a Caucausian American from just about anywhere," Daniel said, "would probably have more experience as a visible minority than his Canadian counterpart. And so feel less threatened to discover himself the only white person, for example, in a crowd at the bank or the post office."

"Certain urbanites excepted," Safiya said. "But nobody who grew up in Canada — black, red, purple or yellow — would ever feel at home in Africa."

"Surely you knew that before you arrived?"

"Yes, but I didn't know that Otherness would teach me so much about myself. That it would throw the recent past into such stark relief."

But I see that I've left too many blanks. Back in New Delhi, after Taggart Oates returned to Sri Lanka to complete his residency, I made up with Daniel and, to his amazement, wangled a visa to Tanzania. I simply placed one hundred dollars American on the right countertop and picked it up next day. Daniel, accustomed to African red tape, bribe or no bribe, couldn't get over it: "It's like magic."

Again Safiya told him, enjoying the irony: "Get used to it."

As a citizen of a Commonwealth country, she didn't require a visa. Likewise Daniel, though anyway he possessed a residency permit. We flew into Dar es Salaam shortly after midnight. When we stepped out of the plane onto the tarmac, whomp! the humidity hit like mid-day in Delhi. Seeing my reaction, Daniel said: "Dar's at sea level, remember? And not far off the equator."

The tiny airport, run-down and over-crowded, looked like an American bus depot except that uniformed guards carried rifles around, and the princes among them automatic weapons. At customs, when a businessman rejected an official's request, an armed guard stepped forward and led him away protesting: "Hey, I'm an American! You can't do this!"

I feared a similar fate, but when I showed my passport and visa, the officer just grinned and stamped them: "*Karibu*! Welcome to Tanzania."

We collected our bags, piled into a battered taxi and made for town, swerving back and forth to avoid the worst potholes. A white moon hung huge in the sky. Palm trees lined the highway. As we drove into the city, rattling and bouncing past tin-roof shacks, I caught a whiff of tar and curry. But mainly I was struck by the number of people rambling the streets, and Daniel explained that the sweltering heat had turned Dar into a city of night owls.

They dropped me off downtown at the New Africa Hotel.

My first morning in Dar, I made my way to Kariakoo market and purchased a beaten-meal skeleton of ominous aspect. Back in my room, I emptied my fabulous green bag and counted my fire-worthy souvenirs: Mesa Verde, New York, Las Palmas, Barcelona, Genoa, Rome, Al-Mayadin, Athens, Meteora, Colombo, Kandy, Galle, New Delhi, Udaipur, Jaipur, Agra, Dar es Salaam. Seventeen. One extra. And magical places? Mesa Verde, Rome, Meteora, Agra, Udaipur, Kandy and now Dar es Salaam, the equatorial Haven of Peace. That made seven.

I was ready. Likewise, Safiya. And Daniel? He'd long since gathered enough mementoes, but begged off setting forth because of Victor.

Also, as he reminded us one late one afternoon at yet another hotel, the Palm Beach: "The time's got to be right. Also the people, the place. You can't force these things."

"Daniel, I've got a daughter lying in a coma."

We were sitting out front on the patio, drinking the local beer — not bad if you could ignore sediment — out of big brown bottles. Safiya said: "Give him time, Bernie. If you'd lost a best —"

As she spoke, a large African man stormed out of the hotel carrying a single suitcase, waving his free arm and yelling at the male desk clerk who'd trotted after him: "The *mwezis* took everything! Even my pots and pans! After I paid the *askari* to keep special watch!"

Lugging his remaining possessions, huffing and puffing and vowing that all of Dar would hear of this carelessness, the furious man made his way to the adjacent taxi stand, climbed into a cab and disappeared into the afternoon.

We all three looked at each other. If I were going to remain in Dar for more than a week or two, for sure I would have to move out of the pricey New Africa Hotel. The Palm Beach, here, was more residential — and just a five-minute walk from the International School. Obviously, I would have to keep a close eye on my souvenirs. But maybe the Golden Flame, and not the Chinvat, had acted to get me a living space.

At the front desk, the clerk said the angry man had vacated a small suite. He clammed up when Safiya said innocently: "What did he say about *mwezis?*"

Reluctantly, after Daniel had offered a dark-sounding proverb, the desk clerk showed us the vacated suite. He pointed out the worn furniture, the peeling paint, the stained carpet. I noted the excellence of the location, far from the noisy bar at the front of the hotel, and checked that the air-conditioning worked. He brightened up when I handed him one month's rent and added an American twenty for his trouble.

In Dar es Salaam, most Westerners live in housing supplied by companies or institutions. To find decent accommodation outside this network is almost impossible. Daniel slapped his forehead in disbelief: "A two-room suite at the Palm Beach Hotel?"

Safiya laughed at his astonishment — and I began to worry: if this synchronistic twist constituted a miracle, how long might I reside at the Palm Beach? Three weeks? I couldn't afford much more. My anxiety increased next day, when Safiya acquired a temporary job. Daniel had arrived home from the school with word that a French teacher had resigned. A Dutch woman in her mid-forties, she'd returned home for a visit and called to say she wouldn't be coming back. The school could keep its bonus.

That afternoon, Safiya visited the headmaster. She couldn't claim qualifications as a teacher, but neither could half a dozen other "Europeans" the school had hired locally, most of them spouses of visiting engineers or university professors. Certainly, Safiya spoke French well enough to teach elementary and junior-high students. Besides, she needed the money.

That evening, when she told me about the job, I responded: "Safiya? We've got a quest to complete."

"Yes, but we can't set forth without Daniel. And he feels the time's not right."

"The time's right, damn it. Something's wrong with Daniel."

Safiya shrugged and showed me her palms: what could we do?

Me, I did a lot of solitary, restless rambling in the downtown streets of Dar es Salaam, where instead of highrises you find a riot of first-floor shops in low-lying buildings, most of them owned by hard-working "Asians" — Patel's Canned Foods, Chandwani's Shoes, Dipti's Fine Fabrics — and carrying goods imported from China or India, colourful saris and silks and knick-knacks.

I remember chasing the whine of a muezzin around street corners and down back alleys to discover an ancient mosque I would never manage to find again. And the people who thronged the streets — women carrying babies on their backs or jugs and baskets and bundles of firewood on their heads, most of them wearing wrap-around khangas, brightly coloured and boldly patterned, while others, despite the heat, wore black.

I remember how, at the sprawling Kariakoo Market, a chaotic city block of narrow walkways and makeshift stalls, men in khaki shorts and torn T-shirts sat cross-legged on mats and tried to interest shoppers in buying stalks of sugar cane or newspaper cones full of peanuts, and the air hung heavy with spices and smoke that rose from charcoal burners over which half a  dozen men held sticks strung with fresh meat, and from a distant corner you'd hear the squawking of chickens, or the voice of a man crying out prices in Swahili, dropping them slowly, reluctantly, incredulous and finally angry, unable to comprehend how a prospective buyer could pass up such a bargain: "Tatu! Tatu shilingi!!"

More than once, from a distance, I spotted Chinvat: young men who looked both familiar and out of place — short hair, tight T-shirts, muscles everywhere. Chinvat — but they made no move. I couldn't figure it out. After a few days, I left off trying and again gave myself over to Africa. I remember sitting under a shade umbrella on the terrace of the New Africa Hotel, drinking orange squash while reading The Daily News. Daniel had drawn my attention to People's Forum, a letters-page stranger and more entertaining than any I'd encountered elsewhere, and also to Action Line, a column that supposedly "solves problems, gives answers, cuts red tape and stands up for your rights," but always ended up reiterating the government line.

Reading The Daily News was like looking into a funhouse mirror. A wire-service article treated an economic summit held in Europe. The story spun nothing too oddly, but an illustration done locally depicted the leaders of the G7, the American president among them. Above this, in seventy-two point, boldface type, the headline blared: "Club of the Rich."

The Otherness of Africa. It surfaced in The Daily News, but also I remember food shortages — traipsing from shop to shop in the heat, hunting a loaf of bread and finally admitting that today, none existed in Dar. I remember the humidity, the stuffiness of the library in the late afternoon, where I'd gone to hunt references to the Golden Flame but found none, and sweat rolling down my back in rivulets until the sky cracked open and down came the rain, falling so hard I couldn't think. The pounding rain would turn streets and back alleys into seaways — and suddenly stop. In minutes, the sun would be blazing down in a cloudless sky. Heavy rain and hot sun, heavy rain and hot sun — a tropical climate.

How did Daniel put it? To live in Dar was to live in a greenhouse. The climate created a nether-world of frangipani trees and cactus gardens, of palm trees and baobabs and bougainvilleas, of flat-topped acacias, papaya trees, lemon trees and a tree whose bean-filled pods Daniel turned into noisy maraccas. Too, I remember the fruit: how you could buy a fresh papaya, halve it and fill it with chunks of mango, banana, orange, grapefruit, tangerine or passion fruit. You could squeeze a lemon over this concoction and call it lunch.

Oh, but tropicality has a downside. To the heat and humidity, other life forms have adapted better than we have. Slugs and snails grow as big as your fist and snakes as big around as your arm. Shiny, black beetles grow big as golf balls, and no matter how I scrubbed the kitchen counter, every morning I'd find columns of ants marching back and forth between cupboard and window.

I remember the spiders — most horribly the grey-brown

tarantulas with fist-sized bodies and eight sturdy legs twinkling with hair. Think dazzling mobility. Think all-star broken-field runners of the giant-insect world. I saw this for myself one evening — an evening I'd long been dreading — when, attracted by the light, a tarantula skittered under the front door into Daniel's ground-floor apartment. It scuttled across the tile floor into the centre of the living room and stopped dead, antennae twitching, suddenly aware of our presence.

First impulse: get your feet off the floor. Second? Daniel cried: "The broom!"

As he dashed into the kitchen, Safiya said: "Poor thing."

The tarantula scooted halfway up a wall and waited, pulsating. Daniel returned with the broom, swung and missed: whack! The spider raced down the wall and disappeared under the sofa.

From the kitchen, with noticeable reluctance, Safiya fetched a bottle of insect spray. She handed it to Daniel, then took the broom, stationed herself at one end of the couch and nodded her unhappy readiness. At the other end, Daniel began spraying. And now I picked up on the tarantula's baleful intelligence. The creature understood that these humans meant to kill it. From beneath the couch, enraged by the relentless spraying, the spider exuded waves of malevolence. I couldn't believe how much spraying it withstood, never mind how much it hated us. I yearned to jump up and cry, "Wait!"

But I remembered how, in my indelible dream, that's precisely what I'd done. This whole scene had evolved differently. No sign of Nathan, for example. Yet I didn't dare act. The tarantula remained the central event and I restrained myself. Perhaps, by not rescuing the spider, I would change the future just enough that Safiya wouldn't disappear while sailing? I didn't like my chances, but neither did I enjoy many options. The tarantula made a break for it, came skittering across the floor, zigging and zagging — but with far less energy than before. Whap! Whap! Safiya nailed it on her third try: WHAP!

She called it "murder" and felt guilty for days. Every time we sat drinking cold beer, she'd say: "Did we really have to kill that tarantula, do you think? Couldn't we have somehow driven it out the door?"

The Otherness of Africa, then: omnipresent, impossible to

ignore. Physical but also pyschological — and, yes, spiritual. And if, for Safiya, this Otherness cast the past few weeks into stark relief, it did the same for me. Evenings, when they weren't taking their respective Swahili classes, Daniel and Safiya would stroll over to the Palm Beach Hotel and together we'd drink beer on the patio. Sometimes, looking over at Safiya, I could hardly bear the proximity: so near and yet so far. Daily, she grew more alluring. I began to wonder whether her distant nearness didn't constitute part of my torture test — a pitiless finale.

Obsessively, and in the welcome absence of Taggart, I analysed the bond between Safiya and Daniel. One evening, when a normal person would have been too far away, I heard her whisper: "You can't imagine how good it feels, Dan, to be back with you, just the two of us."

"Is it me, do you think? Or just being shut of Taggart?"

"Don't be silly," Safiya said.

Even so, my heart started pounding. If Daniel was right, I could hope.

Later that evening, in the washroom, I said to him: "Why do you think, metaphysically speaking, we got involved with Taggart?"

"He was brought in to teach us. His job is done."

"I think you underestimate him."

"*Joka la mdimu linalinda watanudo.*" Drying his hands, Daniel translated: "The dragon of the lime tree guards against those who pluck the fruits."

"Meaning The Shaman will take care of Taggart? I wonder."

But these proverbs, I realized, formed part of an unconscious strategy. Daniel had been more hurt than he knew by Safiya's refusal to come with him to Africa. And her subsequent departure with Taggart? He wasn't ready to explore that pain.

In dealing intimately with Taggart, then, Safiya remained alone. She recognized that her relationship with him was a self-indulgent soap opera. Yet even now she couldn't find a way permanently to free herself. After the debacle in Agra, that horrific drunken scene in the Indian restaurant when I'd punched him out, Safiya might have cried, "Enough!"

Instead, when Taggart sobered up and begged forgiveness, Safiya made it clear all bets were off — and then absolved him.

Yet, before leaving India, the man worked one final bit of voodoo. He accepted that Safiya would now go directly to Tanzania, but implored her not to abandon him: "That would destroy me."

Taggart would return to Sri Lanka and fulfill his commitment. But when he visited Tanzania, he wanted to take Safiya travelling — his treat. While they waited for the right moment, they'd visit Ngoronogo Crater, explore Olduvai Gorge, see Mount Kilimanjaro. Somewhere in those ancient environs, original cradle of mankind, The Shaman made his home — and they would find it.

Finally, to shut him up, Safiya had said, "I'll think about it."

Big mistake. Taggart interpreted this as a commitment.

So Safiya confided to me in Dar. The insanity of it filled me with foreboding, but also guarded optimism: Safiya really did need me. With Daniel, she could no longer discuss Taggart. He'd heard enough. Me, I made it my business to find out more than she realized. From Sri Lanka, Taggart wrote letters, as many as two a day. The early ones remained bright and newsy. He missed Safiya but he'd visited Kandy, he'd found a Hindu temple in Colombo, he'd travelled south and bought a fire mask.

Taggart's letters didn't turn dark until Safiya revealed, belatedly, that she'd taken a job and couldn't go travelling. He replied that he'd fallen into a depression. He'd started a new novel but now he felt sick. He'd had periods like this before. Did she remember her Windigo dream? Last night, he'd seen that insatiable ice skeleton. He'd written a suicide note and sealed it into an envelope. His adult self had felt contemptuous, disgusted, but his child self wanted to lie down on a sandy beach and let the demon have its way.

Taggart had complained bitterly, during the freighter cruise, that Safiya had already left for Africa. Now, in Tanzania, she lived partly in Sri Lanka — though with dread, not anticipation. Where before she'd savored a dream, now she endured a nightmare.

Hers was a different trial by fire than my own, though recognizably of the same genre. She opened Taggart's letters with trembling and trepidation. Always they left her shaken: depressed or angry or both. Yet she couldn't wait to read them. At recess she'd collect them from her mail slot, return to her classroom and close the door. If she'd drawn duty, she'd head out into the school yard and read by the swings, end up standing mired in Taggart's misery while around her uniformed children chased each other in a game of tag, laughing and shrieking, a blue-and-white whirl of happiness.

Taggart speculated that his shaky mental condition arose out of the darkness of the raw material he'd begun exploring in his latest novel, all those skeletons clicking bones in his head. Sometimes he'd write with tears pouring down his face. He guessed he'd been having a nervous breakdown. Brainstorms shook him like a tree in a tempest. He didn't understand the Windigo side of his personality, which proved as destructive towards him as towards other people. He had to keep writing to control it at all.

Taggart wrote (blatantly lying) that he'd never wanted to destroy Safiya's relationship with Daniel. But he didn't want their relationship, his and hers, destroyed either. He remained committed to Saifya. Did she know what that meant? Together, he and Safiya had a great task to perform. Surely she could understand that to ask him to come to Dar es Salaam and NOT spend time alone with her would be asking him to endure an unbearable agony? If Daniel hadn't enjoyed that stretch in Sri Lanka, sleeping with Safiya, being intimate with her, then Taggart might not feel so badly. But he'd expected reciprocity in Dar.

It had never occurred to him that Safiya wouldn't want to make love, given the strength of their bond. He considered himself married to Safiya. They didn't need a ceremony. Maybe Bernie was right and a three-way marriage couldn't work. If not, they needed to find another way. Could Safiya do what she demanded of him? He needed her — and not just to approach The Shaman. He yearned to be with her. It couldn't be all the time and he understood that — but it had to be part of the time.

He didn't blame Safiya for his depression. Yet he felt that, by accepting a teaching job and so precluding a vigorous search of The Shaman's home turf, she'd abandoned him and betrayed their original agreement. Never mind. He'd come to Tanzania no matter what the emotional toll: he needed to see Safiya and that was that.

In responding to this self-indulgent avalanche, Safiya explained that she'd ruled out sex because she simply could not survive another bout of now-it's-this-one, now-it's-that-one. It made her schizophrenic. When Taggart wrote "time alone" and meant sex, he invited her to immolate herself. Look what had happened in India. Ultimately, he'd found three-way sharing intolerable and created that horrible, horrible scene, not incidentally nullifying any "original agreements." She didn't blame him. They'd had no business expecting the extraordinary of themselves. They all three possessed artistic talent, but so what? The rest stood revealed as run-of-the-mill human frailty.

Taggart responded that his mental state was deteriorating. This morning, he'd seen hell in a plate of fried eggs. Safiya remained his only friend in this hemisphere. As such, she bore a responsibility. He was sorry Daniel had gone over to Lanigan, especially after he'd enjoyed that time with her in Sri Lanka. Even so, Safiya couldn't change the rules now. This particular game, the original three wandering amidst alien corn, had long since passed the midpoint.

On Taggart went, ten pages, fifteen, twenty. In refusing to see his point of view, Safiya showed a cruel streak. Daniel had made love with her in Sri Lanka and Taggart felt entitled to equal time. He felt embarrassed to beg. She should send him a telegram, yes or no. Besides, with whom did she think she could approach The Shaman? Daniel hadn't recovered from the death of Victor. Lanigan was a know-nothing poseur who couldn't hang onto his mementoes. Did she propose to invoke The Sacred Fire with one of those two? All he could say was, "Good luck."

Taggart had a quest to complete. He would come to Dar es Salaam no matter who or what opposed him. And if, for two or three weeks, or even a month, Safiya had to shuffle back and forth between Daniel and him, so be it. She owed him that much.

At this point, Safiya visited me at the Palm Beach Hotel. We drank orange squash on the patio. She began summarizing and I said: "Safiya, I've been keeping tabs."

She didn't look surprised: "Bernie, I don't know what to do."

"Oh, I think you do."

"You mean break it off? I'm afraid Taggart might . . . do something to himself."

"That's not all you fear."

"You're right. Taggart's famous for his occult thrillers, but he also wrote a vicious *roman à clef*. The woman he savaged committed suicide."

"You don't look the type."

"You're right," Saifiya said. "That's not reason enough, is it?"

"Anyway, you could write him into the ground."

"What about The Shaman's Fire."

"You, me and Daniel can set forth. We don't need Taggart."

"Yes, but Dan's not ready. He seems . . . oddly reluctant."

I summoned a confidence I didn't feel: "He's bound to heal before too long."

That evening, Safiya wrote telling Taggart that she felt as if he were holding a gun to her head. Thanks, but no thanks. No more agonizing, no more argument: she couldn't do it. He was trying to manipulate her. Or maybe he was right: he'd succumbed to forces he couldn't control. She did understand his point of view, but he wasn't begging, he was choosing. And she couldn't do what he asked.

Maybe Taggart shouldn't come to Dar es Salaam at all, not feeling the way he did. There, she'd said it. He'd spelled out his terms and she couldn't accept them. She couldn't take it anymore. She still hoped he'd change his mind, his state of mind. But if he couldn't, then she agreed with him: he couldn't very well come to Dar. Certainly, given this new situation, they couldn't hope to approach The Shaman together.

Taggart responded with a long telegram. He'd come to Dar no matter what she said — and he'd bring a surprise. He wanted her to send him the address of the British High Commission. He'd come to Dar, not because Safiya was there, but because it was the best place from which to set forth. Anyway, he had to get out of Sri Lanka: people were getting blown up in the streets. Maybe Lanigan would put him up for a few nights? If not, he'd find his own hotel.

If Safiya wasn't going to make love with him, then probably he wouldn't see her. He'd come to Dar and go straight to a hotel. Maybe he'd see her and maybe he wouldn't. If Safiya wanted to see him, she should book him a double room at the Hotel Kilimanjaro. . . .

Of the many letters Safiya sent Taggart from Dar es Salaam, she drafted only one of them twice:

Taggart Oates:

This is an official de-invitation.

If you ever loved me, do not come to Dar es Salaam.

If you love me now, or if you love me still, do not come to Dar es Salaam.

If you come to Dar, I will understand it to mean that you never loved me — that you love only yourself and images of yourself, and I will treat you accordingly.

Taggart, read these words and understand.

I will not meet any airplanes. I will not book any hotels. Can I make it any clearer?

I DO NOT WANT TO SEE YOU HERE.

This is my last communication until you write and tell me that you are not coming to Dar es Salaam.

DO NOT COME TO DAR.

Bongoya Island Bound

Who would have imagined that the four could become five? The lost prophecies spoke of three setting forth. They spoke of two approaching The Shaman and of one "re-emerging." They said nothing of five embroiling themselves beneath the African sun — though in retrospect I see we needed that fifth. If Taggart hadn't introduced Esmeralda into our other-worldly conflagration, which blazed with the intensity that drove Old Nietzsche mad, we wouldn't have invoked The Shaman when and where we did.

Safiya recognized our lucky fifth from the airport lounge, where we waited, looking out across the tarmac: "I don't believe it! That woman walking with Taggart? Wearing sunglasses? That's Esmeralda Esteban."

Daniel said: "The singer?"

"Singer and fellow ashavan."

"Before he met Safiya," I said, "Taggart hoped to approach The Shaman with Esmeralda."

"*Mtaka unda haneni*. He who desires to create something does not announce his intentions."

"Esmeralda Esteban! You've got to hand it to the guy."

Safiya said: "Would you two knock it off?"

To her melodramatic disinvitation, Taggart had responded with a telegram: RECEIVED MISSIVE TOO LATE TO CHANGE PLANS STOP ARRIVE DAR ES SALAAM MONDAY ON AIR INDIA STOP WILL BRING SURPIRSE STOP PLEASE MEET ME AT AIRPORT STOP TAGGART STOP.

Having passed quickly through customs, Taggart enjoyed introducing Esmeralda all around — and why not? Stunningly beautiful, self-possessed, she removed her sunglasses to shake hands. To Safiya, she said, "I hope we'll be friends."

To Daniel: "The man with the sayings."

And to me: "The man with the seeing eyes."

Taggart's "nervous breakdown" began to look like a ruse. He'd been lulling us into a false sense of security while organizing Esmeralda. They intended to approach The Shaman together but needed a third to set forth. Goodbye arithmetic, hello algebra. If

Taggart hadn't raised the stakes, exactly, he'd multiplied the permutations and combinations.

Esmeralda reminded me forcefully of the Safiya I'd met on the Verlandi weeks before when, aware of her physical beauty, her animal vitality, she'd carried her appeal with insouciance. Safiya had lost none of that pantheresque allure — and yet, as she shook hands with Esmeralda, I saw how much she'd grown: she'd developed another side of herself. Where before she'd exuded sensuality and intelligence, now she radiated spirituality as well. The work of the Golden Flame? Or was it me who'd changed and grown enough to recognize an aspect of Safiya that until now had remained invisible.

We collected luggage and made our way through the crowd. Taggart walked ahead with Safiya, talking animatedly. She'd been right to send him those letters, however cruel. She'd thrown a bucket of cold water over an hysteric and for that he thanked her. Mental instability haunted many great writers, but he would conquer this, he knew he would. He hadn't been asking her to save him. He'd needed to talk with a friend, that was all. In the end, he'd thought of Esmeralda.

Anyway, that was history and here we all were: one big happy family. Five ashavans in East Africa, united in the Golden Flame and bent on invoking the power of The Sacred Fire.

"*Panapo wengi hapaharibiki neno,*" Daniel responded. "Where there are many, nothing goes wrong."

Safiya had booked Taggart into the Kilimanjaro, one of the fanciest hotels in Dar es Salaam. Also, one of the priciest. Three nights, Taggart and Esmeralda proposed to remain, while looking around for longer-term accommodation. The Palm Beach, where I stayed, was crowded to overflowing (and frankly too shabby), while the New Africa Hotel, where many foreigners resided, Taggart declared too busy.

I thought he would cave and opt for this last, but Taggart discovered the Bahari Beach Hotel north of the city and rented a by-the-week suite in one of the "traditional" thatch huts. He explained that Esmeralda loved to swim and he wanted to read, write and quaff beer under a beach umbrella.

Taggart worked hard at mending fences. One afternoon, as we strolled along Kunduchi Beach, he told Daniel and me that he'd relinquished all claims on Safiya and felt content to remain her friend. Daniel glanced over and I got a Swahili flash: "One with a scar, do not think him healed." I sought a deeper reading of Taggart, hit an ice-cold fog and could have sworn I heard a chuckle.

Later, during a quiet moment in the lounge at the Yacht Club, Taggart said: "Lanigan, about those fisticuffs in Agra. I do want to say I'm sorry."

"Does this mean we can set forth together?"

He extended his hand: "Business is business."

Safiya thawed first. Initially distant and mistrustful, she began leading expeditions around Dar, showing Taggart and Esmeralda the nooks and crannies we'd discovered, among them the Kilwi Kisiwani or National Museum, which harboured nothing whatever on any Sacred Fire. More than once, Taggart arrived unannounced in a taxi — none of us had a telephone — and insisted that we drop everything to join some excursion.

With Taggart and Esmeralda, we visited the Kunduchi ruins,

where a sixteenth-century mosque reminded us of the greater glories of India; and the Village Museum, with its life-size replicas of various Tanzanian huts; and also the Mwenge Market, where Taggart bought a gleaming, waist-high Makonde sculpture, alive with the family of man: "It's just so us, don't you think?"

The way he laughed made me uneasy.

Esmeralda Esteban became the more interesting conundrum, because look what she did to the theoretical possibilities. By becoming Esmeralda's lover, desirable enough in itself, Daniel or I would double our chances of approaching The Shaman. By playing the lesbian, Safiya could also better her odds — though we all knew that would never happen. And Esmeralda? She knew Taggart too well to wish to remain his property.

Taggart revelled in the confusion. He watched, he waited. And where, with Safiya, he'd shown himself insanely jealous, with Esmeralda he demonstrated cool self-possession. I would have expected him to watch her incessantly. Instead, he encouraged her to ramble around Dar with any or all of us.

I've mentioned the New Africa Hotel. Soon we found ourselves meeting on the terrace almost daily to drink beer or orange squash — late afternoon sessions replete with subtle undercurrents and tensions. We'd all five taken to toting around our fire-worthy souvenirs. Sooner or later, three of us would set forth to invoke The Shaman. Which three? That we didn't discuss. But occasionally one of us would allude to the where and when of a hypothetical invocation. Both time and place had to be right: we all knew what had happened to Victor, and before that to Daniel's father.

Daniel remained committed to Mombasa as the only right place, but insisted that The Time hadn't come. Hundreds of police and paramilitary officers had recently been deployed. Gun battles had broken out in the tropical forests that lined the local beaches. A gang of thugs had burned down two police posts and stolen thirty guns. A few nights later, they attacked Kongowea, eight kilometres north of town, burned down fifty houses and slaughtered half a dozen people.

Editorial writers drew attention to political causes, and once, as a newspaperman, I would have taken a similar approach — but we five recognized the hand of Ahriman. Violence, fires, destruction: who could doubt it? Either way, tourists had been confined to their hotels. Nobody could argue that, in Mombasa, The Time had come. And none of us was would publicly champion any other place — what? divulge our secret thinking?

With the others, I waited. And one afternoon, on the terrace, Esmeralda slipped me a note saying that, come evening, she'd be home alone. Why didn't I visit? Later, as she climbed into a taxi with Taggart, she winked at me.

That evening, in my suite at the Palm Beach, I paced the floor. Why was I agonizing? Esmeralda was gorgeous, accomplished and heading for fame and fortune. Back home in America, she wouldn't have looked at me twice. What did I owe Taggart? Nothing. And Safiya? It broke my heart even to think it, but apparently she'd chosen Daniel Lafontaine. I owed her no allegiance. And by making love with Esmeralda, I would double my chances of restoring Colette — or would I?

Would I dare to face The Shaman with Esmeralda Esteban? I hardly knew the woman. Taggart had told me that the lost Avestan prophecies rambled for pages about "righteousness," which we both understood to mean "integrity." This attribute would certainly be tested at the Chinvat Bridge. Safiya might love Daniel Lafontaine, or she might, as I hoped, secretly feel torn between him and me. Either way, I'd fallen deeply in love with Safiya. How could I become Esmeralda's lover?

I hesitated to define this word "lover" in the context of the prophecies, yet felt certain I could rule out "philanderer." The more I pondered, the clearer it became: by making love with Esmeralda, I wouldn't increase my chances of succeeding with The Shaman. Rather, because of the perfidies and betrayals involved, I would decrease and might even destroy them. In the end, refusing to worry about thieves, the ubiquitous *mwezis*, I went for a long, lonely walk along the ocean. Eventually, kneeling in the sand under the stars, I wept without knowing why: for Safiya? Colette? for myself?

The right answer, I knew, included all three.

To Esmeralda, next time we met, I mumbled something about a previous engagement. She smiled frostily. We'd all five gathered to dine at the Simba Room in the Hotel Kilimanjaro, where on a previous splurge Safiya had acquired a taste for Crab Mornay. After ordering, and while we waited, Daniel noticed a covered piano on stage. He went over and, before anybody could stop him, flipped back the blanket and launched into Smoke Gets In Your Eyes: "They asked me how I knew / my true love was true...." Esmeralda joined him on stage, harmonizing so beautifully that shivers ran down my spine: "I of course replied / something deep inside / cannot be denied." When they'd finished, the Simba Room erupted into applause and shouts of "*Encore!*"

They performed another old Platters classic, and then a tune from Cats, and then broke off and rejoined us as the entrees arrived. They tried to pretend otherwise, but we all knew something significant had happened. Sure enough, later that evening as I returned from the washroom, I caught the two of them whispering. Tomorrow afternoon, Esmeralda said, Taggart would be seeing a man about a sailboat. She'd be home alone.

For the rest of the meal, I agonized. Safiya and I would need a third to set forth. I still believed that ashavan would be Daniel, but his looming intimacy with Esmeralda complicated matters. If he truly loved Safiya, it might well destroy his own chance of winning through — and that would be fine by me. But what of my own integrity? If I offered no warning, I'd become vulnerable to attack. Later that night, when we went to fetch a taxi, I said to Daniel: "Esmeralda's alluring — but I'd think twice about getting involved."

He looked stunned and I received a strange flash of precognition: Daniel trying to convince Esmeralda to abandon the quest. This made no sense — wouldn't he be trying to arrange for a third? Now he flared ominously before stalking off: "*Fadhili za punda, mashuzi; na msihadhari ni ng'ombe.* The gratitude of a donkey is a breaking of wind; one with no discretion is a cow."

I'd done my bit. Chastened, I settled on silence.

That Sunday, Taggart Oates bought a small sailboat. Having lived for two weeks at the Bahari Beach Hotel, he'd grown tired of watching others sail past his doorstep having what looked like "such a jolly good time." Even so, a fourteen-foot sailboat seemed an unlikely acquisition for a sedentary Englishman, and I suspected, though she denied it, that Esmeralda drove the purchase.

She and Taggart took sailing lessons at the Yacht Club, once the heart of the British expatriate community. Having mastered the basics, they christened the boat "The Askari" and arranged to take us all sailing. The sailboat could accommodate only three people at a time. Twice, Taggart took Safiya and Daniel; and once, Daniel and me. The experience exhilarated all of us — something about slashing through the waves off the coast of East Africa.

While sailing with Daniel and me, Taggart mentioned Zanzibar, the fabled island, part of Tanzania and less than one hour away by air. He intended to visit. Daniel, who'd travelled to Zanzibar by hydrofoil, offered an enthusiastic description of the Old Stone Town, the ruined palaces, the palm-fringed beaches: "Before I discovered Mombasa, I thought Zanzibar might be the place to invoke The Shaman."

I said, "What's wrong with it?"

"*Penye kuku wengi, hapamwagwi mtama.* Where there are many fowls, millet is not scattered." Seeing our blank faces, he added: "Too many proverbs, too much magic."

Taggart didn't buy it. Two mornings later, he and Esmeralda arrived at the Palm Beach and rousted me from bed. They'd decided to fly to Zanzibar. But now they'd rented a Jeep for a month and didn't want it sitting idle and vulnerable to *mwezis*. If I accompanied them to the airport, I could return with the Jeep and use it for the rest of the week. I had to hurry, though: their plane left in two hours.

Did Taggart really think to fool me with this ruse? He and Esmeralda were making for Zanzibar to invoke The Shaman. By driving them to the airport, I would become a third ashavan "setting forth." I almost laughed in Taggart's face. But as I opened my mouth to reject his request, I realized something else with the force of premonition: No way any invocation from Zanzibar could succeed. In his visceral response to the island, Daniel had been right. Zanzibar was the wrong place. I said: "Give me a minute to dress."

As we drove to the airport, Taggart gave me the keys to unlock the sailboat: "Might as well get some use out of it." At that, I began to feel guilty. Finally, I said, "Taggart, you shouldn't go to Zanzibar. Not to invoke The Shaman. I've had a premonition."

Taggart took a beat, then said: "You're just realizing."

"No, it's the wrong place. Esmeralda? Any attempt to invoke The Shaman in Zanzibar will end badly."

"Taggart, maybe we should —"

"Don't you see what he's doing? If we succeed, he fails."

Esmeralda remained torn. But we'd never connected and, at the airport, she shook my hand goodbye: "Nice try."

Later that day, over lunch, I told Daniel and Safiya what had happened.

Daniel looked upset but Safiya said: "You've got the keys to the boat? Let's go sailing."

The cloudless afternoon beckoned. None of us had any other commitments. Yet Daniel tried so hard to dissuade us, and with such pitiful arguments, that Safiya said: "You don't want to come, Daniel? Bernie and I will go alone."

"No, no. I'm coming."

Rather than carry a bag of her own, Safiya crammed a few items into my bag and Daniel's. We roared along the highway towards the Yacht Club with the windows open, the wind in our faces and Safiya chattering like a teenager playing hooky. I had a momentary twinge about going sailing with Safiya, the result of my premonitory vision. But look: Daniel was with us. What could go wrong?

I found out at the Yacht Club, soon after Safiya held a wet finger aloft and pronounced the day perfect. We hauled The Askari down to the pier and began rigging her out, a process more complex and challenging than we'd remembered. As we finished, a young man ran down to the dock: "Daniel Lafontaine? We've got an emergency phone call."

Daniel hurried up to the Clubhouse. After a few minutes, he returned: one of his favorite music students had tried to commit suicide. The boy had asked for him. Later, we would learn that the drug overdose had been accidental, and the boy would sleep it off. But now Daniel said, "What should we do?"

He was hoping we'd call off the expedition and go to the hospital with him. If he'd shown less reluctance earlier, Safiya might have chosen to do just that. Instead, she looked at me and said: "We can't do any good at the hospital. Why waste a great afternoon?" To Daniel she said: "You take the Jeep and pick us up later."

"Don't know how long I'll be." He pointed up the hill. "But some guy in the Clubhouse has offered me a lift. You keep the Jeep and I'll catch you at dinner."

That's when it hit me: was this becoming a variation? "Maybe we should just forget sailing," I said. "We'll drive Daniel to —"

Exasperated, Safiya said: "Bernie, go with the flow."

Daniel looked perturbed, but I thought no wonder: he's got to contend with a would-be suicide. Finally, as he turned on his heel, he said: "Promise you won't go out far."

Safiya made a face: "See you at dinner, Dan."

Together, Safiya and I dragged The Askari into the water, and soon we were slashing through swells as if we'd been sailing all our lives. Safiya took the rudder and, as she tacked back and forth, showing me what she'd learned, I told her she looked every inch the captain. She threw back her head and laughed, all sparkling white teeth, and her exultation made me want to hold onto that moment forever: the sun, the wind, the ocean spray and Safiya Naidoo crying: "Bernie, can you believe this? We're sailing off the coast of Africa."

We'd been sailing for an hour, getting farther and farther from shore, when I noticed the swells: they'd grown huge. The sea had turned rough. I surveyed the horizon and saw that the other sailboats, all seven or eight of them, had disappeared or were making for shore.

"Safiya, we're alone."

"Bernie, isn't this wild?"

She hadn't heard me, and this time I shouted: "The other boats have gone in!"

Safiya looked around: "We'd better go back."

In my mind, what followed remains indelibly present.

We're five miles off shore and sailing east, the wind at our backs. To return to the Yacht Club, we must reverse ourselves, travel north and west. That means we have to "jibe," to swing the sail from one side to the other — the toughest maneuver we know. Safiya tells me to duck, then rises and swings the sail. As it comes around, it catches the full force of the wind. The boat tilts ominously, but the maneuver's working when crack! the main mast snaps. The Askari pitches and yaws and here's a huge wave: "Safiya, look out! We're going over!"

Next thing I know, I'm treading water beside an overturned sailboat.

No sign of Safiya and I'm shouting: "Safiya! Safiya!"

At last she bobs to the surface, coughing and spluttering: "I've got your green bag."

"Safiya, you okay?"

"Wha- what happened?"

"The mast snapped. Good thing we're wearing life jackets."

"We've got to right the boat."

I notice blood in the water: "Safiya, you're bleeding."

"S'nothing. We've got to right the boat."

Safiya's slurring her words. She's got a gash in her head. She's bleeding. Despite myself, I think: blood in the water. I think: dangling legs. I think: sharks. And I cry: "Let's right this damn boat!"

We're clinging to the overturned hull, heaving up and down in the swells and I can't believe how much bigger the waves look from here. That's when it arrives, while I'm treading water in the Indian Ocean, washing over me from some other dimension — the rest of the waking vision whose undertow I've been fearing since I arrived in Tanzania....

Through a night-time howling storm, I see Daniel and his two friends arrive at the Yacht Club, the rain sluicing down in sheets so thick they can barely discern the dock. Inside the Clubhouse, whose large windows normally afford a view of the bay, but now reveal nothing but blackness, ten or twelve people hover over a short-wave radio listening to static. Nathan and Rachel join the circle, but Daniel walks out into a screened porch and stands looking out at the ocean. Nothing but blackness beyond the dim lights of the dock. No stars, no moon — no light. Just howling storm and the ocean smashing the beach like some furious beast. He thinks: "What have I done?"

Daniel shunts to a story he heard at an expatriate sundowner, a true story about an American woman who went water skiing. Without warning, a storm arose. The dead-calm sea grew rough. The woman fell, dropped her tow rope and disappeared in the swells. Her husband circled for ten minutes, and then ten more. With their two small children in the boat, finally he turned and made for the Yacht Club.

He dropped off the children and headed back out, but the motorboat flipped and he had to swim for his life, barely made it to shore.

Early next morning, the woman, half-dead, floated up onto the beach at one of the fancy hotels north of the Yacht Club. Drifted ashore like an old piece of wood. She'd spent the night clinging to one of her skis. The story-teller judged her lucky to be alive because sharks lurked just beyond the coral reef that ran between the Yacht Club and Bongoya Island. Usually, sharks didn't approach beyond that reef because, when the tide went out, they'd scrape their bellies on the coral.

Despite himself, Daniel thinks: Safiya's out beyond that coral reef clinging to The Askari. Does Bernard know how poorly she swims? Mentally, he calls: "Bernard! Safiya can't swim."

If the boat capsized, Daniel thinks, and got washed down the channel between the island and the shore, they'll drift out to sea. The Indian Ocean. A Swahili proverb comes to him: "*Avumaye baharini papa, kumbe wengi wapo.* The one who is famous in the sea is the shark; but then, there are many others."

Nathan emerges onto the porch, says somebody telephoned Dimitri, a Greek expatriate who owns the biggest boat in Dar: "He won't try to take it out tonight, not in this storm. But he'll go out at daybreak."

Safiya! Where are you? Alone again, staring into howling blackness, Daniel thinks: Somewhere out there, in those shark-infested waters, pitching up and down off the coast of East Africa, Safiya clings to a sailboat. Safiya! Forgive me!

He borrows a slicker and goes outside, tells Nathan: "Please, I need to be alone."

Oblivious to the ankle-deep puddles, he makes his way onto the beach. The rain hammers down freezing cold and Daniel stands remembering another beach, another terrible night — the night Victor died. And a wizened old man offering comfort as he wept on his knees in the sand: "Daniel, we could help each other."

"Help each other?"

"You want to become famous, Daniel? Isn't that what you hope to achieve with this quest?"

"You're not . . . Verethreghna?"

"No, I'm not."

"Then who are you?"

"Once I was Prophet of the Golden Flame. All you need to understand, Daniel, is that I can make it happen — with your music. I can make you famous around the world."

"How'd you know my name?"

"You seek recognition, do you not? Fame and glory as a musician?"

"You'd want something in return."

"Something in return?" The tiny man took his arm and walked with him along the beach: "Only that you abandon this foolish quest — and dissuade any friends and acquaintances."

"What friends? You've just killed my best friend."

"No, The Chinvat did that."

"So what do you need me for?"

"The Chinvat are stupid and crude, Daniel. Committed ashavans will certainly elude them."

"You come from the dark side."

"The dark side, the light — what difference? The Yin, the Yang — to serve one is to serve the other."

"I wouldn't have to hurt anybody?"

"No, just prevent them from invoking The Shaman."

Now, on the Yacht Club beach, the wind bends towering palms parallel to the ground, whipping their leaves until they flap like clothes on a line. Daniel thinks: this night is retribution — not just for the bargain I made, but for secretly taking up with Esmeralda. In passing, she'd mentioned that Taggart often went sailing alone. . . .

Looking out at the ocean, Daniel sees nothing but raging, ten-foot whitecaps. How can she survive this tempest? Safiya! Please! Then: please, what? Daniel begins trotting along the beach. Please survive? Please forgive me? Please emerge out of this tempest? Daniel realizes he's weeping, mingling salt tears with the rain. He's weeping and shouting: "Please! Please! Not like this!"

Next thing he knows, he's back inside the Clubhouse, exhausted, huddling under a blanket. He feels defeated, bested in some Yin-Yang struggle for life itself. Rachel brings him coffee: "You okay, Dan?"

Flatly, he says: "I'm fine."

"For a while there, we lost you."

"I'd just like to be alone."

Earlier, leaving the apartment, he'd impulsively stuffed the paperback Book of Changes into the pocket of his jacket. Now he takes it out. He re-reads The Thunderclap and looks more closely at where the Tao means to take him: "The Climax of this hexagram is not a zenith, like a sexual climax, but a nadir, a low point in your relationship with Friend."

Safiya is Friend — that much is obvious. "You and Friend are at the end of a trying and almost disastrous time of conflicts and selfish pressures." He thinks: Taggart Oates. He turns to the moksha section, the spiritual interpretation: "Enlightenment comes to some after a close brush with death. Enlightenment IS death of a sort. . . . "

Daniel peruses the "moving lines" and discovers that the second of them carries a special message. The Oracle notes that "disaster has struck close to you," but cautions against becoming "distraught and hysterical." It adds: "Remain calm in the understanding that the material world is always transitory and subject to sudden changes. You will soon regain possession of whatever you need."

Daniel snaps the book shut and stares around distractedly. The headmaster has arrived with his wife. They stand drenched despite their umbrellas. They're decent people — people who'd not only rented him their cherry-red piano, but insisted on hiring Safiya when opportunity arose. Now, they've brought dinner for a dozen — but how can Daniel eat?

He pokes at the beans and rice on his plate. He hears Nathan discussing plans for a morning rescue and remembers another story about Americans. Why always Americans? These three capsized in another sudden storm. They ran aground on Bongoya Island.

There they built a shelter in the trees above the beach. When darkness fell, they slept. In the middle of the night, giant rats woke them — hundreds of giant rats. The men ran screaming into the ocean. They spent the rest of the night waist-deep in water, safe from the rats but freezing cold. Rescuers found them next morning, Daniel believes — though really he just remembers the giant rats.

A big, florid-faced man stomps into the Yacht Club, his hair dripping wet. Loudly, he pronounces this the worst tropical storm he's seen in a decade. Up at Kunduchi Beach, he says, the waves are twelve feet high. Another man glances at Daniel and tells the newcomer to pipe down.

From time to time, the telephone rings: people offering food and blankets. Half the expatriates in Dar have turned up at the Yacht Club — dozens of people, all of them here to express their concern. Daniel hears someone ask: "Where's Taggart Oates? Doesn't he own The Askari?"

Daniel watches Nathan take the man aside. It scares him, the way people are being so careful. Taggart has taken Esmeralda to Zanzibar. Tonight he remains far away and Daniel's glad of that. Mentally, he calls: "I love you, Safiya! I NEED you!"

The night drags on and numbness overtakes him. A Swedish businesswoman promises to fetch her company plane if an air search becomes necessary. Daniel stops hearing what Nathan and the others are saying. Nobody calls from a beach hotel. Rachel takes his hand and tells him not to lose hope.

Eventually, morning breaks. Daniel steps outside and registers the chilly air. The wind blows but no longer rages. Crashing waves have subsided into heavy swells. Still, a thick fog hangs over the ocean, reducing visibility to thirty feet.

Dimitri arrives and prepares his yacht. A burly man, he comes alive when he steps onto the boat, moves nimbly and with great authority. Don't worry about fog, he says. We'll take her out anyway. Heartened, Daniel climbs into the boat and Nathan follows with Rachel. Dimitri waves away the headmaster: "I'm hoping we won't have room."

Daniel starts to zip his jacket against the chill, then stops. He knows it's ridiculous, but does Safiya have a jacket to zip? No, she does not, and he wishes to suffer in sympathy. Dimitri starts the motor. Guided by instruments, he steers the yacht slowly into the fog, making for Bongoya Island: "That's our best hope."

Half an hour later, visibility has improved enough that, as they approach the island through fog, Daniel finds himself staring up at a thirty-foot cliff: nothing but black rock and the odd crevice choked with vegetation.

His voice trembling, he says: "This is it?"

"At the tip," Dimitri says, "there's a bit of beach."

As they motor slowly along the rocky island, Daniel finds himself vomiting over the railing. Rachel tries to help but he waves her away. Staring up at the bleak, rocky face of Bongoya Island, he tries to believe in the Book-of-Changes prophesy: a dramatic finale, a miraculous release — rescue almost inevitable. Almost.

Staring up at the black cliffs of Bongoya Island, Daniel thinks: nobody could run aground here and survive — not Safiya, not himself and not even Bernard Lanigan.

The Chinvat Bridge

This waking vision lasts only an instant, yet it extends into the future and confirms the worst: the rough sea is just the beginning. Safiya's bleeding from the head, an ugly gash above her left ear. Also, she's groggy, keeps insisting that we've got to right the boat, we've got to right the boat. It has airbags under the seats, I remember: bouyancy bags. Once righted, The Askari will bob to the surface like a cork — that's what Taggart said. And so Safiya: "We've got to right the boat."

I move to her side and we try kicking and lifting together, but Safiya keeps losing her grip. In desperation, I scramble up onto the bottom of the boat, grab the rudder and lean back as far as I can. The sailboat rolls and dumps me back into the ocean, but yes! it's rightside up! I pull myself over the gunwhale and haul Safiya into the boat after me.

The Askari's riding so low that every third or fourth wave sweeps more water into the boat: "It bobs to the surface like a cork?"

"The buoyancy bags." Safiya kneels in the water and feels around under the back seat. Finally, she produces the end of an airhose, unstoppered, and stares at it with dismay: "What's this?"

She's not herself: "Safiya, sit tight."

Clearly, the bags are empty. Under a seat I find a tin can attached to a rope. I start bailing, but no way I can compete with these waves. More and more water washes over the side, making the boat heavier, driving it lower. Safiya locates a second tin can and tries to bail but slumps over onto her side, her eyes glazed: "Safiya, hang tough!"

The boat's too heavy. It threatens to roll. I plunge over the side and tread water. The Askari stabilizes with its gunwhales inches above the water line. Safiya slumps chest-deep in water, unconscious but still breathing. She's clutching my fabulous green bag. I cling to the side of the boat and, when the swells carry me aloft, take my bearings. We're six or seven miles from shore and the wind is blowing us still farther out.

Where's that island Daniel mentioned? I look around and, next big swell, spot a smudge on the horizon: Bongoya Island. It's two miles away but that's not bad because we're still inside the coral reef. Sharks remain unlikely. And if Safiya's still bleeding, she's bleeding into the boat. We've got to hit Bongoya, the only land between here and India. The wind is blowing in the right direction but we're churning in slow circles because the broken mast and sail dangle, dragging, off one side of the boat.

I swim around the sailboat — it almost gets away from me — and twist the broken mast so the flapping sail catches wind. I move to the stern hand over hand and seize the top of the rudder. I swing it around, aim for Bongoya and kick hard, trying not to imagine a shark's-eye view of my dangling white legs.

I kick hard for I don't know how long. Slowly, the island grows larger. At roughly five hundred yards, a swell carries me aloft and gives me a good look at where we're heading and I don't like it. I'm staring up at a black cliff, a monolithic mass — nothing but rocks. Wait: at one end of the island, as I recall, there's "a bit of a beach."

When the next swell carries me aloft, I spot a sandspit fifty yards long. That's it? I adjust the rudder and kick like a madman. For a while I fear we're going to smash into the rocks but a gust of wind carries us beyond them: yes! We run aground ten yards from the shore, whitecaps breaking all around. I try to drag the boat up onto the sand but can't budge it — too full of water, too heavy.

Forget the boat, fool! Safiya's slumped over, unconscious.

Twice the whitecaps knock me off my feet. Finally, I manage to haul Safiya out of the sailboat. I drape her left arm around my shoulder and stagger up onto the beach. Beside a driftwood log, I collapse. When I catch my breath, I roll Safiya onto her back and, oh god, at least she's breathing. The gash above her ear has stopped bleeding. I hold my hands over the gash, trying to summon energy, but I'm depleted, powerless, exhausted by the struggle to get us here.

Safiya is still clutching my fabulous green bag, and gently I remove it from her arms. I check for my fire-worthy souvenirs, find them safe enough — and discover hers tucked in with my own. I dig out a T-shirt, perfectly dry because the bag's lined, and use it to bandage Safiya's head. I make sure she's lying comfortably, then take my bearings. No sailboat in sight. No dhow, no ngalawa. Overhead, scudding clouds. The wind is picking up, the sea getting rougher: a tropical storm is brewing.

Behind me, up the beach, palm trees shake their leaves above a tropical jungle of shrubs, vines and grasses. Shelter from the approaching storm? No: giant rats lurk in that greenery. Maybe the boat? I cross the sandy beach, wade into the roaring surf and try again to drag The Askari ashore. Again I can't budge it. The ocean has dumped sand into the sailboat. I check it for food, for anything useful, and settle on the sail. With whitecaps crashing around me, I work away untying, unhooking, and finally manage to tear the sail free.

On the beach, I trot back and forth hunting driftwood. I find half a dozen short sticks, plant them in the sand and prop the sail to dry in the wind. By now night is falling. I collect more driftwood, all shapes and sizes, and pile it near the sail. I feel the first pinpricks of rain. Using the sail and poles, I rig a rough tent over Safiya. From my green bag, I take a book of matches and light a small fire. When the rain begins to fall in great fat droplets, the fire gutters out and I crawl under the sail.

Soon the darkness is utter. The rain pounds down and I shiver with cold. Yet this misery can't compare, I realize, with the horror

Daniel Lafontaine is enduring at the Yacht Club — though that's a horror, I now understand, that he's brought on himself. Eventually, staring out from under the sail at the glowing embers of my small fire, and hugging Safiya for warmth, I drift off to sleep.

Halfway through the night, with the sail flapping and the rain beating down in sheets, Safiya shakes me: "Bernie? You awake?"

"No, go back to sleep."

"Bernie, I had a dream." Safiya hugs me tightly. "It's you I love."

I hesitate, hoping against hope: "Safiya, you hit your head."

"My head's okay, Bernie. In my dream, you healed me."

Safiya pulls the bandage off her head, takes my hand and presses it to her head. No wetness. No gash. I say, "This makes no sense."

"Not unless we've moved into some parallel universe." She moves my hand down onto her breasts, then presses her lower body against me: "Safiya, wait. You're not thinking clearly."

"Oooh, sailor! What's happening here?"

"Safiya, we're already lovers. You don't —"

"You talk a good denial, Bernie." Safiya slips off her jean shorts and everything else fades away: the cold, the wind, the rain, all gone. We've re-entered that magical garden we found in Athens, the place where only we two exist. Safiya undoes my belt and takes out my erect penis: "You talk a good denial, but how do you account for this?"

I pull her onto me and kiss her mouth, and after a moment I try to slide down under her body to bury my face in her, I'm thirsting for the taste of her, but she stops me and pushes me onto my back. Safiya straddles me and gently surrounds me and oh, god, it feels good, so good I might lose control, so for a while we don't move but just lie there holding each and looking into each other's eyes.

After a while, Safiya begins rotating her hips in slow, easy circles, round and round, and together we settle into a slow rhythm, round and round and back and forth and "we're on our way, Bernie," back and forth, "we're on our way over the broken wall," and she picks up the tempo, round and round, back and forth, and says "over the broken wall, the burning roof and tower," and I recognize the immortal lines but I'm giving back as good as I get and this goes on until a great surge of feeling wells up inside me and I revel in being shaken from within and I begin to black out as Safiya cries, "I love you, Bernie, I love you," and I let go and lose myself completely. . . .

What happens next is so bizarre, and so unlike anything I expected, that I hesitate even now to describe it. As I climax I feel reality shift gears yet again and suddenly I'm swirling through a tunnel head first, like in a giant water slide, and I'm thinking what's this? another Near Death Experience? Again I emerge into nothingness and feel myself plummetting and tumbling, tumbling head over heals through a void.

I slow to an easy drift but still discern nothing. Then, gradually, I become aware that I've tumbled into a vast arena, and as my senses adjust I perceive two entities locked in what I recognize as a primordial struggle. Then: my god! Taggart and Daniel! Only here they've been broken down, reduced to their component parts, to thousands and thousands of coloured blocks. This is a battle to the death, I realize, but it's unequal. As an entity, Daniel comprises roughly as many blocks as Taggart, but he stands no chance of winning because too many of them remain colourless, empty: he's too young.

Without thinking, without making a conscious choice, I hurl myself at Taggart and he spins away from Daniel to engage me. Instantly, I find myself transformed, reduced to my own constituent parts, so now Taggart and I have become block-creatures battling, intertwined, spinning away into the void as we lay out our constituent blocks at lightning speed, lay them out in endlessly twisting rows. We lay out everything we are, match each other block for block, until finally Taggart  places his final block and I have one block left and I lay it down crying: "Daniel lives!"

White light explodes into the void with such force that it sends me tumbling, tumbling, and this time when I slow down I find myself drifting in my old familiar astral body. In the distance I see a bonfire blazing against a starry night and three figures talking on a beach. As I drift closer, I realize this is Zanzibar — this is happening now in Zanzibar.

Taggart Oates and Esmeralda Esteban stand before a third figure who gives off a radiant light: Verethreghna! The Shaman himself! Having assumed the form of a shining young man, his least threatening incarnation, The Shaman stands behind a waist-high chalice in which a small fire burns — a fire so brightly golden that, even in my current state, I can't look directly at it: The Sacred Fire of Ahura Mazda!

Taggart and Esmeralda have approached The Shaman through a lesser fire — a bonfire that blazes behind them on the beach. The three are talking but I can't hear a word. The Shaman reaches into the small golden fire and retrieves a silver dagger — Taggart's primary talisman. This he hands to Esmeralda, who in turn passes it to Taggart.

All this time I'm drifting slowly closer.

Now I discern voices. Taggart cries, "Run for the bridge!"

Amazing! Where an instant ago the bonfire blazed, a stone bridge stands now, broad and beautiful. Esmeralda turns and races onto it. Taggart makes his way slowly backwards, brandishing his dagger, but as he wheels to step onto the bridge, a foul-smelling hag emerges from beneath it. Lightning fast and immensely strong, this stinking crone gets a rope around his neck and begins dragging Taggart down an embankment towards a cliff that falls away into nothingness.

Taggart manages to cut the rope with his dagger. He gets his feet under him and stumbles to the bridge. The crone flies after him and leaps onto his back. Taggart fights to keep his balance, takes one step, then another, but suddenly the bridge narrows to a razor-sharp edge and as Taggart takes a third step he slips off the edge and down they go howling, Taggart and the stinking hag, howling and spinning down, down, down into the abyss. . . .

When I open my eyes, I'm back on the roaring, wave-tossed beach at Bongoya Island. Looking out from beneath the sail, I see a fire blazing and can't understand it. The small fire I lit hours ago guttered out in the rain, but now my small fire has become a bonfire and . . . what? I bolt upright: "Safiya! A bonfire."

"Taggart's dead," she says. "I had a dream." Then: "My god!"

We pull on our shorts and emerge from beneath the sail. The rain has stopped falling. I look up, amazed, and realize that's not quite true: it's like we're protected by an invisible dome. The bonfire blazes — and beyond it, some distance away, there burns a smaller fire, brightly, blindingly gold. Beyond that, a shining figure stands. "Safiya! Through the fire!"

"The Shaman! I see him!"

"Where's my green bag?" I grab it from under the sail. "Okay, let's go."

"You mean we . . . approach through the bonfire?"

"Bingo!" I shake my green bag. "Your souvenirs all here?"

She nods: "Bernie, are you sure?"

I get a vision of Colette, the clearest yet, lying unconscious in San Francisco. Simultaneously, I flash on my recurring nightmare, hear the judge roaring: "Repent and redeem yourself! Repent or I'll see that you suffer in love until the day you die!"

I take Safiya's hand: "I've never been more certain of anything in my life."

Together, we step into the bonfire — and feel nothing. We walk through the fire unscathed and emerge into a silent garden. No rain, no ocean. We follow a path that winds gently uphill. At the top stands a shining youth of about fifteen. Verethreghna has assumed the least threatening form available to him, but his presence remains overwhelming, terrifying: The Shaman himself! Before him stands a waist-high chalice in which a fire blazes so brightly gold that we can't look directly at it.

Safiya finds her tongue and speaks an ancient evocation she's never so much as mentioned: "I announce and complete my worship to thee, the fire, oh Ahura Mazda's son! Together with all the fires, and to the good waters, even to all the waters made by Mazda, and to all the plants which Mazda made."

"Speak thou," The Shaman answers, his voice inhumanly deep and rumbling: "Speak thou in order for me to discern that very good thing which has been created for me by truth. Speak thou in order for me to know and bear in mind with good thinking those things of which I am to be the Seer."

"Bernie! The souvenirs!"

We open my green bag and she takes out the two sachets in which we keep our mementoes. She hands me my bag, opens her own and begins depositing souvenirs in The Sacred Fire, which flares more brightly with each trinket. "We beseech thee, Ahura Mazda," Safiya says, indicating that I should follow her example: "We beseech thee to take these souvenirs in token of the sixteen fires. We ask thee to accept seven as magical, one for each of the Amesha Spentas, the Bountiful Immortals, and also to purify one fire-worthy souvenir, one talisman for each of us, that we both may advance in our kwarenahs."

"Ahura Mazda responds with three questions," The Shaman says in that strange, rumbling voice. "You may confer before responding, but know this: even if you answer successfully, only one of you will walk back across the Chinvat Bridge."

Safiya and I exchange a glance, but that's enough to seal a pact: one way or another, we're both returning across that bridge.

"Aboard the Verlandi," The Shaman says, "you learned of the three."

We wait for him to continue, then realize that's it — the first question.

Foolishly, I say: "It's a riddle." And then, turning to Safiya: "The three who set forth?"

"No, I knew about them before leaving home."

"What about the three saviours? One to arrive at the close of each millennium. Taggart told me about them on the ship."

"Me too," Safiya says. "Hashedar and Ashedar-Mah and... and . . . ."

"And Sasoshyant." I face The Shaman: "Hashedar, Ashedar-Mah and Sasoshyant."

Almost imperceptibly, The Shaman nods: "One talisman burns not in The Sacred Fire."

I turn to Safiya: "Does he mean one of them's unacceptable?"

"The talisman you brought from San Francisco," she says. "I think he means, 'Where is it?'"

"It's in Athens," I say, turning to The Shaman. "Or somewhere in Greece. I lost it when — "

Safiya puts her hand on my arm: "The talisman is here, Mighty Shaman." She points to a platform beside The Sacred Fire and for the first time I notice the dead body of Taggart Oates lying there, the handle of his own dagger protruding from his chest: "What the —?"

Safiya steps over to the body. She opens Taggart's shirt and, from around his neck, removes the gold necklace Behroze gave me. She places it in The Sacred Fire.

"What? How did —"

"I figured it out just now, when I noticed the body. Taggart stole the necklace before Chinvat made off with the bag."

"Taggart stole it? Why?"

"To impede you. To reduce your chances of reaching this —"

But again The Shaman rumbles: "Of the challenges you have faced in the Golden Flame, one almost destroyed you."

"The shipwreck." Safiya says. "It's got to be. You saved my life, Bernie. If you hadn't — "

"No, I don't think so." Turning to The Shaman, I fall to one knee and say: "My intellectual pride, Mighty One. It kept me from accepting and loving Behroze as I should have — from surrendering to the forces of the heart and recognizing the healing power of magic. In confronting a ritualized quest which my overblown intellect rejected as foolish and unworthy, I needed constantly to battle my own arrogance. My hubris almost destroyed Colette and Safiya and my last chance for redemption — as once, long ago, it destroyed Behroze. I ask your forgiveness."

"Forgiveness and healing are granted. You may rise." The Shaman thrusts one hand into The Sacred Fire and produces two souvenirs which shine so brightly that at first we don't recognize them. As if in answer to my unspoken question, he says: "These talismans, purified in The Golden Flame, carry the power of Ahura Mazda."

To me, The Shaman hands the necklace I brought from San Francisco. To Safiya, he hands the silver bracelet from Mesa Verde — only now it's not silver but gold. "One of you may walk back across the Chinvat Bridge," The Shaman says. "The other shall remain with me."

Safiya says, "Thank you, Verethreghna."

We bow and step backwards.

"Go ahead down the path," I tell Safiya. "But whatever you do, don't step onto any bridge."

"But what —"

"Please, Safiya. Hurry."

She strides away down the path. I step over to the dead body of Taggart Oates and pull the golden dagger from his chest: "We thank you for the invitation, mighty Shaman. But neither of us wishes to remain."

Verethreghna watches impassively while I hurry after Safiya. As I approach the end of the path I see her waiting. The bonfire through which we passed has become the Chinvat Bridge, wide and beautiful. The Bridge of Judgment. Suddenly, a foul wind rises and a wretched hag, stinking and horrible, emerges from beneath the bridge. She reels toward me with a rope in her hands.

"Who are you?" I cry: "What do you want?"

"I am your own bad actions, you fool. The shadow you've so long repressed. I was ugly at the outset and you daily made me worse, and now you've drawn us both to the brink of the pit of misery and damnation, and together we'll suffer punishment until The Renovation."

The hag darts forward, lightning fast, and gets a noose around my neck. She jerks the rope tight, pulls me off my feet and drags me down the embankment towards the abyss. I fight for breath, clutch at the rope and drop the golden dagger. I kick and thrash but I'm going down when suddenly the rope comes lose. Safiya! Moving like a whirlwind. The hag doubles over and falls to the ground and I don't understand what's happened until I see the dagger sticking out of her chest. "Safiya! You saved my life."

"We're even, Bernie."

Stinking, troll-like creatures scurry out from beneath the Bridge of Judgment, dozens of them waving clubs and howling, and I realize who, in this curious guise, we're facing: "The Chinvat! They've found us."

That's when I remember the wilds of India, travelling during monsoon: "Climb aboard, Safiya!" I brace myself as Daniel did when she stood on the wrong side of the stream: "Climb onto my back."

Safiya gets the message: only one of us can walk across the Chinvat Bridge. She leaps onto my back with such energy that she almost knocks me over, but I keep my balance and reel onto the Bridge. The Chinvat trolls chase after us, waving clubs and howling, and as I stagger forward Safiya grows heavier, I don't know why, until at the three-quarter mark I feel the trolls gaining ground and realize I'm not going to make it, that I'm going to collapse under the weight, but Safiya whispers, "I love you, Bernie Lanigan," and in my mind I hear Behroze say, "I forgive you, Bernie," and then my darling Colette cries, "Help me, daddy, help me," and as lover and husband and father I lurch forward step by step by step and manage two final steps, and then one more, before I stumble and pitch forward onto my face.

Lighting Up Eternity

The twists and revelations that made sense of this shamanistic tumult didn't come until months later. Around the world, the fireworks had subsided. The rash of volcanic eruptions, lightning storms and flashfires disappeared from the headlines, a happy reversal that most people failed even to notice. That the ultimate unwinding should involve Daniel Lafontaine strikes me now as sublime — but I'm getting ahead of my story.

Having staggered to the end of Chinvat Bridge and fallen onto my face, I heard Safiya sing out: "Bernie, we made it!"

I raised my head: Bongoya Island! Gone the Bridge of Judgment, the howling trolls, The Shaman watching serenely from the hill. We'd shifted back into mundane reality. The tropical storm had spent itself. Our sail-tent lay in tatters on the beach. Day was dawning. The fog had dispersed and a mist rose off the Indian Ocean.

"I want you to have this." Safiya handed me her Mesa Verde

bracelet, which sparkled and gleamed gold despite the flatness of the morning light.

I patted my pockets: "But I've got —"

"You lost the necklace when that hag grabbed you."

"No. Are you —"

"Take the bracelet, Bernie. For Colette."

I was still admiring how it glittered when Safiya said: "What's that humming sound?"

Soon, through the mist, we discerned the approaching yacht. I stuffed the gold bracelet into my pocket and, waving and hollering, we dashed into the ocean. Daniel rowed out in a dinghy and brought us back to the yacht, where somebody wrapped us in blankets and gave us coffee.

Daniel said: "You didn't see any — rats?"

Through chattering teeth, Safiya said, "Rats?"

"They stayed in the trees," I said. "Because of the storm."

Safiya looked cold but fully recovered and I couldn't understand it when, a few minutes after we boarded, still wrapped in a blanket, she slumped over and passed out. I examined her head and found no sign of a gash. Safiya remained unconscious after we brought her ashore, though she awoke that afternoon and began coming around. A doctor said: "Exhaustion, exposure: she needs rest."

Safiya was still resting that evening when Esmeralda Esteban, badly shaken, arrived from Zanzibar. Officially, Taggart Oates had drowned. She'd told police they'd gone for a late-night stroll

along the beach. That he'd insisted swimming out into the darkness and didn't come back. Taggart's body never turned up but that wasn't unusual. Zanzibari officials recorded the facts as related and made sympathetic noises. Another tourist dead. Next!

Esmeralda wept when, with Daniel and I, she got to tell the truth. She described the scene I'd secretly witnessed. She and Taggart invoked The Shaman, answered three questions and received two talismans. Esmeralda dropped hers but escaped across the Chinvat Bridge. Glancing back, she

saw Taggart plunge into the abyss. That's when she wept —
describing how Taggart Oates, ridden by a crone, tumbled head-
long and howling off the Bridge.

Daniel dredged up more sympathy than me. My feelings were
mixed because Taggart had stolen Colette's necklace. If, by that
action, he'd threatened only me, I might have been able to forgive
him. But he'd jeopardized Colette. I left Daniel to comfort
Esmeralda and walked into the night.

Next morning, when finally I got a few minutes alone with
Safiya, I discovered that she'd forgotten what happened on
Bongoya Island. She knew we'd succeeded in our quest — that
we'd approached The Shaman, answered his questions and escaped
back across the Chinvat Bridge with a token of our success. Also,
that she'd given me that purified talisman, her Mesa Verde bracelet.

But certain crucial details, I learned to my dismay, she'd utterly
forgotten, starting with the shipwreck itself: "You smacked your
head when we went down."

"Isn't that something? I don't remember."

"You don't remember how we invoked The Shaman?"

"Now you mention it, no."

"We made love, Safiya."

Wide-eyed, she shook her head: "No! That can't be."

She saw the truth in my eyes: "Gee, I — I don't remember. I do
remember standing before The Shaman. But before that's a blank.
I don't remember a thing from the time we arrived at the Yacht
Club. I feel like . . . like I died or something."

Just then, Daniel re-entered the room: "*Siki njema huonekana
asubuhi.* A good day becomes evident in the morning."

"I'd been hoping," I said dolefully, "for more than a good
day."

They both looked at me expectantly, but this wasn't the
moment to declare myself. With time, Safiya would recover her
memory. Then we'd sort out our relationship. Part of me wanted
to wait here in Dar, but no way I could do that while back in San
Francisco, Colette lay in a coma — and finally I possessed the
means to restore her.

Safiya said: "When are you leaving?"

"Tomorrow morning. Otherwise, given the plane schedule,
I'd have to wait a week."

Daniel said: "You're leaving?"

"Safiya's tired. I'll explain outside."

A few minutes later, as we stepped into the sunshine, I challenged Daniel to come clean: "You emptied those airbags, didn't you?"

"What airbags?"

"Dimitri salvaged the sailboat, Daniel. I inspected it myself. You emptied those airbags and sawed partway through the mast to weaken it. You thought you'd catch Taggart but caught us instead."

"I don't know what you're talking about."

"I'm talking about the deal you made on that beach in Mombasa. With a wizened old prophet."

"Ha! Where do you get this stuff?"

"You'd begun to wonder about Bongoya Island, if that wasn't the right place to invoke The Shaman, and so acted to prevent Taggart and Esmeralda from ever reaching it."

"You've gone mad. You've — " He hesitated, staring at me intently, and I saw the realization wash over him: "You did it, didn't you? You and Safiya! You completed the quest."

"If you come clean now, Daniel, and return to the truth, you should be all right."

Suddenly angry again, Daniel said: "You're leaving tomorrow, Bernie? Remember this: *Asiiyekuwapo machoni, na moyoni hayupo.* He who is not in sight is not in the heart."

With that he stormed off.

Early next morning, away I flew: Brussels, New York, San Francisco. The final flight lasted forever but eventually I bounded off the airplane and took a cab to the hospital. I'd missed visiting hours but explained that I'd just arrived from Africa and the head nurse made an exception.

When finally I saw her, my darling Colette, looking so frail and fragile, I fell to my knees and clutched her hand and wept. I detected no bearded men and yet felt a presence: Behroze? The nurse left the room, summoned by name over the public address system, but my dead wife failed to materialize. From here on out, I was on my own. The bracelet! I removed it from my jacket pocket and slipped it onto Colette's wrist.

Nothing happened.

I waited. Still nothing.

I waited all that night and the next day and the day after that, sitting beside Colette's bed. Still nothing happened. Fear seized me and wouldn't let go. Maybe I needed the original necklace? No, that couldn't be. Not unless the Golden Flame had deserted me. Why didn't the bracelet work? I'd seen The Shaman purify it in The Sacred Fire. Then I realized: he'd handed the bracelet to Safiya, not me. Maybe it would function only for her?

The day after I arrived home, I'd written to Safiya in Dar es Salaam. Since then, I'd written twice more. So far, I'd received no answer. I tried telephoning but couldn't get through. Apparently, the city's telephone system had gone down. I sent a telegram asking Safiya to call me. Used the word "urgent." Nothing. Then my second letter to Safiya came back stamped: "Return to sender." Across the envelope, somebody had scrawled, "No longer at this address."

Again I tried calling the International School — no luck. Finally, I got through via shortwave radio. A secretary told me that both Safiya and Daniel had departed. And they'd left no forwarding address. No, she didn't know where they'd gone.

I wanted to find a corner and curl up into a ball.

But what about Colette? Physically, she remained remarkably healthy — miraculously so, the doctors said. I thought: Behroze promised me three months. We passed that deadline and nothing happened. Maybe the bracelet was keeping her healthy? Or maybe Behroze was hanging on, helping. This I knew: Colette was living on borrowed time. Where, oh where was Safiya?

I tried to locate her sister in Montreal, used the phone book and talked with every Naidoo in it without getting a lead. Three long-distance operators failed to do any better. I ransacked my memory, realized that Safiya had never once mentioned her sister's married name. I tried a psychic scan and hit a wall that reminded me of the cliff on Bongoya Island. Where was Behroze when I needed her? A quotation from the Duc de la Rouchefald danced through my mind: "Absence diminishes commonplace passions and increases great ones, as the wind extinguishes candles and kindles fire."

Fire, fire — would I never fly free of this golden inferno?

At home in my kitchen, I fell to my knees and wept. Safiya

had reconnected with Daniel Lafontaine and didn't know how to tell me. Colette remained comatose and I didn't care what the doctors said: I could sense that now, at last, she'd begun to weaken. I cursed the day I'd heard the name Ahura Mazda.

And that's when the telephone rang.

I pulled myself together and answered.

"Hey, sailor." Since Bongoya Island, two months had passed.

"Safiya? Where are you?"

"I'm in Montreal. My sister's married name is Archambault. And she's no longer in remission but strangely recovered."

"You didn't need the bracelet?"

"I've picked up a few of your old tricks, Bernie. And I'm calling to explain. How could you imagine that I'd gone off with Daniel?"

"You . . . you didn't?"

"I certainly did not. Esmeralda Esteban did. They're down in New Orleans. They've signed with a big label and they're getting ready to tour."

"To tour?"

"They're musicians, remember? But that's not why I didn't call."

"You've got my attention."

"First, how's Colette?"

"She's . . . hanging on."

"Bernie, we'll bring her back. I didn't call because I couldn't. Not until today."

"I've missed something."

"I think of it as The Shaman's Reach. I would sit down to write you and literally could not pick up a pen or a pencil. I could not type your name on a keyboard. Anybody else, no problem — as long as I didn't try to mention your name. I'd pick up the telephone and simply could not dial your number."

"That's some reach."

"Still the same old Bernie. Didn't you ever wonder why The Shaman let two of us escape across the Chinvat Bridge? When all he had to do was raise an eyebrow to flip the Bridge onto its side?"

I remembered glancing back as I started across the Bridge. The Shaman stood serene on the hill, enjoying a clear view of all that transpired. He watched our struggle with the foul hag, registered the pursuit by stinking Chinvat trolls. "We'd earned the right," I said into the phone. "Strictly speaking, only one of us walked across the Bridge of Judgment. The Shaman respected the rules."

"Without breaking them," she answered, "he could have flipped the Bridge onto its side and condemned us both to an aeon of punishment. You think he didn't because he felt bound by a human sense of fair play?"

It was like we'd never been apart: "You're taking this somewhere."

"Something strange has happened, Bernie. This morning, a doctor confirmed it."

"Something strange?"

"No, no. It's good news." She took a beat, then said: "Bernie? I'm pregnant."

"You're pregnant?" The kitchen began to whirl. I lowered myself onto the floor. "Uh, congratulations. But I thought you couldn't . . . uh, couldn't . . . ."

"You're right. I couldn't have kids. Or so half a dozen doctors told me. Turns out I'm pregnant anyway."

"I'm sure you and . . . that you'll . . . ."

"Bernie, knock it off. I haven't slept with anybody."

"You haven't slept with anybody."

"That's what I'm trying to tell you. I haven't slept with anybody since . . . well, remember how we invoked The Shaman? I haven't slept with anybody since Bongoya Island."

I paused, letting this sink in, the wonder of it, and through my mind, unbidden, danced a couple of old familiar lines from The Second Coming: "The darkness drops again; but now I know / that twenty centuries of stony sleep / were vexed to nightmare by a rocking cradle." Why those lines? Who cared?

"Safiya, when was the last time you visited San Francisco?"

"Twenty years, give or take. I was a child."

"What if I send you airfare?"

"No need, Bernie. Last week, my agent called. I'd sent him an outline of my next novel? Guess what? He's sold it to the bigs."

"Get out of here."

"Bernie, we're talking six digits."

"Safiya, that's fantastic."

"So you can keep your airfare. The invitation, I'll accept — if only for Colette's sake."

"Tomorrow, Safiya? Can you fly out tomorrow?"

Two days later, Safiya arrived in San Francisco. She'd changed her hair style and wore a short leather coat, an above-the-knee skirt and black tights. We're talking drop-dead gorgeous and oh, so very Montreal. Yet as soon as she spotted me, standing blue-jeaned and dishevelled in the airport lounge, she raced over and threw herself into my arms. I buried my face in her neck as tears scalded my cheeks.

I'd reserved a hotel room so as not to presume, but Safiya insisted we go straight to the hospital. The nurses waved us through: they'd long since given up arguing with me. Safiya knelt beside Colette's bed, bowed her head and took my little girl's hand. Nothing happened. We took one hand each and focused all the magic that together we could summon — and still nothing happened.

Neither of us could understand it. We could feel the heat of The Golden Flame. Why couldn't we restore Colette? Why didn't the purified talisman do its work? Had Behroze misled me? Impossible! Round and round we went.

Eventually, exhausted, despairing, we left the hospital.

Safiya never did see the inside of the hotel room I'd booked. Later, she would enjoy claiming that I never even made a reservation, and cite as evidence that I drove her from the hospital straight back to the house. I would try to explain that I wasn't thinking straight, but invariably listeners preferred her version. Anyway, the day after she arrived, seeing my despondency over Colette, Safiya tried to comfort me by stroking my hair. And one gesture led to another . . . .

The day after that, Safiya's sister called from Canada to relay terrible news. Daniel Lafontaine and Esmeralda Esteban had been performing in some club in Boston, when a gang of thugs burst into the place, identified Daniel and started blasting away with shotguns. The police couldn't understand it. Nobody could. Why would anybody want to murder a piano player on his way to stardom?

Safiya took the news harder than I did. For several days she moped around in a track suit, wondering if she couldn't have done something differently. In our pain, we clung to each other.

Oddly enough, our love-making remained magical. We didn't spin out into the phantasmagoric realms we'd discovered on Bongoya Island, but several times we approached the surreal, and one evening, suddenly, we found ourselves strolling along a tropical beach, just the two of us, with the ocean lapping gently at our feet. Up ahead, we spotted a blond man in blue-jean cut-offs working away at a sailboat. He looked oddly familiar. As we approached, Safiya cried: "Daniel!"

"Hey! I thought you'd never get here."

Daniel hugged Safiya and then extended his hand. "You were right," he said as we shook. "I should have come clean when I had the chance."

"The Chinvat got you?"

He nodded. "But that's not why I've waited."

Safiya said, "It's about the baby."

"Your little boy, yes. I've waited to relay a message. To tell you to call him . . . Hashedar."

Safiya said: "Hashedar? That's the name. . . ."

Daniel nodded: "The name of the first great saviour."

"Give us a Swahili proverb," I said. "To mark the occasion."

"*Uchesi wa mtoto ni anga la nyumba,*" Daniel said without hesitation. "The laughter of a child lights up the house." He took a beat. "In this case, perhaps we should make that the world."

I said: "No, the universe — or perhaps the millennium?"

Safiya, still not satisfied, said: "How do you say 'eternity?'"

"*Umilele. Uchesi wa mtoto ni anga umilele?*"

Safiya spoke the translation: "The laughter of a child lights up eternity."

As if in confirmation, lightning crackled across the sky.

Down the beach, a bonfire flared into existence.

From behind it, a woman emerged and started walking towards us.

I said: "No, it can't be! It can't be Behroze!"

Behroze it was, of course. Thirty yards away, she hesitated, then stopped.

I started moving towards her, or attempted to, and found I couldn't budge.

Safiya nodded: "The Shaman's Reach."

She released my hand and walked down the beach.

I watched, transfixed, as the two most important people ever to enter my life coolly shook hands, then grinned at each other and warmly embraced.

The women talked but I could hear nothing. At one point, Safiya threw back her head and laughed, delighted, and I flashed on the first time I saw her. She embraced Behroze once more, then wheeled and strode towards me and Daniel. As she approached, and despite my best efforts to keep it alive, the scene faded. . . .

And I slippled back into mundane reality, awakened to rumpled sheets and the warmth of Safiya, naked beside me. She opened her eyes and bolted upright: "Bernie! The bracelet!" She jumped out of bed and began pulling on clothes: "Behroze told me what's wrong."

Fearing some mistake or illusion, and afraid to raise my hopes, she refused to elaborate. But she insisted on rushing to the hospital. We made the trip in record time. Safiya stood a moment beside Colette's bed, breathing deeply. This was it. She reached over, took my daughter's wrist and gently removed the gold bracelet. Then she moved to the foot of the bed, rolled up the covers and slipped the shining talisman onto Colette's ankle.

Straightening up, she said: "That's how I wore it as a girl."

We stood holding each other, hoping against hope.

Nothing happened. Clinging to each other, we waited.

Incredibly, Colette's eyes fluttered open: "Daddy? Daddy, where am I?"

"Colette! Oh, Colette!" I fell to my knees and clasped her hand to my face.

"Don't cry, Daddy. What's wrong? Please don't cry."

Three days later, we brought Colette home.

The doctors couldn't believe how quickly she recovered. Two weeks after they released her, Colette returned to school, bent on catching up on the work she'd missed. Also, she resumed her piano lessons. Within weeks, it was like she'd never been hurt.

My own readjustment took longer. With Colette restored, I resumed working at The Statesman — but found I couldn't concentrate. No physical problem: I'd lost interest in event-oriented journalism; indeed, I could no longer take seriously the mundane world. As pretentious as it sounds, I yearned to explore a deeper reality.

When I went to resign, the Managing Editor tried to talk me out of it. She offered me an editorial-page column, something I'd once coveted, and I said thanks but no thanks: "Tell the truth, I've got a book to write."

Because of the role she'd played at the outset, acting on a dream against her better judgment, I'd already told her the basics of my adventure — though not without swearing her to secrecy. Now, the M.E. contemplated me thoughtfully: "You've finally recovered from the death of Behroze."

"No more nightmares, anyway."

The M.E. grinned mischievously: "And look! You've become some sort of Millennial Overman into the bargain."

"That's what I tell Safiya," I answered, straight-faced. "That she's turned me into a pillar of wisdom and clear-mindedness."

"She can't see it?"

I shook my head sorrowfully: "She claims the quest was a Quebecois metaphor. When I pressed her to explain, she handed me The Red Bird of Paradise and told me, 'Start here.'"

The M.E. chuckled and wished me good luck.

What else to report? Against all odds, Safiya and Colette adore each other. They spend whole afternoons shopping — laughing and chattering and hunting for baby clothes. None of us can wait until Hashedar arrives. Having heard the whole story in an expurgated version, Colette has taken to wiggling her ears and declaring: "The laughter of a child lights up eternity."

Then, despite herself, she giggles.

We can only laugh with her, Safiya and I.

As she lights up our life, in the blaze we laugh with her.